Behind me a muffled sound and a sharp intake of breath warned me that I wasn't alone. A sharp pain cut across my shoulders and a rough shove thrust me forward, sending two bags of groceries flying to the floor of the car.

A strong, unpleasant cherry odor followed me and seemed to wrap itself around my face. I couldn't escape it, nor could I see who had attacked me. He was still there. I could sense him closing in on me. A hand yanked my head back by the hair and a gritty cloth dropped down over my face.

I wrenched my body up from the seat and struck out at my attacker, but struggle was useless. The heavily scented, scratchy material cut off my vision. My fists fell against a body as hard as steel. I might as well have been grappling with the storm.

Through pain and nausea I found my voice and the strength to yank the cloth up from my mouth. "Who are you? What the hell do you think you're doing?"

Then another blow to the back of my head split my world into fragments and all awareness vanished in a torrent of white and darkness.

Previously published Worldwide Mystery title by
DOROTHY BODOIN

THE CAMEO CLUE

A SHADOW
ON THE SNOW

DOROTHY BODOIN

W❂RLDWIDE®

TORONTO • NEW YORK • LONDON
AMSTERDAM • PARIS • SYDNEY • HAMBURG
STOCKHOLM • ATHENS • TOKYO • MILAN
MADRID • WARSAW • BUDAPEST • AUCKLAND

A SHADOW ON THE SNOW

A Worldwide Mystery/March 2008

First published by Hilliard & Harris.

ISBN-13: 978-0-373-26631-9
ISBN-10:   0-373-26631-6

Printed in U.S.A.

To the memory of my father and mother,
Nicholas and Helen Bodoin.

ONE

THE RED INTERSECTION LIGHT was flashing, a burst of brightness caught in the swirls of white fog and blowing snow. I braked and turned the windshield wipers up to the highest speed. They whirred into action sending snowflakes flying into the air but visibility still hovered near zero.

All I could see of Huron Station's Main Street were the bare trees of late November strung with miniature lights, the corner drug store, and the Tuxedo theatre, dark and abandoned now with 'Closed' spelled out in black letters on the marquee.

The rest of the block lay shrouded in fog. But I knew the town even though I hadn't seen it in fifteen years. Only the trees that lined the street were new, no more than two or three years old, I guessed.

The intersection was clear now. I stepped lightly on the accelerator and felt the car skidding on a patch of ice beneath the snow. Biting down on my lower lip, I took my foot off the pedal, letting the Taurus choose its own direction, and steered to the right.

Don't panic. There's nothing here to hit, no moving cars, no pedestrians. Don't even think of sliding into a parked car.

The Taurus sailed across the street like a sled following a familiar trail, but now I had control of the wheel again if not my heartbeat. Thank God the intersection was empty.

The only available parking places on the block were in front of Nichols' Drug Store. I pulled into the deep ruts behind a Huron Station sheriff's cruiser and turned off the ignition. My car should be safe enough here with the law so close.

Pulling off my gloves, I tried to rub the ache out of my

hands. I'd been gripping the wheel too tightly for hours, expecting every second to hit that icy patch and spin out of control. That was no way to drive in a Michigan winter.

I knew that I should be relaxed and cautious, ready for anything, and above all have confidence in my ability to control my vehicle. All I could claim to be today was cautious.

My throat was dry and I was in desperate need of a brief rest. Now that I was within twenty miles of the cabin I could stop for a quick lunch and a hot drink. I remembered a small restaurant not far from the theatre. Probably it was still there, or another one like it.

I rolled up the collar of my lavender turtleneck that doubled as a scarf, pulled the hood of my purple coat forward over my hair, and put my gloves on again. Then I reached for my shoulder bag, opened the door, and stepped out into the arctic air.

In the street I walked around the back of the car to the sidewalk, stepping in the tracks left by those who had come before me. The wind promptly blew my hood back and stinging icy flakes hit my face as I climbed over high mounds of plowed snow. The pavement was shoveled and sprinkled with salt. On a day like this walking was infinitely easier than driving.

The restaurant should be in the middle of the block directly across from the Huron Station Savings Bank. Only ten more steps, maybe fifteen. I had no real memory of it, only fuzzy images of a wooden Indian at the entrance, chicken pie, and an adjoining souvenir shop.

When I saw the bank I came to a stop. I was in the right place but the restaurant was now a flower and antique shop named Blooms from the Past. In the window deep pink azaleas and nineteenth century china surrounded a wicker tea trolley filled with pumpkins.

Everything changes, even small northern towns, but there must be another place to eat on Main Street. I walked on, scanning the vintage storefronts anxiously now, ready to take temporary shelter in the first warm and welcoming haven I came to.

I found it nestled between a barbershop and a bakery. Estella's Cafe was a small gabled house, set farther back from the sidewalk than its neighbors, looking as if it had been left in its original location as the stores went up on either side. It was brightly lit, open, and appeared to be doing a brisk business.

Relieved and very thirsty, I opened the door and went inside.

The café was larger than it appeared from the outside with a counter wrapped around three sides and oval shaped tables clustered close together under hanging Tiffany light fixtures. The yellows, peaches and oranges of the color scheme were warm and inviting and a fire blazed in a wood-burning stove.

As I moved farther into the restaurant the temperature seemed to rise at least twenty degrees. I unbuttoned my coat and paused to read the sign that leaned on an oversize brass easel: 'Welcome to Estella's Cafe. Please Seat Yourself.'

The place was crowded with people, some of them still warmly dressed in their cold weather layers. I walked toward the back where I saw a few unoccupied booths. I slid into one of them and occupied myself by observing my fellow diners, the most interesting of whom were the three law enforcement officers.

They had commandeered the best table in the room, alongside the stove. The two state troopers were tall, dark haired and husky, and exuded power. They were so similar in appearance that they might have been brothers. They ate quietly, their eyes fixed on their food. The third man, wearing the tan uniform and badge of a county sheriff, was the most visually appealing part of the décor.

He had a handsome, arresting face with high cheekbones and intriguing angles, tawny-brown hair sprinkled with gray strands, and a hard, lean body. High leather boots reached up to his knees and clung to his long, muscular legs.

He was magnificent. A north woods bear of a man; he was the kind who could banish the winter night's chill for any woman. If I were Estella, I would pay him to eat in the establishment just to bring in the female customers.

He had reached the dessert and coffee stage of the meal and set his cup close to the edge of the table, ignoring the large piece of pie at his elbow, while he studied a map and waited for his lunch companions to catch up to him.

Don't react as if you'd never seen a handsome man, I scolded myself. *Look away now. The next thing you know, he'll turn around and notice you staring at him.*

Or was that what I wanted?

The sheriff continued to read the map as if it were an engrossing news story while the other troopers kept on eating. No one at the table was engaging in casual conversation. The Alcona County lawmen were focused on business.

Wishing I'd taken the time to apply a touch of lipstick and powder, I ran my hand through my hair. It felt damp, snowdrops melting in a tangle of wind-tossed auburn strands, but I knew it looked better this way with moisture creating instant waves.

The waitress brought me back down to earth. She was young, efficient, and apparently oblivious to the nearby display of male beauty. Her crisp orange and white uniform complemented the café's décor.

"I'm Cindy. I'll be your waitress today," she said as she handed me a menu and filled my cup with coffee, creating an instant heat source on the table. "Is it getting worse outside?"

"Every second."

"They say the fog is supposed to clear up after noon."

"That's good. I like to see where I'm going."

The first swallow of coffee burned my throat, but this was what I needed. I sat back and began to thaw.

"It's going to be a long winter, and it isn't even December yet," she said. "Our specials today are turkey pot pie and venison stew. The soup is beef barley."

I opened the menu and scanned the sandwich column. It was still too early for heavy dinner food. I wanted something hot now and a sandwich to take out for later. I didn't know what I'd find in the cabin, but I was reasonably certain it wouldn't be a pantry stocked with staples.

"I'll have a cup of soup and also a sandwich to go," I said. "Make it corned beef on rye."

When Cindy left to fill my order, I sipped coffee and glanced surreptitiously at the lawmen's table. The tawny-haired sheriff had folded the map and begun a conversation of sorts with the troopers. I wasn't close enough to hear what they were saying. Usually I don't eavesdrop, but I thought they might mention some updated information about the weather or the condition of the roads to the north.

Cindy brought my soup then and refilled the coffee cup. I concentrated on my lunch. Aside from any other considerations, the presence of the lawmen was reassuring. I was going to an isolated wilderness cabin surrounded by eighty acres of woods. Although I hadn't seen the farm since my childhood vacations with my family, my Great Aunt Celia had lived alone there without incident for a quarter of a century, and I expected to do the same for two weeks.

Having an active police force in the area could only add to my sense of security, and a man who looked like the sheriff was a definite fringe. I hoped I'd see him again.

Welcome north, I thought. This time I had made the right decision.

A CREAM MINIVAN was parked behind me now, giving me very little room to back up and maneuver my way out into the street. I could only move forward. Unfortunately, I'd pulled closer to the sheriff's car than I should have.

How many sheriffs could there be in Huron Station? This cruiser almost certainly belonged to the tawny-haired officer in Estella's Café. He might come back to his car at any minute or in an hour, as might the driver of the minivan.

I didn't want to wait. The fog was lifting now, but it was still snowing, and I had twenty more miles to go.

As I stood in the street, calculating my chances of extricating myself from this cramped place, it seemed to me that the space between the patrol car and the Taurus had shrunk. An illusion brought about by the snow and fog or an earlier lack of foresight? It didn't matter. I was blocked in.

It would be difficult but not impossible to free myself if I kept turning the steering wheel to the left, moving a fraction of an inch forward each time, until I was in a position to swing out into the street.

I thought I could do it. All the same, I cursed the unknown driver of the minivan who had created this unnecessary obstacle for me.

A thin layer of fresh snow covered all three vehicles. I unlocked the car, started the engine, and turned on the windshield wipers and defroster. My long-handled brush lay on the floor in front of the passenger's seat where I had tossed it this morning. I grabbed it and cleared the snow from the top of the car, using long, angry strokes and wishing I could brush away the minivan or, better still, the driver who had cut off my easy exit.

As soon as I could see through the windows, I turned on the lights and began to ease the car out of the space into the street. The familiar ache rushed back to my hands as I gripped the wheel, once again too tightly, but I paid no attention to it and kept my eyes fixed on the back of the cruiser.

I was sure I could do it now. Turning the wheel one last time, I stepped on the gas pedal, moved a bit forward, and rammed into the patrol car. The crunch of steel smashing into steel cracked open the deep afternoon silence.

Instantly I braked and looked in dismay at what I had done. The shiny blue rear fender of the sheriff's car had crumpled as easily as a model made of cardboard. The damaged area resembled a gaping wound, dripping white snow on the ground instead of blood. My car must be dented too.

Of all the vehicles in Huron Station, why did I have to park behind the cruiser? More to the point, why did I have to run into it?

I glanced out the window, expecting to be surrounded by eager witnesses. In any town downstate, the sheer noise of the collision would have attracted at least a few curious passersby to the scene. Huron Station's Main Street, like the intersection I'd recently slid across, was relatively empty. The people who happened to be in the vicinity were intent on reaching their various destinations and getting in out of the cold. They looked once and walked on.

I wished I could drive away and leave Huron Station and this accident behind, but that was unthinkable. I had damaged a sheriff's car while it was parked and now I had to deal with the situation.

With a shaky hand, I shifted into neutral and got out to view the patrol car's fender more closely. From outside, it looked even worse. Since nobody was going to come to my aid, I would have to notify the police.

When I'd left the restaurant, the town's law officers were still lingering over their dessert. That meant I would have to return to Estella's Café and confess what I'd done, which was the last thing I wanted to do. I had hoped to see the sheriff again, but not like this.

I was reaching across the seat to get my shoulder bag when I heard someone behind me walking up to the car, boots stamping down the snow, the sound magnified in the stillness.

I turned to see the sheriff. He was looking at his cruiser and frowning. "What have we here?" he asked.

He was taller than I had imagined. And brawnier. His hat and jacket were layered with new snow. As he stood waiting for my answer, his hand rested casually on the holster of his gun.

Although his expression hovered between neutral and benign, there was a chill in his voice that had nothing to do with the bitter temperature. I noticed that his eyes were the ice-blue color of Lake Huron in the winter.

He was waiting for me to answer him, to offer an excuse I couldn't possibly give, while the snow blew and drifted between us creating a high, frosty barrier.

"I thought I had enough room to pull out," I said.

He didn't say a word. He was so silent that I could almost hear the snow falling.

I added, "Obviously I didn't. I'm sorry."

Still without answering me, he stooped down in the hard-packed snow and ran his large gloved hand along the damaged fender and then back again as if caressing a loved one.

I wished myself a thousand miles away, anywhere but on the main street of this frozen backwoods town at the mercy of a man whose property I had damaged.

At last he spoke again. "You did have enough room. Are you a new driver?"

I bit back an angry retort. I was the offender here, and the sheriff was apparently a take-no-prisoners kind of man. Not an hour ago in the café I'd thought of him in a vastly different way. The reality didn't match my fantasy, except the part about the bear. That was accurate, except he would be a deadly brown grizzly, not the fuzzy, snuggling kind.

"No, of course not," I said. "I've been driving for years. That minivan parked way too close to me. I'm really sorry. I did the best I could."

Realizing that this defense bordered on belligerence, I ended it and waited for him to respond.

He didn't say "just like a woman driver" or anything remotely similar, but his expression did. I couldn't think of anything else to say. Probably it was better that way.

He was standing up now, brushing snow from his gloves.

"I see. Do you have your driver's license and registration, ma'am?" He paused and added, "Your insurance too?"

It was a relief to look away from him and fumble in my bag for the documents he requested. My hands were definitely shaking as I removed the cards from my wallet. I handed them to him, hoping that he wouldn't notice, or, if he did, would think I was only cold and not intimidated.

He studied each one carefully. Just as I began to think he suspected they were forged, he said, "Krista Marlow, is it? Like Christopher Marlowe, the playwright?"

"Close," I said. "My mother was an English professor."

He removed his gloves and reached for a ticket pad. I didn't expect this. What had happened was an accident. Didn't the concept of "no fault" exist this far north?

Suddenly, my remorse vanished. I hadn't broken any laws or injured anybody, and surely even in Huron Station a policeman took weather conditions into consideration before issuing a citation. Also, my car had its own share of damage. That should be punishment enough.

"You're not giving me a ticket," I said.

"I am, for handling a vehicle carelessly."

"But the minivan…"

"It didn't hit a parked car."

He handed me a pen. "Sign here, please."

I had no choice. But as I wrote my name I felt resentment welling up in me and willed myself not to let him sense it. This was a small town, after all. Maybe they needed the income collected from downstate tourists who broke their laws. Or their handsome sheriff could be a male chauvinist in which case I didn't have a chance.

Silently I handed him the signed citation. Even then there wasn't the slightest hint of friendliness in his face, only the self-satisfied look of a lawman who has done his duty. Or a bear that has captured his dinner.

I liked that last comparison better.

"So you're from the big city. Are you going to stay in Huron Station long, Miss Marlow?" he asked.

"I'm just passing through."

"Didn't I see you at Estella's?"

"Probably. I was there."

"I thought so. Be careful," he said, making no attempt to disguise the condescension. "These roads can be tricky for a city girl."

I dropped the ticket into my bag. "I'll keep that in mind. Is it all right if I leave—and would you move your car, please?"

"Sure, Miss Marlow." He tipped his hat and a shower of

snow fell against his jacket. Now that I was on my way out of town he looked positively congenial.

"And drive safely. You're in dangerous country now."

TWO

OVER THE YEARS landmarks vanish and restaurants turn into flower and antique shops, but the white Victorian house on the hilltop was still there. So was Lake Huron, a smooth expanse of water as ice-blue as the eyes of the arrogant sheriff.

Only something was wrong. I should have left the lake behind and found the turn off half an hour ago. On a clear stretch of highway washed in weak afternoon sunshine, I had managed to miss the byroad that angled northwest through acres of woods and eventually led to the cabin.

There were still three or four hours of daylight left, but suppose I was really lost? If I were still wandering through the forest when night fell, I would be in trouble. The last gas station was five miles behind me. With no one in sight to provide directions, I had to rely on my instincts.

They were telling me to turn left on the first road I came to and hope it would connect with the one I'd missed. I could also backtrack, heading south all the way to the hilltop Victorian, if necessary, and try again. I had to find that elusive turn off. It couldn't just disappear.

By now the sun had burned off the last wisps of fog and driving was easier. Still, black ice might be hiding under the snow layer that covered the pavement. I drove slowly, not wanting to attract the attention of a state trooper or, worse, spin out and crash into a tree.

I was in deep woods now, with miles of towering trees and gray, cloud-filled sky, but little else. The only indications of human presence were the 'No Trespassing' signs posted at intervals.

Before long I came to a narrow road that looked promising

and I turned left, hoping I wasn't invading private property. Long ribbons of snow, deeply imprinted with tire tracks, glistened between borders of thick dark woods. I steered to the right, keeping my wheels in the groves so that only the left side of the car rode on the slick surface. I was looking for a name I could cross-reference on my roadmap of northern Michigan.

Gradually I became aware of a familiar sound in the distance, and then I saw the headlights, weak but unmistakable. Another car was coming toward me, moving at a high rate of speed. To give it room to pass I pulled over to the side as far as I could.

The gray Crown Victoria was almost completely covered in snow. From the small cleared area of the front window I barely caught a glimpse of the driver's face. Like a great white-topped machine designed for destruction, the car rapidly closed the distance between us.

Driving this fast and with obstructed vision was lunacy. I held my breath as it sped past me, thankful that it hadn't crashed into the Taurus. Then, stepping lightly on the gas pedal, I returned to the security of the tire tracks.

The driver was guilty of speeding and failing to clear his windows of snow, but there was no lawman around to whip a ticket pad out of his pocket and cite him for reckless driving. Probably the Sheriff of Huron Station was back in the café having coffee.

· I had to stop thinking about that man. Our first encounter had been a disaster, I didn't know his name, and almost certainly I wouldn't see him again. Strange, though, that he had mentioned Christopher Marlowe. Maybe at heart he was an English scholar or a fan of the theatre.

He was handsome enough to be an actor. I could see him on stage in an Elizabethan costume, the bright colors and antique style suiting him better than officer's tan, but that picture was wrong. The sheriff had no charm, no charisma. He was exactly what he appeared to be—a north woods lawman with a tyrant complex.

Ahead about thirty yards, I noticed a splotch of blue suspended in midair, brilliant against the stark black and white landscape. It must be a flag or a scarecrow. Flying out here in the middle of nowhere? Keeping birds away from a non-existent field?

More likely it was a leftover Halloween decoration, put up to scare the infrequent travelers on the isolated road, nothing more than straw or pillows formed into a vaguely human shape and dressed in old cast-off clothing.

But as I came closer, I saw that the clothes weren't old and the shape wasn't vague. The object looked like a man hanging from the branch of an oak tree.

Slowly I applied the brake and brought the Taurus to a stop in a drift of snow. From where I sat, safe inside my car, I couldn't tell if I was looking at an ultra-realistic Halloween figure or a person who had met with a gruesome end. There was only one way to find out.

I ran my hand along the top of my off-white boots and retied the top sets of laces. If I walked about fifteen yards into the woods, I would know for certain if what I suspected was true.

For a moment I hesitated. If a man had been killed here, this might be a dangerous place for a passerby to linger, but I didn't see anyone lurking nearby, and I couldn't just drive on.

Leaving the motor running and the door open, I got out of the car and walked across the road, taking short, careful steps around the ice. Once I reached ground, the way was easier, as someone had traced a rough path in the snow. It appeared to have been created by two sets of footprints and something large being dragged to the tree.

Alongside the prints I saw a trail of bright red drops. It looked as if a hunter had shot a deer and transported the dripping carcass this short distance, but I didn't think I was looking at the blood of a slaughtered animal.

I was close enough now to see what was hanging from the oak branch. The body faced away from me, turned to look with sightless eyes into the dark woods. He was wearing jeans and a flannel shirt of deep cobalt blue, but neither a jacket nor a hat. At the base of the tree, blood formed a crimson pool in the snow, indicating that he hadn't been dead long.

Once again looking around to make sure that I was alone in the woods, I walked around the tree and steeled myself to look up at the hanging man. Attached to the branch by a rope that was knotted around his neck, he was definitely and horribly dead.

Not too long ago, an arrow had pierced his chest, breaking through the thick flannel and the flesh, sending blood streaming from his body to soak the blue shirt and smear the writing on the sheet of poster board that was propped up against the tree trunk. I was able to make out the words: 'Stop the Kill!'

A wave of nausea gripped me, and a sour taste of barley and carrots rushed up to my throat. I covered my mouth to keep my lunch from gushing out onto the snow.

Don't be sick yet, I commanded myself. *You have something to do.*

I stepped back, trying not to surrender to the weakness, taking deep breaths, looking away from the dead man's contorted face, concentrating on the curious words lettered on the poster. How did that terse command apply to what I was seeing?

I couldn't remember ever being so cold. I ran back to my car, away from the macabre scene, stumbling over fallen branches and almost losing my balance on the ice. When I was inside, I locked the door and dialed 911 on my cell phone.

SHERIFF MARK DALBY touched me. His hand on my shoulder was strong and heavy, warm and comforting. I was still shaking from the cold even though I was sitting beside him inside his cruiser with the heater turned on high. I was trying to convince myself that I wasn't going to be sick and wishing I was on my way to some familiar place instead of a cabin I hadn't set eyes on in fifteen years. At least the interrogation was almost over.

In a controlled chaos of flashing strobe lights and noise, half a dozen men were busily turning the isolated wooded area into a crime scene, while a scattering of others milled around. Cruisers and an ambulance were lined up behind the Taurus, and a rusty red truck idled in the middle of the road, its driver apparently the sole civilian spectator in the area.

The victim was gone, transferred to the ambulance, and a photographer was taking pictures of the oak tree. The blood was still there, crimson splattered on the white snow. I saw the color red even when I closed my eyes.

Although nobody said so, I had the impression that everyone at the scene knew the identity of the murdered man. As soon as my nausea lifted, I planned to ask the sheriff about the significance of the slogan on the sign.

'Stop the kill' was a peaceable message connected to a grisly, ritualistic murder. I suspected that Sheriff Dalby knew why the killer had left the poster beneath the body. Then there was the matter of the man in the gray Crown Victoria.

In the seconds after I'd discovered the body and locked myself inside my car, I remembered him. Even with snow-obscured windows, he couldn't have missed seeing the man in the tree. Maybe he was speeding down the road to alert the police.

Or maybe he was the killer. That was what frightened me.

Sheriff Dalby appeared to be studying me as if I were a valuable piece of the puzzle.

"Are you sure you're all right?" he asked. "You look pale."

His voice was as strong and comforting as the touch of his hand had been.

"I'm fine," I said. "Just a little shaky. It isn't every day I discover a body, and it was so horrible—the way he died."

"I won't disagree with you on that. Do you usually gravitate toward trouble, Miss Marlow?"

The brusque remark pushed his kind gesture and words of concern into the past. He was again the man I remembered: a brisk, no-nonsense officer, now in charge of a murder investigation. As the one who had found the victim, I was part of his job. It was fortunate that he'd seen me at the café a while ago, or I might be a suspect myself.

"Only since I passed Standish," I said. "It must be something in the water. If you recall, you were the one who said this was dangerous country."

He almost smiled at me then. "You can identify the make and color of the car, but not the driver. Tell me why."

"Because I didn't really look at him. I was wondering how he could see with all that snow on his window and hoping he wouldn't slide into me. I remember thinking that he should get a ticket for driving so fast in unsafe conditions. Lots of things."

He did smile then, and a fan of fine lines appeared at the edges of his eyes. It filled me with warmth, and I no longer felt sick.

"Alcona is a big county, ma'am. We can't be everywhere. You're sure the driver of the Crown Victoria was a man?"

"Not really. Probably. He must have seen me, though."

I wished that Sheriff Dalby would lay his hand on my shoulder again.

If the owner of the gray car was the killer and if he thought I could identify him, I was in serious trouble. The great cold was coming back along with the feeling that I was going to be ill.

"We'll catch him," he said. "Now, Miss Marlow, you're not really lost. You say you're going to the old McLaughlin place? Stay on this road. In about five minutes you'll pass the first of two crossroads. Turn left at the next one you come to and keep going, about ten miles. On your right, you'll see a burned-out house with the whole second floor gone. That's where you turn, right this time, not left. If you don't take any more detours, you'll reach the cabin safe and sound."

"Thank you." I tried to remember everything he'd said. With the specter of the dead man inside the cruiser with us it was impossible.

He took a pen and pad out of his jacket pocket and scrawled a few lines on it. Ripping out the sheet, he handed it to me. "Here. This is as good as a map." He paused and added, "I'll send one of the deputies to escort you."

"Thank you," I said, "I accept. Incidentally, it was never the McLaughlin cabin. Doctor McLaughlin only rented it during the hunting season. It's always belonged in my family."

He opened the cruiser door for me and held it as I got out of the car. A gush of bitterly cold air engulfed me. We stood facing each other, and a few snowflakes landed on the sleeve of my purple coat. I stared at them, watching them melt, wondering if they were the first of many.

The sheriff looked up at the sky, shading his eyes with his large gloved hand.

"It's starting to snow again. Are you going to move up north or is this a winter vacation?" he asked.

"I'll be staying for two weeks, maybe longer. I'm not sure."

"Good. If I want you, I'll know where to find you."

Turning around, he surveyed his men quickly and then, settling on one, called, "Rusty! I have a job for you."

A tall lanky young man with lightly spiked red hair detached himself from the group that had gathered around the oak tree and jogged up to us. I was being dismissed, but I wasn't ready to go yet.

"Wait," I said. "I want to ask you something, Sheriff Dalby. You all seem to know the victim."

"He was Randall Scott. Didn't you recognize him?"

"I never saw him before today."

"Scott was a local celebrity. Back in the seventies, he had his own television show, 'Texas Rogue.' He was famous all over northern Michigan. Everyone liked him."

"Except the killer," I said.

The deputy, Rusty, waited a discreet distance away from us, absently kicking the snow from a large fallen log. I imagined he'd rather remain at the crime scene than escort me to the cabin. Sheriff Dalby looked impatient, too. Now that I'd served my purpose, no doubt they were anxious to be rid of me.

"About the poster, sheriff," I said, "what does the slogan mean?"

"It refers to the deer kill down in Millennium Park. The anti-hunting activists had dozens of signs just like this one. I saw them myself. 'Stop the Kill!' was their rallying cry."

"Isn't it hunting season now?" I asked.

"Sure is, but this is different. There's been a lot of opposition to bringing in hunters to thin out the herds. The protesters claim there are more humane ways to control the deer population. That may be true, but it's easier to kill them outright."

"I guess it isn't much different from what happens in hunting season, but this sounds so calculated and inhumane."

"It's a controlled deer harvest. And when it's over the meat is given to the hungry."

I had no doubt on which side the sheriff stood in the dispute.

"Do you think this murder is connected with the deer harvest?" I asked.

"I didn't say that, Miss Marlow. This little sign strayed a ways up north. That's all I know."

"And it's covered with blood."

"So it is."

I thought of the sign under the dead man's body. Whoever had left it had meant to send a definite message. I made another attempt. "Was Randall Scott one of the hunters?"

"Yes, he was." Sheriff Dalby's expression was grim.

"So this is a message from one of the anti-hunting activists who wanted to make a point?"

"That's the obvious interpretation, but we have to wait until the investigation is over."

"He could have been killed by accident. And the activists took the opportunity to string him up as a warning to other hunters," I said.

"That's pure conjecture. Scott's jacket and cap are missing. When we find them we'll have some answers."

"How did they kill the deer in the Park?" I asked. "You can tell me that."

"With bows and arrows."

Sheriff Dalby glanced at the sky again. The snow flurries were increasing but they were light and fluffy, manageable stuff.

"You'd better be on your way," he said. "It gets dark early now."

I knew he wasn't going to tell me anything more. After all, why should he? Discovering the body didn't admit me to the sacred ranks of the law in Alcona County, but if I were in danger of becoming the killer's next victim, I had a right to know as much as possible about the murder.

As we walked over to the Taurus, he said, "Have a safe trip to the cabin. Follow Rusty and you'll be all right."

He stood back and tipped his hat once again as he had in Huron Station when I was leaving town. He didn't look congenial now, only anxious to return to his investigation.

The deputy was already starting the cruiser's engine. Soon I'd be far away from this place, and the long day would be over. I wanted that, of course, but I felt safe here in the company of the law.

As Sheriff Dalby said, it was a big county. A killer with a dark twisted mind was on the loose. I could only hope that if he were the driver of the Crown Victoria, he had been too intent on fleeing the scene of the crime to notice me.

"Don't forget to lock your door," he said, "and keep up with Rusty."

The deputy was moving slowly out into the road, waiting for me. I started the engine and set the map the sheriff had given me on top of my shoulder bag. With Rusty leading the way hopefully I wouldn't need it.

"Thanks for the escort, Sheriff. I hope you find your man."

Standing tall against the darkening sky and trees with his brawny arm within reaching distance of his holster, the sheriff seemed capable of accomplishing any feat. As he waved to me a sudden gleam appeared in his eye and a look that was almost, but not quite, arrogant.

"I always do, Miss. Marlowe," he said. "Ask anybody in Alcona County."

THREE

DAYLIGHT WAS FADING when I made the last turn on the wide path that led to the cabin. Snow lay on the roof like a heavy white comforter and provided a striking contrast for the dark brown logs. The scene reminded me of a Christmas card, but the emotions it evoked were sorrow and loss.

No welcoming light flickered in the window, no smoke rose from the chimney. This was the strangest, loneliest arrival I'd ever experienced.

At one time Aunt Celia would have come slowly down the path to meet my parents and me, often limping from the pain in her hip. I could almost see her now in her blue cotton dress, her silver hair wound in a loose bun with stray strands framing her face.

In my memory it was summertime, her smile was warm, and the woods that surrounded the cabin on three sides were green and fragrant. When I jumped down from our car—in those days it was a blue Plymouth Volare—and ran toward her, I always thought I was moving into the sunshine.

That was a long time ago. Aunt Celia was dead now as was Dr. McLaughlin, the hunting season tenant. The cabin belonged to me simply because I had outlived the other heirs. I would gladly trade it all, though, to have everything back the way it was and everyone alive again.

As I approached the property, the Taurus plowed with ease through the three inches of new snow that lay on the ground. I soon drove past the two old barns. They were weathered and empty, crying for a fresh coat of paint. Where the haystack had been there was a high drift of snow. The cows and two horses were only distant memories, snapshots in an old album.

I hoped the doghouses behind the cabin were still standing. I hadn't thought about Aunt Victoria's old brown and white collie, Ranger, in years, but as a child I'd loved him. I'd thrown sticks for him to retrieve and longed for a dog of my own.

That was in another decade and season. Now the farm was a ghost of its former self, and all the people and animals were gone. I forced myself to rein in the runaway nostalgia. There would be plenty of time for reminiscing later, after I'd opened the cabin and settled in.

I parked as close to the front porch as I could and turned off the engine. For a moment I sat still behind the wheel, fumbling in my bag for the key to the cabin. I began to feel a growing apprehension. Did I really want to stay in this isolated place where the atmosphere was thick with memories and I would be alone? I wasn't sure, but I was here now; and, in any event, I had no choice.

In spite of its roughhewn appearance, the cabin was wired for electricity and had indoor plumbing and a wood-burning stove for heat. With the flashlight, bedding, and the coffee-maker I'd brought along, I considered myself well prepared for wilderness living. I had food too: a tin of Classic Roast coffee, a dozen doughnuts still in their box, a bag of apples, and the corned beef sandwich from Estella's café, although it must be nearly frozen by now.

Krista Marlow's survival kit, I thought. *Let's see how soon it'll be until I discover that I've overlooked some essential item.*

It was time to stop thinking and go on in.

I stamped through the snow on the stairs, pushing it to one side with my boot, and opened the outside door to the porch. Eight windows protected the enclosed space, but the trapped air inside was frigid. Moving quickly, I unlocked the front door and stepped into dark space and bone-chilling cold.

I was in the dining room. The cabin had a simple floor plan designed by the farmers who had cleared ten acres and built it in the 1930s with logs chopped down from the woods. All of the amenities came later.

If I turned right and took five steps, I would be in the living room. The kitchen was ahead, alongside the cabin's two bedrooms. In the back was a small bathroom that had been added in the sixties and a sleeping porch used for storage and clothes washing.

I ran my hand along the rough surface of the wall, found the switch and turned it on. The room filled with weak light and shadows. On my right I saw the fireplace with a shotgun mounted on the wall above the mantel.

The bulb in the antique overhead fixture must have been twenty-five watts, if that. Tomorrow I'd have to buy a supply of hundred watt light bulbs and candles. But for tonight, any illumination was better than the darkness. Good God, it was going to be spooky living here.

I set my shoulder bag down on the antique sideboard beside a kerosene lamp and stood staring into the shadows. Aunt Celia's beloved mahogany table was covered with dust and all six chairs were pushed in.

The hunters had used the cabin for sleeping, meals, and coming in out of the cold while they waited for an unwary deer to wander into their range. But in those long ago summer days whenever we came up north, Aunt Celia would bring out her best linen tablecloth and plates with a delicate pink and green floral design.

She had inherited the dishes from her mother who had collected them piece by piece as giveaways at the movies. That was in Detroit during World War II. Every article in the cabin had a story attached to it. I wished I'd listened and remembered more.

She fed us with pork that she'd canned herself, or roasted a chicken with vegetables from her garden, and baked loaves of homemade bread. For breakfast we had eggs, fresh milk, and cream, all plain country fare, but impossible to duplicate today.

Absently I dabbed at my eyes with my glove. The cold was making them water.

Along with the garden and animals those laden tables of

summer had vanished. But with the corned beef sandwich, doughnuts and apples I wouldn't starve.

I didn't know how I could think about eating so soon after finding the body of Randall Scott. In the flood of memories and impressions I had almost lost those grisly moments. Now, like a bolt of winter lightning, they were back: the speeding Crown Victoria, the body hanging in the tree, and Sheriff Dalby looking at me with appraising ice-blue eyes, asking me if I usually gravitated toward trouble.

I shivered, suddenly aware of how cold it was in the cabin. Instead of standing in the living room indulging in past remembrances, I should be building a fire in the wood stove before I froze to death.

Thank heavens I knew how to do it. A stack of old newspapers lay on the side table. Dr. McLaughlin must have left them there, not knowing that he would die of a heart attack before the next hunting season. I was glad that I'd remembered to bring matches. All I had to do now was start moving.

I WORKED QUICKLY and by seven o'clock had the car unpacked and a fire blazing in the stove. It sent warmth radiating through the front rooms, but did little for the cold in the back of the cabin.

It was dark outside now. Inside the cabin, moving shadows filled the dimly lit rooms. I tried to stay in the present and not think about the past.

I had come up north one last time to pack my aunt's personal possessions and list the property with a realtor. Eighty acres of woods and a vintage log cabin in good condition were a valuable asset and the only one I had. With money from the sale, I would be able to start working toward my doctorate in American Literature and eventually teach English at a college.

This was what I really wanted to do, and, at twenty-four, I thought that my time to make another career choice was running out. Fortunately, I now had the means to make my dream a reality.

Now that I thought about it, my plan sounded as cold-blooded and calculated as the Millennium Park Deer Kill. The cabin was my inheritance and a priceless part of my past. Something of my aunt and every lost relative who had ever visited her still lived here. But my real life was four hundred miles south of Alcona County. Only a fool would hold on to a relic from yesterday while a dream for the future slipped out of her hands.

Well, I'd been a fool before.

As I explored the cabin, I discovered a surprising renovation. Since my last visit the wall between the cabin's two bedrooms had been knocked out to create one large shadowy area. Two double beds, one with high maple posts, faced each other across opposite corners. They were covered with loosely draped cotton spreads that had once been ivory but were now dusty and yellow with age.

The room also contained a chest of drawers, a matching dresser, and a cedar chest that apparently served as a nightstand for the bed with the posts, the one in which I was going to sleep. On top of the chest was a medium-size mirror set in an ornate brass frame.

Leaning forward, I studied my reflection behind the thin coating of dust. Only my hair pleased me. The soft peach blush and light blue eye shadow I'd applied this morning had vanished, leaving my eyes looking gray, a color I disliked. My lipstick was gone, too. I hadn't given a thought to my appearance since leaving the café and had turned into a dull, washed-out version of my usual self.

I lifted the lid of the chest and found the cabin's supply of spare blankets, sheets, and pillowcases with embroidered designs. The towels and washcloths were here, too, along with Aunt Celia's crocheted doilies and scarves. On top of everything lay a cheery quilt pieced together with bright squares of materials in solids and prints in bold primary colors.

Aunt Celia had made it herself. I had a hazy memory of being covered with it once as I lay on a cot out on the sleeping porch.

A low voltage bulb in a dust-coated overhead fixture

provided the bedroom's only light source. I brought an old-fashioned milk glass lamp from the living room, set it on the cedar chest and plugged it in. It added fifteen watts to the light show.

What the cabin needed were accessories in fire-bright colors, candles, and more powerful illumination. How Aunt Celia had remained so cheerful in these dim surroundings was a mystery. But the cabin had never seemed dark to me when she was alive.

I turned back the covers, fluffed the pillows and walked back into the kitchen. This was the one room in the cabin that felt familiar to me. If ever my aunt returned to earth, surely she would come here.

The dishes, many of them chipped now, were still neatly arranged in the glass-fronted cupboards. Except for a tarnished copper teakettle on the stove, the pots and pans were crammed into a tiny cabinet next to the sink.

I opened the refrigerator expecting to find it empty, but Doctor McLaughlin had stayed here last November. Not knowing that he wasn't going to come back, he'd left a few provisions behind.

One by one, I took them out and examined them: four bottles of beer, a sausage ring, a jar of grape jelly with a two-year-old expiration date, and an unlabeled container filled with an unidentifiable yellow glob.

In the freezer compartment I found two empty ice cube trays and a plastic bag of doughnuts. There was no way to tell how old they were. Wondering how to dispose of garbage and trash in Huron Station, I added them to the other throwaways.

Aunt Celia's old radio was in its usual place on the drop leaf maple table under the kitchen window, still plugged in. This was a true relic of a bygone age, a genuine antique. The sleek mahogany-stained table model had graceful lines, three dials and stations behind a circle of glass. The brass handle on top turned it into a portable, but it never left the table.

Here my aunt used to eat breakfast, look out at her vegetable garden, and listen to the news. She would turn it on in the evenings while the adults sat around the fireplace talking and the children played games on the floor or read.

I ran my hand lightly over the top to brush away the dust and turned the on knob, hoping to fill the cabin with music, but there was no audio. In spite of its mint condition appearance, the radio was dead. It must be sixty years old at least. Once again, my expectations were too high.

I should have something to eat. Too many hours had passed since I'd walked into Estella's café and dined on soup and crackers.

I filled the coffeemaker and unwrapped my take-out order. A high stack of thinly sliced corned beef on rye bread lay on a soggy napkin, alongside a kosher dill pickle in a plastic bag and packets of mustard and horseradish. None of it appealed to me.

Corned beef is best when it is hot. I realized that I wasn't very hungry after all. Nevertheless, I ate half of the sandwich and drank two cups of coffee. I didn't even untie the box from the bakery.

The stress and trauma of the long day had caught up with me. All I wanted to do was to go to bed and sleep for at least ten hours.

You're not cut out to be a country girl, Krista, I told myself, *just like you're not suited to be a high school teacher or any man's lover. Wind up your business here and head home. That'll be best.*

DURING THE NIGHT a strange, eerie sound woke me. It was beautiful but at the same time chilling. There was no need to turn on the lamp and search the cabin as I quickly identified the source. Somewhere out in the night the wolves were howling.

I hadn't known wolves lived in the woods, but the high, thin sound was unmistakable.

Under the blankets and the thick quilt, the now familiar cold reached me again. The pack must be very close to the cabin. I could only hope they'd keep their distance by day. The prospect of being torn apart by wild canines was even more unpleasant than being hunted down by a murderer.

Those horrors were only going to happen in a nightmare. I'd think of the howling as a lullaby, a little night music. I was locked in an impenetrable wilderness cabin and nothing could possibly get inside.

After a while the wolves stopped howling and I slept, but later I was awakened again, this time by a sound that originated inside the cabin. In the kitchen the old radio had come to life. Maybe when I had touched it or turned the knob I'd jarred some hidden mechanism loose, causing it to turn itself on.

I was listening to static and a deep male voice, but the words were muffled. Probably the broadcaster was giving the news and weather report or perhaps a warning about wolves in the area.

I intended to get up and turn the radio off. In just a minute…

But I was too tired to move. Soon I was asleep again, wandering frantically through the streets of an unfamiliar city looking in vain for the door to home. In my dream I could hear the music Aunt Celia used to listen to on the radio.

I WOKE TO A dazzling vista of glittering white. Through the log-framed window across the room I could see a wide border of sparsely spaced trees and beyond them the meadow where the cows once grazed. It swept down to thirty acres of dark, mysterious woods all covered in snow like the rest of the county. The other forty acres were in the back of the cabin and to the west.

Morning sunlight poured in through the dirt-streaked glass pane, but the air around me was incredibly cold. The fire in the stove had died and the cabin had no thermostat to turn up a few notches.

I should have gotten up and dressed quickly, but instead I pulled the quilt up to my chin and looked out the window again at the trees closest to the cabin. With their leafless branches stark and black against the pale sky they resembled arms raised in supplication.

The wolves had run away to their den and the woods were silent and still. The cabin was quiet, too. The radio must have died again unless someone had turned it off.

Someone like—who? I didn't know where that idea had come from. I was alone.

Pushing the covers back, I scrambled out of bed and covered the short distance to the kitchen without even noticing the cold under my feet. There was the radio in its accustomed place on the drop leaf table, undeniably silent.

Holding my breath, I turned the on knob. Nothing happened. The radio was as dead as it had been yesterday and the silence in the cabin was so thick I could almost touch it. Maybe I'd just dreamt that I'd heard a man's voice last night and had associated it with the radio. Maybe the wolves weren't real either but ghostly creatures howling in the streets of my nightmare city.

I wasn't ready to believe that Aunt Celia had come back to earth in the middle of the night to listen to the radio, nor that it had magical properties. The loose mechanism theory was the only one that made sense. For now I was going to forget about it and have a cup of strong, hot coffee and something to eat.

I regarded the doughnuts with disinterest. They had survived the jolt when I hit the sheriff's car with only the loss of a few sprinkles, but I wanted a real breakfast this morning. Bacon and eggs, ordinary foods, never failed to restore a measure of normalcy to my life.

Besides I was hungry and had a sudden craving for company. I was curious too. I wanted to know more about the murder of Randall Scott and the status of the investigation.

I closed the doughnut box, put the lid back on the coffee tin, and reached for my car keys. I was going to drive into Huron Station and have breakfast at Estella's Café. And this time I wouldn't park anywhere near the sheriff's patrol car.

FOUR

THE BREAKFAST SET out in front of me was enormous, more suitable for a farmer or north woods lumberjack than a woman who occasionally remembered to watch her weight.

The Sunrise Special at Estella's café, so temptingly pictured on the cover of the menu, translated into two scrambled eggs, six strips of bacon, country style white bread, thickly sliced and toasted to a golden brown, and a ten-ounce tumbler of fresh orange juice.

"Let me know if you'd like anything else, Miss Marlow," the black-haired waitress said.

I looked up from the sumptuous morning feast in surprise, wondering how she knew my name.

"Only more coffee, please."

"Certainly," she said. "I'm Estella Marten. Let me be one of the first to welcome you to Huron Station. You're going to love this town. I came up here for the winter sports seventeen years ago and never went home."

She wasn't a waitress, then, but the owner and maybe a spokesperson for the Chamber of Commerce. That explained her bright red sweater and blue jeans that contrasted sharply with the crisp orange uniform of the waitress who had taken my order.

Estella was distinctive in other ways, too. Although it was only eight-thirty in the morning, her eyes were outlined in kohl and shaded with shimmering blue. And she had the most unusual hair I'd ever seen. It was jet-black except for the shorter layers in front that curved forward at her shoulders. They were silver. I couldn't tell whether they were dyed or natural, but the effect was stunning.

"Are you on vacation?" she asked.

"In a way. This is the coziest little restaurant I've ever seen. It looks like a country parlor. I love these centerpieces."

The orange and peach carnations on the table matched the shades in the Tiffany fixtures overhead. Happy flowers for every season, they served as a reminder that one day spring would come again.

"Thanks," she said. "It gets so cold up here that we need some warm colors to look at. You'd better eat your eggs while they're hot."

As she turned to go, I picked up a piece of toast and broke it in two. "There's one more thing. I was wondering how you knew my name."

For a moment, I thought she looked flustered, but she recovered quickly.

"I heard how you ran into the sheriff's car yesterday. Talk about getting off to a bad start with the law."

"Yes, I guess I did. He gave me a ticket."

"Mark loves that old cruiser. You'd think it was a horse."

"It was more of a fender bender than a collision," I said. "In this snowy weather sometimes they're hard to avoid."

I pierced a piece of scrambled egg with the sharp edge of the toast, wishing the sheriff were the silent type. "I didn't realize he would broadcast it to the town."

Estella's expression turned serious. "Oh, he didn't, honey. He only told me and he happened to mention your name."

She seemed eager to go back to work and my breakfast wasn't going to stay warm indefinitely. I picked up my fork and coaxed a bit of egg onto it.

"I'll try to avoid the sheriff in the future," I said.

"Most women do just the opposite."

Well, I'm not most women.

Estella's smile suggested that she had heard my thought and didn't believe it.

"Come back for dinner tonight," she said. "This week our

special is turkey with stuffing and sweet potatoes. The dessert is pumpkin pie. We'll be closed on Thanksgiving."

I said, "I may do that."

She smiled, apparently pleased that I approved of her café. "I'll be back in a minute with the coffeepot."

Left alone, I turned to my bacon and eggs. I was trying to eat slowly although I was ravenous. Suddenly the breakfast seemed just the right size.

As I ate, I looked for Sheriff Mark Dalby in the crowd. Neither he nor his trooper friends were there. I hoped they were somewhere out in the cold, hard on the trail of Randall Scott's killer.

The two women at the next table were talking about the murder in hushed voices, dwelling on the sensational aspects, gleefully mixing graphic details with requests to pass the salt and sugar, and speculating on the likely guilt of someone named Roy Yarrow.

I didn't think Sheriff Dalby had told Estella that I was the one who had discovered the body. If she knew, she would probably have talked about the killing instead of my ill-starred meeting with the local sheriff.

I didn't want anyone to know about my inadvertent involvement in the murder case, but since almost a dozen people had been present at the crime scene, that was unrealistic. Still, I could hope that the sheriff hadn't mentioned my name to anyone, especially not to a reporter.

Little towns like Huron Station weren't known for keeping secrets, and I suspected that Estella was a gossip. The café appeared to be a popular gathering place for natives and tourists, as well as those who were passing through town. Maybe Estella knew the name of the person who drove a gray Crown Victoria recklessly over icy roads and didn't take the time to clear the snow from his windows. I'd ask her later this afternoon when I returned for my turkey dinner.

As I APPROACHED the cabin path, I saw a man riding toward me on a sleek chestnut horse. He wore a heavy brown jacket and a red plaid scarf that flapped in the wind. The Stetson hat that covered his hair gave him an appealing western look, but it couldn't be protecting his head from the bitter cold.

He waved to me and turned into the drive of a neat gray brick and cobblestone ranch house that was landscaped with tall blue spruces. To the east of the property I saw a weathered barn.

I had a neighbor within walking distance and he appeared to be friendly. Last night, when I'd pulled beside the deputy's car to thank him for the escort I hadn't noticed the house across the road. If I had a chance to meet the rider, I'd ask him about the wolves.

I drove up the road to the cabin, parked, and sat still for a moment, savoring the black and white beauty of my surroundings. There were so many things I wanted to do: go for a walk in the woods although not far because it was too cold; see if the root cellar was snowbound; do a little light housecleaning— that was at the bottom of my list—explore the barns...

I used to love to breathe in the sweet scent of hay and stroke the long brown face of Aunt Celia's horse, Dasher, who smelled of sawdust and pine. She had another horse, too. I tried to remember his name but couldn't and finally settled for another pleasant recollection. Sometimes I'd climb up the wooden ladder to the loft and read one of Aunt Celia's old books or look down on the farm and the woods in the distance.

My memories were mainly of the first barn. The other barn was older and smaller and contained grain and other farm essentials. Both of the barns were padlocked, but nothing is more fascinating than a bolted door.

Last night, I'd seen several keys labeled and hanging on hooks on the sleeping porch. I'd have to start referring to this area as a storage room or laundry, for that's what it was. The bathroom was an afterthought, replacing the old outhouse. It occupied a third of the space that had once been the porch.

I doubted that anyone had used the porch as a bedroom in years, except maybe in the summer, but the cot was still there. Like the beds, it was covered with a faded spread. The single length of clothesline knotted around two hooks would prove useful, as would the washer that looked new but couldn't have been, since I recognized it as the one Aunt Celia had used.

The mops and brooms were here, too, along with the cleaning supplies, a basket of rags, and a snow shovel. The real treasures were the antiques: a washing board leaning on a large metal tub, a vintage iron, and an ancient churn that Aunt Celia had kept as a conversation piece.

No memories lived in this coldest section of the cabin, or so I thought. But when I saw the two steamer trunks and innumerable boxes wrapped in brown paper and tied loosely with string, I knew that I was wrong. Someone had come before me to pack Aunt Celia's belongings away. That made my job easier.

I would sit in the living room beside the stove and sift through the boxes. If I could keep warm while handling the objects my aunt had touched, perhaps I wouldn't miss her so much.

First, though, I had to unpack the groceries, change all the light bulbs, and fill the rooms with candles, just in case the power failed as it had a way of doing back home during severe storms. Then I was going to dust the sideboard and table and move the radio to the dining room.

When my work was done, I planned to relax with a cup of coffee and read the *Huron Station Press*. The front page carried a picture of the victim, Randall Scott, holding a black puppy. Scott had been an attractive man with a friendly smile, a person I'd like to have known. That was the image I wanted to keep.

THAT EVENING I began my task of examining Aunt Celia's possessions by choosing the smallest box I could find. Once it had contained two pounds of Sanders candy. As I opened the lid, a faint scent of chocolate drifted out.

It contained at least a decade's worth of greeting cards. I spilled them out on the table and picked up a lacy Valentine, the largest and most elaborate in the collection. It was exquisite, lovely enough to be framed. At present the walls were bare. I tried to remember the last time I had seen the cabin. When Aunt Celia was alive, she used to hang family pictures on the walls and framed needlework of autumn leaves and flowers, as well as my childhood artwork.

Where were the wall decorations now? Probably packed away in one of the boxes on the sleeping porch, in which case eventually I would find them.

A loud knock on the door startled me and summoned me back to the present. I dropped the card and it fell back into the box to lie alone upon a bed of red and silver glitter.

As I walked across to the living room window, I glanced at the shotgun above the mantel, making a mental note to see if it still worked soon. Pulling back the heavy beige curtains, I saw the sheriff's patrol car parked a good distance behind the Taurus.

He knocked again. It was a loud impatient sound that seemed to be saying, 'You're under arrest.'

What could he want with me now? Maybe Estella had reported my comment about him broadcasting my accident to the town. I hoped I hadn't unintentionally antagonized him again. I took a deep breath and told myself that I was imagining things. When I had returned to the café for dinner, neither the sheriff nor the troopers had been there, and Estella had looked too busy to chatter with the customers.

I opened the door and tried to keep the alarm out of my voice. "Sheriff Dalby. Come in."

The sheriff looked even taller and brawnier than I remembered, but more relaxed. His ice-blue eyes were sparkling tonight. Or maybe it was the dusting of snow on his hair creating an illusion of light. He removed his leather gloves and slapped them together, sending a shower of white flakes into the air.

"Evening, Miss Marlow," he said. "I thought you were going to leave me out here to freeze."

"I wouldn't do that, Sheriff, and please call me Krista."

He stepped past me, stamping the snow from his boots on the bare wood floor, and moved silently into the living room, to the stove.

"I was driving by and saw that you were in," he said. "There's no prettier sight on a snowy winter night than a log cabin that's all lit up."

"You sound like a poet," I said, feeling a little more at ease with him.

He was looking at the sideboard. Inspired by the café décor, I'd bought six candles in shades of peach and orange, Estella's warm colors, and set them close to one another on an ornate silver tray I'd found in the top drawer. They were all burning, bathing the old radio in a soft golden glow.

"Nice radio," he said. "Is it a replica?"

"No, it's authentic, but it's broken."

In an instant, the sheriff's mood seemed to change. He seemed almost disapproving, but whether it was of my decorations or me I couldn't tell.

He was looking at the shotgun hanging above the fireplace. "This sure is a godforsaken place for a woman to be all alone," he said. "You are staying alone here, aren't you?"

"For the present."

"Did you come up north to go hunting?" he asked.

"I'm not a hunter, Sheriff. I couldn't kill an animal."

"The woods are crowded with deer," he said. "Doc McLaughlin got one every year."

Hadn't he heard me? I felt as if I were under interrogation. I didn't know how to make myself any clearer, but I tried again. "I came to Huron Station for a vacation."

"It's usually hunters who rent the cabin."

"Not anymore. It belongs to me now. By the way, I wondered about something. Maybe you'd know. Are there any wolves in the area?"

"They're in the Upper Peninsula, but not this far south," he said. He paused and frowned, as if reconsidering. "Not yet. I should say, none that I know of. Why?"

"I thought I heard wolves howling last night. They woke me up."

He smiled then, no longer floundering, sure of his answer.

"You heard my dogs, Tasha and Timber. They like to howl, night or day."

"They're dogs then, not wolves?"

"You were partly right. Timber is a hybrid; he's half wolf. Tasha may have some wolf in her. All I know is she looks like a husky-collie mix. I gave her a home when she lost her owner."

I decided that I could like this man. He had a heart after all.

"Did her owner move away or die?" I asked.

"You might say he moved away when I sent him to jail," he said with a wry smile. "He asked me to find a home for Tasha."

"It was nice of you to take care of his pet."

"She's a good dog. I live in an old farmhouse over on Huron Road. That's why you could hear the howling. You might say I'm your neighbor."

We were still standing in the living room, talking around the stove. It occurred to me that I wasn't being very hospitable, but then this couldn't be a social visit. Sooner or later Sheriff Dalby would tell me why he had come pounding on my door. I didn't believe his driving-by-the-neighborhood story.

"Will you have a cup of coffee with me?" I asked. "I think it's almost ready."

"That sounds good."

He was looking at the newspaper lying on the side table. "I see you've been reading about the murder." He followed me into the dining room. "I came by to ask if you remembered anything more. Anything at all."

"Only what I told you."

"It sure would help if you could give me a description of the driver."

"I'm sorry. I can't. I wish I'd taken a good look at him but I couldn't know it was going to be important. Did you find the Crown Victoria?"

"The state troopers did. It was abandoned a few miles west of a freeway exit ramp stuck in a snow bank. There's no sign of the driver."

"But you can still identify him, can't you?"

"Maybe. Someone stole the Crown Vic from a used car lot in Saginaw last night. The lab has it now. If the driver left a shred of evidence behind we'll find it."

He sounded confident, but then he was the sheriff. I was the one who might be the target of a killer since I was a possible witness.

"That isn't good," I said. "I hoped you'd have him in custody by now."

"There's a chance that the driver and the killer aren't the same person. But I have another lead. Nothing I can talk about," he added quickly.

He pulled out a chair at the head of the table, official business concluded, ready for refreshment. I could only hope he didn't consider me his other lead.

"I guess I'll have to keep reading the paper then," I said. "Sit down and I'll bring the coffee in."

I found another mug and washed the dust off it. Perhaps if I plied Sheriff Mark Dalby with good fresh coffee and day-old doughnuts he'd slip and tell me something about his lead. I found a plate, ran it under the hot water tap, and spilled the dunkers, crullers, and cinnamon fries onto it.

The Valentine lay in the empty candy box. A coy Cupid in a surround of lace-edged hearts and red roses, he held a berib-boned banner that bore the sentiment 'Truly Thine'. The sheriff was looking at the card collection.

"I haven't seen one of those old Sanders candy boxes in years," he said.

I set the plate of doughnuts in front of him. "There can't be many of them around. The cabin belonged to my Great Aunt Celia. Did you know her?"

"That must have been before my time," he said. "I only knew Doc McLaughlin. You said you weren't moving in, Krista. It looks like you're settling in for a long winter's stay."

"I'm on vacation. I'd like to go cross-country skiing on my own land."

"Did you say you have a friend coming up to join you?"

"I don't think I did. Why?"

He chose a chocolate-covered cruller from the platter. "Like I said before, it's pretty isolated out here for a woman on her own. This looks good. Thanks."

"After her husband was declared missing in action in Vietnam, Aunt Celia lived on the farm alone. I'm sure her neighbors looked out for her."

For some reason my appetite for doughnuts had returned. Food always tastes better when eaten outside or with a companion. I helped myself to a plain cruller and said, "I have a neighbor I haven't met yet."

"In the gray house? That's Craig Stennet. He's nearby all right, but he's kind of strange. Don't count on him for protection."

There was that note of condescension in his voice again. I didn't like it.

"I don't intend to. I'm really self-reliant."

"Is that shotgun in good working condition?" he asked.

"I'm not sure, but I'm going to find out."

"Do you know how to use it?"

"Yes. You say that Craig Stennet is strange. In what way?"

He shrugged. "Stennet keeps to himself. He's a writer. He had an article about native predators published in *Michigan Up North* last month. You might ask him about wolves if you want a second opinion."

I said, "I'll do that when I meet him."

I was more interested in what the sheriff wasn't saying. "Do you think I'm in danger?" I asked. "Anyone could have found Randall Scott's body, whoever happened to be on that road."

"You're assuming that the driver and the killer are the same person again. I told you…I have another suspect."

Consumed with curiosity about his lead I said, "Have another doughnut, Sheriff. I'll pour you some more coffee."

He handed me the empty cup and leaned back in the chair. He was at ease, willing to offer me a sliver of confidential information now, or make it appear that he was.

When I came back with his coffee he said, "Maybe a kid stole the car, took it out for a joy ride and then abandoned it. Lots of people leave their cars on the road when they get stuck. We're going to get Scott's killer, Krista. Maybe we'll have him tomorrow. Keep reading the paper," he said. "Listen to the news."

"I would but the radio is broken."

"Maybe it can be fixed. There's a young man in town who does that kind of work. In the meantime you can listen to your car radio. If you see anything unusual or if something happens let me know right away."

"I'll do that. And I won't open the door to any stray men who are just passing by."

He took a gulp of coffee and another doughnut and said, "Those stray men should watch out for you, Krista."

His blue eyes were sparkling again and for a moment I thought he was going to laugh.

FIVE

I STOOD OUTSIDE the back porch knee-deep in drifted snow looking up at the old maple. For years the tree had been allowed to grow unchecked. Now it was so close to the cabin that its lowest branch leaned heavily on the section of wall alongside the window.

In a strong wind the branch would whip around in the air and repeatedly strike the glass. That was the probable cause of the pounding that had awakened me last night—it was neither the sheriff knocking at my door again nor a ghostly manifestation, but a restless tree limb.

It was about four feet beyond my reach. Of all my problems this would be the easiest one to solve, but I needed a saw and a ladder. I glanced toward the barns. That's where the tools would be stored—at the end of a path that probably hadn't seen a snow shovel in years.

I'd been standing outside for only five minutes but already my face was beginning to burn and my fingers were aching in spite of the heavy gloves I wore. Not wanting to add frostbite to my list of things to deal with, I hurried inside where I found the keys labeled 'Barns.' After waiting for a few minutes in the kitchen until I stopped shivering and my hands thawed, I headed back outside, stepping deep into high snow, moving as quickly as I could.

Last night's wind had died down, leaving a cold, clear day without a hint of a breeze. In the brilliant morning sunshine, the snow sparkled like the silver glitter in Aunt Celia's candy box or like the sheriff's eyes on the few occasions when he'd been in a congenial mood.

What was it about the man that made me think about him so often? Heaven knows I had enough to do, and the last thing I needed was another nowhere-bound romance. I forced myself to put Sheriff Dalby out of my mind and concentrate on my surroundings.

My car was blanketed in glistening white and all traces of the sheriff's cruiser had vanished, buried under a fresh ground cover. Deer tracks crisscrossed the area in front of the cabin, but I didn't see anything that looked like the paw prints of a wild canine.

My own section of the world was beautiful and bright, but this sunlit splendor had a dark side. The trees were duplicated in the snow as shadows. The one lying ahead of me, right across my path, was the strangest shadow I had ever seen. It resembled a gigantic arrow.

I came to a standstill and looked up at the tall poplar on my right. A branch had broken in the middle and fallen. The portion that was still attached to the trunk was pointed like a sharpened pencil and surrounded by trapped deadwood.

That was what had caused the arrow-like shadow. I forced myself to look away. Was I becoming paranoid? In a minute I'd be imagining the ominous shape of a hanging man.

At times I didn't think about Randall Scott and the way he died, but the memory was never far away. I could happily immerse myself in my own affairs, and then, without warning, the image of the dead man would insinuate itself into my thoughts.

Instead of seeing Randall Scott as he had looked in death, broken and bleeding, I would see the man in the newspaper photograph, holding a puppy and smiling, a person anyone would want to know.

Stop thinking about him, I ordered myself. *Forget about shadows. Concentrate on what you're doing.*

As I plowed through the snow, I took the keys out of my pocket. With luck I'd be able to unlock the door quickly, find a ladder and saw, and retrace my footsteps back to the cabin where it was relatively warm. But when I reached the first barn, I saw that my project wasn't going to be so easy. Over the years, the lock had frozen and turned to a chunk of rust. Before I could open the door, I would need a can of lubricating oil, an essential I'd neglected to bring.

Frustrated by this unforeseen obstacle, I imagined that I might get the door open only to discover that the barn was empty. With this possibility in mind, I changed my plan for the day in favor of a trip to Huron Station. The branch wasn't going anywhere and it was too cold today to climb a ladder and saw through wood. A shopping trip was a more appealing activity. I'd buy whatever I could think of that might prove useful, and in a day or two, when the weather moderated, I'd take care of that pesky branch.

I SAW THE HUNTER as soon as I came out of the cabin. A small splash of orange against the stark background, he stood across the meadow at the edge of the woods. He was about five acres away from me. Squinting against the glare of sunlight on white, I saw that he was carrying a rifle. He seemed to be watching the cabin—or me.

I tried to ignore the icy fear that began to creep over me. After all, Sheriff Dalby said the woods were thick with deer. Doctor McLaughlin and his hunter friends had made my aunt's farm their headquarters. Maybe one of them had returned to the familiar territory.

Or the hunter might be interested in another kind of prey.

"It's pretty isolated out here for a woman on her own," the sheriff had said.

Then, as if aware that he'd been observed, the man turned around and walked back into the woods. I watched the dark tangle of trees swallow up the orange and breathed more easily.

Good riddance to the curious deer killer. I wouldn't have to deal with him today. Later, though, as I brushed the snow off my car, I decided to visit Sheriff Dalby when I was in town. He had asked me to alert him to any unusual occurrences. If the man on my property wasn't hunting, this incident certainly qualified as one.

With deer, wolves, a solitary watcher in the woods, and a strange writer living across the road, I wasn't as alone in my wilderness cabin as I thought.

SHERIFF DALBY'S DISPATCHER had long oval-shaped fingernails painted bright green with a silver quarter moon-and-stars design. They were a perfect match for her cowl neck sweater and emerald ring. As she wrote my name and cell phone number on a message pad the jewel sparkled in the harsh overhead light.

Vibrant color and glittering makeup must be a local woman's key to survival in the long northern winter.

"The sheriff will call you as soon as he comes back," she said in a perky, professional voice that grated across my frayed nerves.

I was getting hungry. I planned to have dinner at Estella's Café while I was still in town rather than drive in later.

"I may not be home for a few hours," I said, wishing I'd remembered to take my cell phone. "Will you ask him to call me after four?"

"Well, okay, no problem. He'll call you then."

"Do you know where I can find a hardware store?" I asked.

"Turn west on Main Street and drive out of town. It's on the right. You can't miss it."

But I wasn't so sure fifteen minutes later when I still hadn't found the place. Just as I was about to pull into the Sunoco station ahead and ask directions, I saw the sign on an aging two-story building: 'Drayton's Feed and Hardware.' The store was attached to a barn and set far back from the road with shovels and snow blowers leaning against a faded red brick exterior and a frosty window. I'd nearly missed it.

I parked close to the entrance and went inside. The shelves were stocked with additional reminders of what I'd need when the real winter arrived next month. I collected a bag of rock salt, an extra flashlight, and a package of batteries, and headed for the back of the store where the all-weather items were kept.

As I moved through the aisles, inhaling the potent odors of

paint and rubber, I found everything on my list. Carrying a shiny aluminum ladder that would give me the extra four feet I needed to reach the branch, I made my way to the cash register, took my place in line, and studied the impulse items on display around the counter.

"Are you going to do a little renovating to the cabin?"

The voice was behind me. I turned and recognized my neighbor. He was wearing the same brown jacket and red plaid scarf he'd worn for riding when I'd seen him yesterday. In his hand he held a box of faucet parts.

Now that he was so close to me I could see that his wavy hair was mostly gray with the slightest sprinkling of black. The scar that curved from his left eyebrow to his high cheekbone enhanced his ruggedly attractive features.

He smiled at me and waited for my answer. "I'm Craig Stennet from the gray house across the road," he said. "I waved to you yesterday when I was out riding."

"Hi. I'm Krista Marlow." I moved the saw further down the counter. "I'm only going to do a little tree trimming."

"In this weather?"

I told him about the branch that had kept me awake by scraping against the window. "My cabin appears to be haunted, Mr. Stennet. It's filled with strange noises that only come out at night."

He nodded. "I'm not surprised. The place has been deserted for years, except during hunting season."

"It used to belong to my Great Aunt Celia. Did you know her?"

"No, but I've only lived here for seven years. I talked to Doctor McLaughlin a few times. I assumed that he owned the cabin. He talked about it as if it were his place."

He glanced at my saw. "I'll trim the tree for you, if you'd like. I was going to come over anyway and introduce myself."

So this was the strange neighbor Sheriff Dalby described? Maybe he was wrong about the wolves, too.

"Thanks, but I can do it," I said, not wanting to appear to be a helpless female. Then, realizing that my reply amounted to a rejection, I added, "Could I have a rain check? I'm sure something will come up that I can't do."

"Sure, Krista," he said. "Anytime, and it's Craig. Let's get together some day soon for a drink or dinner. Neighbors are few and far between in Huron Station."

"I'd like that."

"We'll do it then. Soon."

"Miss?" The young blond man behind the checkout counter was trying to get my attention. While Craig and I had been talking, I'd moved to the head of the line and he'd finished ringing up my purchases. I handed him a fifty-dollar bill.

"Do you want help carrying that ladder out to your car?" the clerk asked.

"I can manage…"

"I'll take it for you," Craig said, "unless you're in a hurry."

"No, I'll wait for you, and thanks again."

While Craig paid for his faucet parts, I studied my new neighbor's face. He was easily twice my age, at least fifty, and seemed a trifle old-fashioned, not at all like the men I was used to. He belonged to a whole other generation, that of my late parents. Maybe he was a little pushy about offering his services, but having someone so helpful living nearby would be pleasant.

I couldn't imagine why Sheriff Dalby had described him as strange.

MY LAST STOP WAS Estella's Café for an early dinner. The time was three-thirty now, the snow was falling lightly, and the lunch crowd had trickled down to a few solitary customers. The restaurant was a quiet and pleasant oasis of warmth in a frozen world. No wonder people lingered here over dessert and coffee.

Although I had been in the café a few times, the place seemed oddly familiar to me, almost like the quintessential Grandma's parlor. With the irresistible aromas of turkey and pumpkin drifting out from the kitchen, I could imagine my whole family home for Thanksgiving dinner, a nostalgic Norman Rockwell print come to life.

Estella was sitting at the counter reading the paper. She turned around when I came through the door. Her eyes were shadowed with smoky gray today, but no makeup could conceal the fact that they were bloodshot. It looked as if she had been crying, but her greeting was so cheerful and friendly that I decided I must be wrong.

"If you're here for the turkey dinner, we've added something special today," she said. "It's a surprise course."

She was reading the *Huron Station Press*. The boldface headline dominated the front page: 'Archery Murder Suspect Questioned.' That must be Sheriff Dalby's other lead.

I peered over her shoulder. "Thank heavens the sheriff arrested somebody. That's fast work."

"Roy didn't do it."

I sat down beside Estella, now in no hurry to be seated at a table. "Do you know the suspect?"

"I guess I know Roy Yarrow as well as anybody in town. Poor Randall didn't deserve to die like that, slaughtered like an animal and left in a tree, but Roy didn't kill him. I'm sorry you were the one to find his body."

"Did the sheriff tell you that?"

"He may have, or it might have been one of the deputies."

I said, "It's true. I was on that road by accident. If I hadn't found him somebody else would have."

"There hasn't been a murder in all the time I've lived here, only hunting accidents."

"It sounds as if you knew Randall Scott, too."

"I did," she said. "He was a good man—a wonderful man."

"Sheriff Dalby called him a local celebrity. What exactly did he do besides his television show?"

"I wouldn't say that Randall Scott was famous, but most people around here knew him. He was rich and generous with his time and money. He was going to build a ski resort here in Huron Station…"

She trailed off and dabbed at her eyes, smearing the gray.

"I read that he'd been married three times and had four children," I said.

"That's true. He and his present wife were getting a divorce. You may have seen his daughter, Renie. She's on a television station downstate."

"Renie Scott. Sure. I've seen her. She's the Channel Five meteorologist. Tell me, Estella, did Randall and this suspect know each other?"

"Yes, unfortunately. They were exact opposites who disagreed about practically everything, especially hunting. The deer kill was only a part of it. They came to blows last month, and Roy threatened to kill Randall. Plenty of people heard him, but I think Roy was just talking. He can't stand to hurt an animal, much less a human."

I remembered the sheriff saying that Randall Scott had participated in the deer kill at Millennium Park. "Was Roy Yarrow one of the anti-hunting activists?"

"Yes. That's why I'm so sure he's innocent. Roy isn't a violent man. He advocates kindness to animals and tries to fight cruelty wherever he finds it. Activists are for peace, not violence."

"Not all of them. Some have been known to resort to murder to call attention to their cause."

"That's not Roy, but no matter. He's everybody's favorite suspect. Roy has been in trouble before. I'm sure Mark would like to put him away. I wish Roy had never threatened Randall. Mostly, Roy was all talk."

I didn't think Sheriff Dalby would arrest a man on the basis of threats. "There must be other evidence."

"There may be." Estella folded the *Station Press* and set it aside. Either she had exhausted her supply of knowledge or feared she had said too much. As she reached across the counter for a menu, she said, "You came in here for dinner, Miss Marlow, not to talk about murder. Do you want the turkey special again?"

"Yes, but call me Krista. I don't have any Thanksgiving plans. This dinner will be it."

"You're not going to stay alone in that old cabin over the holiday, are you?"

She must have been talking to Sheriff Dalby about me. How much had he told Estella? Fortunately, he knew very little.

"I may go cross-country skiing," I said.

"That sounds like fun. How about this table, by the stove?"

I followed her to the choice spot that Sheriff Dalby and the troopers had occupied on my first visit to the café.

"I knew your Aunt Celia," Estella said. "Mark told me you're her niece. She was a sweet lady."

"Everybody thought so. The cabin isn't the same without her bustling around in her kitchen."

"I suppose you know you resemble her. You have her pretty gray eyes and her hair used to be the same shade of red as yours."

"My mother often said so."

"Your aunt is probably looking down at you right this minute, glad you're here."

"That's a nice thought," I said. "I'll keep it in mind."

"If you're going skiing watch for the hunters," she added. "Wear something orange if you have it so they'll know you're a person and not a deer. I'll swear some of those fools shoot at anything that moves."

She left me with that alarming thought. While I waited for her to bring my order, I took my paperback mystery out of my shoulder bag. But instead of reading, I mulled over what Estella had said. Were her tears for the victim or the suspect, or perhaps for both men? I couldn't tell. Maybe her eyes were just rebelling against the high intensity liner and shadow.

I still hadn't decided when Ruth, Estella's other waitress, came out of the kitchen carrying a tray that contained a large bowl filled with thick liquid. Its color was an unappetizing pale orange.

"This is pumpkin soup," she said. "Your turkey will be out in a few minutes."

I was eyeing the first course warily when Sheriff Dalby

came into the café, bringing a rush of Arctic air with him. He headed straight for me with a determined look in his eyes. Estella intercepted him at the stove.

"Just a cup of coffee today, Stella," he said. "I came to see Miss Marlow."

He pulled out a chair, sat down, and leaned forward, elbows on the table. A trace of snow lingered on his tawny hair. His voice was brusque and hurried. "I got your message and took a chance you'd be here. What happened?"

"I saw a hunter on my land this morning. I thought you'd want to know."

From his frown, I realized I'd said that all wrong. "He might have been watching the cabin. It made me uneasy, but then he just left. It's probably nothing. I only meant for you to call me when you had time."

He continued to stare at me. In the deepening silence that followed, I realized that he must think I'd called him away from official business to relate a virtual non-incident. Growing uncomfortable under his scrutiny, I pushed the soup away. At the moment it was more than I could face.

"It tastes better than it looks," he said. "Stella gave me a sample this morning."

"I like my pumpkins on piecrust or hollowed out with a candle inside. I'll just let it cool for a while."

He said, "If you're concerned about this man, it's something, Krista. But don't forget that this is the hunting season. You can post 'No Trespassing' and 'No Hunting' signs. If you see men on your property chase them away."

"And they'll just listen to me and go? What if the man wanted something else?"

"You said he went away."

"Yes, but he could come back."

There was that twinkle in his eyes again. It didn't appear often, but when it did, the stern lawman look vanished. Everything about him seemed lighter.

"If he does, let me know," he said.

I leaned forward to meet his gaze. "And what will you do?"

Before he could answer, Estella set a cup of steaming coffee on the table. "Sure you won't have a bowl of pumpkin soup, Mark? Something to warm you up?"

"Maybe later," he said. "Thanks, Stella. Now, Krista, let's wait till this hunter of yours makes another appearance. You call me then, and we'll see."

"That's a nice, safe answer, Sheriff. I hear you have your man."

"Just like I said. I always get him."

"Estella thinks he's innocent," I said.

"She has a soft heart for drifters and losers."

"Don't you think it's little too obvious? An activist murdering a hunter during hunting season?"

"That doesn't mean it didn't happen that way. Aside from strange men trespassing on your land, how are you getting along in the deep woods?"

"Just fine. I love the cabin."

"It isn't too cold for you up there all by yourself?"

"Not at all. I have the wood stove."

His sudden smile melted a little of the ice in his blue eyes. I wondered if he found some secret humor in my remark.

"I'll drive over to see you in the morning," he said. "I want you to look at a picture of someone. He was seen driving a gray car on the day of the murder."

"All right, I guess I'll be home."

He pounced on that. "Home? I thought you were on vacation."

"It's just an expression." I looked up at him and smiled. "I'm not your suspect—or am I?"

"I just need to ask you a few questions," he said.

With that oblique comment, he touched my arm lightly and stood up.

I watched him stride boldly through the aisle and out the door. It looked as though I would be seeing more of Sheriff Mark Dalby. Whether or not that was good remained to be seen.

SIX

THE SOUND WAS a faraway murmur, breaking through the stillness that surrounded me. Lying in bed, safe and warm under Aunt Celia's quilt, I knew that the old radio had come alive again.

I heard two male voices, one of them heavily accented, and frequent bursts of laughter, followed by music that swelled to a crescendo. It seemed to fill the entire cabin, and then died like the last ember in the wood stove.

It's only a dream, I told myself. But suppose it was real?

If I got out of bed and walked the short distance to the dining room, I'd know for certain. But I couldn't do it. The quilt was as hard and cold as an ice-crusted snowdrift pressing down on my body. It was much easier to lie still under the covers and relax.

Think about falling snow; surrender to the frigid night air trapped in the bedroom; burrow deeper into the flannel sheets.

In the end, I didn't resist. I didn't want to.

DEAR LORD, that radio is haunted.

The time on my traveler's clock read five-thirty in the morning. Inside and out, the cabin was steeped in darkness and a heavy, pre-dawn silence. I couldn't stay in bed enjoying the last few minutes of warmth and rest while the cabin was the target of a supernatural manifestation. When I'd examined the radio earlier I must have missed something. The need to investigate the eerie phenomenon propelled me into action.

I searched for my slippers and found one under the bed and the other halfway across the room. *And how did that happen?*

When I'd gone to bed, they were together. I hoped the cabin wasn't haunted, too.

I tried to remember. I'd been up once during the night for a glass of water. Probably I'd kicked them off when I returned to bed and one had traveled farther than I'd intended. That was a nice, acceptable explanation.

Shivering, I scrambled across the bare hardwood floor to the bathroom. I needed warm water, toothpaste, and a fresh perspective, and this part of the cabin needed its own wood stove.

I wished I wasn't alone in the middle of eighty acres of woods. I didn't doubt the validity of otherworldly happenings, but I never thought I'd experience one. There had to be a rational explanation for a vintage radio that turned itself on and off at will. It made sense to eliminate every possible natural cause before leaping to the supernatural, but I had to be awake and alert to do it.

First things first. I started a fire in the wood stove and filled the copper teakettle. A little later, when the flames were blazing and the water was boiling, I made a cup of tea and took it into the dining room.

There on the sideboard was the radio, silent and broken. In the strong morning light that streamed through the window, its mahogany case was lightly covered with dust.

But how could that be? Only yesterday I'd cleaned the entire dining room. I ran my hand across the shiny surface of the sideboard. That was dusty too, but I decided there was nothing mysterious about it. I wasn't a thorough housekeeper, and the bright sunshine magnified every stray mote. Now, on to the major mystery.

In the hope of restoring the audio, I began to play with the radio, turning all three knobs in a fruitless search for the morning weather report or an update on the archery murder, anything at all to prove that my ghost was a faulty mechanism or connection.

Nothing happened. The sound was definitely gone, but I hadn't dreamed last night's broadcast. I was sure of it.

Exasperated and confused, I returned the knob to the 'off' position. Mark had mentioned that someone in Huron Station had a repair service. Before I accepted the idea that the radio was haunted, I'd have it thoroughly dissected by an expert.

WHILE I WAS DRINKING my second cup of tea and planning the day's projects, I heard a car door slam and the stamping of footprints on the porch. Guessing that my caller was the sheriff, I rushed to the door to let him in.

It seemed that whenever Mark entered a room, he brought a bit of the weather with him. A blast of cold north air, a swirl of snow, and the power of the winter wind—they were all inside the cabin with us now, eagerly reaching toward the flames in the stove.

"Morning, Krista," he said. "You're up bright and early."

"I'm a morning person, Sheriff. Come in and have a cup of tea with me."

Without realizing what I was doing, I stepped back from the door and touched the radio, willing it to remain still, afraid it would turn itself on.

Let it. Then I'd know I wasn't imagining things.

It was hard to think about Sheriff Dalby and the supernatural at the same time. His powerful body and the sheer force of his presence filled the room. No phantom would dare invade his space.

"Or would you rather have coffee?" I asked.

"Make it coffee." He set a manila envelope on the table and pulled out a chair, gripping its solid maple arm firmly with his large hand. "Did your hunter make another appearance?"

"Not last night. I haven't been outside yet this morning."

"I didn't see anyone around the cabin except Stennet out for his daily ride," he said.

"You'd think he'd be afraid his horse would fall on the ice. I didn't realize people went horseback riding in the winter."

"That road is in good condition. Stennet must know what he's doing."

Our conversation was trapped in a vortex of small talk. The sheriff was staring at the radio. He must be wondering why I still rested my hand on it.

His blue eyes sparkled with the humor I'd seen before. "You don't have to protect your valuables from me, Krista."

"I—I'm not. Sit down and I'll get your coffee. Then I'll see if I can identify your suspect, but I have to remind you again. I didn't really look at the driver that day, only the snow on his car."

"You may have seen something that you forgot."

With one last glance at the radio I said, "I'll start the coffee."

The books I'd brought along to read on snowy winter nights were on the sideboard, too. When I returned with a plate of cinnamon rolls and two paper napkins, he was holding my leather-bound Dickens volume.

"*A Christmas Carol*," he said. "You're going to take a long vacation."

"Well, 'tis the season."

"You have a good selection of reading material."

Besides the Dickens classic, I'd chosen my favorites: collections of poetry by Stephen Vincent Benet and Emily Dickinson and a science-fiction time travel novel. The mystery was still in my shoulder bag.

"I think so. I wish I'd brought more. While we're waiting I'll look at your picture."

He helped himself to a cinnamon roll. "You've discovered the Station Bakery, I see."

"I sure have. I'm going to live on take-out sandwiches from Estella's Café and pastries from the bakery. The stove works but I'm not going to cook. I'm on vacation."

He wiped his fingers on a napkin and took six pictures out of the envelope. "These are snapshots of three different men. Two were taken at the deer kill protest last month. Look at them carefully. Take your time."

I knew what he wanted me to say. He was clever, but he couldn't conceal the eagerness in his voice. According to Estella, the sheriff was determined to send Roy Yarrow to jail.

He had called the suspect a loser and a drifter. His words had created an image in my mind that threatened to dull my objectivity. I'd envisioned a man wearing faded Levis and a tattered jeans jacket. He would have long, unkempt hair and the burning eyes of a fanatic. Blocking out this mental picture I went back in time to the day I found Randall Scott's body…the treacherous drive on the icy road, the gray car coming toward me like a machine gone berserk, my fear that it would hit me.

Sheriff Dalby said, "There's no hurry, Krista."

I held the pictures up to the sunlight. It was easy to tell which one of the suspects was Roy Yarrow. He had attractive features and his dark hair was cut short. He looked as if he only had time for life's serious issues. I could see him in a college classroom more easily than a picket line. The other men were older than I imagined Roy to be and they had a rough, disreputable look.

"I've never seen any of them before," I said.

The left windshield wiper had cleared a wide arc of snow, just enough to frame the driver's face. His features were still a blur, but now he was wearing a cap.

I said, "He was wearing a cap."

"But you couldn't see his face because of all the snow on the window," he reminded me.

"That's what I thought until this lost detail just resurfaced."

"What color was the cap?" he asked.

"White or gray, I think, or maybe it was the snow on the front window. I can't be sure of the color. I wonder what else I forgot?"

"Give it time, Krista. There may be more."

"Memory is a strange thing. It scares me," I said.

"Don't let it. In its own good time, it'll come. Now, how about that coffee?" Apparently satisfied, he put the pictures back into the envelope.

"You'd like to get this case closed, wouldn't you, Sheriff?" I asked.

"That's going to happen."

"I don't want to help you railroad an innocent man—if Roy Yarrow is innocent," I said.

"That's *not* going to happen. I have a good piece of evidence against Yarrow and I'd like to get more. Scott's daughter is going to be in town tomorrow. I want to have something to tell her."

"Which daughter? Renie Scott or the one who lives in California?"

"Renie," he said. "She just got to know her father recently when he came to Michigan. After her parents' divorce, she moved to St. Clair Shores with her mother."

"Is she coming to investigate the murder for Channel Five?"

"No, Renie is their weathercaster. She's here on her own. Tomorrow is Thanksgiving and she has a few days off. Huron Station will be closed down for the holiday except for my office," he said. "I'm not going to rest until I see Yarrow behind bars."

"Who are the other men in the pictures?" I asked.

"They've been in trouble with me before. Consider this a pictorial lineup. I don't want anyone to accuse me of putting ideas in your head."

"That'll never happen." Before he could respond to my comment I asked, "Where is the radio repair shop located?"

"Over at the Feed and Hardware. Albert Drayton is a jack of all trades. If he can't fix it, he'll know where you can take it." He looked toward the living room and frowned. "Without television or a working radio you're cutting yourself off from the rest of the world."

"There's one in my car, but you're right. I need a radio in the cabin, if only to listen to those chilling weather reports. Since tomorrow is a holiday, I'd better go into town today."

"Yes. Get in some supplies for that big blizzard that's coming."

For a moment I imagined myself snowbound in the middle of eighty acres with nothing to eat and only the ghost in the radio for company.

"Don't look so alarmed," he said. "I meant, sometime this winter. Call me if you remember anything else, or if that trespasser shows up again. Thanks for the help and the breakfast."

He put his pictures back into the envelope and walked over to the door. It seemed as if he couldn't wait to leave and resume his search for evidence. But then I remembered: the dead man's television star daughter was on her way to Huron Station. Sheriff Dalby wanted to give her a progress report.

As I TOOK THE CUPS and plate into the kitchen I half expected the radio to turn itself on. But with the sheriff's departure the cabin returned to its normal super-silent state. Apparently inexplicable noises and impossible happenings were reserved for the nighttime hours.

I wrapped the last two cinnamon buns in waxed paper and held the dishes under the hot water faucet until they were clean. My goal was to keep household chores to a minimum. So far I'd been successful.

My work with Aunt Celia's belongings was moving along in slow motion. I'd decided to use the 'Keep, Discard, Set Aside and Decide Later' method, but so far I hadn't found anything I wanted to throw away except a stack of paid bills dating from the year of her death.

I'd slipped the Valentine into my *Selected Poems of Emily Dickinson* to use as a bookmark until I could find a frame for it. There was no signature or verse inside, only the two words 'Truly Thine." But who needed more than that?

Maybe Aunt Celia had known the identity of the sender or considered the card too pretty to throw away. Most likely her husband, Kent, had given it to her. I supposed it didn't matter now, except to me.

You tend to remember people as they looked when you were last with them. I saw my aunt as plump and silver-haired, with rosy cheeks and a warm smile that reflected her loving nature. To a young girl, she'd seemed ancient, but at one time she had been my own age and had cherished a romantic Valentine.

There was so much about Aunt Celia that I didn't know. An entire story, in fact, but she could no longer tell it. If I intended to finish my sorting project I had to move on.

I put the card collection in the 'Keep' stack and turned to

the next box. Feeling as if I were opening a gift of my own, I raised the lid and carefully lifted a miniature silver sleigh from the layers of white tissue paper.

I set the trinket on the sideboard next to the radio and stepped back to admire its soft glow in the sunshine. It measured about a foot in length and had a height of three or four inches. Although it was badly tarnished, a dab of polish would restore its former luster. The workmanship was intricate and the sleigh was embellished with fanciful scrolls. In a subtle way—the toss of a head, the position of a paw—each of the reindeer was unique.

On Christmas, Aunt Celia used to put up a balsam fir tree chopped down from her own woods, unfold a white sheet around the tree stand, and sprinkle a glittering substance that looked like snow all around it. Then she would place the silver sleigh under one of the lower branches, making sure that only white lights were shining on it.

That couldn't be a memory, because all my trips to Huron Station had taken place in the summer. My mother must have mentioned it, or maybe I'd seen a picture in one of the old family albums labeled 'Christmas on the Farm.'

As I held the silver sleigh, the thought came to me that I should really experience one Christmas in the cabin before I left Huron Station to begin that other life as a doctoral candidate that I wanted so much. I would be more than doubling my planned two-week stay, but it was possible. There was no one waiting for me to come home and I could find another substitute teaching job at any time.

I made a few swift calculations. My money should last until the middle of January if I was careful with it. Once I enrolled in a doctoral program it would be a long time before I could take another break. And besides, then I'd no longer own the cabin.

It made sense to extend my vacation. At the moment I couldn't think of a reason not to stay in Huron Station for Christmas.

ON THE AFTERNOON before Thanksgiving, Drayton's Feed and Hardware was deserted except for the blond man behind the cash register. He looked bored, but he brightened considerably when he saw what I was holding.

"I inherited this radio from my aunt but it doesn't work," I said. "I'd like to have Albert Drayton take a look at it."

"What a beauty! You came to the right place. I'm Albert Drayton."

"The store's owner?"

"I'm his nephew and maybe his partner one day."

He examined the radio carefully, lovingly, as if it were a handsome living thing brought to him to be petted and admired.

"For a minute, I thought you had a replica. One of those collectors' editions," he said.

"No, I'm certain it's an antique. Do you think there's any hope for it?"

"If anyone can get it working, I can," he said. "That's my hobby—tinkering with old radios and phonographs."

"I'll leave it then."

He pulled out a receipt pad, scribbled the information I gave him, and ripped out a copy. "Give me about a week," he said.

"A friend of mine described you as a jack-of-all-trades. What else do you do?" I asked.

"I'm majoring in agriculture at State. I'd like to take over our family farm but there's no living in that. I'll do almost anything you need done, and if you have any small appliances that don't work, bring them in. I make house calls, too, for the ones you can't carry."

Along with the receipt he gave me his card.

"You sound too good to be true," I said. "I may call you, Albert."

When I left him, he was playing with the knobs as I had done. How would he react if the radio suddenly turned itself on? He'd probably be fascinated. In any event, whether I ended up with a radio that worked and an explanation for its strange behavior or a genuine haunt, the thought of having an ally on this otherworldly exploration was reassuring.

SEVEN

A LIGHT SNOW was falling and it felt colder, as it always does without the sunlight. Still, I loved the northern winter and the constant promise of fresh snow. It seemed to me that each additional layer was a separate new beginning.

Albert Drayton had the radio and I could look forward to seven nights of sleep undisturbed by a broadcast from beyond. Now all I needed was something to eat.

Huron Station was as white and still as a glittering snow scene on a Christmas card. The tire tracks and sludge-stained mounds that had lined the road were covered once again. In front of St. Sebastian's Catholic Church, two men walked around the outdoor manger they were constructing, drinking from thermoses and making notes. Along Main Street, several of the shops had already closed for the day. I parked in front of the café, leaving myself ample room to pull out, and went inside.

I didn't see Estella, but Craig Stennet sat at a secluded table in the back reading a book. The only other diners were three rowdy hunters in bright orange jackets and the two state troopers I had seen on my first day in town. As she served the officers, Cindy exchanged light banter with them, but she was obviously trying to avoid the hunters. Everyone else in town must be getting ready for the holiday or in the woods stalking the deer.

I sat down at the counter, unbuttoned my coat and pushed back the hood. The café had no formal take out window, but Ruth had seen me, and with so few customers, I knew I wouldn't have a long wait.

A discarded *Station Press* lay on the stool beside me. Once again a boldface streamer blared the day's top news story:

'Two Hunters Killed in Alpena.' A more modest headline was equally grim: 'Flu Claims First Fatality.'

Sheriff Dalby had said that I was in dangerous country. With four deaths in a single week and the hunting season in full swing, I was ready to believe him. The grisly killing of Randall Scott was different from the others, though; and if Roy Yarrow were innocent, as Estella claimed, the archer killer was still out there somewhere. He might be the man I'd seen at the edge of the woods.

"Hi, Krista. It's nice to see you again."

Estella came out of the kitchen, patting back a strand of silver hair that had fallen over her left eye. She was a little breathless, and her face was flushed only a few shades lighter than her fuchsia turtleneck.

"We just had a little oven fire, but it's under control," she said. "I can hardly wait for this day to end. Are you here for dinner?"

"No, I came for two days' worth of take out."

Estella walked over to the door and peered outside. "It's snowing again. That'll make everything pretty for Thanksgiving. The snow covers up a multitude of sins, don't you agree?"

"I suppose so. I never thought about it that way," I said before realizing that I'd had a similar idea only a few minutes ago, but without the sins. Nevertheless, it was a strange statement to make, unless in some way it was connected with the killing of Randall Scott.

"Do you know if Roy Yarrow is still in custody?" I asked.

"I assume so. He usually comes to the café at least once a day for a hot meal. Do you want to take out the special?"

"Not today. I'd like two sandwiches, turkey on whole wheat with lettuce and tomato."

"How about two pieces of pumpkin pie to go with them? Two coffees?" As if on command, a heavenly pumpkin-ginger-cloves scent drifted out of the kitchen.

"The pie sounds good. I'll take two slices, but I make my own coffee at home."

"You're having company for lunch?"

I hesitated for a second before replying. From our first conversation I'd sensed that Estella was a gossip, but in this case, her question was harmless enough. Why not give her an equally innocuous answer?

I said, "They're for my dinner. I'm not cooking tomorrow."

"Is Celia's stove still working?" she asked. "It must be at least twenty years old."

"It seems to be. But so far I've only made coffee and tea."

"How Celia used to love to cook and bake. I still remember her pies. She used lard for the crust. Celia often said she'd come work for me in the café, but she didn't want to leave the farm."

"My aunt didn't really have to work for a living. She loved staying home and taking care of her garden and the animals."

"Wouldn't it be great if we could all do that?" With a sigh, Estella returned to the present. "A sandwich isn't much of a Thanksgiving dinner for you, Krista."

"I don't mind," I said. "I expect to be busy tomorrow."

"Are you going skiing?"

"Probably, if it doesn't get any colder."

I was growing uncomfortable with this pleasant interrogation and beginning to feel trapped in a conversation that was going in a dangerous direction. Even though Estella and my aunt had been friends, I didn't want to talk to her about myself, lest my activities become common knowledge around town.

Ruth was coming my way with a glass of water and a menu and the troopers were getting ready to leave. My window of opportunity to escape Estella's questions was opening but I only had a short time to act.

"Craig Stennet is here," Estella said. "He lives across the road from you. Have you met him yet?"

As Ruth set the water and menu down on the counter in front of me, I glanced toward the back of the restaurant where Craig was still reading. The hunters, who had finished their dinner, were growing increasingly louder. Since there were so few people in the café, their noise was particularly annoying. I didn't know how Craig could concentrate over their racy jokes and raucous laughter.

Offering her a tidbit, I said, "I met him at the hardware store the other day. He seems nice."

"Craig Stennet is a genuine gentleman. He's been coming to the café for lunch for years, but I don't really know him. He never says more than he has to." Her gaze strayed to the hunters and she shook her head. "If they don't calm down I'll have to go over and speak to them. That tall one is so belligerent."

"They look like they're getting ready to go. Sheriff Dalby told me that Craig is a writer," I said. "I guess he values his solitude."

"There's plenty of that in Huron Station. So, you've been seeing Mark?"

The question startled me. I'd thought we were talking about Craig Stennet. "Only on sheriff's business. I ran into his car, remember?"

"But he must have taken care of that when it happened."

She was certainly persistent. I tried to distract her. "I had the impression that Sheriff Dalby doesn't like women," I said.

"Mark? It's just the opposite."

"I'll bet he wouldn't have ticketed a man."

"Maybe not."

I ignored her knowing smile and gave Ruth my order. "While I'm waiting for this, I think I'll go over and say hello to Craig."

"And I'll take care of Mike and Jerry," Estella said. "Our jolly hunters are leaving, too. Ruth will have your take-out order ready in ten minutes."

So saying, she descended on the troopers who were waiting at the cash register, while Ruth disappeared behind the kitchen doors. Left alone, I took a few hesitant steps toward Craig. I didn't want to intrude on his reading time, but I could hardly leave without speaking to him.

As I drew nearer, he looked up and smiled. He was reading a worn paperback edition of *Walden,* a suitable choice for a writer who lived in the woods.

"Hello, Krista. Come, sit down." He closed the book, marking his place with a napkin, and transferred his jacket and scarf to the next table, nearly tipping over his full glass of ginger ale in the process.

Craig's blue flannel shirt was rolled up to his elbows and open at the neck to expose another scarf that curved across his shoulder blade until it was lost in the folds of material. The colors of the shirt brought out the dark blue of his eyes, but the plaid reminded me of the garment Randall Scott had worn. I suppressed a shudder and the memory as well.

"I don't want to disturb you," I said. "I just came over to say hello. I see you like Estella's cooking."

"It beats what I make for myself. Usually I have dinner at the American Legion. Did you saw off that branch yet?"

"Not yet."

"Are you sure you don't want any help?" he asked.

"I'm going to do it this afternoon."

"You're like me, a born procrastinator. Just be careful. If you fall, they won't find you till the snow melts."

"Very funny. I won't let that happen."

"I haven't forgotten about our drink or dinner," he said. "Let's make it dinner. After Sunday, I'll be able to take a short break. Can we do it then? Say around the first of the week?"

When Craig had first mentioned our getting together, I'd assumed that his invitation was a friendly overture to a newcomer to Huron Station. Now it sounded alarmingly like a date. But he couldn't be thinking of me in that way. He wasn't the right age for me.

I said, "Sure. I'm making my own schedule these days. I hear that you're a writer."

"You can't run away from fame, even up here in Huron Station." He laughed. "I'm not serious, Krista. One thing I'm not is famous. I'm writing a series of articles on native predators for *Michigan Up North* right now. Alcona County is my headquarters. What do you do?"

If Estella had asked me this question, I would have given

her an evasive answer, but Craig's earnest expression inspired confidence. I felt sure he'd never listened to or repeated gossip in his life.

"Well, I'm on an extended vacation," I said. "I taught English in a high school for one year and did a bit of subbing in September and October, but I'm going to start working toward my doctorate in American Literature this spring if things work out."

"I hope they do. Once that was my ambition, too, a quiet life in a northern college introducing young people to the great American authors, but events sidetracked me."

"Into writing?"

"And other places. I'll tell you about it sometime, when we know each other better."

That didn't sound like a friendly, neighborly remark, but it reminded me of a question I wanted to ask him. "The other day Sheriff Dalby and I were talking about wolves. He said they don't live around here. As a nature writer, what's your opinion?"

"The sheriff is wrong. That wasn't his hybrid I saw when I was riding last week."

"How could you tell?"

"By its size. Then I stopped and looked at the prints. They were enormous and the trail they made was straight, not curving like the kind a dogs would make."

"I'll have to tell him."

"Do that," he said with another laugh, a strange one this time that didn't hold the slightest trace of humor. "The more Sheriff Mark Dalby knows about our woods, the easier it'll be for him to keep the peace."

Another cryptic comment. And from his tone, it was obvious that Craig wasn't one of the sheriff's fans. It appeared that the feeling might be mutual. What was going on here?

Before I could ask Craig what he meant, Ruth appeared at my side and set a large white bag down in front of me.

She handed me the bill. "Please pay at the register. Have a nice Thanksgiving."

"Thanks, Ruth. You too. Well…"

I buttoned my coat all the way to the top and pulled my hood over my hair. I had no reason to linger. "I'll let you go back to *Walden,* Craig."

"I'll get in touch with you," he said. "If you decide you need help with that branch after all, I'm right across the road."

"Okay. Till then."

I picked up my bag and turned to walk away, and Craig reached for his book. I *had* disturbed him, then, but he'd been very polite. As Estella claimed, he was a genuine gentleman.

What a pleasure it was to enjoy a casual conversation with a man who shared my interests and had no hidden agenda. I couldn't help wishing that he were closer to my age.

As I paid my bill, I tried to ignore the scowl lurking in Estella's smile. She'd been too far away to hear our conversation, but I had a feeling that she knew Craig had asked me to go out with him and she wasn't particularly happy about it.

LATER THAT AFTERNOON, I leaned the new ladder against the side of the cabin, climbed to the fifth rung and sawed the maple branch. The grating of the saw against wood was the only sound in the white silence until the gunshots exploded, ripping it apart. Although I couldn't see anything through the falling snow, I knew the hunters were on my land.

Damn them. I hoped the deer got away. As I sawed through the last inch of wood, the image of a graceful animal, fallen and wounded but not dead, haunted me.

Feeling unhappy and powerless to change the situation, I dragged the branch to the back of the cabin and left it on a log stack that was rapidly disappearing under the falling snow. It was so quiet now that I could hear my breathing and the crunching of my footsteps as I tramped back to the newly trimmed tree to check my work. Then I heard the gunshots again.

On my next vacation, I'd follow the sheriff's suggestion and post 'No Trespassing' signs to keep the hunters out.

I amended that thought. I wouldn't be here next year. When

hunting season came around again, I'd be hundreds of miles away, sitting in a classroom at Michigan State, and the farm would belong to someone else. My eighty acres of woods would be divided into smaller parcels or the new owner might be a hunter. As visions of sixteen vacation houses that all looked alike flashed in front of my eyes, the prospect of handing over Aunt Celia's beloved farm to a stranger no longer seemed appealing.

I took the ladder and the saw inside to the back porch and hung my coat and gloves on the clothesline. The rest of the afternoon I worked in the cabin, opening the small boxes that were stacked on top of the steamer trunk, all the while listening for the sound of gunshots.

From time to time I heard them, but they were far away, and I forced myself to concentrate on what I was doing. The chance of discovering another treasure like the silver sleigh lent an air of suspense to my task. But most of the boxes were filled with miscellaneous bric-a-brac packed with no thought for organization. Nothing intrigued me or told me anything new about my aunt, and soon I was feeling tired and overwhelmed.

Then, in the last one, I found a stack of letters and some postcards. They were the best kind of treasure. But after examining several of the cards, I found myself reading variations of the same "having a good time" sentiment. I turned to the letters but was so tired that the faded handwriting blurred in front of my eyes. I was getting drowsier with every passing minute.

In the end I left them on the table for tomorrow's project and got ready for bed. I had all day tomorrow with nothing else to do but pour over my findings. I'd be able to think more clearly after a good night's rest. The winds were picking up, but with the radio and the branch gone, I knew I'd sleep well. Hunters didn't shoot in the dark, and if I heard a broadcast in the night, I'd either be dreaming or losing my grip on reality.

As soon as I opened the door to the front porch the next morning, I saw an arrow embedded in a drift that covered the bottom stair. Quickly I stepped down, sinking into deep snow, and pulled it out. I brushed the arrowhead clean. It felt unfamiliar in my hand, smooth and cold—and as deadly as the gunshots in the woods.

To shoot an arrow into the snow at this angle the archer would have to be standing on the roof. But that was the unlikeliest of scenarios. I was dealing with a flesh and blood man, not a north woods version of Cupid.

Maybe there was another arrow buried in the snow. I looked around the foundation but couldn't see any more. A fully developed and terrifying explanation leaped into my mind and took hold. In the night, someone had invaded my land and left me a deliberate message that I couldn't possibly misinterpret. Randall Scott's slayer thought I could identify him and had chosen this way to warn me not to say anything. If he didn't want me to talk, it was too late. I'd already done that.

Perhaps he wanted to frighten me into leaving town. But if he considered me a threat, wouldn't it make more sense to kill me outright—the way he had killed Randall Scott, with an arrow in his chest?

I left that morbid thought dangling and went on to the important question. Who was the arrow-armed invader? Roy Yarrow was locked up. There was the hunter I'd seen watching the cabin from at the edge of the woods and the man who had fled the crime scene and later abandoned the car. Maybe they were the same person.

Last night's wind-driven snowfall had only partially obscured the deer tracks around the cabin and the large impressions made by boots. Since the intruder hadn't dropped down from the sky, there must be tire tracks from the road to the cabin.

If there were a clue in the snow, Mark would be able to find it. Even though it was a holiday, I knew he'd be in his office working on the Scott case. When I showed him the arrow, he'd realize that my danger was real and do everything in his power to protect me because that was his job.

How fortunate I was to be on a first name basis with the sheriff of Huron Station. Then I remembered: if I hadn't run into his cruiser and been delayed while he wrote the ticket and lectured me, I wouldn't have been on that lonely country road to cross paths with Randall's killer just as he was fleeing the scene of the crime. Sometimes blessings are mixed.

EIGHT

HURON STATION resembled a frozen ghost town, forlorn and forgotten under an overcast sky, with all the people gone and snow pressing heavily on the rooftops and crushing the branches of trees.

Only one building showed signs of habitation. The lights burned in a second floor office of the Huron Station Police Department, and a sheriff's patrol car with a damaged fender was parked in the unplowed lot. I pulled into a reserved space a good three yards away from it and reached into the back seat for the arrow.

The front door of the building was locked, but I found a side entrance open. Feeling like an intruder, I let myself in. The echo of my footsteps in the deserted hall, combined with the unnatural quiet and inadequate heat, made the building seem unfamiliar today.

I passed the elevator and walked up the single flight of stairs, waiting for some hidden camera to detect the weapon I was carrying, but if the building was equipped with a security system, it wasn't turned on. Everyone must have the day off for Thanksgiving, except the town's sheriff who had a crime to solve.

He'd probably be busy. Maybe I should have called to report the incident instead of appearing unannounced in his office with an arrow in my hand. The sight of the damaged patrol car in the lot reminded me of how unbending Sheriff Dalby could be, how infuriatingly condescending.

Still, he'd told me more than once to contact him if anything unusual happened and he'd taken my report of the hunter sighting seriously. Moreover, the arrow might be a valuable piece of evidence. He wouldn't dare be anything but grateful.

Nothing is spookier than a chilly, shadowy stairwell in an almost deserted public building. I was relieved when I reached the second level and pushed open the heavy door. Walking briskly now, eager for contact with another human, I followed the trail of light to the office at the end of the hall and rapped once on the frosted door pane.

It opened immediately, and the sheriff stood in front of me. Strong and powerful with ice-sharp blue eyes he was everyone's picture of the ideal vigilant lawman. A trace of a frown lingered on his face, but I didn't think it had anything to do with me.

"Morning, Krista. Come in. I've been waiting for you."

Behind him, a wide window offered a view of Lake Huron and the lot with my car parked in a choice reserved spot near the building.

"I don't think you've taken up hunting," he said. "Why are you bringing me an arrow?"

"Somebody left it on my doorstep last night."

"Tell me about it," he said as he ushered me into his office, "and sit down. Here."

He pulled out a chair and took the arrow from me while I looked around, curious to see the place where Huron Station's chief law officer worked. It was a large, airy room with freshly painted white walls. Diplomas and awards interspersed with laminated news clippings decorated the walls. A towering Norfolk pine in an enormous clay pot gave the room a touch of soft green color.

His desk was impossible, though…an untidy jumble of file folders, reports, loose papers, pictures, and scattered pens. Only the space in front of the computer was clear.

He held the arrow up to the overhead light before setting it down on top of the paper mess. "Beautiful and lethal. Are you an archer, Krista?"

"No, this is the first time I've handled an arrow—oh, my fingerprints are on it," I said. "I didn't think."

"So are mine, now. You say a hunter lost it in front of your cabin?"

"No, someone put it there deliberately on the bottom step of my porch. It looked as if were planted in the snow."

"Have you seen that hunter lurking on your property again?"

"Only the one time."

"Hmmm." He picked the arrow up, turning it over, saying nothing, putting it down again.

I couldn't have imagined a more lackluster response. In a minute, he was going to suggest that some wild animal had dragged the arrow in from the woods and then dropped it on my doorstep. It was time I gave him a little help.

"I think it's a warning from the man who killed Randall Scott. Since your suspect is in custody, it has to be someone else."

He looked away from me and through the window to the parking lot, silently studying the wintry scene and the snow that was covering the footprints leading up to the cabin. The extra set of tire tracks I'd found, the additional proof of my story, was being obliterated.

Finally he said, "My suspect isn't in custody. We had to let Yarrow walk. He's left town."

The sheriff managed to keep the anger out of his voice, but his expression had a will of its own. He was furious.

"Have you checked the café? Estella said he usually comes there for a hot meal."

"He didn't yesterday and today it's closed for Thanksgiving."

"You said someone saw him driving a gray car. Couldn't you hold him on that?"

"It turned out to be a gray Olds that belonged to a friend of his. Besides, he has an alibi provided by that same friend."

"So he was free last night?"

"Yes, but I can't see him dashing out to your place with an arrow. That's not Yarrow's style."

"You don't think he's the killer anymore, do you?"

He sidestepped my question. "I don't have any proof that he did it. Supposedly he was in another county at the time."

I glanced at the arrowhead and felt a sense of relief. I was glad the sheriff had it now. At the same time I was certain the arrow was a clue that was slipping out of my grasp. How important he considered it, I couldn't tell.

"So you'll look for someone else?" I asked.

"That's my plan, but, alibi or not, I'm not forgetting about Yarrow."

"Can't you do anything to help me now? I don't want to wait until it's too late and I end up like Randall Scott."

He had the audacity to laugh. "You won't, Krista. I'll be out to your place to have a look around in about an hour, maybe sooner. In the meantime, stay inside and keep the door locked."

"If I do that, it won't be because I'm afraid," I said. "Maybe I'm a little apprehensive, but I'm willing to trust you. Didn't you say that you always get your man?"

"Yes, and don't forget it. I haven't let a criminal get away yet."

"Then I hope you won't break your record with this case."

He laughed again, his earlier anger at Roy Yarrow now by replaced by confidence and determination. Two desirable qualities for a sheriff to possess.

"I'll see you later at the cabin," he said. "In the meantime, don't worry about Yarrow. He's probably heading for the Canadian border. But he's going to be back in Huron Station lockup before he has a chance to settle in. I'm going to shoot holes in that alibi of his."

"But you will look for somebody else, just in case…"

"I said I would."

He walked over to the door and held it open. I was being dismissed. In spite of his reassuring words I had the impression that he was already pursuing another lead, maybe even considering how best to reduce Roy Yarrow's alibi to powder and take him into custody again.

"I'll be watching for you then," I said. "Are you going to have Thanksgiving dinner somewhere?"

"That won't be until much later. Thanks for bringing the arrow in, Krista, and try to keep an open mind. It's still possible that the driver you saw that day had nothing to do with Scott's murder."

"But if he stole a car and then abandoned it…"

"Then he was up to no good, but it could be unrelated."

"I hope so," I said.

The sheriff was thinking like a detective while I was reacting as a potential victim would. That made me feel vulnerable. The case and now my contribution, the arrow, were in capable hands. I should leave them there and enjoy the holiday.

That wasn't so easy. For the first time since coming up north I wished I had some place to go this afternoon. I needed the distraction. I was half way to the parking lot when I remembered that I'd forgotten to ask Sheriff Dalby if he'd interviewed the victim's daughter, Renie Scott, yet.

THE MEADOW WAS a vast snowscape, shimmering in the light of the sun and sloping down to the dark woods that surrounded it on three sides. It was much larger than I remembered from those childhood summer vacations and one of the few memories that didn't shrink and fade as I grew older.

My new cross-country skis were on the porch, stored with the rest of my luggage. This was an ideal place to practice walking on the snow. I had endless acres to explore and the time to do it. There was no reason for the gnawing feeling of deprivation that had come upon me. None except for the holiday.

My family was gone, my parents killed long before their time in a car accident, and the day-old turkey sandwich from the café had lost its appeal. Last Thanksgiving I had been dating Ned, who also taught English at my school. He'd taken me out for a traditional dinner in an upscale restaurant. It wasn't really my idea of the way to keep the holiday, but at least I'd had someone to be with.

Ned and I had since gone our separate ways and I hadn't found a suitable man to take his place. Nor had I made any plans for the holiday other than to drive up north to the cabin. Even the busy sheriff was planning to celebrate with a Thanksgiving dinner while I was alone.

Disgusted with the whiny turn of my thoughts, I ended this stream of self-pity. I was exactly where I wanted to be: in Aunt Celia's home in Huron Station. If I felt depression closing in on me, it was only the thick atmosphere of nostalgia, surrounding the cabin like winter fog, drawing me back into the past.

By tomorrow Thanksgiving would be just another memory. In the meantime, exercise and fresh air would drive away all dark thoughts. I could ski across the meadow and look around, hiking as far into the woods as I could. By the time I returned, I should be too tired to brood about the past.

Just at that moment I heard gunshots, rumbling in the distance like winter thunder, and reconsidered. I hadn't bought an orange jacket yet. As I crossed the snowy terrain, somebody was likely to mistake me for a deer. As long as hunters were in the vicinity, it would be safer to work inside. I had all those waiting boxes, the prospect of the sheriff's visit, and a cold turkey sandwich with Estella's pumpkin pie. If that was insufficient activity to occupy the hours, I could review my life and romantic history and figure out what I wanted to do differently in the future.

Inside the cabin, I spilled a tumble of letters out on the dining room table and rearranged them in chronological order. I counted twenty-three, a few still in their envelopes. In the oldest one, addressed to Aunt Celia's mother and dated April 2, 1925, a girl named Melinda described the highlights of a long ago spring: a vague family quarrel, a blue party dress, and an exciting new romance with a boy who worked at the Detroit News.

Melinda would be close to a hundred now, or more likely dead. If she were still alive, would she remember the young man she had described with such youthful ardor? Maybe she had married him.

Idly I rearranged the letters in the shape of a fan, and selected one with a February 1965 date. The Detroit postmark and the unfamiliar street name of the address, Pinegrove, puzzled me until I remembered that Aunt Celia hadn't always lived on the farm.

I knew the writings were a treasure trove of period detail and well worth keeping but I wished I could read the letters my aunt had sent instead of the ones she'd received. That was impossible, but why not invent a little game to amuse myself? As I read, I'd try to imagine what my aunt had written in return.

I must be going over the edge. I needed a television or, better still, someone to talk to. An exciting romance like Melinda's would be better yet. At the very least, I would benefit from a night out.

I was letting the past wrap itself around me like a soft warm blanket. When my greatest source of entertainment was a trip to the local café, it was time to take action. I was glad I had the prospect of dinner with Craig to anticipate.

LATER THAT AFTERNOON, Sheriff Dalby and his deputy, Gil, provided a diversion of sorts. Gil was a husky, fresh-faced rookie with wavy brown hair, a sprinkling of freckles on his nose, and a quiet, respectful demeanor.

I waited on the porch steps while they examined the tire tracks leading up to the cabin. The hunters were in the woods again, and their sporadic gunfire grated on my nerves.

At last the sheriff came stamping through the high snow up to the cabin. He stood at the foot of the stairs, looking into the depression made by the arrowhead's entry and what remained of the footprints around the cabin.

"You had an intruder during the night, but his tracks are buried in the snow," he said. "We won't be able to trace him."

"That's what I said. What I was afraid of, I mean."

Gil was making wide arcs in the snow around the foundation with his boot.

"You won't find any clues there, Deputy," I said. "I already looked. What now?"

"We wait. You call me if something else happens, and I do

my job. With Sheriff Dalby on the case, Huron Station is going to be the safest county in the state of Michigan."

"That sounds familiar," I said. "Kind of like a campaign slogan."

"So it does, but I got elected without using it."

Another series of gunshots shattered the silence. They were closer now, in the woods behind the cabin.

"I wish you'd get rid of those hunters," I said. "They make me nervous."

"That's one thing even a sheriff can't do, Krista, but the firearms season will be over before you know it and then we can all look forward to a long quiet winter."

"As soon as you catch the killer," I reminded him. "Until then I think I've landed in one of the deadliest places in the state."

NINE

THE DAY AFTER Thanksgiving I drove into town and wandered down Main Street, mingling with the people who had drifted in from the outlying areas. Huron Station had come to life again. It was a little past ten o'clock, and all the shops were open, hoping to claim their share of the Christmas shopping trade.

In front of Blooms from the Past, the drab harvest decorations and the wheelbarrow were gone, replaced by bright red poinsettia plants and beribboned ivy topiaries. A painted fireplace backdrop and a real wicker rocking chair suggested the beginning of a living room display.

Christmas was in the air and the snow was falling again. A large wreath decorated with wooden gingerbread people adorned the door of Estella's café. As Albert Drayton outlined the window with a string of multi-colored lights, he hummed 'Jingle Bells'. He saw me coming and moved the ladder away from the entrance.

"Watch your step, Miss Marlow. It's still a little slippery there. If you need any outside decorating done I have a few free afternoons this week."

I stopped to breathe in the fragrance of fresh balsam, that most magical of Christmas scents. "Thanks, but I'm going to try for simplicity this year," I said. "Did you have a chance to look at my radio yet?"

"I've been tinkering with it. I'm sure I'll have it working again, but modern technology would give you a better sound. You wouldn't want to sell it, would you?"

"Oh, no. That radio is a link to my past."

"An antique, you mean?"

"Yes, a family heirloom. Even if you can't repair it, I'll never part with it."

He nodded. "I understand. Stop by the store tomorrow and I'll have it ready. By the way, if you're ever in Huron Station after dark, drive past St. Sebastian's and look at the trees. I did the blue lights."

Promising to do so, I took another deep breath of balsam and opened the door. As always, the warmth and charm of the café drew me in. That and the savory smell of sausage browning on the grill. I felt as if I were returning to a beloved familiar place. Best of all were the people and the sound of talking and laughter. I hadn't realized how much I missed being part of a crowd, even a small one.

The fire blazed in the wood stove, and the tables closest to it were unoccupied. I made my way to the smallest one and eased out of my coat. Ruth wove through the aisles, expertly balancing a large tray laden with plates of pancakes, eggs, ham, and sausage, while Cindy waited on a large party that included several children.

I had timed my arrival to coincide with that brief lull between the breakfast and lunch rush, hoping to have a chance to speak to Estella. On my last visit, when she had told me about Roy Yarrow, I'd seen the wisdom in encouraging her to talk. A gossip is annoying when she pries into your life, but she can also be a good source of information. All I had to do was ask the right questions, deflect personal queries, and keep a few steps ahead of her.

I wondered how much Estella knew about Renie Scott. Since Randall's daughter should have arrived in town yesterday, she would probably come to the café for breakfast or lunch. She might be here now.

For her television appearances, Renie favored soft pastel suits, often pink. Her blonde hair was full and springy with never a strand out of place except when the studio sent her outside in blustery weather. For a fall trip up north, I thought she'd probably be wearing wool pants and a bulky sweater.

None of the women in the café remotely resembled her. The two state troopers were here again, but without Sheriff Dalby. The sheriff was most likely in his office giving Renie a report. A scene unfolded in my head, like part of a movie reel.

Renie Scott wore one of her winter pastel suits with her blonde hair as freshly styled as if she had just left the hairdresser's. The sheriff's eyes sparkled as he gave her a detailed report, which would be difficult since he didn't have much information. He'd take her to lunch and maybe dinner as well and afterward give her a personal tour of Huron Station. After all, she was a celebrity with expensive clothes, jewelry, and cosmetics. Who could blame him if he was impressed with her?

And why should I care if he is?

Then I looked up and saw him sitting alone at a booth against the wall drinking coffee and watching Cindy serve the party at a nearby table. He had to see me. I was sitting directly across the room from him. Why was he ignoring me?

It wasn't as if the sheriff and I were friends, even though we had seen each other often in recent days. I remembered what Estella had said and told myself that, in truth, Sheriff Dalby was the last man I'd want to socialize with. Let him pretend we'd never met.

As I glanced at him again, I realized that something was wrong. I was slower than usual this morning not to have seen it at once. He was wearing a dark blue policeman's uniform and he looked different. Overnight, he seemed to have added about five years and gained some weight. His face was fuller, his hair a little grayer.

Just as I realized that this wasn't Sheriff Mark Dalby but a man who closely resembled him, he noticed my scrutiny and smiled as if he understood my confusion. No, he definitely wasn't Mark. This man seemed friendlier, was probably nicer, and appeared to be more approachable—not that I intended to approach him.

"Hi, Miss Marlow. Would you like to see a menu this morning?"

I turned to see Cindy waiting patiently for me to acknowledge her presence. She'd seen where my attention strayed and seemed to be amused by it.

"No," I said quickly. "I'll have the same breakfast I had before. One of the specials..."

"I remember...the Sunrise Special. That's everybody's favorite. With coffee?"

"Yes, black, please, and a glass of water."

It couldn't have taken me a minute to place my order, but when I looked toward the booth again it was empty. Sheriff Dalby's double was going through the door.

ESTELLA CLEARED UP the mystery, as I suspected she would. Stopping by my table to inquire about my Thanksgiving, she added, "Mark's brother just left. Did you notice him?"

"That policeman sitting in the booth who looks like him? Yes."

"He's the splitting image of Mark, but older. Those Dalby men are real hunks, but Mac is more fun than Mark. The town is always livelier when Mac is here."

"Where is he from?" I asked.

"Downstate in Foxglove Corners. He's with the police department there."

"I hope I'll get to meet him," I said.

"You'll have to hurry then. He's only here for a few days."

Like her waitresses, Estella was wearing orange today and she'd found lipstick in a soft, frosted shade that matched her blouse. She appeared to be in the mood for conversation.

"Did you get a chance to go skiing yesterday?" she asked.

"I decided against it. Those hunters are all over the place and I don't want to get shot."

"I'll be glad when firearms season is over. Hunters are my least favorite customers."

"You know about Roy Yarrow being released I guess," I said.

"Yes, but I haven't seen him yet. Maybe he'll be in later."

"I hear he has an alibi."

Estella's expression changed subtly. Her eyes narrowed and suddenly that citrus orange lipstick shade didn't flatter her.

"Yes, that girl, Lily, came through for him again. She's always on hand to give him whatever he wants."

Since Estella didn't try to conceal her disdain for the person named Lily, naturally I wanted to know more about her. "Don't you believe her?"

"Not for a minute. Lily hangs out with the activists, but she isn't really one of them. I believe in Roy, though. He has a right to get out of Mark's clutches any way he can."

"I assume Lily was with Roy when Randall Scott was killed?"

"That she was. According to sweet Lily, they were together that day and all night, too. In her dreams."

"Does Lily ever come to the café?"

"Not much, but you may see her here. Who knows? She's easy to recognize. She used to be passably pretty, but now she lets herself go. She always wears faded old jeans and baggy sweaters. She does have nice hair, if she'd do something interesting with it instead of wearing it in a ponytail. How she thinks Roy would ever give her a second look, I don't know. And she never wears any makeup," she added, making it sound like the ultimate fashion sin.

This was more than I needed to know about the unremarkable Lily, but it told me plenty about Estella. She must be envious of Lily's connection with Roy. But I thought she was fond of Randall Scott. Perhaps she cared for both men, but in different ways.

It occurred to me that Estella might be a good person to ask about the murdered man's daughter. "Do you know if Renie Scott arrived in town yet?"

"I've been here all morning, Krista. Unless Ms. Scott comes to the café and introduces herself, how would I know?"

There was an edge in Estella's voice when she spoke of Renie. Surely she couldn't be jealous of her, too.

"Maybe she'll have some idea about who her father's enemies were," I said.

"Renie Scott doesn't know anything about Randall and she isn't an investigative reporter. Her job is to give the weather report. I don't know why she bothered to come here now. Her father sure would have liked to see her when he was alive. But she wasn't interested then."

"You sound as if you know her."

"I never met Renie, but I know Randall wanted to have a relationship with his daughter. Her mother kept them apart when she was growing up, so they were strangers. No, Renie Scott might as well stay away now. Nobody wants her here."

During this tirade Estella's voice had risen and I noticed the people at the next table were glancing in our direction. As if suddenly remembering where she was she said, "I'd better get to work. Enjoy your breakfast, Krista."

As she walked quickly back to the kitchen, I realized that I had just seen a different side of Estella. If the right name were mentioned, the genial restaurant owner of Huron Station could turn uncharitable and judgmental.

But maybe she was the sort of woman who reserved her kind words for men. It would be interesting to hear how she described me to other people. I had a suspicion that in the right circumstances Estella could be a formidable enemy.

I FOUND THE ANSWER to one of my problems on the way home. I must have driven past the Station Roadhouse many times without noticing it. Today, on the way home from the café, I did notice it and decided it was time for a change.

In the spirit of being prepared for anything, I had packed a sleek black dress in my suitcase. Tonight in the interest of balancing my long hours of seclusion in the cabin, I would have a hot meal and sample Huron Station's after-dark activities.

I couldn't understand how my great aunt had survived so many snowbound winters. She had an old Plymouth, but she seldom left the farm she loved. That was her choice. Instead she filled her life with correspondence and her radio and she lived for the spring. I had been up north less than a week and

I was getting restless. But then again I was young and craved action.

The prospect of dining at the Roadhouse cheered me considerably until I turned onto the path to the cabin. Even from this distance, I could see the figure dressed in safety orange at the edge of the woods. Although the man carried a rifle I knew he was no random hunter. He was as still as any tree, looking up across the meadow at the cabin. The watcher had returned to find me away from home.

He must have heard my car, for in the next instant he bolted back into the woods. Fervently I wished that I could turn and drive down into the meadow, all the way to its end, and then on into the woods. It was impossible, of course, and futile. I would never be able to catch him. Even if I did, the situation might turn on me. This was a matter for the sheriff to investigate.

Once I was safe inside the cabin with the doors locked, I took the old shotgun down from above the mantel. Since I had a rudimentary knowledge of firearms, I suspected that no one had fired this gun in two decades. But it was loaded. I was about to take it outside and test it on some hapless branch when I was startled by a loud knock on the door.

That's why you should never have a loaded gun in your hand unless you intend to use it.

Thinking that Sheriff Dalby had intercepted the watcher, or perhaps Craig was here to set a date for our dinner, I flung open the door without glancing through the window first. That was foolish, one more precaution I'd ignored, because the man standing on the porch was a stranger. I was glad that I was still holding the gun.

He was portly and very handsome with white hair, sparkling blue eyes, and a friendly smile. He wore an orange jacket and an odd fur cap with earflaps. I wasn't sure why, but I didn't trust him a bit.

I kept one hand firmly on the doorknob and the other around the gun. "May I do something for you?" I asked.

His smile widened. "Maybe. I'm not coming in, ma'am, don't worry. I heard you were going to sell the cabin. I might be interested if the price is right."

He took a few steps toward me and I tightened my grip on the knob.

"My name is Hal Brecht," he said. "I'm one hundred percent safe. People around here know me."

I started to close the door. "I can't imagine who told you that my property is for sale. It isn't."

"Oh. Sorry to have bothered you then. You sure?"

"Positive."

He tipped his hat and made a half turn.

"Wait," I said. "Were you in the woods a little while ago, over there beyond the meadow?"

"No, ma'am," he said. "I just got here. I walked up from the road."

He sounded sincere, but that could be an act. Still, I thought that the watcher was shorter and thinner, even though I couldn't be certain since I'd never seen him at close range.

During this conversation, Hal Brecht had edged closer to the door. "Why do you ask? Is some man giving you trouble?"

He sounded sincere, but my common sense told me that he didn't know me and had no reason to be concerned about my safety.

"Only the hunters," I said. "I wish they'd stay away from my property. I don't like listening to gunfire and I hate the thought of all those deer getting killed."

He glanced at the gun in my hand. "Excuse me, ma'am, but you sound like one of those activist people." It was a statement, but he made it sound like a question.

To avoid getting into a conversation about deer hunting pros and cons I said, "Do you remember where you heard about my cabin being for sale?"

He gave a vague wave of his hand. "Somewhere. Around town, maybe. If it isn't true, it doesn't matter." He turned to go. "Good afternoon. Take care."

As he tramped back to the road, making a second set of foot-prints alongside his previous ones, I looked for some vehicle-a car, a truck, even a snowmobile. I didn't see any form of transportation, but Hal Brecht hadn't dropped from the sky. And wouldn't it make more sense for him to drive up to the cabin than leave his car some distance away and walk?

The whole affair was curious. Maybe Estella had been gos-siping about me, but no one in Huron Station knew my plans. Only Craig knew anything about me at all.

I closed the door and walked over to the window in order to watch Hal Brecht walk away from the cabin. Even after he reached the road and moved out of sight, I stood looking out at the view of my land wrapped in winter white.

I was unprepared for the intense feeling of possessiveness that had crept up on me when I'd heard Hal Brecht's offer. It was with me still. In spite of the drawbacks of living up north, I was growing too attached to my home in the woods. That was unfortunate since I wasn't willing to abandon my dream of earning a doctorate. I couldn't afford to keep a summer place and go back to school as well.

I wished that I could live without ever making another major decision. And, more importantly, that I could figure out what Hal Brecht really wanted. I didn't think for a minute that it was my cabin.

TEN

THE STATION ROADHOUSE was one of those multi-purpose establishments where a woman on her own could dine on prime rib or filet mignon and sample the delights of the bar, dance floor, and gaming rooms. In other words, it was the opposite of a lonely north woods cabin. Since I didn't have a dancing partner or enough money to risk losing, I sat alone, waited for my steak, and sipped mineral water.

Every now and then I looked out the window. Either Albert Drayton or someone with a similar vision had strung the spruce trees in front of the Roadhouse with blue lights. It was a pleasure to watch their soft cool glow in the darkness and to know that the Roadhouse walls and its company protected me from haunted radios, mysterious watchers, and a dangerous man whose face I wouldn't recognize even if I were to see it again. That was a fact of which the stranger was most likely unaware.

There was no need to feel threatened as long as I had a shotgun and a fresh supply of ammunition. Now, just in case the radio resumed its supernatural ways, what could I use to ward off an agent from the other world?

The thought amused me. It was easy to treat the matter lightly in a lively place like the Roadhouse. As I took another sip of mineral water, I heard a familiar voice behind me and felt a strong hand on my shoulder.

"Unless you have a designated driver you'd better lose the drink, Krista. The roads are getting icy and you don't want to run into another car."

Without waiting for an invitation, Sheriff Dalby sat down

at my table. He was wearing his uniform. In spite of his high-handed words, his eyes couldn't hide his amusement.

He was still on duty and wandering around in a roadhouse that served alcohol and hosted gambling. Maybe this behavior was ethical up north, but I didn't think so.

"You're a comedian, Sheriff," I said. "Do you expect to find the killer in a roadhouse?"

"You never know. Stranger things have happened. I'm serious, Krista. You need all of your wits to navigate these roads on a night like this. I thought you'd be in your cabin wrapped up in a blanket."

"I didn't realize you thought about me at all."

The glimmer of approval in his eyes was my reward. I was a match for him and now he knew it. In the future he wouldn't be so quick to underestimate me. I decided to give him one concession.

"This is mineral water, but I was thinking about ordering a Tom and Jerry because it's winter in Huron Station and the roads are icy."

"That's brandy and rum, very potent stuff…"

"I know…and eggs, powdered sugar and nutmeg. Don't forget the boiled water. It's a traditional Christmas drink. I'm going to have one instead of dessert."

He must be wondering if I was serious. I wish I hadn't told him that I was drinking mineral water. It would have been smarter to keep him guessing.

"I saw your brother at the café this morning," I said. "At first I thought it was you."

"Estella must have filled you in. Mac came up for Thanksgiving. He's leaving in the morning."

"Is he in here now?"

"He's around here somewhere."

I glanced at the bar and the dance floor beyond, but Mac Dalby was nowhere in sight. That left the gambling area. The Roadhouse must be a favorite hangout for off duty officers of the law.

"I saw the hunter again this morning," I said. "Later, a stranger came to the cabin."

I described my visitor and his supposed reason for seeking me out. "He said his name was Hal Brecht. I don't think he was the trespasser. But if he came in a car, I didn't see it."

"Hal Brecht? You're sure?"

"That's what he said."

"A tall, white-haired guy in a fur hat, sort of jovial looking?"

"That's as good a description as any."

Sheriff Dalby smacked the table with his hand and laughed. "Well, that crafty old son of a—gun."

"What's so funny?"

Instead of answering, he asked, "What did you tell him?"

"That the cabin isn't for sale. Do you know him?"

"Sure. He used to be the sheriff before I won the election."

"That's interesting. What happened?"

He waited, and I thought he was trying to make up his mind about something. Then in a quiet voice, he said, "Hal Brecht was involved in a scandal and had to leave office. You don't have to know the details, but nothing was ever proved. Old Hal likes public life, though. He thinks he can make a comeback in spite of everything."

"He wants your job, you mean?"

"He'll never get it. Brecht and I aren't rivals. Not serious ones, anyway. We go way back. I don't know why he's interested in your cabin. He already owns two houses."

"I have eighty acres, too."

"I'll ask him the next time I see him. Did that hunter bother you?" he asked.

"It was the same as before. He heard me coming and took off into the woods."

He frowned. "I don't like that."

"Neither do I. But there's a gun in the cabin."

"All right. Just keep it as a last resort," he said.

The waiter set a large dish of mixed greens and a basket of rolls in front of me. "Are you going to join the lady for dinner, Sheriff Dalby?" he asked.

"Not tonight. I just wanted to check on my friend," the

sheriff replied. The waiter nodded and stepped away from the table.

"You must be very busy," I said. "You can talk to me any time."

"So I can," he said, "but, believe it or not, I'm working right now. Try the rum cake instead of the Tom and Jerry. And drive safely. Those roads are hell for beginning drivers."

"One of which I'm not."

He smiled, gave me a quick pat on the arm, and left. I watched him as he walked toward the gambling rooms in the back. A slender woman with long light brown hair intercepted him at the door. She wore a purple dress embroidered with a trailing silver vine design and had a warm, inviting smile. She obviously knew Mark well and seemed anxious to prolong their encounter.

They stood together for several minutes conversing with the familiarity of old friends who have met by chance after a long absence. The sheriff of Huron Station was working tonight. If he hadn't said so, I wouldn't have believed it.

HE WAS RIGHT ABOUT the roads, though. In places they were solid ice and the snow cover made them even more treacherous. I had intended to mull over Mark's comments about the dishonored Hal Brecht on the way home but that was impossible now.

I turned on the bright lights and drove slowly, keeping my right tires on the snow for traction. If Huron Station had a salt truck it hadn't reached this section of the county yet. Fortunately I didn't have far to go and traffic was non-existent.

The heavily falling snow obscured my vision. Even with the windshield wipers racing back and forth on the window, visibility was poor. Fortunately, I was halfway to the cabin and there was nothing on the road to collide with.

Or so I thought. Behind me two pinpoints of light broke through the darkness. As I glanced in the rearview mirror to track the vehicle's progress the pinpricks turned into headlights and then the car burst through the snow screen like a giant silver creature bearing down on its prey.

That fool driver was going to try and pass me. He was two car lengths behind me now and was swerving into the opposite lane. Then, in a flash of light, he skidded on a patch of ice, veered toward the Taurus, and spun out, turning around and around on the icy pavement. I pumped the brakes lightly and steered farther to the side of the road.

What the hell was wrong with these northern drivers?

He started sliding across the ice toward me. Without thinking, I stepped down hard on the brakes. The Taurus went into a spin of its own, skidding giddily across the road and coming to rest in a snowdrift in front of a stand of spruces.

The seat belt kept me from being thrown against the dashboard, but its tight grip sent a bolt of pain cutting across my chest. I freed myself from the restraint and rested my head against the wheel. I didn't think I was hurt, and the car appeared to be undamaged but the near collision had scrambled my nerves.

I turned in the seat to look back at the road. The speeding car was long gone. But in the split second when my world had turned into a dizzying confusion of ice and terror, I had seen enough to know that I'd just relived a familiar experience.

The gray car looked like a Crown Victoria, but I couldn't be certain. And I hadn't seen the driver's face.

How likely was it that I had encountered another reckless driver in Huron Station? With the long hard winters, most people would know how to drive safely on ice. What if this had been a deliberate attempt to run me off the road?

I didn't know whether or not I was going to tell Sheriff Dalby about this incident. He'd probably say that after drinking a Tom and Jerry I'd had a predictable mishap on a slippery road, an incident that he had foreseen. I would point out that I'd only eaten a piece of the rum cake he'd recommended. Then he'd either make a remark about my poor driving skills or take me seriously. I couldn't wait for our next meeting to find out.

I put my car in reverse and tried to back up, but it wouldn't budge. The snow bank held my front tires in a tight grip. This latest setback was one I could fix. With my emergency shovel I cleared the snow away, a little at a time, and soon I was on my way again.

Nothing else happened on the trip home except I caught a brief glimpse of Craig who was pulling into his driveway as I reached the road to the cabin. He waved and brought his truck to a stop as I made my turn. I wanted to tell him about my experience on the road, but I wouldn't do it tonight. I'd had enough drama and danger to last for a while. And besides, I'd probably be seeing him soon.

THAT NIGHT I HAD a frightening dream about ice and snow that never stopped falling. I lay in bed, safe under the quilt, and replayed my near accident. My dream version was different in two major ways. Instead of sliding into a snowdrift, I'd driven off an icy bridge into Lake Huron. And this time I could see clearly that the other car was a gray Crown Victoria covered with snow. The driver's face was a blur wearing a white cap.

I was reluctant to face the day until I had thought through this latest brush with danger. The shadow on the snow that I'd seen on my first trip to the barn was one hundred percent my imagination. The hunter could have a rational explanation for appearing at the edge of the woods and the driver last night might simply have been a reckless jerk. Finally, there must be thousands of gray cars in the state.

Still, I sensed that someone was out to get me. That feeling was what mattered.

Maybe I should pick up the radio, throw my clothes into the car, and go back downstate before I was trapped by that big blizzard Mark had mentioned. I could have the rest of my aunt's belongings shipped and arrange for the sale of the cabin by telephone.

But that would be running away, which amounted to failing. I wasn't going to do it. If someone meant to harm me, let him come. I was forewarned, and I'd be ready. Feeling in control again, I got up, got dressed, and set out for the hardware store to deal with one more unknown—the phantom radio.

The bright morning sunshine didn't offer much warmth, but it was good for my frame of mind. The daily snowfall hadn't begun yet and the road I'd slid off last night was in better condition this morning.

As I approached the place where my car had skidded into the evergreens, I slowed down. There was a large impression in the snow and a few broken branches that I hadn't seen in the dark. Except for the other driver, I was the only one who would know what had happened here last night.

THE RADIO SAT ON the counter, freshly polished and shining. I could hardly believe that it was over half a century old.

Albert plugged it into an outlet behind the counter. "I got it going. They couldn't have done it in a regular repair shop. Radios had tubes in those days. Lucky for you, I have all kinds of old stuff lying around."

"What was wrong with it?" I asked.

"The tubes were shot. I replaced them."

"So it couldn't have worked at all before?"

"Not at all."

He turned the 'on' dial and sound filled the hardware store. "Four additional inches of snow are expected by tomorrow morning…"

Albert turned down the volume and changed stations. Then he turned the dial in the opposite direction and the store was quiet again. The way a place should be when a radio has been silenced.

He said, "Like I told you, you can get better vocal from a modern model, but the radio is working. That's what you wanted. I'm only charging you for parts, not labor, because I had fun tinkering with it."

He pulled the plug out of the outlet and started writing the bill.

I opened my checkbook. "I'm so happy to have it working. I'd like to ask you a question. It's sort of related."

"Go ahead."

"Did you see anything unusual when you looked inside, something that would cause the radio to start playing by itself?"

"Just dead tubes. It was dusty. Otherwise everything looked pretty normal to me."

I wished I'd resisted the impulse to ask that question. I thought Albert was looking at me strangely, but it might just have been my imagination. "I just wondered, since it's so old."

"All I can say is you've got yourself an antique with a second life. It should go on for another fifty years. If it doesn't, bring it back. I stand behind my work."

"I'm sure it'll be fine," I said. "Thanks again, Albert."

He wrapped the cord neatly around it three times. *Three times was a charm.* I remembered Aunt Celia saying that. I gripped the radio with both hands. The case was warm and the radio seemed heavier now. For a moment I had the absurd idea that it was glad to be going home.

ELEVEN

AT LAST THE GUNFIRE ENDED. The hunters packed their gear and headed south, many of them taking home a cold, lifeless animal body. Once again the woods were silent and peaceful. Best of all, when I looked out the bedroom window, I didn't see a man in an orange jacket watching the cabin from across the meadow. Maybe he had gone home, too.

Still, there was something out there. I could feel it. I had never been close enough to the man to see his face, but I could imagine dark and hungry eyes trained on me, waiting as patiently as any hunter for a deer to stray into his rifle range. I couldn't assume that I wouldn't see him again.

The bow and arrow season would continue until the end of the year. An arrow flying through the air would be quieter than a bullet but just as deadly.

In my bedroom, the hardwood floor felt like a block of ice beneath my bare feet. My flannel nightgown might as well have been made of gossamer for all the warmth it was giving. Although I was shivering, I stood at the window for a few more minutes looking at the now familiar scene.

The sun shining on the white landscape created an illusion of scattered diamonds. There would be shadows on the snow again today, arrows and shapes of hanging men, all of them trying to tell me something if only I could understand their message.

My imagination was running amok this morning. I needed to be with other people. Soon I would make a return visit to the Roadhouse. In the meantime, I'd find other entertainment wherever I could. My date with Craig Stennet could be as early as Monday. After the weekend, he'd said. That should provide a little diversion.

Wishing that I'd bought another party dress, I turned away from the window. Today I was going to the twelve o'clock mass at St. Sebastian's church and then to the café for an early dinner. Following this schedule of strictly normal activities and being part of a crowd should keep dark thoughts away for a while.

Cheered by my plans for the day, I poured boiling water in the teapot and gave the loose leaves a vigorous stir. The sound of light footsteps on the porch and a soft rapping on the door broke into my thoughts. I rushed to the window. An unfamiliar red Saturn was parked behind my car.

Deciding to take a chance that today's visitor would be a person I wanted to see, I opened the door halfway.

An attractive blond woman in a rose parka stood on the porch, turning her car keys around and around in her gloved hands. She wore blue jeans and a pink turtleneck sweater. The cold gave her cheeks a becoming flush. Although we'd never actually met, I knew her immediately.

"Good morning, Miss Marlow," she said. "I'm Renata Scott, Randall's daughter. I hope you'll forgive this intrusion, but I'd like to talk to you if I may. It won't take long."

I opened the door all the way. "Come in, Ms. Scott. I've seen you on Channel Five."

"Thanks. Call me Renie."

She unzipped her jacket. Over her sweater she wore a vest embroidered with pastel colors reminiscent of spring. Renie was shorter than she looked on the television screen and even prettier without the heavy makeup.

She glanced beyond me into the living room where the fire in the wood stove burned energetically. "This is the coziest log cabin I've ever seen," she said. "You're so lucky to have it."

"I think so, too. I guess everyone in the state dreams of owning a rustic cabin up north." As I took her coat and pulled out a chair for her, I realized with a pang that once I put the house on the market I would have to stop thinking of it as mine.

"Yes, or a cottage on the lake," she said. "That's what I want to have some day. Aren't you afraid, living here all alone?" She caught her breath, and the flush deepened. "Oh, I'm sorry. I shouldn't have assumed…"

"That's all right. I'm on vacation. I don't think I could last through a whole winter. Would you like to have a cup of tea with me? I'm afraid I can't offer you sugar and cream, though."

"Black is fine, and tea sounds nice and warming." She sat down and held her hands above the candles I'd moved from the sideboard to the table. The amenities completed, she moved quickly to the purpose of her visit.

"Sheriff Dalby told me that you're the one who found my father. I hope you don't mind."

"No, but I don't want it generally known."

"I understand. Would you tell me about it?" she asked.

The last thing I wanted to do was relive that day, but I didn't see how I could deny Renie's request. I said, "It was pure chance. I was looking for a turn off I'd missed when I drove down that road. Excuse me, I'll be right back with our tea."

While I washed a cup for Renie, I wondered how much of the story I could omit. The memory of that day burned as vividly as a candle in my mind. The image of the dead man's face was frozen in my memory and the blood pouring out from the chest wound was as red as fire. All the emotions I'd felt when I found Randall Scott's body were with me still.

I decided there was no need to add every gory, extraneous detail. The plain facts were horrible enough. As I set the teapot on the table I said, "I noticed something blue in the woods ahead of me…"

I busied myself with pouring the tea and tried to avoid looking directly at Renie as I finished the story. Except for pink lipstick, she wore no makeup and she looked young and vulnerable, unlike the poised weathercaster I remembered. Not at all the person Estella had described.

Renie nodded. The color in her face had faded perceptibly. "I read the coroner's report and what that monster did to him was all over the news. I hope my father lost consciousness quickly."

"I'm sure that's what happened."

"They never found his jacket," she said. "His wallet is missing, too, and maybe some money. But they don't think it was a robbery."

"I agree. I think the killer left his body in that state as a message."

"It had to be one of those anti-hunting people."

"It's possible. The jacket may be buried somewhere under the snow. If that's the case it won't turn up until spring."

"Yes, and every day more snow keeps falling."

It didn't sound as if the sheriff had told Renie about the man in the Crown Victoria. Since I'd turned that matter over to him, I didn't mention it.

"It hasn't been long. Only a week," I said.

"Then I'll have to be patient. I wanted to come to the place where it happened and talk to the people he knew."

"I never met your father," I reminded her.

"I didn't really know him either. My parents divorced when I was four and we were apart for most of my life. We were planning to make a new beginning."

I began to listen more intently now. According to Estella, Renie had refused to reconcile with her father.

"Did he plan to stay in Michigan permanently?" I asked.

"Yes, he was starting over again with the ski resort. He'd met a special woman and was thinking about getting remarried as soon as his divorce from his last wife was final. They were coming down to Detroit so we could all get acquainted over Thanksgiving dinner."

"She must be devastated."

"Probably she is, but I don't know even know her name. My father wanted it to be a surprise for Thanksgiving."

"I read about a possible wedding in Randall Scott's future, but the account didn't mention the future bride's name," I said. "Someone must have seen them together or met her."

I was thinking about Estella who knew everyone and every-thing that happened in Huron Station.

"You'd think so, but nobody can tell me anything about her, and she isn't making herself known," she said. "Why should she now?"

"Maybe she hasn't heard about the murder yet. Wait and see. She may still get in touch with you."

"I'm not expecting her to. I suppose I'm no worse off now than I was last year when I hardly remembered my father, but that doesn't change the way I feel."

"No, of course not. Are you going to stay in town long?"

"I have to leave tomorrow," she said. "I'm flying out to California on Tuesday for the funeral and the reading of the will."

Renie finished her tea in one gulp and stood up, looking as if she were about to take flight herself while she still had some control over her emotions. "Thanks for your hospitality and for talking to me. I appreciate it."

"I only wish I could tell you more. I hope they find the killer soon."

She managed a weak smile. "Sheriff Dalby tells me that he always gets his man."

"He's told me that, too. Maybe it's true."

"I'm coming back to Huron Station," she said. "Even if they find out who killed my father, I have a feeling that this story isn't over."

As we walked out to the porch together, I thought about that. When the sheriff found the murderer there would be a conclu-sion. But would the whole truth be known even then? I sensed that there was more than one mystery swirling around us. Renie and I and even Estella were a part of it.

I stayed on the porch, watching and thinking, while Renie got into her car and drove away. In spite of the circumstances that had kept them apart, it was obvious that she was affected by her father's death. As for Estella, I considered her comments completely off target. I wondered what had prejudiced her against Randall Scott's daughter and if she would change her mind when she met her.

It might be interesting to delve further into Estella's relationship with Scott. What if she were the mysterious new woman he had found? If he hadn't been murdered, that Thanksgiving dinner might have been unpleasant for the women in his life.

THREE VIGIL LIGHTS BURNED softly at the side altar of the Christian martyr, Saint Sebastian, who had been slaughtered for his faith around the third or fourth century A.D. I'd forgotten how he had been killed until I saw the life-sized marble statue with two arrows piercing the chest.

Now I remembered another version of the story. After Saint Sebastian had been shot with arrows, a kind Christian woman nursed him back to health. Afterward, he confronted the Romans again, whereupon the Emperor ordered him cudgeled to death. In either version, he took a roundabout and painful way to martyrdom.

The sculptor had created a handsome face with realistic features and a strong young body for his subject, for Sebastian had been a Roman soldier before his conversion to Christianity. I could almost see the saint standing above me, serene even in his suffering. I blinked. For a minute it seemed as if the pale marble had taken on flesh tones and deepened into red for his blood. But this was only an illusion, probably caused by the flickering vigil lights.

Mass was over. The priest and his altar boys had gone along with most of the congregation. An elderly woman remained in the front pew saying her rosary while the organist played a poignant melody. It sounded vaguely familiar, almost like "The Streets of Laredo," but then I remembered. The carol was "Jesu Bambino," the Christmas Rose.

I tried to pray but my mind kept straying to the tales of the martyrs I'd read about as a child. Those stark accounts of Christians being torn apart by wild beasts, boiled in oil, and burned at the stake hadn't lost their power to terrify me over the years.

I'd thought of them as fairy tales. Now I believed they were true. But those atrocities belonged to a distant century. My world was slightly more civilized. Randall Scott's slaughter was the work of one demented man.

When the sheriff arrested the killer he would have a fair trial. If a jury of his peers found him guilty he'd be sentenced to life imprisonment, or committed to an institution for the criminally insane. As a society, we'd come a long way from barbarism—in some respects.

I lit a fourth vigil candle and said a silent prayer to Saint Sebastian for the soul of Randall Scott and the deceased members of my own family. Feeling closer to Aunt Celia at the altar of the martyr than I had in her cabin, I sent a silent plea her way: *Tell me if I should find a way to keep the cabin and protect me from this evil that has come to Huron Station.*

There was no answer. Already people were arriving for the one o'clock mass. Quietly I left the altar and made my way through the incoming crowd to the entrance, stopping along the way to dip my fingers in the basin of holy water.

Outside, the glare on the snow almost blinded me. The manger was finished but empty. It was a large, impressive structure that could easily house the Holy Family, as well as a beast or two. I imagined the church had life-sized nativity figures and animals stored away in the basement.

Albert had strung lights around the roof as well as on the trees behind the manger. I promised myself that some evening I'd come back to view the display when the statues were in place.

ON SUNDAY Estella's café offered a traditional dinner of roast chicken with stuffing, mashed potatoes, and string beans. The dessert menu was pared down, with a choice of apple or cherry pie. Then, promptly at four, the restaurant closed its doors, giving Estella and her waitresses a long leisurely evening.

I had finished my dinner and was now sitting at my table near the counter waiting for dessert and the duplicate take-out meal I'd ordered for tomorrow.

Estella replaced the top of the glass cake holder that was now empty, as she'd just cut the last piece of pie for me. "I love the café, but everybody needs a break. We're closing for a week between Christmas and New Year's, so we're decorating early."

She looked toward the entrance where a tall, unadorned balsam filled the air with the rich, fresh scent of its needles.

"The girls will decorate the tree in the morning," she said. "I was hoping you'd stop by today, Krista. I have something for you."

She reached behind the counter and handed me a paper plate of cookies covered with green plastic wrap. Mixed with traditional rollout stars and bells sprinkled with red and green were fancier confections covered with powdered sugar. Some of these were twisted into ties. Others were shaped like horns.

"They look wonderful, thanks," I said. "Mmm. They smell good too."

"I think you'll especially like the horns," Estella said. "Your aunt baked them every Christmas. I used her recipe."

"I don't have to wait until Christmas to eat them, do I?" I asked, trying to conceal the stab of pain I felt at the mention of my aunt. I wished that I could keep the cookies forever in memory of her, but I knew she'd want me to eat and enjoy them.

"Not at all," Estella said. "Just taste one and see how fast they'll disappear."

I lifted the cover and helped myself to a horn.

"That has poppy seed filling," Estella said. "They were your aunt's favorite. Didn't she ever bake them for you?"

"No, we never came up north in the winter. And Aunt Celia rarely left the farm."

"You're in for a treat then. They don't taste exactly like Celia's. I don't know why."

I took two more horns and ate them, one after another. The sharp sweet taste of poppy seed lingered on my tongue, but the sensation was pleasant.

"These *are* delicious, Estella. They literally melt in your mouth."

"Some of them are filled with strawberry preserves," she said. "I was wondering, Krista, did Celia ever tell you about me?"

"I don't think so. She would have talked to my mother about the people she knew. That was grown up conversation. Mostly she told me stories about her dog and the farm animals."

Estella looked so disappointed that I added, "I was only a child at the time. Even if she mentioned you, I wouldn't be likely to remember. Are you going away for Christmas?"

"I'll probably go down to Detroit for the holidays unless the roads are bad. Excuse me, I'd better see what Roy wants."

"Roy Yarrow?"

"Yes, he's back in town, over there in the last booth. Don't look now."

But it was too late. I did and saw Roy sitting beside a slender girl whose long dark hair tumbled down to the collar of her white ruffled blouse. Around her neck she wore a sparkling pendant suspended from a chain.

"Is Roy's companion the one who gave him his alibi?" I asked.

"Who else? That's Lily. He'll never be rid of her now that he's in her debt."

Even from a distance I could tell that Roy and Lily appeared to be enjoying each other's company. The young woman was hardly the unkempt hanger-on described by Estella. She was fairly attractive. Estella was wrong about the makeup. Lily just applied it with a lighter hand.

Why had Estella presented so unflattering a picture of Lily? At the moment I could think of only one reason, the oldest in the world. She was jealous of the attention Roy was giving another woman.

Still, I thought she had cared for Randall Scott. Possibly she had strong feelings for both men or just didn't like young women, although she'd always been nice to me.

I didn't know yet how I felt about Estella, but the cookies were a thoughtful gesture, even though I suspected she'd only befriended me for my aunt's sake. She was still talking to Roy and Lily when Cindy brought out my order, so I left without asking her about Randall. There would be other opportunities to do so.

Eventually I supposed all the players in this bleak drama came to Estella's café. Maybe the killer himself stopped by from time to time for a corned beef sandwich and a cup of coffee. He could even be one of the people with whom I'd been associating. That was a chilling idea but a real possibility. Once again, I hoped that he didn't consider me a threat.

TWELVE

THAT NIGHT the radio turned itself on at ten-thirty. I was certain of the time because I'd glanced at my traveler's clock before settling down for the night under the quilt and it was only a few minutes later that I heard a familiar, droning sound.

I made my way on bare feet into the dining room, following the voice and the static. At the moment I was more curious than frightened. I'd never thought the haunting would go away so easily.

The radio light was a small glowing circle suspended in mid-air above the sideboard. Everything else was dark and suddenly unfamiliar and dangerous. I stumbled over the chair I'd pulled out for Renie and grabbed the edge of the table to keep from falling. When I turned on the wall switch, the room was flooded with a ghostly light that seemed even more unsettling than the darkness.

The radio was playing but the reception was extremely poor and the broadcast sounded wrong. I sat back in the chair listening and wondering what troubled me about it, aside from the supernatural element.

Beyond the barrier of static, I could hear a deep male voice. His words were indistinct, almost muffled, as if they had traveled a long way to reach me, losing a portion of their clarity along the way.

I was able to catch a half dozen of them as they whirled by like airborne puzzle pieces: casualties…Viet Cong…offensive…helicopter…troops…bombing…

That was all. I couldn't put them together or grasp the gist of the newscast, but my senses were functioning in high gear.

I continued to listen and when I heard the word "Vietnam" repeated several times, I began to suspect that I was listening to a newscast that had originated in another era.

I don't know why I was so ready to seize on this unlikeliest of explanations. It just felt right. I wasn't old enough to have firsthand knowledge about the war in Vietnam, but the radio was. And it had unique powers. I became aware of a sense of horror as I realized the implications of that thought and quickly backed away from it.

Maybe I didn't have to look for a solution in the Twilight Zone until I had no other choice. For all I knew, it was 'Remember the War' week on the nostalgia station. Or Albert Drayton might have installed a modern tape player in the radio as some kind of weird initiation for the new person in town.

That second idea made sense and would explain everything. Anyone could order tapes of old radio programs and broadcasts from a catalog. For a skillful, imaginative technician like Albert, turning the radio into a combination tape recorder-time machine would be a simple task.

But maybe I was being too quick to blame him. He might have inadvertently triggered some rogue mechanism that connected the radio to the past. I'd already considered a similar theory but dropped it when Albert assured me that there was nothing out of the ordinary about the radio.

Tomorrow I was going to return to the store on some pretext and question Albert again in such a way that he wouldn't think I was losing my mind.

And good luck with that.

The 'Albert the meddler' theory was the least frightening and I knew of a sure way to test it. If Albert had slipped a vintage tape into the radio the other stations should be normal. I turned the dial to the right, stopping when I heard the poignant strains of "Scarborough Fair." I left the station on hoping the next selection would be new age, rap, anything modern. But it was Peter, Paul and Mary singing "Where Have All the Flowers Gone?"

I could think of one rational explanation for the music from the sixties. Suppose that up here in the north a majority of the listeners preferred ageless classics to contemporary music and this station was simply pleasing its audience? And here was another one, a variation on the 'Remember the War' theory. The stations might be airing old broadcasts of programs and news-casts to commemorate some special occasion. I could ask Albert about that and he'd never suspect the true reason for my inquiry.

As I moved the dial slowly to the left I found a weather report. Static still distorted the broadcast but for some reason the words were clearer now. "…temperatures will fall below zero for the sixth night in a row." There was nothing unique about this kind of forecast. It could apply to any town in Michigan on any winter night during the last four decades.

Finally, I turned the dial as far as it would go in both direc-tions, but all I could hear now was static. The lost in time aspect of the phenomenon had played itself out, at least for tonight.

What was I dealing with? I didn't have the answer yet, but I had intuition. It was clamoring that the answer lay in the Twilight Zone. Somehow I'd tuned into yesteryear's news and music and probably a decades-old weather report as well.

All of my ideas were running together in one unintelligible jumble and my head was beginning to ache. With a sigh of ex-asperation I turned the radio off and as an added precaution un-plugged it. Now it would have to be still.

I went back to bed, and nothing else disturbed me for the rest of the night.

CRAIG STENNET LOOKED UP from his plate and glanced through the window where there was nothing much to see except darkness.

"Sometimes I have to be near the lake," he said. "I can't explain it. The need is just there."

We were having dinner in a small restaurant called the Captain's Table. The water of Lake Huron was a dark expanse under a black, starry sky, its reflection, along with ours, captured in the window. On the beach, lights twinkled closer to the surface. Inside our surroundings were elegant and atmospheric.

We drank white wine that was chosen by Craig to accompany the Rainbow Trout we'd both ordered. We were getting to know each other. Rather, he was getting to know me. Craig was an expert at drawing people out.

"If you like the water you're living in the right place," I said.

"I think so. You look very pretty in that black dress, Krista. I may be old-fashioned, but I don't like to see a woman wearing jeans or pants—ever."

He handed me this compliment as casually as if it were the saltshaker. He was really sweet, if more than a little quaint.

I couldn't resist saying, "You are old-fashioned, Craig. There's no doubt about it. But thank you. This is the only dress I brought with me. I didn't think I'd be going out much."

"What are you doing with your time? I'll confess I'm curious."

He was easy to talk to. With Estella, the gossipmonger, and the arrogant Sheriff Dalby, I'd kept my plans to myself, but Craig had a way of putting me at ease. I'd already told him about my chaotic English classroom and my disastrous first year of teaching that had seemed to go on forever. I wanted to confide in him about the phantom radio but resisted the impulse.

I couldn't tell that story to anyone until I knew what was going on.

"I've been going through my aunt's papers and possessions and packing them in my car," I said.

"Are you leaving soon then?"

"I'm not sure. Maybe."

He poured the rest of the Chardonnay in the glass goblets, filling them to the top. I watched, afraid that the wine would spill on the white tablecloth, but it didn't happen.

"I hope you'll stay for a while, but I wish Dalby would hurry and catch Scott's killer. I worry about you living alone with that lunatic still on the loose."

"He has no reason to kill me," I said, hoping it was true.

"Even so. Luckily, I'm just down the road. You can call on me anytime, day or night."

"Thank you, Craig. I may surprise you and do that, but I think I can protect myself. There's a gun in the cabin."

"I've heard a theory that Scott was hiking in the woods when he was killed," he said.

"Well, I won't do that, not until the snow melts anyway. I'm sure the sheriff will have his man by then."

"I certainly hope so. Why don't you know how long you're staying?"

"I can't make up my mind. I could leave tomorrow. One of my cousins already sorted and boxed my aunt's possessions. It's just a matter of deciding what I want to keep. When I go, I'll leave the furniture and dishes in the cabin."

"So you'll have everything you need when you come back in the spring," he said.

It was obvious what Crag was doing, so why resist? He already knew I was an ineffectual teacher with an uncertain future, the facts I'd intended to keep private. So far, all he'd told me about himself was that he liked horses and boating in the summer.

I said, "I may sell the cabin. But then I remember how beautiful Huron Station is in the summer. I haven't made up my mind yet."

"Tell me about it," he said.

"I hate making life-altering decisions and this one isn't easy. The inheritance came as a surprise to me. I hadn't even thought about the farm for years. Then one day all those acres and the cabin were mine. I saw them as a way to finance my degree. I didn't think I was so attached to the cabin. I've been wondering if I could keep it and still go back to school."

I'd revealed much more than I intended to. I'd better stop talking. Next I'd be telling him about my unsatisfactory love life and the long line of losers I'd left behind me.

I looked down at my plate. Half of the trout and baked potato were gone, and I was no longer hungry. That left the wine. I lifted the glass and took a few sips as I waited to hear Craig's response.

"I understand, Krista," he said. "Money is a powerful lure, but living up north grows on you, and what you're talking about selling is a family place."

"That's it exactly."

"You could apply for an assistantship and a loan. Then all you'd have is living expenses."

"I thought about that. Last year I cut way back and saved every penny I could, and I still have most of the money I made subbing in September. I can do it again."

"That's what you should do then." He paused, as if trying to make a decision of his own. He then added, "But if you do decide to sell, I'd like to make you an offer. I'm only renting the house I live in. The owner is retiring next year and he plans to move up north."

Hal Brecht wanted to buy my acres too, even though he already owns two houses. The knowledge that others coveted my property reawakened my sense of possessiveness and made me determined to hold on to it.

"All right, Craig," I said, "but I'm not sure what I'm going to do yet."

"Whatever you do, you can still have an old-fashioned Christmas in a country cabin—since you don't have any pressing reason to go home."

For him the matter was settled. I was staying in Huron Station for the holidays, keeping the cabin, and still going back to school.

"Are you ready for dessert?" he asked. "They specialize in anything cherry here. Their Traverse Cherry Pie is my favorite."

"That sounds good."

"It does to me, too."

Our evening was drawing to an end and I remembered that I had my own agenda, one that didn't involve talking about myself. Sheriff Dalby thought that Craig was strange. So far I hadn't seen any evidence of unusual behavior except for his eccentric views about women wearing pants and jeans. As for Craig, whenever he mentioned the sheriff, his dislike of him was apparent. Hoping to catch him off guard, I changed the subject.

"Don't you have any faith in Sheriff Dalby's ability to catch Randall Scott's killer?" I asked.

"Like you about your cabin, I'm undecided, Krista. For one, I don't like the company Dalby keeps. That Hal Brecht is a consummate scoundrel."

"The former sheriff, you mean? I've heard he had to leave office. Exactly what did he do?"

"Oh, a little embezzlement, a charge of rape. He was stockpiling weapons and cozying up to the Michigan Militia."

"All of that? Good grief."

Craig backtracked slightly. "The rape charge was never proved. But the embezzlement was. And he had enough weapons in his house to equip a small army."

"Was he a member of the Militia while he was serving as sheriff?"

"That they couldn't prove. He claims that he wasn't."

"What does any of this have to do with Sheriff Dalby?" I asked.

"Maybe nothing, maybe everything. When Dalby was elected, he promised to return integrity to the office."

"Has he done anything illegal?"

"Not that I know of. But the company he keeps is highly suspicious."

"Well, maybe he's just loyal to old friends."

I didn't know why I was defending the sheriff. After all, I had only my impressions of him and the little he had told me about himself. Craig had known him longer than I had and was familiar with his background.

I'd once thought of Sheriff Dalby as a male chauvinist, though. There was that.

"In the end, what's important is that he catches the killer," I said.

"Agreed."

The waiter took our plates and gave us the dessert menus and a little time to study them. I noticed that Craig was studying me instead and decided to forestall any more personal questions by launching one of my own.

"Why did you never get your doctorate, Craig? You were going to tell me when we knew each other better."

He seemed surprised at the direction I'd given our conversation, but he covered it with laughter.

"Did I? Well, I guess that's now. And it's no secret. After I graduated from the University of Michigan, I enlisted in the army. Then, after my tour of duty, I went back to college, but by then my interests had changed. War can do that to you. I majored in journalism and here I am, years later, a freelance writer. It's a good life. I don't have any regrets."

Hoping that Craig wasn't as old as I imagined I asked, "Were you in the Gulf War?"

"You're an outrageous flatterer, Krista. It was Vietnam. What's the matter? You look startled. Did one of your relatives die in the war?"

His words had brought my night with the phantom radio crashing back into my memory. For a while I'd been able to push the haunting to a far corner of my mind.

"No, it's just…" I searched for an appropriate comment and said, "I thought you were much younger, that's all."

"Did you? I'm old enough to be your father, but I don't look on you as a daughter."

I'd intended to say that he must have been very young when he went to Vietnam, only a boy, but after this comment, I decided against it. Earlier in the evening, I'd been thinking how pleasant it was to go out with a much older man, a father figure. There'd be dinner and companionship with no romantic expectations or entanglements, no tension, and no awkwardness at the end of the evening. Then Craig had complimented me on my dress. And now there was this additional remark that didn't need elaboration and a certain look in his eye that any woman can recognize.

I had to say something. "I'm over twenty-one myself, Craig, and besides, age doesn't matter."

"You're kind, Krista, very tactful and nice, but you're not fooling me. I can read people. I can tell what you're thinking right now."

"I hope not."

"I'll tell you what. It's still early. After dessert, let's take a long drive along the lake. I can't remember when I've had such a pleasant evening. I don't want to see it end."

Now what? I went back to my repertoire of appropriate comments to search for one that would express my true feelings, only to find it empty.

"That sounds like fun," I said.

While I closed the menu, Craig signaled the waiter that we were ready to order dessert.

"Cherry pie, Krista—a la mode?"

"Yes, but without the ice cream," I said.

I wondered when the sparkle had appeared in his dark eyes. It made me think of the sheriff. I hoped I wasn't going to lose my only friend in Huron Station tonight.

THIRTEEN

THE HAUNTED RADIO was on its best behavior. It had stayed quiet during the night and waited for me to turn the 'on' dial this morning. I finished the last of my doughnut and listened to a grim forecast of a rapidly approaching blizzard, but I wasn't in the least unhappy. The weather report was current. The winter storm was targeting Huron Station in my own century and year.

I didn't relax completely, though. The radio was bound to revert to its supernatural ways when I least expected it. However, in other respects, my life was satisfactory. The big snow was twelve hours away, giving me ample time to gather survival supplies, and I still had Craig Stennet as my friend.

I couldn't help but smile as I remembered the end of our evening. I didn't have to worry about any awkwardness between us. His goodnight kiss was definitely not fatherly, but he appeared to be satisfied when I briefly returned it in a chaste manner before pulling away. Only now I knew I wouldn't call on him if that undefined future trouble materialized. I didn't want to encourage him.

You're giving yourself too much credit, Krista, I told myself. *Craig is a man of the world, even if he lives alone in a house in the woods. And you're not exactly irresistible. You just happen to own a sexy black dress.*

Nonetheless, Craig might misinterpret a request for help— the one I wasn't going to make because I could take care of myself. And, besides, I had a rifle in the living room. On the other hand, spending days in the company of an intelligent older man who shared my interests would have been pleasant. Days yes, but not the nights.

I sighed, wondering if I would ever find a man who was right for me in every way. The men I usually met weren't interested in a committed relationship, only in having a good time. 'Only in scoring,' as my friend, Diana, often said.

Two sterling exceptions were Matt, the policeman, whom I had met in the Student Union when I was a senior in college, and Ned, the one bright memory from my first year of teaching. But Matt was too serious and dedicated to his profession, almost a martinet. He was a little like Mark now that I thought about it. Their names even sounded alike. I couldn't imagine my life with Matt in it. He broke too many dates because of his work schedule and eventually we stopped seeing each other.

Ned was the opposite: blond and handsome, very easygoing and charismatic. Before long, another girl discovered this and Ned turned to her. Since I hadn't been in love with him, only temporarily infatuated, I soon got over my disappointment and resigned myself to being alone again

I liked to think of the men I'd dated as the loser brigade, but in truth not one of them was right for me. And, in the interest of being strictly honest, there weren't many of them. The one man to whom I would be the most important woman in the world was still out there somewhere. And as nice as Craig Stennet was, in my view, his age eliminated him as a relationship prospect.

I cleared doughnut crumbs from the table and took my empty cup into the kitchen. I'd had enough of reviewing my dismal romantic history. My plan for today was to stay inside and explore the contents of the steamer trunk. More than once I'd been tempted to open it but instead forced myself to go through the boxes stacked on top first. I was convinced that Aunt Celia's most treasured possessions were stored in the trunk and wanted to save the best for the last as a reward for all my hard work.

Now I had to consider the approaching blizzard. Before

settling down with antiques, I'd have to go into town and buy some food in case I was snowbound and couldn't go to the café. I needed fresh vegetables for salads, fruit, and cans of soup to heat up on the stove for quick meals. I'd need extra bread, too. But first I was going to open the trunk and take a quick look inside just to satisfy my curiosity.

I dodged a spray of water as it hit my sleeve and left the cup in the sink to drip dry. Filled with energy and eager to begin the day, I headed toward the back porch, moving farther away from the heat with every step. I found the key and turned around to unlock the trunk. But it was already open.

Last week it had been locked. I was certain of that. Some intruder must have broken into the cabin while I was away and tampered with my property. He would have seen the clearly labeled key and thought there was something valuable inside. Or maybe now I had a haunted trunk that opened itself.

I pushed up the heavy lid and peered inside. The top tray was divided into three sections and filled with photograph albums. Unlike the cards and letters in the boxes they were jumbled together. Some of them were open with snapshots slipping out of their slots. I lifted the tray and set it on the floor. Beneath I saw more of the same. It looked as if someone had rummaged through the contents hurriedly. Or the albums could have been tossed out of order when the trunk was moved out here from another room.

That didn't explain how a locked trunk was now open.

Trying not to give in to the anger I felt at this apparent invasion, I moved through the cabin methodically, checking the doors and testing the windows for signs of a forced entry. As far as I could see, the cabin was impenetrable. But then, in the kitchen, I found evidence of an intruder. The loaf of bread was missing at least four slices. And in the refrigerator the jar of strawberry preserves that I kept on the top shelf was now on the one below.

I supposed I was dealing with a hungry burglar who couldn't resist peeking into a locked trunk. I didn't like the idea but it was better than dealing with another weird phenomenon.

In the living room, I took the shotgun down from above the mantel. I needed to see if it still worked and the best way to test it was to shoot at something. Just then I heard a preemptory knock on the door.

Setting the gun down on the table I opened the door a crack. Sheriff Dalby stood on the porch, stamping the snow off his boots. He had been pounding on the door as if he intended to break it down. I should have known who it was.

As I let him in I said, "Good morning, Sheriff. Come in before you wake the dead with that infernal racket."

"It's not so loud. You can hear more out in the country, especially with all the snow. You're up bright and early again, I see."

"Always. This is the best part of the day."

He pulled off his gloves and stepped inside, leaving a trail of melting snow in his wake. His face was wind burned and so were his hands. He dropped the envelope he was carrying on the sideboard. Standing in front of the delicate silver sleigh he seemed like a giant in a toy log cabin: powerful but restrained.

"I just stopped by to see if you got home all right," he said.

"After dinner? Sure. We went for a ride along the lake first."

His smile froze. "We?"

"Craig and I."

"Was he at the Roadhouse too? I didn't see him."

I could see that the sheriff and I were talking at cross-purposes. It would be amusing if his frown weren't so forbidding.

"If you're referring to the evening at the Roadhouse, that was four nights ago. I arrived home in one piece. But you were right about the roads. I ran into another reckless driver…"

The frown spread to his eyes and turned them darker. I'd better watch what I said to him. He was the law, after all.

"Not literally," I said. "I lost control of the steering for a few minutes but no harm was done."

"Maybe when you want to go some place you should let someone else do the driving."

"It was nothing. No matter how slippery the roads get, there are plenty of trees to stop you from crashing into the lake."

"Those trees can do a lot of damage to a car and a body."
He walked calmly past me and picked up the gun, examining
it with the ease of one who has handled firearms all his life.

"Someone took good care of this baby," he said. "Are you
going hunting out of season? I'm going to have to give you a
ticket if you are, even if it's your own land."

His voice was gruff but he wasn't serious now. His frown
was gone and the gleam in his eyes hinted at his lighter side,
a side that he seemed to like keeping out of sight.

"Only for impertinent males," I said. "I'm glad you're here,
Sheriff. Someone broke into my cabin."

He was instantly alert, his blue eyes sharp, ready for action
of any kind. Putting the rifle down he asked, "Were you here
when it happened?"

"Not unless he came during the night. I think I would have
heard him, though."

He pulled out two chairs and took a notebook and a pen out
of his pocket. "Sit down, Krista—please." All of a sudden, our
roles were reversed. I might have been a visitor in his office.
"Now, what happened? Start at the beginning."

I told her about the trunk, the missing slices of bread, and
the misplaced jam. Said aloud, they sounded insignificant. But
the sheriff was taking me seriously. At least he was writing in
his notebook.

"Did that hunter ever come back?" he asked.

"I haven't seen him."

"Is anything else missing?"

"Not that I noticed," I said. "There isn't much here to take."

I hadn't made a thorough search yet, but the silver sleigh and
the radio were still on the sideboard. To my knowledge they
were the most valuable objects in the cabin and the most important ones because I wanted to keep them.

He walked slowly to the back of the cabin. I trailed after him,
pausing to close the bedroom door on the way.

"Let's see how good your security is," he said.

On the sleeping porch he examined the lock and then pushed the door open. I stepped quickly back into the kitchen to avoid the waves of cold air that rushed inside.

"This is old but it passes inspection," he said. "What about the windows?"

"I already checked them."

He walked past the cot and lifted the lid of the trunk. "What's in here?"

"My aunt's photo albums."

"Not exactly what a thief would be looking for. You're sure it wasn't open all along?"

"I'm positive. Absolutely. It was locked."

"All right. I'm not doubting you, just asking. It looks like you had a burglar here…maybe a vagrant who came this way before. He made himself a snack and thought he'd find warm clothes in the trunk."

"That's what I thought. But how did he get in?"

"There's always a way," he said. "No lock is one hundred percent foolproof."

Casually he walked through the kitchen and stopped to open the bedroom door. I noticed how fine he looked in his uniform and how its color complemented his tawny hair. He stood on the threshold and looked around, taking a long time to do it.

This was the one room in the cabin that was in utter disarray. I breathed a sigh of relief that I'd made my bed neatly and folded a clean nightgown on top of the pillow. But my suitcase was open on the other bed, its contents spilling out in a jumble of sweaters, jeans, and frilly lingerie in my favorite colors of ivory, black and red.

Why hadn't I finished hanging my clothes in the closet? There was no reason, no excuse for this negligence. In the relentless sunshine that streamed through the window every intimate item looked brighter, almost garish. I wished I could jam every one of them back into the suitcase and slam it shut, but it was probably better to act as if I didn't care. Anyway, the sheriff wasn't interested in my underwear. He was conducting an investigation.

"Did you bring any jewelry or money with you?" he asked.

"Only two pairs of earrings. They're in my bag on the cedar chest—oh, I forgot to check it."

He handed the bag to me. I unzipped it and moved my hand through the contents, identifying each object. When I felt the bristles of my hairbrush slide under the soft flesh under my fingernail, I emptied everything out on the bed. My wallet was unfolded, but I usually left it that way. Hastily I counted my money. Why hadn't I thought to do that earlier?

"It's all here, including an extra ten dollars I didn't know I had," I said. "Maybe the thief left it to pay for the food. But it would make more sense for him to leave money in the kitchen."

"Maybe," he said. "It's good that nothing else is missing." He moved silently into the kitchen and picked up the loaf of bread. "You're sure you didn't just forget how much you ate?"

Was he serious or joking now? I couldn't tell. "I'm sure."

"I'll take a look in the refrigerator then—my God, girl, don't you have anything to eat in the house? Don't you know there's a blizzard on the way?"

"No woman cooks when she's on vacation. I am going shopping today," I said.

"If this is the best you have to offer I wonder why your burglar stayed. I don't think he'll be back for a couple of jam sandwiches. All right, Krista, I've seen enough. I'll make a report, but I don't think you have to worry about a return visit. These break-ins happen frequently when houses are left untended for long periods of time. Whoever broke in saw that somebody's living here now and took off."

That was a satisfactory explanation. "I hope you're right."

"If you're going to the grocery store, you should leave soon before the snow starts," he said.

I followed him into the dining room, noticing again how large he was, like a great bear only without the fur. In certain select circumstances I felt certain that he could be dangerous.

But he was the sheriff now, a representative of the law, a man who had sworn to protect the people of Huron Station. For a while that included me.

"All these things that have been happening could be coincidences," I said. "But what if they're not?"

"What things?"

"The arrow I found in the snow and the man who watches the cabin from the woods. That car could have been trying to run me off the road."

"Are you talking about the Crown Victoria?" he asked.

"The man who passed me when I was driving home from the Roadhouse. He had a gray car. I told you about it."

"You said it was nothing."

"Maybe it was. All I'm saying is, 'what if?'"

"When we know what we're dealing with, I'll take care of it," he said. "Trust me. You sure you know how to use this gun, Krista? I don't want you to fire at me some day when I stop by."

"I can shoot. I have excellent eyesight and it would be hard to miss you."

As he emptied the chamber on the table his frown came back. "You don't want to rely on this gun. The bullets have gone bad. If you're serious about using it have Albert over at the hardware check it out for you and buy some fresh ammo. You don't look like a girl who could handle a gun to me," he added.

"That's a snap judgment and a sexist crack rolled into one. Try me."

He chuckled. "I might do just that, but not today. I came here on business. How about a cup of coffee?"

"Sure, coming right up."

I didn't have any left from breakfast. I wanted to serve him fresh coffee anyway so I decided to make a fresh pot. As I measured the coffee I glanced back to see him in the dining room, looking intently through the window. I joined him but didn't notice anything unusual.

"What's in the barns?" he asked.

"In the big one some old tools and a ladder and saw I bought. My aunt used to keep feed in the other. I hope it's all gone."

"After all these years you can be sure of it. I'll have a look at them on the way out."

"Do you think someone could be hiding there?"

"I didn't say that."

But that's what he meant. Either barn would have been a safe place for a stalker to watch and wait. I should have explored them thoroughly myself.

The coffeemaker was bubbling merrily in the kitchen, calling me back to my hostess duties. It was fortunate that I had an immediate task to occupy my hands and mind instead of contemplating what might be lurking inside the old barns.

"Sit down, Sheriff. I'll get the coffee. I'm sorry I can't offer you a doughnut. I ate the last one for breakfast. Oh, I almost forgot. Estella gave me some Christmas cookies."

"I'll never turn down Estella's cookies," he said.

When I came back, he had transferred the envelope he'd brought in earlier from the sideboard to the table and taken out a black and white photograph.

I remembered then. He'd come here for a reason. "Do you have another suspect for me to identify?" I asked.

"Maybe. See if you recognize him."

The man in the picture had an unkempt black beard and small beady eyes in a combination that screamed 'villain.' He was scowling into the camera and looked as if he were about to swear at the photographer. I didn't think I'd want to meet him in any dark place, and I was certain I'd never seen him before.

"Sorry, no," I said. "Who is he?"

"The only name he gave us was Ben. We're running a check on him."

"Do you think he might be Scott's killer?"

"He says no, claims he never even heard of him, but he took Scott's jacket to a dry cleaners over in Abbotsville yesterday and asked if they could get the bloodstains out. Scott's wallet is still missing."

"That doesn't make any sense," I said. "If Ben were the killer he would have burned or hidden it."

"We don't have a bright man here. He's a vagrant. His story is that he found the jacket in a deserted cabin and figured somebody had left it behind. He claims there was nothing in the pockets. The trouble is he can't give us any location. Are you certain this couldn't be the man in the Crown Victoria? Think. Imagine him with a cap on."

I took the pictures over to the window where the light was better. If only Ben were the killer then the sheriff could keep him in lockup and I could concentrate on the radio and whatever ghost had taken possession of it.

"I wish I could say yes but I don't know."

"What if you saw him in person?"

"I'm sorry. I just don't remember."

"Okay. Thanks anyway. Let's see what today brings. You make good coffee, Krista."

"I'll bet you say that to all the ladies in the county."

"Only the ones who give me coffee. I'll look in on you tonight on the way home."

I hadn't expected Mark to make a return visit. "I don't want to inconvenience you, Sheriff."

"It's no trouble. I live close by. Not as near to you as Stennet, though. He's practically on your front doorstep. Do you still hear my dogs howling at night?"

"Sometimes. But it's like the wind, a pleasing sound."

"I'm that close to you," he said. "Within shouting distance."

"Now you're exaggerating."

"Not by much. When the snow melts you could walk to my house. Don't forget to fill the refrigerator. I see you have plenty of candles. Good. You'll be all right."

Except for the haunting. I imagined myself telling him about the sixties broadcast I'd heard and the music from long ago. Would he be so cavalier then?

"Do you give everybody in Huron Station this kind of hands-on attention?" I asked.

"Only the ones who need it."

That intriguing gleam was back in his eye again, and suddenly I remembered Estella's allusions to Mark's fondness for women. Maybe I'd better keep my flippant remarks to myself.

Flippant? They're downright flirtatious. Backtrack before you regret it.

"Thanks for everything, Sheriff. I can't tell you how much safer I feel now."

He lifted the coffee mug in my direction. I could almost believe he was toasting me with an elegant crystal flute.

"Anytime, honey," he said. "It's part of my job."

FOURTEEN

LARGE WIND-DRIVEN SNOWFLAKES drifted down from the sullen gray sky, turning the air around my car into a white cloud. I cut off the engine, killing the radio and the doomsday voice of the weathercaster. I'd heard enough.

The winter storm that was predicted for seven o'clock was ahead of schedule. The forecast included dire warnings of winds gusting up to seventy miles an hour. Thank heavens I'd made it home with enough food to carry me through a dozen snowstorms. In the trunk I had Aunt Celia's cleaned and newly loaded rifle that Albert swore was better than anything he had to sell me. Now all I had to do was unload the car and settle down in front of the wood stove to ride out the blizzard.

I could hardly see the cabin through the falling snow. It was only an impression of shape and darkness, but I could tell that I'd parked farther from the front door than usual. That meant a longer walk and several trips lugging two bags of groceries at a time. Maybe I could carry three. Maybe I should pull the car closer to the door.

Just make a decision, I told myself. *Get inside where it's warm before you freeze.*

I pulled my hood forward, opened the door, and sank into the deep snow that hadn't been beaten down by the sheriff's cruiser. The cold seared my face and wet snowflakes stung my eyes. This was pure misery. It was no time to be moving in slow motion but I couldn't seem to hurry with the force of the storm working against me.

Except for the rifle, everything was in the back of the car. I tried to open the rear door, but it was almost frozen shut. Using all my strength, I pulled the handle toward me several times. It finally broke free. I leaned across the seat, reaching for the box of pastries from the bakery.

If Mark showed up tonight I'd have something to offer him besides coffee: fresh bread, apple pie, and pastries, along with baked ham from Estella's café. But I didn't really expect to see him. With a blizzard added to the murder investigation and whatever else he did, he'd be busier than usual.

Then something changed.

Behind me a muffled sound and a sharp intake of breath warned me that I wasn't alone. Before my mind could identify the flash of movement just beyond my peripheral vision, a sharp pain cut across my shoulders and a rough shove thrust me forward, sending two bags of groceries flying to the floor of the car.

A strong, unpleasant cherry odor followed me and seemed to wrap itself around my face. I couldn't escape it nor could I see who had attacked me. He was still there. I could sense him closing in on me.

I lay face down on the back seat with one arm dangling over the edge and the other one bent under my chest. The cans that had spilled out of the fallen bags shifted in and out of focus, their labels a blur. Before I could cry out a hand yanked my head back by the hair and a gritty cloth dropped down over my face.

I wrenched my body up from the seat and struck out at my attacker, but struggle was useless. The heavily scented, scratchy material cut off my vision. My fists fell against a body as hard as steel. I might as well have been grappling with the storm.

Through pain and nausea I found my voice and the strength to yank the cloth up from my mouth. "Who are you? What the hell do you think you're doing?"

Then another blow to the back of my head split my world into fragments and all awareness vanished in a torrent of white and darkness.

I AWOKE IN THE BARN, lying on the hard floor. I felt that I hadn't been unconscious long; only the few minutes it had taken my assailant to drag me across the snow and throw me inside.

There was a different cold in here, the dead, airless kind I'd always imagined would be found in a mausoleum. I pulled myself up and stumbled over to the front wall of the barn. An unfamiliar weakness set the floor in motion. I had moved too fast. Leaning against a post, I took long, deep breaths.

As soon as I felt stronger, I pushed on the heavy wooden door. It was barred from the outside. Days ago when I'd opened the barn I decided to leave it unlocked. In the semi-darkness, I looked for the shelf where the combination lock had been. Except for the new can of oil, it was empty and already festooned with trailing cobwebs. My attacker had planned carefully.

Assailant and attacker were anonymous words. I would feel more in control of my life if I could attach a name or description to the person who had handled me like a sack of oats. Plenty of suspicious people lurked in my recent past, but Hal Brecht was the only one I'd met.

Still, I'd learned an elementary lesson today. A loaded rifle in the trunk of a car is worthless when an assailant creeps up behind his intended victim in the snow.

He could hardly have moved in silence, plowing through the high drifts that surrounded the cabin. I should have heard boots tramping through the snow or a giveaway crunching or snapping of twigs. But I didn't have a warning of his approach until it was too late. I'd been thinking about Mark and that had landed me in danger. A second lesson was embedded in that bit of folly.

Now I had to use my wits and whatever resources I could find inside the barn to escape from my prison. I needed to act quickly. In this case delay might be fatal.

Slowly I looked around at the empty stalls hoping to find an object I could use as a weapon. Although the animals were long gone the scents of horse and cow, wet dog and sweet hay lingered, mixed with the sickening cherry smell that still seemed to cling to my hair.

An old wooden ladder led up to the loft where a single window provided the barn's sole source of illumination. It offered a magnificent view of the meadow and the woods. Now all I could see were sheets of slanting snow.

Dear God, it was cold. If I stayed much longer in this vast unheated structure I would die. But probably that was what my enemy intended. Maybe he planned to set fire to the barn. At this very moment, he might be striking the match.

That was possible but unlikely. Who builds a fire in a blizzard, especially if he can't afford to attract attention? It would be simpler to leave me here to freeze or starve to death, whichever happened first.

The barn wasn't entirely empty. As I surveyed my surroundings again, I noticed the pathetic collection of throwaway tools almost hidden by a stack of rotting, mismatched boards. My choices included a broken pitchfork, a rusty shovel with half a handle and a misshapen broom. The hammer on top of the discarded wood looked the most promising. I could use it to break the window and then jump out into the snow.

When I was a child I'd climbed that ladder many times, but it had been old then. How reliable could it be now? Also I had weighed less, and someone was always waiting below to catch me if I fell. I didn't have that safety net now. I didn't have an alternative either.

Don't stop to think or you'll never do it.

I picked up the hammer, stepped back, and pitched it high up onto the loft. It landed with a resounding thud.

Now for the hard part. Just do it.

Gripping the ladder by its rough, weathered sides, I put my foot on the first step to test it. The old wood creaked in protest but it seemed sturdy enough. I ignored the renewed pain in my shoulders and, not looking down, climbed up to the loft and swung my body over onto the boards just like I used to do. Only this wasn't child's play.

The smell of hay was stronger up here and the air was thick. Carefully avoiding sections that looked as if they were rotted, I walked over to the window. The hammer had landed underneath it in a pool of straw-colored powder.

Fortunately the window wasn't built into the wall. Unless it had frozen shut over the years, I could simply open it. I moved fast now, so close to freedom that I couldn't wait another second.

I tried to push the window up but it remained firmly in place. For a moment I considered smashing the pane. Impulsively I raised the hammer to do so, but then put it down. It would make too much noise, and I could cut myself on the glass. As a last resort, though, I might have to risk detection or injury.

Keeping the alternative clearly in my mind, I gripped the hammer and pounded the frame in all four of its corners, hoping the sound would be contained in the barn. Bits of wood flew back into my face but I was able to raise the window, all the way to the top.

Nothing held me back now except the pain in my shoulders and the nagging fear that I was about to throw myself off a cliff to my death. I sat on the sill and swung my legs over the side of the barn. All I could see was white.

Think of what you're about to do as jumping out of an airplane, drifting down through the clouds with the snow. Some people do it for fun. Now!

I let myself drop through the air and almost immediately hit snow. Stunned by the jolt of the impact I lay still for a minute. I hadn't fallen far. The snow on this side of the barn had drifted halfway up to the window, and the frozen mass beneath the newest layers kept me from going all the way down to the ground.

You did it. You're still alive. Now get up.

That was even harder, but I managed to do it. I stood breast deep in the snow, having landed at the drift's highest point. Holding on to the side of the barn, I started moving forward, traveling downhill. By the time I reached the corner the snow came up to the top of my boots.

I took another step and heard a car door slam. The sound was magnified in the deep snow-filled silence. I froze, wondering if I should take cover in the nearest drift. Then a familiar voice shouted my name.

It was Mark.

"CHRIST ALMIGHTY. You look like a snowman. What happened to you?"

I was so cold that I couldn't speak. I could hardly breathe. Now that I had come through the ordeal, feeling in my body started to creep back. My shoulders were throbbing and thin needles of pain danced behind my eyes. I couldn't stop shivering.

Mark came tramping through the snow and looked down at me. The frown darkened his eyes, but I couldn't read his expression.

"Never mind. Let's get you inside."

That seemed like a good idea. The prospect of warmth and the presence of someone at my side revived me. With his arm around my shoulders, Mark guided me slowly through the blowing snow to the cabin.

At last he said, "Here we are. Inside now."

"Wait. Did you see anybody just now? Someone locked me in the barn. I had to jump out of the window."

He opened the door to the porch and practically pushed me inside. "I haven't seen anyone but you. What were you doing in the barn in this weather?"

"I didn't…" I started to explain but Mark cut me off.

"Where's your key, Krista?"

"In my purse in the car. I hope whoever it was didn't take it."

"Wait here, and I'll get it."

Before I could reply he was gone. I didn't have the energy to do anything except wait. I wished those old lawn chairs were still on the porch. If I didn't sit down soon I was afraid I'd fall. Mark came back before that happened. He had my bag and the key. As he opened the door I stood behind him, brushing the snow from my coat.

"Your car door was open," he said. "Those grocery bags are

getting snowed on. I'll bring them in for you as soon as I get you inside and then you can fill me in."

"Leave them. Someone must need you for something more important tonight."

"Like I said, Krista, saving city girls who lock themselves in barns is part of my job."

"It didn't happen that way," I said.

"Tell me, then."

"I didn't see anybody. One minute I was reaching for a box, the next I felt a pain. He hit me with something hard, tried to gag me, and tossed me in the barn."

"Are you sure?" he asked.

When I nodded he said, "Where did he hit you?"

His voice was that of a sheriff on official business. A cold mask had slipped over his face, making his expression impossible to read.

"On my shoulders." I showed him. "And higher, back here."

"And then you jumped out of a window? That was a stupid thing to do. You could have been killed."

We were inside the cabin, standing in front of the wood stove where it was slightly less cold. Now that I was safe my fear turned into anger. Because Mark was the only other person in the cabin I directed it toward him.

"I could have died in that barn. I did what I had to. The fall probably saved my life. How dare you call what I did stupid?"

"As soon as I get you warmed up I'll take you to the hospital," he said.

"Absolutely not. I don't want to go back out in this storm. Everything hurts but I'd know it if I broke something."

"What about hypothermia? Frostbite? You said this attacker hit you on the head? You might have a concussion."

The concern in his voice melted my anger a little.

"I don't think so," I said. "I can remember exactly what happened. I'm going to have a cup of steaming coffee. That's all I need: something hot to drink and a couple of aspirin."

"Good idea. I'll go back outside and look around."

He stamped out, slamming the door. The sudden silence inside the cabin was overwhelming, almost unsettling. I pushed the thought out of my mind. In the bathroom I took my aspirin and lingered at the small mirror over the sink to brush my hair and apply a touch of powder and lipstick. Then, instead of making coffee, I sank into the rocker by the wood stove and willed the medication to take effect quickly.

When Mark returned and joined me at the fire I asked, "How did you happen to come by the cabin so early?" By now my anger had gone and I could feel my apprehension beginning to slip away.

A slow smile stole the chill from his eyes. "I was just driving through the neighborhood," he said.

"In a blizzard?"

"You don't think the sheriff sits in his heated office while a snowstorm buries his town, do you?"

"No, but I could see you in an all night diner over coffee and doughnuts."

"You're sort of sassy for a girl who's just had a near brush with death."

"I'm giddy with joy. Glad to be alive."

"Sit still," he said. "I can make that coffee you wanted as soon as I get the fire going. Do you have anything stronger in those bags?"

"I wish I did."

A bottle of rum, I thought, *or brandy.* A Tom and Jerry. A snowbound cabin. The sheriff. Cozy, tantalizing images went spinning through my mind.

Mark said, "There must be tire tracks or footprints, but they're already snowed over. I didn't find anything and there's no chance of apprehending your attacker in this storm. You're sure you didn't hear another car? Anything?"

"I'm sure. Only sounds…breathing…when it was too late. I was focused on—carrying in my groceries."

And thinking about you.

"It's all right, Krista."

For a moment I was afraid that Mark had read my thought.

"Let's get some more heat in this old cabin," he said.

I sat on the sofa and watched Mark replenish the fire in the wood stove. He worked quietly and efficiently with the skill of a man who knew what he was doing. I looked at his strong hands arranging the elm wood and I stared at the first flames. My ordeal wasn't over. This was only the first major skirmish.

"He came after me in a blizzard," I said. "The other things that happened could be explained away. This was deliberate."

"There's no doubt about that. I think you should get away from this place. Like I said, it's too isolated."

"If Huron Station had a hotel I might consider it," I said. "I'm not going to stay in one of those seedy motels, though."

"Miss Krista, we don't have any seedy motels in Huron Station."

"I wonder if he knows I got out of the barn? Maybe he'll come again."

"That's why you should leave the cabin. Just for a few days."

"Huron Station is going to lose its reputation as a pretty little resort town if you don't catch the killer soon," I said.

"That's what I plan to do."

The unspoken thought that the person who had attacked me might be the archer killer hung heavily in the air. Mark crumpled a newspaper and threw it into the blaze with unnecessary force. I suppose I'd angered him. My intent wasn't to criticize his methods or progress. I didn't relish a repeat performance of the barn incident but I wasn't going to run away either.

"What are the places around town where people get together to talk and have a good time?" I asked.

"Estella's Café gets a lot of business," he said. "There's the Roadhouse and the casino when cabin fever really sets in. The American Legion has a good fish dinner every Friday night. Why?"

"I want to make some more friends. I'll let you carry in the groceries if you still want to. My rifle is in the trunk. Would you bring it in too, please?"

He looked up from the fire. The anger I thought I'd heard in his voice had vanished. Perhaps it was never there. But he was quiet for so long that I thought he was regretting his offer or had suddenly remembered another piece of urgent sheriff's business that awaited him.

"Or I can get it," I said.

"You stay here. When I get back I'll make that coffee. And as soon as the blizzard is over I'll go after the man who attacked you. I'll get him, too."

It sounded more like a promise intended to make me feel good than something Mark was actually going to accomplish. And it did make me feel better. I had a plan of my own, however, and I could hardly wait to implement it.

FIFTEEN

"I FORGOT to tell you something," I said as Mark handed me a steaming mug of tomato soup.

He had made himself at home in my kitchen, making coffee, heating a can of condensed soup, and even opening a box of crackers. The fire in the wood stove was burning, filling the cabin with a delicious smell of apples or bacon. I could never decide which. And the rifle was on the wall again. Now he was buttoning his jacket and pulling his leather gloves on, getting ready to go back out into the blizzard.

In the midst of all my newfound comfort I'd remembered a detail that had slipped out of my mind.

Mark turned around, instantly the efficient sheriff again. "What did you forget?"

"During the attack, I smelled a strong cherry scent."

"Do you think the man was wearing after-shave or cologne?" he asked.

"No, it was a smoky odor like cherry-scented tobacco."

"That's a clue. He may be a pipe smoker."

"Or maybe it was a sore throat lozenge. He was so close to me that I could hear him breathing. It's probably nothing."

"You don't know that. Everything is important, Krista."

He laid his hand on my arm as he had done before and for a moment I felt as if everything was going to be all right.

"I don't want anyone else to know what happened to me," I said.

Again I thought I'd angered him, but he smiled and said, "You're confusing me with Estella. I'll have to make out a report, but I agree. It's better to keep this incident under wraps."

"And keep the villain befuddled."

"Yes."

"Have you heard how long the blizzard is going to last?" I asked.

"Until sometime tomorrow morning."

"If there are any tracks, they'll probably be gone by then."

"The way the snow is falling, I'm afraid so. I didn't notice any tire tracks, only yours."

"He didn't drop down from the sky."

"No, but maybe he was on skis."

"There would be ski tracks then." A sliver of fear came back as I remembered the man in the orange jacket at the edge of the woods. "He could have been behind the cabin waiting for me," I said. "Maybe that's why I didn't hear him."

"I'll check it out," Mark said, and once again he touched my arm. "It's over. You'll be more careful the next time. I'm on my way now. No, don't get up."

He let himself out. I stayed on the sofa close to the fire, warming my hands on the mug and listening to the wind. Outside the cabin a wild winter storm was raging, but I was safe. For tonight at least.

As soon as it stopped snowing and the roads were cleared, I intended to make an effort to get acquainted with everybody in Huron Station whose name was linked to the archery murder case, no matter how remote the connection. As a beginning, I'd try to arrange a casual meeting with Roy Yarrow the next time he came to Estella's Café.

Although Lily had given Roy an alibi it didn't necessarily exonerate him. My other targets were Hal Brecht, the dishonored sheriff, and Ben in Abbotsville, both of whom might be more difficult to track down, but I would do it.

Any one of these men might have fled the crime scene in a Crown Victoria and later watched my cabin from the woods, leaving an arrow in a snowdrift for me to find. Any one might be the burglar.

But I wasn't going anywhere tonight or even tomorrow. As

soon as I finished the soup and coffee, I took a hot bath and put on my warmest flannel nightgown. After my misadventure in the barn and Mark's visit, I was too wired to sleep, but I wasn't afraid.

My attacker would be unlikely to return in the middle of a blizzard. If he did I had my rifle. He was probably miles away, confident that I was still locked in the barn. Eventually he would know that I was still alive. That was when I had to be on my guard.

I was certain that Mark meant every word he said about catching the man, but he wasn't a Lone Ranger figure dedicating to righting the world's wrongs. I had to take responsibility for my own safety. So far I thought I'd managed well enough.

At ten o'clock I turned on the radio and listened to the latest weather report. Eight additional inches of snow were expected to be on the ground by morning and people were urged to stay off the roads. Night classes at the community college and choir practice at St. Sebastian's were cancelled. Tomorrow all schools in Alcona County would be closed. I assumed that meant Huron Station would be shut down as well.

Once again I comforted myself with the thought that the snow was keeping me safe. Not even a desperate killer would be likely to brave the elements on a night like this. Grateful for a brief respite, I turned off the radio and lights and checked the embers in the stove. All was well.

As soon as I started moving around the events of the day caught up with me. I was exhausted and the pain in my shoulders throbbed with renewed intensity. I took two more aspirin, drank a glass of milk and went to bed. Maybe I'd sleep away the pain and the blizzard would turn into flurries, while somewhere in Huron Station Mark would stop for pie and coffee at a diner where the villain was taking refuge from the storm...

In the hours before dawn, I heard soft music in the living room but I didn't get up. The songs were "Blowin' in the Wind" and "Cruel War." The radio had turned itself on again and slipped back into the sixties.

WHEN I WOKE UP the next morning I realized that it would take more than painkillers and sleep to ease the all-over soreness in my body. I felt as if I had fallen from the sky and landed on a block of ice.

The only visible sign of the attack was a bruise on the side of my face that neither powder nor a rearranged hairstyle could conceal. All things considered, though, I was in good shape. The blizzard was tapering off and the winds had died down, leaving behind a landscape filled with fantastic snow sculptures. The view from the living room window was breathtaking but disheartening.

Like a river of snow, the earth had risen to a dangerously high level. Only the top of the Taurus was visible, and the long drive leading out to the road was drifted over. I wouldn't be going out tomorrow, either. Unless Huron Station had a remarkably efficient snow removal service, I might not be able to leave the cabin for a week.

Inside I proceeded as though it were a normal morning. After taking a bath I got dressed and listened to the radio while I ate breakfast. The big story was Huron Station on the morning after the first major snowstorm of the season and how people were coping with it. This was definitely news from my own time, not the sixties.

Since I couldn't begin my investigation until the roads to town were cleared I spent the morning going through old photograph albums. Before her marriage to Uncle Kent and the move to Huron Station, Aunt Celia and her family had lived in Detroit on Pinegrove, a tree-lined street of handsome old Victorian houses. In these earliest pictures, the neighborhood looked new and fresh. It would be interesting to see how it had aged in later decades when my aunt was growing up.

One album was filled with pictures of Aunt Celia and Uncle Kent in the first years of their marriage, before he went to Vietnam. One black and white snapshot of Uncle Kent occupied an entire page. He was in uniform posing in front of a helicopter with other soldiers in the background. How young he looked and how strange to think that in some misty after-life he would never change while on earth his wife had grown older with each passing year and finally died.

I set the album aside. My activity had just gone from inter-esting to sad. It might be simpler just to pack the rest of my aunt's pictures in the car and take them home with me when I left—whenever that happened. The lure of yesteryear had lost much of its luster for me. I had immediate matters to deal with now, and, in spite of the danger, I wanted to see how things turned out here in Huron Station.

And by "things" you mean?

I left the rest of the thought unfinished.

In the interest of taking responsibility for my own life and well being, I buttoned a bulky beige cardigan over my turtle-neck and put on my coat. Thank goodness the usable shovel was on the back porch instead of in the barn.

WHILE I WAS CLEARING the hood of the Taurus, I heard the roar of a snowplow in the distance. Moving slowly down the road, it passed Craig Stennet's house. Craig was in the driver's seat.

Liberation was at hand and sooner than I'd hoped. But with over an acre of unplowed snow separating the cabin from the road I was still marooned. Nevertheless, I continued to clean the car and became so absorbed in my work that I didn't notice when the plow turned down the path to the cabin.

With his Stetson hat and the red scarf flapping in a continu-ous spray of white, Craig looked like a modern cowboy on a range-clearing mission. Shielding my eyes from the last of the flurries I watched as the plow sent high waves of snow crashing to the sides of the road.

When he reached the front of the cabin he waved to me and took the plow back to the road. On his next trip he brought it to a stop next to the Taurus and jumped down. I now had a tunnel between high walls of snow, wide enough for a car. My way out.

"Here, I'll do that." With a warm smile he took the shovel from my hand.

I stood aside, watching him widen the path from the car to the cabin. A sliver of light broke through the clouds, and occasional flakes floated in the air around us. Craig tossed more snow up into the air to meet them. My shoulders throbbed and my legs ached. Without anything to do I was more intensely aware of every ache and pain.

Finally he leaned the shovel against the cabin and reinforced the knot on his scarf.

"I can't thank you enough, Craig," I said. "Come inside and get warm."

"I think I will."

He followed me through the porch. As I opened the door he started to remove his jacket and boots.

"Don't worry about getting snow on the floor," I said, leaving my own boots on. "Let me take your jacket."

This morning I had found an antique coat rack lying behind the trunk and moved it close to the front door. This small addition to the décor and the ability to put a guest's coat in a proper place made me feel that I was truly at home in the cabin.

"I see you weathered the blizzard in one piece," he said. "That's a nasty bruise on your face. How did you get it?"

"I ran into something." I thought it best not to be specific about how I had injured myself, not even with this kind man. "At times, I thought it would never stop snowing. I didn't expect such service."

"Here in Huron Station, we take care of ourselves," he said. "That plow is the best investment I ever made."

"How can I thank you?" I asked.

"Don't worry about it, Krista. Up here neighbors help each other. Besides, I like the exercise. I can't ride my horse until the rest of the roads are plowed."

"Stay and have a cup of coffee with me then," I said.

"That I'll say yes to. I've only been inside your cabin a few times before, when Dr. McLaughlin was hunting, and it was rather plain. The candles and kerosene lamps give it a nice old-fashioned feeling. You're turning this old place into a real home."

"Thank you. That's the way I remember it. The cabin is too wonderful to be used only as a rest stop for hunters."

"It's been crying out for a woman's touch." He moved over to the wood stove and held his hands over it. "These are great, aren't they?"

"They're indispensable. Do you have one?"

"Not at the present. I burn logs in an open fireplace. The simple life suits me."

"I think I could get used to it, too," I said. "Sit down while I start the coffee."

In the kitchen I opened the large box from the bakery. Two dozen mixed doughnuts had seemed excessive to me at the time, but I was happy to have them now. A man who had just moved a ton or more of snow was entitled to a few chocolate-iced dunkers with his coffee. And I'd have plenty left to offer Mark.

When I came back with the doughnuts Craig was standing at the sideboard examining the silver sleigh.

"You don't see such intricate work today. How old do you think this piece is?"

"Maybe sixty or seventy years. It belonged to my aunt."

I set the plate of doughnuts on the buffet. Arranged on Aunt Celia's antique silver tray, they looked like the beginning of a breakfast buffet.

"Have one," I said. "They're necessary for surviving the snow."

"You've been visiting the Station Bakery, I see. They always outdo themselves around the holidays. Are you going to decorate the cabin for Christmas?"

"I think so. I have acres of balsam trees—oh, I forgot. They're all buried."

"You may be able to find a nice fir growing closer to the cabin where the snow isn't so deep."

"Or it might melt before Christmas."

"Don't count on that. We're not officially into winter yet. I admire you, Krista. Not many young women are brave enough to stay alone in an isolated cabin in the winter. You must come from pioneer stock."

He was so earnest that I almost laughed. "I don't know about that, Craig. I told you why it's in my best interest to stay."

He nodded. "I remember. Still, it's unusual. I'm glad you're here."

"Why thank you. I'm glad I came."

"I'd have plowed you out in any case," he said, "but I wanted to see you. I went to Abbotsville yesterday for a supply of copy paper and my buddy gave me a side of venison. Will you have dinner with me?"

"At your house you mean?" I asked. "Deer meat?"

"Yes. Have you ever eaten it?"

"Only once."

And I didn't like it. Not at all.

I couldn't tell him that. As I didn't see how I could turn down his invitation without offending him I said, "That would be nice. When?"

"How about tomorrow evening? The venison is thawing as we speak."

"I'll drive over at—what time? Six?"

"No, you won't," he said. "You're my guest. I'll come by for you. How about five?"

I had almost forgotten what a gentleman Craig was and his preference for women in dresses. I'd have to wear the black sheath again. I wondered where Aunt Celia's clothes were? If I found them maybe I could create a vintage outfit to augment my wardrobe—a skirt and blouse, perhaps.

In the midst of contemplating appropriate clothing I remembered Craig's goodnight kiss. Was I going to regret this hasty acceptance? I was encouraging a man I thought of as a father figure. But maybe I was wrong in assuming that Craig's interest in me was more than neighborly.

He was waiting for my response, no doubt wondering why I was hesitating.

"Neighbors help each other," he'd said.

Someone else once pointed out that everything in life has a price attached to it. Even liberation from the snow?

"Whatever you say, Craig. I think the coffee is ready. I'll be right back."

ALTHOUGH IT WAS now possible for me to drive into Huron Station I decided to wait until tomorrow. Craig had said that the roads were passable but most of the town was closed down. Even Estella hadn't opened the café, which was unusual for her.

To pass the time, I kept the fire in the stove burning, read *A Christmas Carol*, and occasionally jotted down decorating ideas. Later, after a lunch of chicken broth, salad and a French roll, I had another visitor.

Through the window I saw an unfamiliar beige Jeep, but the impervious pounding was Mark's trademark. There was no doubt about it.

As I opened the door he tipped his hat. "Morning, Krista. You look lively for a girl who jumped out of a barn yesterday."

I smiled, glad that I had decided to wear my turquoise turtleneck. My mother often said that the color brought out the green in my eyes.

He stepped inside but didn't take off his gloves, which he usually did first.

I said, "I'm bruised and battered, but I'll live. I was lucky."

"I'll say. Who plowed your road?"

"That was Craig. He just left."

"Stennet? He never plowed anyone's private property before."

"You're forgetting that the cabin was vacant for years, except during the hunting season. How are things in Huron Station?"

Even though the door was open and cold air was blowing in he made no move to come any closer. "Improving every minute. This little storm is a rehearsal for the real thing."

"I hope you're joking. By the way, thanks for taking such good care of me yesterday."

"I'm glad to it. It's part of my job."

Of course it was. I was a citizen who had been in trouble, not a faint-hearted damsel in distress. There was no reason for me to feel like a balloon that had just encountered a needle. "May I offer you something?"

"No thanks. Before I head back to the office I want you to get your coat and come with me."

That took me by surprise. I hadn't thought this was an official visit. "Where?" I asked. "Why?"

"When I tell people to come with me they usually don't ask questions," he said.

His voice was gruff and his expression serious, but there was a contradictory gleam in his eyes.

"Before I go along quietly, I'd like to know my destination—and if I'm under arrest."

Instead of answering me directly he said, "We're not going far. I want you to see someone."

"You have another witness for me to identify?"

"God almighty, girl, you sure want to know a lot. Just hurry and get ready. I have to get back to work."

"All right." There was no point in continuing to question him. He wasn't going to reveal anything until he was ready. I grabbed my coat and shoulder bag from the rack and pulled on my boots.

As he hustled me out to the porch he said, "I think I've found a solution to your dilemma. Let's see if you agree."

SIXTEEN

MARK AND I drove silently through a hushed white world. The atmosphere in the Jeep was charged with mystery. If I weren't in the company of a lawman I'd think I was being carried off to a seduction in the snow.

And wouldn't that be an intriguing way to end the day?

Except that wasn't Mark's style. I sensed that he was different from former Sheriff Hal Brecht who had been accused of rape. The opposite, I hoped. I didn't entirely understand him. At times he seemed inscrutable.

"We're almost there. One more turn," he said. "I'm taking you to my house. I told you we're practically neighbors."

I took a deep breath. What was Mark up to? Despite my best efforts to remain calm I felt a surge of excitement. "Shouldn't you be on duty?" I asked, almost reluctant to remind him of his work.

"I am, kind of. You'll see what I mean in a minute."

He turned down a narrow byroad that looked as if someone had cleared it with a shovel. We passed a small balsam forest and came to an old white farmhouse with classic lines. It stood alone, surrounded only by vast stretches of lightly wooded land drifted high with snow.

As Mark parked the Jeep, I heard a chorus of barking coming from the back of the house. I'd forgotten that he kept dogs. They sounded like an entire pack.

"Is this where you live?" I asked. "It's beautiful."

"It will be when I have time to fix it up. I shoveled just enough in the back to get out to the run."

"Why did you bring me here?" I asked.

"I want you to see my dogs."

"That sounds interesting. But why?"

"Because I'm going to lend you whichever one you like," he said.

In the past Mark had demonstrated his power to surprise me. This time he outdid himself.

"You can't lend a dog to someone the way you would a car," I said. "Besides, I don't want a pet. My life is complicated enough."

"How so?"

"I can't go into that right now."

Without a word Mark got out of the Jeep, opened the door for me, and extended his arm to assist me down. "Here, take my hand," he said. "You must be feeling the effects of your jump yesterday."

I hadn't been aware of them until he reminded me. My body only rebelled when I moved from one place to another. During our short ride I'd been sitting in the same position and was too preoccupied with my thoughts to notice any discomfort. I held on to him and stepped down from the Jeep, relieved to find myself on a cleared surface.

"You're going to change your mind when you see them," he said.

We were walking around the western side of the house now which gave me an opportunity to look through the windows. I didn't see any curtains or shades, but one sill was filled with green plants.

"Before this viewing, would you please explain why you think I should keep one of your dogs?" I asked.

"For your protection, Krista. Just until I catch the man who's threatening you."

All this time the dogs kept barking. Fortunately, Mark didn't have any neighbors nearby. As we rounded the corner, I saw a large fenced area enclosing a homemade shelter that looked more like a small barn than a doghouse. Three excited canines, their noses pressed to the fence, were pushing one another out of the way in an attempt to attract their owner's attention and be the first to greet the newcomer. They all looked like wolves.

"Oh, they're gorgeous!" I said, admiring the furry canines' energy and devotion. "Aren't you afraid somebody will steal them when you're away from home?"

Mark smiled with pride and reached in to pet them. "Not at all. Everyone around here knows they belong to me. Would you raid my dog run?"

In spite of the wagging tails, the barking sounded ferocious. "I'm not that brave," I said.

"All right. The big one is Timber. He's my hybrid."

"I've read that they're too unstable to make good pets."

"That's true in some cases, but Timber is one of the successful crosses. He combines the best of wolf and dog. The other male is my new malamute pup, Blizzard, and this pretty little girl is Tasha. She's a husky-collie mix."

I moved closer to the fence but resisted the impulse to put my hand through the wire and pet the dogs. I knew enough about canine behavior to proceed with the greatest of caution.

"I don't think this is a good idea," I said. "Whoever I choose will miss you and be lonely for the others."

"Maybe, but it's only a temporary arrangement." Mark reached over the top of the fence to give each one of his dogs a quick pat. "Tasha is very protective. She has a sweet personality. You'll fall in love with her."

I had the feeling that the decision was already made. My visit to the dog run was only a formality.

"I remember you telling me about her," I said. "You sent her owner to prison."

"Tasha was quick to adjust to a new home," he said. "She's well trained and obedient, more so than the males. She listens to me."

I gave him a sidelong glance, wondering if he was talking about something other than his dog. I wasn't sure but it didn't matter.

Tentatively I held my palm up to the wire for Tasha to sniff. She was a lovely creature with sparkling blue eyes, a shiny coat and the slightest hint of collie in her expression.

"They must be lonely with you gone from home so much," I said.

"They're together and I spend as much time with them as I can."

"What would I have to do if I took her?" I asked. "I'm not saying I will."

"She's housebroken, so she doesn't have to stay outside all the time. Talk to her, feed her. Make sure she has fresh water to drink. You can take her for walks since Stennet was nice enough to plow the road. She doesn't have to be on her leash. She'll always come when you call her. You can take her with you when you go into town, too. She loves to ride in a car."

It sounded like a lot or work but I knew I could do it. Suddenly it seemed like the best idea I'd ever heard. Between Tasha's blue eyes and Mark's powers of persuasion, I knew that I was going to accept his offer.

"You've convinced me," I said. "I'll take her. The other two look too rough for me to handle."

"I had a hunch you'd like her."

"Isn't she used to living outside though?" I asked.

"They come inside when I'm home, all except Timber. He gets restless in the house."

Mark unlocked the gate and the dogs converged at it in a flurry of hair and noise. In the stern voice he must use often in his line of work he said, "Back, Blizzard, Timber! Tasha, come. You're going home with Krista."

"I wonder if she's good at sniffing out ghosts," I said.

"I don't think she's ever done that, but it's a living intruder you have to worry about. Tasha is the best protection you could have."

It was all settled. Although fostering a dog hadn't been my idea, I could see the advantage in having a canine guard. The next time my nemesis came skulking up to the cabin, Tasha would sound the alarm. With those impressive fangs she might even bite him.

At the moment, though, she was acting more like an excited puppy than a guard dog. As soon as Mark freed her she ran up to me eagerly and offered me her paw to shake.

I reached down to take it. Underneath it felt rough and cold, but it was as soft as velvet on top. She wagged her tail and regarded me gravely. I wouldn't have believed how warm I felt knowing that this lovely creature had accepted me on sight.

I looked up and saw Mark smiling down at us. "That's the collie in her," he said. "See, you're going to be friends. You wait in the Jeep with her while I get a dish and food. There's a pail for water, and she has her own brush. I'll give you her leash, too."

"Aren't you afraid I'll want to keep her?" I asked.

"I'm sure you will," he said. "Yes, this is going to work out well."

That sounded ominous. I wondered what he had in mind.

"THE FIRST THING I want to do is find out where Roy Yarrow was when I got locked in the barn," I said.

Tasha lay next to the wood stove, regarding me with a level blue-eyed gaze.

'Talk to her,' Mark had said. I'd been doing that, and I was convinced that Tasha understood what I was saying. Unfortunately she was unable to give me any advice.

In less than twenty-four hours the dog had made herself at home, just as her owner had done in my kitchen when he had made coffee and heated the soup. If she missed Mark she gave no indication of it. Her favorite place to lie was beside the wood stove.

Last night she had slept at the foot of my bed and neither music nor voices from the past had disturbed me. I didn't know how there could be a connection, but having a dog in the cabin made me feel better. She would be here when Craig brought me home tonight after dinner. I wouldn't have to return to an empty house.

I was waiting for Craig now, wondering if I was too dressed up for a casual dinner with a friend in a country house. I was wearing the black sheath again and turquoise earrings that made my eyes look green instead of gray. But my aqua cashmere sweater was dressy, too, and I had a short straight matching skirt that might be more suitable for the evening, especially with my high black boots.

It would only take a few minutes to change clothes and I could keep the earrings on. But now I was out of time. I heard a soft rapping at the door, a different sound from the pounding of Mark's fist against the wood.

Tasha heard it too and began to growl a warning. I put her on her leash and said in my most soothing voice, "It's all right, Tasha."

She was stronger than I thought and she didn't like being restrained.

Holding tightly to the leash I said, "This is a friend," and I opened the door.

She tried to lunge forward and Craig stepped back in alarm. Whatever he had expected, I'm sure it wasn't an angry blue-eyed dog.

"Where did you get that, Krista?" he asked in a stern voice that couldn't quite hide his fear.

"She belongs to Sheriff Dalby. He thinks I'll be safer with a dog for protection."

He took a step backward. "Thoughtful of him. She looks vicious. Does she bite?"

"I don't know. Do you, Tasha? Sit, girl."

She obeyed me and stopped growling. Her eyes darted warily from me to Craig as if she had her own thoughts about the intruder. She wasn't going to be so easily won over by a man who hadn't said a word to her yet or tried to pet her.

"You look pretty tonight, Krista," Craig said. "If you're ready, we should leave now. I left our dinner cooking on the stove."

"You go out first and wait on the porch," I said. "I'll close the door and let Tasha off her leash. Then I'll join you."

Tasha began to growl softly again. I could see that keeping her was going to make having company awkward. Fortunately, there weren't many people in Huron Station who were likely to visit me.

"That dog is like Dalby," Craig said. "Dangerous and tenacious."

Ignoring that comment, I closed the door and set Tasha free, telling her to watch the cabin, assuring her that I wasn't in imminent danger. She lay down by the wood stove and watched every move I made until I slipped quietly out of the cabin.

Craig was waiting for me at the porch door.

"I guess I should be glad she let me out," I said.

"I'm surprised that Dalby is taking a personal interest in your safety," he said.

Craig didn't know how I had come to be involved with Mark, and I wasn't going to enlighten him. "Well, he is the sheriff. I guess he thinks that heading off trouble before it happens is part of his job."

"Maybe. He likes women, too. Especially flashy ones."

As far as I knew, nobody had ever used that adjective to describe me. If that's what Craig was doing. On the other hand I didn't take his words seriously. He had a problem with Mark. It was as simple as that.

"How could you know that?" I asked.

"I've seen him at the Roadhouse and the casino. He never lacks for female companionship. Here we are. Let me get that door for you."

"Sheriff Dalby's interest in my safety is purely professional," I said, although I was curious about this other side of Mark that Craig was showing me.

"Don't be so sure."

I had hoped that Craig would tell me more about Mark, but instead he opened the car door for me. I slid inside. The interior was like a freezer, the heater in 'just turned on' mode.

"Are you cold?" he asked. "This car takes its time warning up. We'll be at my place in a minute. I've got a good fire going and the oven is heating the house up nicely."

He turned the car around and in record time sped down the

narrow drive and crossed the road. Before I knew it we were going through his front door.

Inside the house was almost unpleasantly warm. The fireplace was on the right wall, close to the entrance. I turned around to see the flames and found myself staring up at four mounted stag's heads, two of them on either side of the mantel.

As Craig took my coat his eyes lingered approvingly on the square neckline of my dress. "Sit down while I check to see if anything's on fire," he said.

I sank onto the soft cushion of a brown leather couch and looked around. Craig's living room reflected the taste of a male who was attuned to nature. The maple furniture was simple in design and functional. The lamps were brass and the only wall decorations were the unfortunate deer on the wall. There was also a display of pipes on a whatnot shelf made of logs.

I couldn't stop looking at the pipes and remembering the scent of cherry tobacco.

He may be a pipe smoker, Mark had said.

Was it possible that Craig was the man who had attacked me and locked me in the barn? He lived near enough to me to be aware of my comings and goings and was probably familiar with my property.

On the surface it didn't seem likely. But I couldn't afford to dismiss the idea without making a few subtle inquiries. I'd do it later and in such a way that he would never suspect I was interrogating him.

From where I sat I could see into the dining room. The table was set with white china, unembellished flatware, and wineglasses. Everything was plain and serviceable, a nod to Craig's preference for simplicity. I was happy to see that he hadn't added candles as they would have altered the ambience. But then decorative candles would be too frivolous for a man with Craig's tastes.

He came in from the kitchen carrying a wooden plate filled with trail mix and sat down at the opposite end of the sofa.

"Nothing's burning," he said. "Dinner won't be ready for

about fifteen minutes, though. I hope you're not too hungry."
He passed the trail mix to me. It looked as if he'd tossed in a
cup of Tasha's kibble.

"I'll wait," I said. "I don't want to spoil my appetite. I
thought you didn't like to cook."

"I don't. Making dinner for one is wasted time. But I
couldn't pass up venison or the opportunity to share it with my
new neighbor. Did I tell you how nice you look tonight?"

"Yes, you did. Did you shoot those deer on the wall?"

"No, I don't hunt. They belong to the owner. Most of the
furnishings are his. Mine are in the study."

"Well…" I searched for a safe, generic topic. An awkward
silence began to grow between us. I wanted to keep the conversation away from my appearance and also from hunting, if
possible. Craig stepped in to fill the void.

"In the summer I try to get in two or three days of fishing
every week. There's nothing like sitting at the water's edge to
help the thinking process along."

We'd wandered into another dead end.

Relax, I ordered myself. I had never felt uneasy with Craig
before. I wished I'd changed into the aqua outfit. My black
dress was more appropriate for an after-hours place or an
elegant restaurant.

Floundering, I pulled a topic out of mid-air. "Do you think
they'll ever find Randall Scott's murderer?"

"Not in the foreseeable future. He gave Dalby the slip and
got out of town."

I said, "Roy Yarrow is a likely suspect. He's still here."

Now we were on safer ground. Apparently Craig wanted to
talk about the murder case.

"Yarrow's girlfriend swears they were together when Scott
was killed," he said.

"Which nobody believes."

"Maybe not, but Dalby has her sworn statement."

"Who had a better motive?" I asked.

"Renie Scott, for one."

"Scott's daughter? She was devastated."

As I saw the look of surprise cross his face I realized my blunder. I had wandered blithely into a trap of my own making. In ordinary circumstances Renie and I would never have met. I couldn't tell Craig why she had come to the cabin to visit me.

"You've met her then?" he asked.

"I've seen her on television," I said quickly. "I'm assuming that's how she'd feel. She did look a little sad."

"She could just be pretending to be the bereaved daughter. Her parents went through a nasty divorce. Even though it happened years ago, Renie grew up resenting her father and her half brother and sisters. She didn't want anything to do with them."

He agreed with Estella then. What about my own impressions of Renie? Could I trust them? I had leaped to judgment on the basis of one short visit.

"Do you know Renie Scott?" I asked.

"I've met her. Her mother and I were friends. Ella had an unforgiving nature. She passed that on to Renie."

I couldn't imagine Channel Five's sophisticated weathercaster shooting an arrow through her father's chest and hanging him on a tree. And why would she come back to the scene of the crime as the grieving daughter? So that no one would suspect her of the murder?

"Renie as her father's killer sounds all wrong," I said. "Do you think she could fool the sheriff?"

"Sure. She's a beautiful woman, the kind Dalby likes."

"I didn't think she was all that beautiful—when I saw her on television, that is. That makeup and the cameras probably have a lot to do with her appearance."

"She has an entirely different look when she's out on the town. Rather wild."

"But to murder her father? That's a stretch. No, I'm back to Roy Yarrow," I said, hoping to turn the talk away from Renie.

"As fascinating as all this murder talk is, I think our dinner should be just about ready," he said. "Would you like to see my kitchen?"

Interpreting that as a request for help, I followed him through the hall and into a spacious black and white room. The kitchen was at the back of the house. I didn't see a single extraneous pan or flowerpot. The kitchen was much hotter than the other rooms. The aroma of the cooking meat was strong and unfamiliar to me, but not entirely unpleasant.

"What can I do?" I asked.

"Bring in the salad, if you will. It's in the refrigerator. Oh, and see if I put the saltshaker and pepper mill on the table. I'm not sure I seasoned the venison enough."

He lifted a large aluminum pan out of the oven and set it on top of the stove. "This is going to be a simple dinner. I cooked rice and we'll have olives, dill pickles, and some of Estella's corn relish."

"That's plenty," I said.

I watched him as he transferred chunks of brown meat onto a platter. I hoped we weren't about to dine on one of the beautiful deer that had wandered freely in my woods. But I'd better stop thinking about that or I wouldn't be able to eat at all.

"I roasted the venison for a long time, so it's going to be tender," he said. "I have a nice Cabernet to go with it."

He carried the platter into the dining room and carved the meat while I brought in the rest of the dinner. Then, before he could direct me to a particular seat, I sat down in the chair that faced away from the mounted stag heads.

"It all looks wonderful, Craig," I said.

He let his arms rest on mine as he pushed in the chair. "It will be."

SEVENTEEN

CRAIG DECANTED the second bottle of wine and filled the glasses to the top. The liquid was a strong dark red color, a good choice for the main course and a cold winter night.

"Nineteen ninety-seven was a good year," he said. "I should have a candle behind the bottle to watch for sediment."

"You put together a wonderful dinner, Craig. You don't need anything else."

I had left most of my venison on the plate. It was tender and well seasoned, but too gamy for my taste. I'd cut it into small pieces and moved it around on my plate. Craig was thoughtful enough not to comment on it.

"There…now," he said. "We were talking about motives for murder. Most of them are pretty run-of-the mill. Often people kill members of their own family. I've made a study of the criminal mind."

"How gruesome."

"Not at all. I find the subject fascinating."

"What about people who kill for the thrill of it?"

"They're in a separate category. This murder in Huron Station is unique. I've never heard of another one like it."

"Thank heavens for that," I said. "My first choice for chief suspect is Roy Yarrow."

"Supposedly he's against hunting."

"Maybe he just applies his beliefs to animals. Let's assume that the killer is a hunter, someone who knows how to handle a bow."

"Plenty of people around here do," he said. "Albert Drayton from the Hardware gives archery lessons. He was a champion archer in high school."

This gave me a new angle to explore. I added Albert to my list of people to question. I intended to go back to the store anyway to ask him about the radio.

"Is there anything Albert doesn't do?" I asked.

"Yes, farming his land. He can't make a living at it. You're not drinking the Cabernet, Krista. Don't you like it?"

I'd already had half a glass. To placate him I took a few dutiful sips. "It's very good, but if I drink too much wine I get sleepy."

"We certainly don't want that."

"Besides, I'd rather talk. I'm enjoying our discussion." I wasn't really, but there was no reason to be rude by letting Craig know how uneasy he made me feel.

Craig said, "I often think about killing these days because of my work."

"Your nature articles, you mean?" I asked.

"No, the novel I'm going to finish when I have enough money in the bank to take a year off."

"Is it a murder mystery?"

"No, mainstream. The story is about a soldier who can't stop killing people when the war is over."

Again, I was at a loss for an appropriate response. When Craig talked about his novel he seemed different. The change was subtle, hardly noticeable. It was a faint flickering in his dark eyes and a barely suppressed excitement in his voice. Recalling Craig's involvement in the Vietnam War, I hoped his book wasn't in any way autobiographical.

"I'm going to call it *Addicted to Murder*. Shall we go sit by the fire?"

The light in Craig's eyes when he mentioned the title was unsettling. I wanted this odd dinner engagement to be over. It was too hot and strange in Craig's house, too easy to let my imagination roam free.

I stood up. "Let me help you with the dishes."

"I'll do them later. I'd rather continue our conversation."

"About murder?"

"Why not? Specifically, the Randall Scott case. Perhaps you and I can do some brainstorming and help Dalby solve the crime."

Never before had I dated a man who wanted to talk about death all evening. It was positively weird. I reminded myself that this wasn't a date but a quiet evening with an older neighbor whose idea of after dinner conversation was unusual.

I tried again. "It's getting late, Craig."

"It's not even seven o'clock. Come. Humor me, Krista. I have another idea. Suppose Scott was murdered by someone who was opposed to having a ski resort built near his property."

"Surely there would be easier ways to derail a construc-. tion project."

Craig picked up the wineglasses and moved them to the coffee table in the living room. I had no choice but to follow him. He sat down in the middle of the sofa. As I settled myself in a leather armchair, I happened to look up at the assortment of pipes on the shelf above the mantel. The thought of cherry-scented tobacco drifted through my mind like smoke.

This was an ideal time to ask Craig about his pipe collection. The idea of my neighbor as the murderous archer wasn't so farfetched, and yet I was reluctant to accept it. He was an intelligent man, gentle and solicitous.

When he was near me I smelled Old Spice, not the scent of cherries.

Still, my suspicions wouldn't go away. I had to know the truth.

"That's an impressive pipe collection you have, Craig," I said. "Do you smoke?"

"I used to. These days I'm striving for a healthier lifestyle. I'll never part with those pipes, though. Some of them belonged to my father, and there are a few my grandfather used."

"They must mean a lot to you then. I always picture a male writer in a tweed jacket with a pipe in his hand. When the blizzard started were you writing? Or maybe working on your novel?"

"I was in Abbotsville buying a case of copy paper and picking up the venison," he said. "I made it home just in time."

I picked up my wineglass and stared into the dark liquid. Craig couldn't have been the assailant who had locked me in the barn unless the copy paper and venison were clever fabrications. But I had just eaten the venison or tried to, and a writer would have to keep a supply of copy paper on hand, especially since he had to drive to another town to purchase it.

He could have acquired both the day before. Half a glass of wine and a little murder conversation and I was letting my imagination run amok. But forewarned is forearmed, I reminded myself.

I set the glass down on the coffee table. It was too warm in the living room. I wanted to feel the cold fresh air on my face.

"Have some more wine," Craig said, reaching for the bottle.

"No," I said quickly. "No thank you, Craig. I really should go home now."

"Please stay a while longer, Krista. We'll talk about something else."

I stood up and tried to look regretful. "Another time, Craig. At the cabin, maybe. Could I—could you get my coat please?"

He was silent for a long moment, his expression unreadable. Finally he said, "If that's what you want, sure." He opened the closet, took out my coat, and held it for me. Belatedly I remembered to thank him for his hospitality.

"My pleasure, Krista," he said as he opened the door to a rush of cold air. "I'll be looking forward to our next meeting."

IN THE BRIGHT morning light my suspicion of Craig began to fade. Surely he wasn't the only man in Huron Station who had a collection of pipes. And if he seemed strange at times—well, he was a writer. *Addicted to Murder* was his work in progress. I didn't have to worry about him making unwanted advances, either. Last night he'd plied me with wine, but in all ways he behaved like a gentleman.

Another kind of man appealed to me more, someone else…

His eyes were the color of the lake in winter and his tawny hair was lightly streaked with gray. I could see his face as clearly as I could see the street where I was driving and the place where I'd damaged his patrol car.

In a few short minutes I had wandered away from my main idea. I told myself that if I was going to discover who was out to get me I needed to stay focused.

I parked my car in front of Estella's Café and left Tasha asleep in the back seat with the window partially open. The day's temperature was expected to climb into the forties. For mid-December that was practically balmy. The countryside was still blanketed in snow, but in Huron Station the streets and sidewalks were cleared and bustling with activity.

The prospect of a breakfast that didn't come out of a box cheered me. And being able to get out of the house and go somewhere after a bout with cabin fever was the best morale booster there was. Here everything was familiar. I had a strange but good feeling that I had just walked into my second home.

Also, now I would be able to start my investigation. Estella's Christmas tree was decorated and strung with multi-colored lights. I stood in the café entrance and surveyed the room, hoping to see someone I knew.

The place was crowded. There were only a few empty booths at the back. I didn't see Roy Yarrow, but Estella was talking to the two state troopers. They must be permanent fixtures.

She noticed me and waved. I was close enough to see the gold bangles on her wrist and the long chain around her neck. The jewelry gave Estella's bright green dress a festive look. As I made my way through the aisle, she held her hand out to detain me. The bracelets clanged together like tiny cymbals.

"Hi, Krista," she said. "I thought you were buried alive out there in the country. I'm glad you could make it in this morning."

"It isn't that bad. I'm tired of my own cooking."

"We were closed for two days. You just missed Mark."

Reminded of Estella's passion for gossip and apparent interest in my love life, I wished I could say that I'd seen Sheriff Dalby yesterday at his own home, just to see how she would react. Naturally I didn't.

"The farther I stay away from the law, the better," I said. "I'm sure you understand that."

One of the troopers, the one who was a shade huskier than his companion, gave me a sidelong smile and went back to eating his pancakes.

"How did you get that bruise?" Estella asked.

I touched the tender spot on my forehead. "While I was shoveling snow, I guess. I can be pretty clumsy."

"It looks like someone hit you."

"I guess it does, but there was nobody around to do that."

"I'll lend you a good foundation that covers blemishes if you like. You blend a little into your makeup, dust some powder over it, and nobody will ever know it's there."

The noise level in the café was higher than usual this morning. While we were talking, it rose several notches. Estella scanned the room.

"Excuse me for a moment, Krista."

I watched as she walked over to a corner table where three men were arguing and cursing in loud voices. I recognized them as the hunters who had been in the café earlier in the season, disturbing the cozy atmosphere then as they were doing now.

I couldn't hear what Estella said to them, but their reaction was immediate and furious. One of the men, a red-haired, bearded giant, got up, giving the table an angry forward shove. While a coffee cup overturned and spilled its contents on the floor, splattering Estella's dress, he stood glaring down at her.

"Is that so? Well, you're disturbing *us*. How about that? We ain't going nowhere, you dumb, crazy bitch."

His stance was menacing, his tone belligerent. Estella stepped back as if she had been physically assaulted, but the trooper who had smiled at my remark about staying away from the law was already at her side. He didn't say a word. His size, uniform and weapon made language unnecessary.

Their argument forgotten, the three men appeared to band together in the face of a common foe.

"Let's get out of this hick joint," his companion said with a snarl. The men exited the café with remarkable speed. As the surly red-haired man left the table, he knocked over a chair.

Ruth silently picked up the chair and broken pieces of china. A voice from the back of the café called out, "That's right. Throw 'em out with the trash."

Estella whispered a remark to the trooper and made her way back to the counter. In spite of her vibrant makeup, she looked pale to me. As she reached for a napkin her hand shook. In seconds, though, her composure and bright smile were back in place.

"I hope they stay away," I said. "Thank heavens for the state police."

"From now on they won't be welcome here. Usually our customers are civilized, but every now and then we get the other kind." She began to dab at the coffee stains on her dress. "There. Almost as good as new. Now about that makeup…"

"Thanks, Estella," I said. "I barely notice the bruise. Probably because the mirrors in the cabin are so small and the lighting is poor."

Estella frowned. "Celia had a big full-length mirror in the bedroom."

"Are you sure?"

I would have noticed something that large, even if Aunt Celia had moved it to another room.

"It was there the last time I visited her. Sometimes I'd drive out to take her dinner from the café and we'd sit and talk. It seemed to cheer her up."

"I guess I'll have to look around for it then. I don't know where it could be, though. I've explored every inch of the cabin except for the root cellar," I said.

"It was a full-length mirror with an octagonal-shaped mahogany frame, if I recall."

Two women sailed past us and made their way to the table the hunters had vacated. I noticed that while we were talking someone had taken one of the two available booths in the back.

If I didn't claim the other one in a hurry, I'd find myself back at the entrance waiting in line for the next party to leave.

Hastily I said. "I'll look for it. Excuse me, but I'm going to grab that booth in the back."

"That's a good idea," she said. "Ruth will be with you in a second."

I congratulated myself on once again escaping from Estella without revealing any of my personal business. I wondered if anyone else felt the same way. Maybe Estella's other friends weren't so private. For all I knew, the townspeople might regard gossip as a good way to spice up the dreary winter days.

The unpleasant altercation with the hunters apparently forgotten, Estella stopped to exchange light banter with the troopers again. Then she swept up to the cash register in a swirl of bright green. Like one of her own ornaments, she was a bright harbinger of good cheer. It was no wonder that people flocked to her café.

I ordered an omelet with a side of bacon and a pot of hot tea. I watched the front door, wondering who would drop in for one of Estella's Sunrise Specials or perhaps a Danish and coffee take-out.

As it turned out, it was Hal Brecht who came through the door next. He was a larger-than-life figure in a brown suede jacket and a Stetson hat similar to the one Craig Stennet wore. Like the perennial politician, he had a warm, ready smile and a hearty greeting for the people who recognized him. Estella allowed him to give her an enthusiastic hug.

It was difficult to believe that Hal had left the office of sheriff in disgrace. It was as if everyone had erased the scandal from memory. Just as he'd come into the café, the people sitting at the most coveted table in the café, the one closest to the wood stove, got up to leave. Ruth rushed over to clear the dishes away and wipe the table clean. In a millisecond, Estella had seated him and handed him a menu.

I felt as if I were witnessing a combination of Homecoming at the café and the prodigal son being welcomed back into the embrace of the town. I wondered if something strange was going on in Huron Station. Could there be another layer under the surface that I had yet to explore?

My plans for making contact with Roy Yarrow and Hal Brecht were fuzzy and unformed. Instead of fabricating excuses and contriving meetings, perhaps I could just talk to them if they happened to come into the café. That would be easier, but I soon saw that I had no hope of approaching Hal this morning. Even after Ruth served his order he entertained a constant stream of visitors at his table.

It didn't matter. Now that he was in town, I would probably see him in another place. In the meantime I'd move on to the next name on my list.

I finished my breakfast quickly, looked again for Roy Yarrow on my way to the cash register, and decided to visit the hardware store next. Albert Drayton was bound to be more accessible than Hal Brecht.

As I went out through the door I heard a dog barking. It was Tasha, awake and wagging her tail. She was trying to squeeze her head through the three-inch opening of the window while Mark rapped loudly on the glass.

Coming quietly up behind him I asked, "Aren't you disturbing the peace, Sheriff?"

He turned around. "Krista! Good morning. I just want to make sure you're taking care of my dog. I stopped by the cabin last night."

"I went out for dinner," I said. "Tasha and I are getting along fine. She's adorable."

"I hope you're not coddling her. She doesn't need petting and treats—just companionship." Mark's voice was stern, but he wasn't serious. I knew this because of the gleam in his eyes.

"You don't have to worry," I said. "I don't think she's a big stuffed toy if that's what you're thinking."

"I'm just having fun with you, Krista," he said. "Seriously, is everything okay?"

Realizing that she had lost her owner's attention, Tasha lay down again. But she continued to watch us as if we were the most fascinating people in her world.

"So far fine," I said. "Hal Brecht is inside having breakfast. From the way everyone is treating him you'd think he was royalty."

Mark frowned. "I didn't know he was back in town. Now that his partner is dead he'll probably be spending more time at the store."

"Does he have a business here in Huron Station?" I asked.

"It's a sports outfitting place over on Willow, Scott-Brecht's, but everybody calls it Brecht's. Hal's partner was Randall Scott. He has a good manager. But if you own a place you have to be around some of the time."

"That's interesting. I wish I'd known about Randall's connection to Hal."

Mark didn't respond right away. I wondered if the idea of Hal Brecht as the archer killer had occurred to him.

Finally he said, "Brecht is a scoundrel but he isn't a killer. Besides, he and Randall Scott were like brothers."

"People have been known to kill family members. Did you ever ask Hal why he wants my property?" I asked.

"I haven't had a chance. He's been in Nevada."

If that were true he couldn't have locked me in the barn. But the first time Hal had come to my door, inquiring about my property, Mark was surprised to find out that he was in town. Maybe he'd come back sooner than Mark had realized.

"How did things turn out with the man you arrested?" I asked. "The one who had Scott's jacket?"

"We couldn't hold him. No evidence. We had no proof that he hadn't just found the jacket like he'd claimed."

"So you're back to square one. Could you use a little help?"

"I sure could, honey. You stay out of trouble and I'll have more time to do my job."

This time he was serious. The gleam in his eye was tinged with ice. I had better retreat while I was ahead. But not before I told him something I'd meant to say before.

"I don't like to be called *honey,* Mark. Most women don't—unless it's from someone very close to them."

"Okay—Krista. Whatever you say." His voice was agreeable, but his devilish grin was more effective than any last word.

EIGHTEEN

As I PULLED AWAY from the curb I glanced in the rear view mirror. Mark was still standing on the sidewalk…not exactly the picture of a busy country sheriff working around the clock to solve his case.

I wished I hadn't implied that he wasn't doing his job. Except that wasn't what I'd said. I only asked him if he needed any help. I hadn't locked myself in the barn. And I'd managed to extricate myself from danger without any help from the slowpoke sheriff of Huron Station. I was the one who should be offended by his cavalier remark about staying out of trouble and his liberal use of the word 'honey' when he addressed me.

There. I felt better now. The man could be infuriating and unreasonable. Still, he had lent me Tasha. She was sitting in the back seat, refreshed after her nap and looking out the window as if mesmerized by the passing scenery. Mark probably never took her anywhere.

Realizing that I was only a few miles from the hardware store, I reviewed what I was going to say to Albert. First, I'd tell him that I was interested in taking archery lessons. If I were lucky, he might mention a few of his previous students who had known Randall Scott. With that information I would be able to add a few names to my list.

For a moment I entertained the possibility that Albert himself was the archer killer. I would keep that in mind as I slipped in a subtle question about the radio. I'd have to buy something, too. I could always use more batteries. And I needed polish to restore the antique sleigh to its former glory. Also, if the hardware carried pet supplies, I'd buy a toy or a rawhide bone for Tasha. Mark had given me an ample supply of dog food but nothing else for her. As he said, he didn't believe in coddling his pets.

The only other vehicle in Drayton's lot was a truck painted a garish mustard color. Leaving Tasha in the car again, I went inside and gathered an assortment of batteries, a jar of silver polish, and an extra-large rawhide bone. The other customer was browsing in the furnace filter aisle, leaving Albert free to drink hot chocolate from a paper cup and read the morning comics.

"Did you find everything you need today, Miss Marlow?" he asked.

"I think so. I heard that you give archery lessons, Albert. Are you taking any new students?"

"Not until spring," he said. "We just finished the fall session. Are you going bow hunting?"

"Not this season. I've been interested in archery ever since I read *The Black Arrow* and *Robin Hood*. I thought it would be good exercise."

"You won't get much of a workout in my class. If you're still interested in the spring, I teach a class two nights a week over at the high school. You'll get plenty of hands-on practice. A lot of girls take my class," he added.

My inquiry wasn't going the way I'd intended. I had to learn to ask the right questions. "I'd like to talk to someone else who took the class. Are most of your students from around here?"

"Some of them. I've had people come from as far away as Abbotsville."

"And they're all ages?"

"Sure, but mostly they're young. The ladies from the café took lessons last year. Don't worry, you'll fit right in."

"The waitresses, you mean?"

"Yes, and Miss Marten, too. And Cindy's older sister."

The time had come to play my last card. "I hope the person who killed Randall Scott wasn't one of your former students."

He began to ring up my purchases. I opened my bag and looked for my wallet.

"I don't think so," he said. "My guess is an inexperienced bow hunter who missed his target and then panicked did that. He probably high-tailed it back to wherever he came from."

"Interesting," I said, "but how would you explain the fact that he left the body hanging from a tree?"

"I wouldn't, ma'am. That's Sheriff Dalby's problem."

"Did you know Scott?" I asked.

"He came to the store a few times, but I can't say I knew him. How's that radio working?"

"Just fine. There's one more thing, though. I thought I heard it playing the other night when I was in bed."

"That's how I like to go to sleep, too," he said, "with some good soft music on. It helps me relax."

"No…" I was going to have to make myself clear and risk the consequences. "What I meant was that I didn't turn it on. It was playing by itself."

He gave me a strange look.

"I must have been dreaming. It made me wonder, though. Is such a thing possible?" I asked.

"Not that I know of. You asked me that once before. It must be something like cabin fever. When you're trapped inside your house for a long period of time you get to where you're imagining things."

I felt my face grow warm but forced myself to smile. "That must be the explanation then."

He was scanning the last item now: Tasha's bone. "Are you going to get a dog? That'll help some."

"It's for my friend's dog," I said as I tried to read my total on the register. I took a twenty-dollar bill out of my wallet and added, "I may see you in class in the spring."

"WELL, THAT WAS brilliant, Tasha," I said. "I've just labeled myself a mental case to that nice young man. He couldn't have shot an arrow into Randall Scott. At least I don't think he could."

Tasha didn't answer. Busy eyeing the package that held her

bone, she was resting her paws on the back of the passenger's seat. I supposed she could smell it. I considered turning around and driving back to Huron Station. By now Hal Brecht would be finished with his breakfast. Whether or not he went back to his store he would probably stay in town. I might run into him.

But where? A chance meeting and conversation on the street were impractical in this cold weather. If Brecht returned to the café he would most likely be mobbed by his admirers again. I'd meant to visit the sports shop but hadn't done so yet. I could stop by today and exchange a few words with him there, something like "I'm looking for a warm pair of gloves and equipment for bow hunting. Could you show me what you have?" Then I could ask him for a demonstration.

Or maybe I could ask Mark to introduce us—or maybe not, until he was in a better mood. I moved Hal Brecht to a lower line on my list. The man I really wanted to target was Roy Yarrow, but now I couldn't wait to get back to the cabin. I had something else on my mind.

The matter of Aunt Celia's missing mirror troubled me. The kind of object described by Estella was too large to go unnoticed. Had I searched the cabin thoroughly enough to make certain I knew what was there? Yesterday I would have said yes. Today I wasn't so sure. If I'd overlooked one item, what else might I have missed? Besides, I could use a full-length mirror. Tonight when I dressed for dinner at the Station Roadhouse it would be helpful if I could view my whole figure.

I left Tasha in the kitchen with a pail of fresh water and her bone and set out to search the back porch again, hoping to find a storage place I'd overlooked. I had been pretty thorough the first time I'd explored this area. Satisfied after another look, I moved on to the bedroom and opened the closet door. The narrow cramped space inside was empty except for my clothes. The only other place to look was under the bed.

I knelt on the floor and flashed a light under the mattress. There was nothing here but dust, a grim reminder that I'd better do some housekeeping soon, especially in this part of the cabin where I slept. The space under the bed would make a good hiding place for someone or something. Not since I was five had I given a thought to what might be hiding under my bed. This was no time to revive old fears.

Aside from the root cellar, which was inaccessible until spring and the least likely place anyone would store a mirror, I didn't know where else to look except in the other barn, the only place on the farm I hadn't explored.

The sudden coldness that came stealing over me had nothing to do with the temperature inside the cabin. I remembered only too well my frantic leap from the loft. At times I still felt the effects of it, but it would be different now. I was forewarned, and I had the best protection available, my borrowed dog, Tasha.

It was settled then. I'd better do it now before I found another more appealing task that required my attention. Even with all my hastily assembled assurances, tramping over the snow to a dark and icy outbuilding wasn't my idea of a good time.

No SHADOWS LURKED ON the snow this afternoon. The sun had gone into hiding high above thick gray clouds and light flurries danced through the air, blown about by the wind. The day was cold and dreary but not forbidding.

Tasha ran in front of me like a joyful puppy, occasionally stopping to roll in the snow and then shake her silvery coat free of the tiny twigs and leaf bits that littered the white ground. She was part husky. This was her kind of weather.

I was as certain as I could be that no one lay in wait for me behind a stand of trees or more likely in back of the barn. Still, I took the precaution of surveying the surrounding area before venturing farther from the cabin.

Between the barn and the road the land sloped downwards. The snow was lower here and dozens of balsam firs grew close together competing with one another for space and light. In this section of my acreage it would be easy to cut greens or even saw down a tree. That was a project for another day.

I took the keys and the can of oil out of my pocket and headed toward the second barn. Once I kicked the snow from the entrance and drowned the combination lock in oil, opening the door was easy.

Glancing around once again to make sure I was alone, I told Tasha to stay and stepped inside. As I did, I almost stumbled over a small maple table before my eyes grew accustomed to the dim interior.

It lay upside down in the entrance as if it had been thrown inside as an afterthought. The other pieces of furniture, apparently all castoffs, were jammed together in no particular order. Where was the rest of the furniture? I remembered that there used to be more of everything in the cabin.

Shivering in this different kind of cold, I moved farther inside, using my flashlight to illuminate the scene.

A dark blue sofa with frayed cushions, a mahogany rocker, a dinette set and two twin beds filled one corner. They were all familiar. An old portable phonograph and the vintage sewing machine that had belonged to Aunt Celia's mother were here, too, along with several tables and lamps and even a Christmas tree stand. Nowhere did I see a mirror.

Someone had stored more boxes in the barn. I counted ten of them, all larger than those inside the cabin. Apparently my work wasn't done after all. But I didn't think I could go through them any time soon. They looked too heavy for me to move and it was too cold to stay in the barn for an extended period of time.

After one last sweep of the area to make certain that I hadn't missed the mirror, I turned around. Tasha had moved slightly forward and was now blocking the entrance so that nobody could close the door and trap me inside

That was all I could do today. As I locked the barn the mystery of the missing mirror insisted on taking its place along with the other strange happenings I'd experienced since arriving at the cabin. While it wasn't in the same league as the haunted radio or the deadly assailant, I knew I wasn't going to rest until I'd solved it, if that were possible.

Every time I turned around the mystery changed. Sheriff Dalby's investigation remained at a standstill and my sleuthing techniques faltered. It was discouraging. Fortunately, I was going to combine business with pleasure at the Roadhouse tonight. I needed a change of scene.

I FOUND HAL BRECHT at the Roadhouse, or rather, he found me. I was returning from the restroom, looking at the tiny clear lights twinkling in the garlands that were draped on the walls. He was emerging from the gaming area in the company of a gorgeous dark-haired woman who wore an extremely low-cut blue dress.

He nodded and favored me with that warm smile, the kind that he'd dispensed to his admirers in the café. Then he led his companion toward the bar and settled her on a stool.

Although Hal and I were together under one roof, I suspected that prying him loose from his date wouldn't be easy. They appeared to be extremely comfortable with each other. He had his arm around her waist and she was listening attentively to every word he said, laughing at his jokes and often touching his shoulder or arm in a familiar way.

I returned to my table to wait for my dessert, while keeping an eye on him. Although Hal Brecht had long since left his youth and even mid-life behind, he had an intriguing face, a booming voice, and enough charisma to carry him to any heights and compensate for past indiscretions, short of murder. He wasn't attracting any special attention at the Roadhouse tonight, except from the lady in blue who appeared to be fascinated by whatever he was saying to her.

The waiter brought my dessert, a generous square of Holland Rusk. Hal's companion slipped away, leaving him alone at the bar. As I broke off a small piece of the confection with my fork he sauntered over to my table, drink in hand. I couldn't have contrived a smoother meeting.

He favored me with a campaign-bright smile. "I was sitting over at the bar and I said to myself, 'I know that attractive redhead in black.' It's Miss Marlow, isn't it? We met before. I'm Hal Brecht. Mind if I join you?"

He was already sitting down, but then that was the idea.

"I remember," I said. "You wanted to buy my land. I told you it wasn't for sale."

"That's right. I heard somewhere that you wanted to sell."

"But you didn't remember who told you."

"I still don't. Your dessert looks good. Is it a cake?"

"Sort of. It's custard, meringue, and the Holland Rusk crust, served with whipped cream. My mother used to bake it for special occasions."

"I think I'll order some too."

Wonderful. That should give me ample time to question him.

He signaled to the waiter who was instantly at his side, eager to take his order.

"And a drink for the lady," he said. "What will you have, Krista?"

"Just Club Soda, thanks. I'm driving."

I was still interested in knowing who had told Hal that I wanted to sell my land, but obviously he wasn't going to enlighten me. He'd changed the subject and would probably continue to do so if I kept mentioning my property. But one question he couldn't dodge.

"What would you do with my cabin if I sold it to you?" I asked.

"That's easy. I always wanted to live in a place with plenty of undeveloped acreage attached to it."

"So you could have your own private hunting ground?"

His great loud laugh was drawing attention to us. "You guessed it."

"Then it's my house you want?"

"Not exactly. It's too rustic and old. I'm going to build a new log house. It'll have all those things that make life worth living. I want a wraparound porch, a deck, a game room, a hot tub, a swimming pool, whatever I think of."

"That'll cost three or four hundred thousand dollars."

He laughed. "Krista, my dear, you're naïve. Double that figure."

"You can't call that rustic living," I said.

"I don't intend to. It's luxury."

As the waiter served his dessert and my drink, I found myself wondering about Hal's source of income. But I couldn't think of a polite way to pry into his finances. Instead I asked, "Did you go hunting this year?"

"I would have but I've been out of town, chasing another game, you might say."

Instead of pursuing that interesting bit of information, I asked, "Do you hunt with a rifle or bow and arrow?"

"Both. I may still try to get my deer this year. Have you ever eaten venison?"

"Twice," I said. "It's not my favorite meat. I'd rather see the deer run free."

"I don't much like the taste either, but I love the sport and the country up here. It's the closest thing to Paradise in the United States."

"Except when someone gets murdered," I said. "Did you know Randall Scott?"

"He was my friend. We were partners."

"That was a horrible way to die, like something out of the Roman Empire," I said.

"You can say that again. If he'd gone to Nevada with me the way we planned he might still be alive. He changed his mind. Something about a woman and family business."

Finally I had a promise of new information. Unfortunately Hal had lapsed into a moody silence. The waiter brought his dessert and he ate it quickly, all the while casting longing looks at the gaming rooms. Also bearing down on him like a bird of prey was his date. Hal saw her, too.

"I have to go now," he said. "Thanks for the conversation. I'll see you around, Krista."

I watched as he met his companion halfway across the room. He kissed her and put his arm around her shoulder. They walked back together through the doors, talking and laughing as if their activities had never been interrupted.

It was time for me to leave, too. As I waited for my check I decided that it was premature to remove Hal Brecht from the suspect list. He had claimed that he was in Nevada at the time of Randall Scott's murder but alibis could be false. And sometimes people killed their friends.

Then there was Scott's last-minute business that had kept him in Huron Station so that he could cross paths with his killer. For the price of a good dinner this had been a profitable evening. I planned to come back to the Roadhouse soon to see what else I could learn.

NINETEEN

I STOOD ANKLE DEEP in snow where the land sloped down to the road, ready to begin my search for the perfect Christmas tree.

Earlier, Tasha had slipped into the first barn when I'd opened it to take out my saw, and there she stayed, barking. I'd gone in after her and looked carefully around but couldn't see anything. She'd probably discovered a mouse or some other creature nesting in the remnants of the hay. It was all right. I could look for a tree without her.

Now I was so close to the slope that the trees appeared taller than I'd thought. The slope was definitely larger, spread over at least two acres. At this point I was nearer to the road than the cabin.

Usually in the morning I would see Craig riding by on his horse but nobody was in sight now. The rolling white landscape was covered with some of the prettiest balsam firs in Alcona County, their branches drooping under the weight of heavy scarves of snow that glittered in the sunlight.

The drifts were lower here, making it easier to walk. As I moved deeper into the small forest, I felt like a small child wandering around in a maze. The evergreens grew close together, leaving little room for a human to navigate. The air was thick with the spicy scent of balsam.

I wanted a tree with a nice shape and one that I could manage. But every time I spied a likely prospect I saw another one I liked better just beyond it. Finally, when I'd made my way almost up to the road, I'd found the ideal fir. It was full and symmetrical with silvery, snow-dusted green needles. I walked around it twice and decided. This was the one.

Kneeling on the ground, I gripped the trunk with my left

hand and started sawing. At first the blade moved easily through the wood. But soon my right arm began to ache and the tree seemed to have turned to stone. Also the pain in my shoulder was coming back.

Maybe I should just cut branches for decorating instead. Bunches of greens would be festive if I tied them together with red ribbon. With very little effort on my part they would fill the cabin with the scent of balsam. Besides, sawing down trees was men's work. At a time like this, I didn't mind falling back on sexist stereotypes.

I brushed the tempting thoughts away. *Don't even think about quitting,* I told myself. *You're three-fourths of the way there.*

I was miserable, though. The temperature was at the freezing mark. It was the mildest we'd seen in days, but my eyes were still watering from the cold and the potent fragrance of the firs. As I laid the saw down and reached into my pocket for a tissue, I heard a thin whistling sound in the air. Something as hard as a rock whizzed past my upper arm. Instinctively I jumped back to avoid it and fell into the tree.

Sharp needles raked my face. The balsam scent forced its way up my nose the way the odor of cherry tobacco had. As I turned my head away from the branches and tried to cover my skin, I lost my balance and rolled on my side. My hand brushed against the cold steel teeth of the saw.

Not a foot away from me an arrow stood upright in the snow, its tail still quivering.

Ignoring my better judgment that told me to freeze in that position, I scrambled to my feet and took refuge behind the tree. I didn't see the archer, but he couldn't have gone far. In which case I was still in danger—and Tasha…

I called her name loudly before I realized how idiotic that was. Suppose the archer shot his next arrow at her? I felt an overwhelming need to protect Mark's dog. Then, with a high-pitched yelp, Tasha came running through the maze of ever-greens up to my side and pranced around me in a state of high excitement. She had a dead mouse in her mouth. In my sternest voice I told her to drop it. She did so reluctantly but stood sniffing at it and poking it with her nose.

Taking a firm grip on her collar, I held my breath, waited, and listened. I couldn't see any movement among the trees. The only sound I heard was the dog's panting.

I felt certain that I was alone now, but was worried about how far I could trust my senses. I hadn't been aware of a hostile presence in the area earlier. When I'd checked the area around the barns no one had been there. The archer must have come up from the road using the thickly growing trees as a cover.

The problem with that theory was obvious. How could he know that I'd go roaming among the balsams on this day at this particular time? He couldn't, unless he'd been watching me for a long time, waiting for just such an opportunity.

Tasha began to voice her displeasure at being restrained. Above her barking I heard a revving engine. I hurried toward the road to the edge of the trees but couldn't see any vehicles or anything else that shouldn't be there. The only sound was the distant hum of a car speeding away.

The immediate danger was over now, but I didn't doubt that there would be another attempt. In the future whenever I left the cabin, I resolved to take the shotgun. I should have had it with me today. But how would it have helped me when I'd had no warning of an attack?

I ran my hand over the wool material of my coat. An arrow could easily have punctured the cloth. I felt my neck behind the loosely fitting collar. Maybe this had been the archer's target. If so, he was an unskilled marksman, which was fortunate for me. I had survived being locked in the barn and this cowardly attack. The next time I might not be so lucky.

I stooped down and picked up the arrow. It was long, cold and deadly, a weapon in common use in the distant past. But that didn't make it any less lethal today.

My enthusiasm for gathering greens was gone, destroyed by the reality of what might have happened and the fear that was overtaking me. This was another matter for Mark, who would probably claim that I'd gotten into trouble again just to delay his investigation.

He wouldn't dare! I might have been killed, along with Tasha!

"Let's go back to the cabin, Tasha," I said. "How would you like to see your master? I'm going to call him."

MARK SAT WITH ME on the opposite end of the sofa close to the wood stove while Tasha gnawed her bone, her treasured mouse already forgotten. He was annoyed with both of us.

"Bad girl, Tasha," he said. "You're supposed to watch Krista, not go chasing after vermin. And you, Krista. Why were you out in the middle of nowhere making yourself a target?"

Only one of us was moved to remorse by his words. While Tasha laid her ears back and looked sufficiently cowed, I said, "This must be the only county in Michigan where the victim is blamed for getting attacked. Or is that just your way, Sheriff Dalby?"

"I know you're not serious," he said in that stern tone he reserved for life-and-death situations.

I wasn't. I hadn't been able to rid myself of the fear yet. Sitting in my own living room with the highest lawman in Huron Station, I still felt vulnerable. And I was cold even though the flames in the stove were crackling. Mark's patrol car was parked outside behind the Taurus, but soon he would be gone.

"I get upset when I know that somebody wants to kill me," I said. "It's happened three times now."

"What else was there, besides this attack and the incident in the barn?" he asked.

"That night I drove home from the Roadhouse. When someone tried to run me off the road. I told you about it. I'm not sure about that one, though."

"Then let's deal with what we have. This time there's a set of tire tracks that aren't ruined and a few footprints. Your archer came from the road."

"Do you think anyone saw him?"

"I'm going to question Stennet, but this area doesn't see much traffic even in the summer. I think I'll take Tasha home and give you Timber instead. He's older and more reliable."

"No," I said. "I want to keep her. I mean if it's all right with you, I'd like her to stay. You told me that you always get your man. I'm counting on it."

"That's true, Krista, but this case is taking longer than I expected. Some of them do. That doesn't mean I won't get him. In the meantime you're in danger here."

"I think that'll be true wherever I go until you find the killer," I said.

In the brief silence that followed, I stared at the fire that always cheered me and at the empty space in front of the window where I'd planned to set up my tree. Then I glanced at the silver sleigh, my link to Christmas past. The cabin was home to me now. I had grown very attached to it, which was going to make selling it very hard.

After a while Mark said, "The Hollow Oak Casino and Resort has a popular Christmas package. I think you could still get reservations."

Anticipating a suggestion of this sort, I was ready with a response. "I can't afford to pay for a hotel room and meals when I have a perfectly good cabin and food here."

"You wouldn't be alone at the Casino. It's always crowded there." He was silent for a moment. "If living in a hotel doesn't appeal to you, I have several empty rooms in my house. You could stay with me for a while. I won't charge you anything. Maybe you could cook me an occasional dinner."

Once again I didn't know if he was serious or teasing me. Without the gleam in his eyes I couldn't tell. But whatever he was doing, his proposition was outrageous. I think he knew that.

"Sorry, Sheriff. Don't expect a home cooked meal from me. In case you haven't noticed, I'm not the domestic type."

He slapped one of his leather gloves against the other. "I thought you'd say something like that." Again he lapsed into a brief silence. "Almost every crime is solved eventually, Krista. Down in Foxglove Corners where my brother, Mac, is on the force, they just broke a twenty- seven year old murder case. You can read about it tomorrow in the Station Press."

"If it takes you that long I'll be long dead with an arrow through my heart and you'll be too old to do whatever it is you do."

"You're pretty sassy for a girl who wants my help," he said. Then he softened his words with a teasing half-smile. "There's going to be an arrest soon."

"Thank heavens. Who?"

"You know I can't tell you. That's why it would be safer for you to stay out of sight. Just for a couple of days."

Even with this new information and the prospect of an end to the nightmare, I wasn't inclined to leave my cabin. "If this is going to happen tomorrow or the next day I think I can survive till then," I said.

Mark patted Tasha's head and she wagged her tail once. She lay down at his feet, her bone forgotten for the moment. Tasha was back in his good graces again, and all was well again.

I suspected that sometimes Mark didn't mean half of what he said. He must be as frustrated by the slow movement in the case as I was. Only I had more to lose. My life.

"All I wanted to do was cut down one of those balsam firs for a Christmas tree," I said. "That's what I was doing out in the middle of nowhere, as you said. I'm not going to hide inside my cabin, and I'm not running away. So you'll have to catch the killer. I hope you arrest the right man this time."

Ignoring that he said, "I'll come by tomorrow evening and chop the tree down for you."

I would have liked to accept his offer but I didn't want to be in his debt. I said, "Thanks, but I'm just going to cut some greens and make swags. There are some nice balsams in the back."

"Farther from the road and behind the cabin? That's an even better place for an ambush."

"You *really* know how to make a woman feel safe, Mark. I think I told you that before."

If I kept listening to Mark's warnings, I'd be looking under the bed at night and seeing man-shaped shadows in the snow by day. Perhaps before long he'd have the killer in jail and the danger would be over. I was going to focus on that.

Recalling my suspicions about Huron Station's dishonored sheriff I said, "I meant to tell you that I ran into Hal Brecht at the Roadhouse last night."

"I haven't seen him since he got back to town. Did you ask him why he wants to buy your farm?"

"For the hunting, he says. He'd like to tear the cabin down and build a fancy log mansion in its place."

"That sounds like Hal."

"I wonder where he gets his money. If he was in all that trouble you'd think he'd have a mountain of legal expenses."

"Hal is a gambler," he said. "Usually he's broke. But that doesn't stop him from talking. Why do you ask?"

"I'm just curious."

"Oh, about Scott being his business partner. I remember."

"I hope you do. It was only yesterday that we were talking about Hal."

"So it was."

He sat still, watching me. His expression remained unchanged, his eyes like the water of the lake in the winter touched with miniature ice floes. He was a master at keeping his thoughts hidden.

To break the awkward silence I said, "You told me to stay out of trouble."

"I'm glad to see you've listened."

He gave Tasha another pat. I thought she looked dejected. She probably sensed that Mark was about to leave. Maybe she missed him after all.

He stood up and slowly pulled on his leather gloves, taking longer than was strictly necessary. "How would you like to check out the Hollow Oak Casino with me?" he asked. "If you're free we can go tomorrow, have dinner, make a night of it. When you see the place, you might change your mind about staying there."

"This isn't some diabolical plot to drug me and stash me there against my will, is it?"

"Good God Almighty, girl! Where do you get such strange ideas? Call it a date."

I hadn't expected Mark to ask me out on a date, but secretly I was pleased that he had. "Won't you be busy with the case?" I asked.

"I can take a dinner break," he said. "Will you go with me?"

"Yes, I will. Happily. That'll be one night I'll be safe, I think."

"I'll make sure of it." His voice grew stern again, but he was talking to the dog. "Tasha, I want you to be on guard. Do you hear me? No more fooling around with mice. Understand?"

She yelped and wagged her tail. I could only assume that meant 'yes.'

As I walked with him to the door Tasha trailed after us, nudging his hand. In spite of my happiness at the prospect of a date with Mark, I wondered what I was getting myself into.

THAT NIGHT I DREAMED about the hanging man in a new and sinister way. I was in the balsam grove again cutting down my tree. The temperature had risen to an unbelievable fifty degrees and I worked without the slightest discomfort, sawing with ease all the way to the last woody fibers.

Just as the fir came crashing to the ground, I looked up and saw Randall Scott suspended from one of the fragile top branches like a grotesque ornament.

He was still attached to the branch when it hit the ground, but the arrow flew free from his chest and landed at my feet. It lay in the snow, long and sleek and deadly in a widening pool of crimson blood.

I turned on the bed and reached down to pick it up just as the dream fragments broke apart. I was clutching the edge of the sheet and my breathing was rapid and heavy. Part of the quilt was bunched around my ankles, and the rest was on the floor.

Then, from the front of the cabin, I heard the droning

voice of the radio announcer. His words were too muffled for me to make them out. The haunting had chosen this traumatic time to return.

TWENTY

THE RED CARNATION CENTERPIECES and holiday atmosphere inside Estella's Café provided a bright contrast for the cold, blustery morning. It was the twenty-first of December, the first day of winter, and I needed a big country breakfast and a double dose of Christmas cheer to offset the uneasy feeling I had after last night's mix of nightmare and ghost broadcast.

I couldn't cast off a premonition that disaster was on its way and my enemy might strike again before Mark could arrest his suspect. That was assuming they were the same man, which was what I had suspected from the start.

Still, I was determined to be optimistic. I had a date with Mark tonight and I was going to live to keep it. Then, in a few days, whoever was trying to kill me would be behind bars, or so Mark had implied.

Since my last visit, four small presents wrapped in peppermint-striped paper had appeared under the tree. A small stack of mail lay on the counter in the shadow of a towering red poinsettia plant. By the shape of the envelopes I imagined that they were Christmas cards.

I recognized the man sitting alone at the counter as Roy Yarrow. He was drinking coffee and reading the paper. The sleeves of his wrinkled brown shirt were rolled up to the elbows and he needed a shave.

Deciding to postpone my breakfast, I sat down beside him. He didn't look up, but that was good because I needed a moment to decide what I was going to say.

Cindy handed me a menu. "Don't you want a table, Miss Marlow?"

"In a while," I said. "I'd like to relax with a cup of hot coffee first. I slid all over the road on the way to town."

Weather was always a good conversation starter. Roy folded his paper and said, "I've already had enough of this winter. Think we'll get that big snow they're talking about?"

"I suppose so," I said. "How much was it again?"

"Twelve inches by the weekend. Just what we need."

"Well, there's nothing we can do about it," I said.

"Those damn snowmobiles will just keep on tearing through the land. They ought to be banned. If I have my way they will be."

This was going to be easier than I'd thought. Apparently Roy had a new cause. Although I was sure he hadn't abandoned the deer.

"That's interesting to know. I always thought they glided over the snow and didn't cause any damage."

"Sometimes. But they ruin the trails. And you can't hear yourself think when they're out on the lake."

I didn't know how Roy could garner support for his cause with vague explanations and accusations but I said, "I like to do whatever I can to keep our state beautiful."

"Then you'll want to sign my petition. I'm Roy Yarrow, in case you're wondering."

"Hello, Roy. I'm Krista Marlow. I've heard your name somewhere."

"I get around," he said.

"You sure do, Mister Yarrow. You're practically notorious." It was Cindy with the coffeepot. As she filled my cup she added, "Estella wants to talk to you, Miss Marlow. She'll be over in a minute."

"I've been written up in the newspaper, too," Roy said. He held up the *Station Press.* "In this very one in fact."

"Do you live in Huron Station, Roy?" I asked.

"Off and on. I've been downstate for a couple of weeks. Only been back in town a few days."

If that were true it would place him elsewhere when I was locked in the barn, but not during the arrow attack.

"Were you anywhere near Rochester?" I asked. "That's where I'm from."

"I didn't go that far," he said. "I stayed with a friend in Flint."

He shuffled on the stool and reached for his newspaper.

"I remember now. I read about it," I said. "You were one of the protesters at the Millennium Park Deer Kill. So, you like animals and want to ban snowmobiles. I guess you're not a hunter then?"

"I don't believe in killing, especially not helpless creatures."

"It's still the bow and arrow season. I wonder if that's a more humane way to hunt than with a rifle."

"It's all slaughter no matter what weapon you use," he said. "Too many people are out to destroy our planet and its denizens for their own pleasure. We have to stop them."

"Are you talking about protecting the deer or outlawing snowmobiles now?" I asked.

"Both. Preserving the land is as important as saving the animals."

"Well, I certainly can't argue with that."

"About that petition, then…"

He took a long paper out of his pocket. It was blank.

"Don't you have any signatures yet?" I asked.

"The rest of the petitions are filled. This is a fresh one. You can be the first to sign it."

He handed me the pen. I turned it around in my hand for a second and then gave it back to him. "Oh—I'm sorry. I'd like to, but I can't. I just remembered I'm not registered to vote in Alcona County."

"No harm done. You can help in some other way."

He tucked the paper under his arm, took out a fifty-dollar bill, and laid it on the counter.

Was this the way he paid for a cup of coffee? Somebody had told me that Roy Yarrow was usually unemployed. He must have found a money source somewhere. In Randall Scott's missing wallet, perhaps? I was taking a giant leap to reach a conclusion I wanted. That was no way to conduct an investigation.

Apparently Cindy didn't see anything unusual about Roy paying for a cup of coffee with a large bill. She took his tab and money and returned shortly with a handful of dollars and change. In the meantime, Roy had lapsed into a moody silence. Perhaps he minded losing my signature. I hoped he wasn't suspicious of my true motive in talking to him.

Estella came up behind me and laid her hand on my arm. The silver charms on her bracelet jingled together and the fragrance of her perfume lingered in the air. It was a spicy scent that reminded me of carnations. She was wearing a long crimson dress that matched the holiday centerpieces.

"I have some mail for you, Krista," she said. "If you didn't come in today I was going to drop it off at the cabin after we closed. We won't reopen until after New Year's."

"It looks like your café doubles as the post office."

She glanced at her tables decked out in their Christmas finery and at her customers dining quietly. Everybody was served and everything was under control. She smiled. "You might say that. In the winter when the roads are bad Sheri brings the mail here and folks who live out in the country pick it up for themselves and their neighbors. It's a Huron Station tradition."

"Are you going to deliver all those letters tonight?"

"Only to my special friends. I'll leave the rest at the bakery next door. People will know where to find them."

It seemed as if a lot of mail was going to get lost in the process, but I wasn't one to question tradition. I watched as she spread several envelopes out on the counter. Roy took one last swallow of coffee, stood up and stretched.

"Ah, here they are, Krista. These two are for you," she said. "Roy, you're not leaving without having a good hot breakfast, are you?"

"I've got things to do, Stella," he said. "I'll be back for lunch."

While they were talking, I looked at my cards. One was from

Diana, the only person who knew where I was. The other was a large green envelope with my name scrawled across it in fine line black marker.

Two of the cards belonged to Estella. I noticed the smaller one because the address, 714 Pinegrove, Detroit, Michigan, was familiar. I remembered seeing the street name on one of the old envelopes in Aunt Celia's candy box.

"Wish me luck, ladies," Roy said. "I'm off to brave the elements."

"Hurry back then," Estella said. "Now, Krista, I'll bet you miss all your friends from downstate. You must be getting pretty bored with wilderness living."

"Not at all," I said. "I keep busy. Things happen."

"Oh? Like what?"

In spite of my better judgment, I decided to give her a tantalizing tidbit.

"I had dinner with Craig Stennet the other night. He cooked venison for us."

"My, you're a fast worker. Craig has never given me the time of day. By the way, did you ever find your aunt's mirror?"

"I looked for it but I don't think it's there. Maybe she broke it and threw it away."

"A big heavy thing like that would be hard to break unless you pounded on the glass with a hammer. Are you going to keep looking?"

"Maybe. I have a lot of other things to do, though."

"I can't imagine what happened to it," she said.

"Well, consider it a mystery. Maybe it'll turn up one day." I didn't want to be considered a snoop but couldn't resist the impulse to ask Estella about the address on the small envelope. "I see you know someone on Pinegrove in Detroit. My aunt used to live on that street."

"So she told me once. That was a long time ago before she moved up north."

"But you met her in Huron Station, not in Detroit?"

"That's right, when I first came to town."

"That's quite a coincidence, you knowing someone who lived on my aunt's old street."

"It is, in a way, but Pinegrove is a very long block, intersected by a boulevard." Estella scooped up her letters and slipped them into her pocket. "My cousin bought one of those old Victorian houses on Pinegrove. She's planning to renovate it. I'll take country living any day."

She glanced toward the kitchen doors. "I'd better give Ruth a hand in the kitchen." But she didn't move. She shuffled her envelopes as if they were cards and she was looking for a winning hand.

Now that Roy was gone there was no reason for me to stay at the counter. I saw an empty table near the wood stove and picked up my coffee cup and cards.

"I think I'm ready to order breakfast now," I said and deftly slipped in another question. "Is Roy still with Lily, do you know?"

"He didn't say, but I think Lily is gone. Good riddance."

"You're fond of him, aren't you?" I asked.

Estella's eyes narrowed slightly and a subtle edge came into her voice. Apparently, she didn't like talking about her own relationships. I'd taken her by surprise.

She said, "Roy and I are old friends and he's loyal. That's an important quality in a man. Betrayal is unforgivable."

"Those are two good reasons to like him." I couldn't resist adding, "Roy is sort of cute, too. I hope I get to know him better."

"Since you have Craig Stennet cooking dinner for you, who knows? Maybe you will. You must have something men like," she said.

IN THE MIDDLE OF our dinner at the Hollow Oak Casino Mark asked, "What do you think, Krista? Would you like to get a room?"

"Excuse me. What did you say?" I searched for the telltale gleam in his blue eyes. It wasn't there.

Before I could toss a flippant remark at him he said, "Until I make that arrest. Remember?"

Thank heavens I hadn't answered him immediately. I was always making a fool of myself with Mark. This would have been my worst and most embarrassing blunder yet.

"I don't think so," I said. "There's too much activity here. It's too noisy. I like a quieter place."

"Like your isolated cabin in the woods? You don't make my job any easier, honey."

"I'm not trying to, and Mark, please, I asked you not to call me 'honey.'"

"Sorry. I forgot—Krista. I already lost a high profile entrepreneur on my watch," he said. " I don't want to lose a city girl, too."

"You won't."

We were back in familiar territory and I was holding my own, or trying to. Once again I was wearing my black dress, but tonight I'd added a long rope of shimmering pearls that I'd found in Aunt Celia's cedar chest. My dress looked different, almost new. Mark didn't seem to notice. He didn't dispense compliments as freely as Craig Stennet did.

The Hollow Oak Casino and Resort was much larger than I had thought and farther from Huron Station. We had driven over an hour through a light snowfall. When we reached the wide brick complex with its bright welcoming lights in every window we were both very hungry. So far all I'd seen of the place was this pricey restaurant known as the Fisherman's Cove.

"You seem to be familiar with the Casino," I said. "Do you come here often?"

"Sometimes," he said. "Usually I'm too busy. We held our sheriffs' convention here last summer. They have good steaks."

He was eating the thickest Porterhouse I'd ever seen and a mound of cottage fries. Well, that made sense. Mark was a meat-and-potatoes kind of man if ever I saw one. I'd chosen the poached salmon, a lighter entrée.

"Do you like to gamble?" I asked.

"I don't do it. Gambling leads to other vices."

"And you want to be above reproach?"

"I have to be," he said. "I'm the sheriff."

"I guess Hal Brecht didn't worry about a little thing like that."

"I'm not Hal. This is his favorite hangout in the state. I wouldn't be surprised if we saw him tonight. How about you, Krista? Are you a gambling woman?"

"No," I said. "I like to hold on to my money. I can see why casinos are so popular up north, though. When I was a kid, we used to play games in the cabin. The adults liked cribbage and poker, and we kids had Monopoly. It kept us amused for hours."

"You never told me what you do for a living, Krista," Mark said, changing the subject so abruptly that I was almost at a loss for words.

My life seemed rather unglamorous and I wasn't sure I wanted to discuss it now. "Do you want me to tell you?" I asked.

"If you like. Unless it's something illegal."

"I taught English last year, but I didn't like it very much. Earlier this fall I worked as a substitute teacher. That was even worse."

"Let me guess," he said. "The classroom was too noisy."

I almost dropped my fork into the salmon. Had Craig been talking about me to Mark? But that was unlikely. The two men didn't care for each other.

"How did you guess?" I asked.

"You like solitude. The other women I know wouldn't last two days in that old backwoods cabin."

"You're talking about my home, Sheriff. I don't mind being there alone," I said.

"You live in another place, though, don't you? Downstate somewhere?"

"I own a small house in Rochester. There's a little noise, but I have neighbors."

"Are you going to continue to work at that teaching job you don't like?" he asked.

"I'm not sure what I'm going to do next. This is a transition time for me."

"I see. And you need country quiet to think about your future."

"That's it. But mystery and danger keep intruding on my life and it's all your fault," I said.

He frowned. "How so? Because I haven't caught Scott's killer yet?"

"Partly. If you hadn't given me that ticket I'd have driven through the crime area before the murder took place."

Mark obviously found that amusing. The gleam was back in his eyes and the laughter as well.

"I'm happy to know that I'm entertaining you," I said.

"You're censuring me for doing my job. Let's go further back. If you'd learned how to get a car out of a tight space…"

His humor was infectious. Sometimes in retrospect a tense, resentment-filled incident can be viewed in a lighter way.

"All right," I said. "Let's say it was fate. I surrender."

"Good," he said. "That's what I like to hear."

TWENTY-ONE

MARK AND I walked together through a brass-bordered red door into a bright carnival world of clinking coins and loud cheering. Smoke filled the air and the machines were alive with whistles and bells. Here dreams were the best antidote for a winter night's chill. And if a gambler had a losing streak he still had a night of fun to remember and the promise of better luck tomorrow.

In a sense, gambling was a little like life.

"I've never been inside a casino before," I said. "Even if I don't play I'm looking forward to seeing the action."

"Then I guess it's up to a country sheriff to teach a city girl about northern living."

I let that last observation pass by, mainly because I couldn't think of anything relevant to say.

Mark placed his hand firmly on my back and steered me past a row of brightly painted game tables. "You can play for two dollars or even a nickel," he said. "What do you say, Krista? Blackjack, Let It Ride, Poker—what'll it be?"

"I'd rather walk around and watch for a while first," I said.

"That's what we'll do then."

He moved his hand up to my shoulders and we joined the people who were gathered around the Roulette Wheel. I gazed at the chips neatly stacked in their circles and squares on the green felt and at the numbers as they whirled by. Twenty, eleven, zero, two…

It would be fun to place a bet if only I had money to spare. For once in my life I might be lucky. I toyed with the idea.

Inside this room of games and dreams it seemed only natural to hope for instant wealth. Then I could keep the cabin and still go back to college.

Except when had I ever been lucky?

So many people came up to greet Mark that it was hard to believe he was a stranger to the Casino as he claimed. Most of them were women.

"They're all from around here," he said. "They recognize me."

"That must be it. You're a public figure."

"And this is a popular place. Everyone comes to the Hollow Oak sooner or later."

At that moment, I looked across the room and saw Estella feeding coins into a machine. She had on the same crimson dress she'd worn at the café, but she had opened the top buttons and added three long silver chains. By her side was a husky young man in a blue ski jacket. I recognized him as the trooper who had stood by her during her confrontation with the obnoxious diners at the café.

"Estella looks like she's winning," I said.

"That's Jerry with her. I'm surprised."

"Why do you say that?"

"Because he's shy and serious, something of a loner. And she's the exact opposite."

I told him how Jerry had supported Estella in her efforts to restore order to her café.

He nodded. "Any one of us would do that. Not that there's much trouble in the café. Estella takes good care of us lawmen. She always has extra eggs or pancakes for us and the coffee is free."

Just then Estella's machine rang out. She clapped her hands and hugged her escort.

I said, "That's generous of her. But it sounds like an ongoing bribe to me."

Mark smiled. "We think of it as special privileges for overworked law enforcers. Estella is good to everybody. She's been giving that no good Roy Yarrow meals on the house for years."

"He had a fifty-dollar bill to pay for his coffee this morning," I said.

"He did? I guess even Roy Yarrow has to work sometime."

Across the room Estella engulfed her escort in another exuberant embrace. Then they parted company and she headed directly toward us, radiant in red and shining silver.

"Well, Mark—and Krista. This is a surprise," she said.

She gave me a long, level look that told me she didn't appreciate being kept in the dark about my date with Mark. When she returned to the café, everyone was going to know that Mark and I had gone to the Hollow Oak Casino as a couple. Like the coming snow, there was nothing I could do about it. I didn't really mind.

Estella gazed at Mark from under her long black eye lashes. Her voice was as smooth and sweet as a warm, rich drink. "You look so good, Mark. I haven't seen you out of your uniform in ages. I can't remember how long it's been."

Mark put his arm around her. "You're looking mighty fine yourself, Estella," he said.

"Now that the café is closed for Christmas vacation, I guess we'll all be meeting at the Casino regularly," Estella said. "Are you playing tonight, Krista?"

"No, not yet."

"You should." She flashed three ten-dollar bills at us. "I just won thirty dollars. I'm going to see if I can triple that. Then I'll go Christmas shopping tomorrow. I'll see you two later."

"Good luck, Stella," Mark said.

As Estella strolled back to her machine, Mark took my hand. "Estella always brightens up a place. There's Hal Brecht heading for the Blackjack table. Don't expect him to come over and talk to us. He's preoccupied."

Looking in the direction Mark had indicated, I saw Hal with two glittering female companions, one for each arm. He saw us and waved, but Mark was right about him being preoccupied. He kept on walking, laughing and talking with his ladies.

"Hal likes high stakes poker and beautiful women," he said. "We won't see him again tonight."

"This is like Grand Central Station. Maybe we'll see Craig Stennet next or Albert Drayton," I said.

"Don't count on it. They're not the casino type."

"Am I?"

"You tell me," Mark said. "If you had, say, two hundred dollars to spare, would you spend it here?"

"I don't think so. If I had two million dollars, maybe I could spare a few hundred. But it's fun to watch others win. Would you?"

"I might. I didn't say I never gambled in my life. I can find other uses for my money. Let's sit down for a while."

He led me to two red chairs beside a potted plant, a space with a good view of the Money Wheel. We were slightly apart from the main action, in a good place for an intimate conversation. All we needed was a fireplace with a roaring blaze.

"What do you like to do in that spare time you don't have much of?" I asked.

"I watch sports, especially the Lions and Red Wings. When I was in the Marines, I used to play a little football. In the summer I go fishing. And there's dog sled racing some day when I have the time. That's about it."

"Is that why you have Timber, Blizzard and Tasha?"

"It's one of the reasons. I just like dogs."

I sighed. My own interests were reading, music and a little light gardening in the spring. Cross-country skiing was the closest I'd ever come to a sport. It didn't look as if a future with Mark was in the cards for me. An hour ago he had referred to himself as a country sheriff and he often called me a city girl. Along with the entire lower peninsula of Michigan our interests separated us. But we were sharing this evening happily enough, and there was a lot of it left. I was sure neither one of us was thinking beyond the night's end.

You're kidding yourself now, Krista, I told myself.

The Money Wheel came to stop and a memory made its way to the surface, scattering my thoughts. *In the cards* was one of Aunt Celia's favorite expressions. I hadn't thought about that in years. I never used it myself.

A cold draft came through the smoky haze and sent a chill racing over my body. Mark's hand on my shoulder felt as if it were weighted with lead.

Maybe I wasn't going to be able to build a relationship with him. Maybe all we were going to have would be this one night.

"What's wrong, Krista?" he asked. "Do you still think I'm going to drug you and lock you in one of the rooms?"

I forced myself back to the present and into that light, bantering mood Mark seemed to like. "Maybe. Are you?"

He laughed and moved his hand slowly over my back. "No. I have other plans for the evening."

"I hope I'll like them."

"You will."

"You're pretty sure of yourself aren't you, Sheriff Dalby?"

"Only of you, Krista. I've gotten to know you these past few weeks. For a city girl, you're okay."

"Well, that's a low-key compliment, but I guess I'll take it."

"I can do better," he said. "If you'll be all right here for a minute, I'm going to buy us some chips."

"I'll be fine."

"Okay, I'll be back in a few minutes."

I sat watching the players for a while and then threaded my way through the tables and laughter to the windows. The snow was still coming down and the outside lights threw my own reflection back at me with a thick slice of the Casino in the background. Gamblers, guests, and red-uniformed attendants with trays in their hands passed behind me like gaudily dressed wraiths.

This was a different side of Michigan, one I might never have discovered if Mark hadn't brought me here tonight. I closed my eyes and concentrated on darkness and blackness, allowing my mind to receive a parade of sensory impressions:

white snow falling silently outside, bells with melodious tones, shrill whistles, loud clapping, laughter, and red, black, and gold colors at every turn.

Insinuating its way through the smoke was a strong odor of cherry-scented tobacco and a terrifying memory of being locked in a barn.

I whirled around, looking away from the reflections. I searched the crowd for the source of the smell. At this particular moment no one was near me, but I was standing beside the door that led to the restaurant where people were constantly going in and coming out. Someone who carried that cloying scent on his body had passed near me and then walked on quickly.

How many people were at the Hollow Oak Casino tonight? Probably hundreds, possibly over a thousand. I had seen only a small part of the complex.

The chance that the person who smelled of cherry tobacco was still in the immediate area was slim. And how likely was it that he was my attacker? Not very. More to the point, I didn't know what the man looked like. I couldn't go through the casino searching for a scent.

Nevertheless I surveyed the room, looking for one man that might stand apart from the others. Except for the casino employees, almost all of the people in my view appeared to be in pairs or part of a small group. No one looked the least bit sinister. This was a place where camaraderie flourished, not treachery.

Mark came up behind me quietly. "Here you are, Krista. I thought you were trying to give me the slip."

In his hand he had a large mug with the Hollow Oak logo on it. He carried it carefully by the handle as if afraid of spilling the contents.

"You brought me coffee?" I asked. "Hot chocolate?"

"Neither, it's a Tom and Jerry, your Christmas drink. Here take it, but don't scald yourself. I almost did."

"You remembered."

"Rum and brandy," he said, "and don't be afraid. I didn't put a drug in it."

I took a sip. It was hot, sweet, delicious and strong—all those ingredients I needed to ward off the chill of fear.

"Now, tell me what's wrong," he said, leading the way to our chairs.

They were empty. Nobody comes to a gambling casino to sit on the sidelines and talk except a country sheriff and a city girl on their first date.

"Just a while ago, I smelled that cherry tobacco scent," I said.

"You're thinking about the man who locked you in the barn." Mark's eyes grew sharp and he scanned the people in our view. "I don't know, Krista. It's just plain smoky in here."

That was true. "Well, I don't smell anything now except nutmeg and sugar so let's forget about it. But I have to say, if this is the place you wanted me to stay, I think I'll be better off in the cabin."

"You're safe now," he said. "I won't leave you alone again."

I didn't want Mark to think I was a clinging female. I was afraid I'd given him that impression over something as elusive as a remembered scent. I took a deep breath and tried to sound confident.

"Thanks, Mark, but I don't need a round-the-clock body-guard. I already looked around and didn't see anyone suspicious lurking behind me. That scent reminded me of being locked in the barn and I'm afraid I overreacted."

"Maybe," he said. "How's your Tom and Jerry?"

"Delicious. Thanks. I think I'll buy my own rum and brandy and whip up a bowl for the holidays. I'm planning to have a quiet country Christmas in the cabin."

"All alone?" he asked.

"I guess so. Except for Tasha."

"Well then, let's have some action now." He took four chips out of his pocket and placed them in my palm. "Never let it be said that Sheriff Dalby takes a date to a gambling casino and doesn't let her play. Did you decide what it'll be?"

Smiling up at him I said, "The Roulette Wheel. I feel like living dangerously tonight."

TWENTY-TWO

ON THE WAY BACK to Huron Station, Mark navigated the icy roads with skill and ease while managing to carry on a conversation at the same time. Confident in his ability to keep the car from skidding into danger, I leaned back on the seat and listened as he told me about his older brother, Mac, and the mischief they had gotten themselves into as they were growing up.

"Mac and I were always friendly rivals," he said. "After I graduated from college, I followed him into the Marines and later into law enforcement. Some day when we retire, we're going to start a private security agency. Do you have any brothers or sisters, Krista?"

"No. I was an only child. You're lucky to have Mac."

"You were spoiled, I'll bet," he said.

"Certainly not," I said quickly, even as I wondered if he was right. My parents had always been good to me, but then I'd been a good daughter. "Why would you think that?"

"You're a little sassy," he said. "I like my women docile."

"Well…" Since Mark was looking straight ahead, I couldn't see his expression, but I was certain he wasn't serious. "I never thought of myself as being sassy or spoiled. I don't think of myself as one of your women either, if that's what you are implying. I don't think you can find a docile woman today. Use that word to describe a sheep."

He laughed. "All right, I will. What does your boyfriend think about this extended north woods vacation of yours?"

"I'm not in a serious relationship right now."

"How about your parents? Don't they worry about you?"

The question was innocent, but I felt as if I were being inter-rogated again. Mark wasn't subtle and he didn't possess Craig Stennet's skill at drawing out a person or making confidences seem natural. He'd offered a few details about his relationship with Mac and their boyhood pranks, but mostly he'd grilled me about my life. As soon as I gave him his answer I planned to ask the questions.

"My parents were killed in a car accident," I said. "A kid who didn't have a license ran a red light and crashed into them. It was a head-on collision. They died together, which is the way they would have wanted it."

Mark reached across the seat and crushed my hand in a comforting grip.

"I'm sorry, Krista. When we first met, you mentioned that your mother was an English professor. I assumed she was still alive. Did the accident happen recently?"

"During my last year of college. They didn't live to see me graduate."

"I'll bet they'd be proud of you now," he said.

"I hope so."

His warm tone surprised me as did the approval implicit in his statement. At times I'd thought that Mark disliked me or asso-ciated with me mainly because of our mutual involvement in the murder case. Even our date this evening had been his opportunity to show me that the Hollow Oak would be a safe house for me.

But I was seeing another side of Mark tonight. Maybe I'd been wrong about him. I liked to think that he was different from the loser brigade that haunted my past. If so I might continue to see him after he arrested his suspect and solved the Randall Scott case.

Warmed and cheered by the prospect of having Mark in my life, I was eager to know more about him.

"And what does your girlfriend think about your dangerous job?" I asked.

"You might say I'm between girlfriends," he said. "Call it good timing."

That sounded as if he was referring to our relationship. I

stole a glance at his handsome profile in the dark. Ever since we'd first met I hadn't been able to think of any other man. I hoped he felt the same way about me.

THE AIR WAS ALMOST as cold on the front porch of the cabin as it was outside, but the faint light of the lamp in the living room window created an illusion of warmth.

While Mark turned the key in the lock I waited close behind him, wishing that our date didn't have to end so soon. I had a modest windfall in my evening bag and a night of Technicolor memories. The contrast between the razzle-dazzle atmosphere of the Hollow Oak Casino and the darkness and silence surrounding the quiet cabin was overwhelming.

I heard the faint click of the key and a soft welcome-home bark on the other side of the door. Reaching past Mark for the doorknob, I said, "Thank you for everything. It was a wonderful…"

He turned me around and pulled me roughly into his chest, holding me tightly and bending his mouth to mine for a long, crushing kiss. Instantly the temperature on the porch rose and continued to climb. I moved my hands up to his shoulders and touched his face and hair, letting him bring me closer still, allowing the sudden fire to envelop us. Like our date, I didn't want this moment to end. But nobody has ever found a way to stop time.

After a while, he pushed me gently back and traced the outline of my lips with his finger. It was cold, which was surprising since his touch could create such heat. "Haven't you ever been kissed by a country sheriff before, Krista?" he asked.

"Not this year," I said. "Not like this. I think I'd better go inside now."

"Alone?"

Why was I always confronted with decisions clamoring to be made? For once I wished my choices would be easy.

We could spread the quilt on the floor in front of the wood stove and let nature take its course. So why was I hesitating when I wanted him as much as he wanted me, if only for this one night?

He moved his hands down my body to my waist in slow caresses that seared through the warm layers I'd piled on. I wanted to feel his hands on my flesh, but that wasn't going to happen unless I let him come inside with me.

I couldn't do that. This was our first date. Aside from our exchanges about the murder case, we'd had only one real conversation, and that was only a short while ago. Mark should realize this, too.

In the darkness his voice was clear and firm. "Krista?"

"We'd better say goodnight, now, Mark," I said.

He trapped me against the door while he kissed me again. "I know you want me. I can tell. Don't try to deny it."

"You are sure of me, Sheriff Dalby. I wish I could be so sure of you."

"I'm exactly what you think," he said, "a man who wants to go to bed with you."

"That's all?"

"God almighty, Krista. What do you want?"

"To wait until we know each other better," I said.

In the weak light I could see his face with its intriguing planes and lines and his icy blue eyes. I had no trouble reading his expression tonight. He knew that I wanted him. I wasn't fooling him, not even a little bit.

"Okay, honey," he said. "It may not be tonight, but I always get my woman. Remember that."

I couldn't resist saying, "Like you always get your man?"

"Like that. Yes."

There was the slightest glimmer in his eyes, not the teasing gleam and yet not quite anger. I couldn't give it a name. The mood had definitely changed.

He opened the door part way and gave Tasha a stern command to back up and stay.

"Goodnight, Krista," he said. He turned and stamped across the porch, pushed open the porch door and disappeared into the snowy night.

Inside the cabin I leaned against the door, parrying Tasha's excited greeting, and marveled that once again I had done the exact opposite of what I wanted. Because of my strict adherence to convention, I might have scared off a good man, even though I'd been right to refuse him. I didn't doubt it, but that didn't alter the fact that a man like Mark wouldn't appreciate having his ego battered. I wondered what he was thinking of me right now—if he was inclined to spare a thought for me at all.

That was something I couldn't know. Well, I'd made my decision and I felt that it was the right one. I would resist the impulse to second guess my refusal and get ready for bed. This was an unhappy ending for an otherwise enjoyable evening. It effectively cancelled out the mellow feelings generated by our conversation in the car.

I hung my coat on the rack and moved listlessly through the cabin, turning on lights. That helped a little. I let Tasha out into the snow and while she was gone, set out a bowl of fresh water and a bedtime biscuit for her. In the small, cold bathroom I washed off my makeup and put on my warmest cotton nightgown.

That was all I was going to do tonight. If the radio turned itself on again in the hours before dawn, I'd just ignore it.

THE NEXT MORNING I woke to a light but steady snowfall. The blizzard Roy Yarrow had fussed about was scheduled to arrive over the weekend, which meant the possibility of a snowed-in Christmas. Now we were having light precipitation, a harbinger of the big storm moving in from the West.

I had a dull, persistent headache that could only be cured by breakfast at Estella's Café. Then I remembered. The café was closed. I'd have to eat cereal and toast, and for lunch toss a salad or heat a can of soup. If the roads weren't too bad I could drive to the Station Roadhouse for dinner this evening.

I tried to find my usual enthusiasm for the beginning of a day but it was gone. One minute I didn't think I'd ever see Mark again and the next I was sure that I would. After all, I had his dog.

Cheered by the thought that he would have to come back sometime and get her, I cleaned the cabin thoroughly. Then, when the snow tapered off into showers, I went out through the back door, armed with shovel, saw, and pruning shears.

The trees grew sparsely here. Aunt Celia had told me that at the time the cabin was built this entire area had been cleared. To the north, another meadow sloped down to thick, dangerous woods. They were filled with poisonous snakes—instant death waiting in the rotting leaves to strike out with their fangs and inject venom into the bloodstream of little girls.

That was the claim of my cousin, Douglas, who was two years older than me. For some unfathomable reason when we were children, he'd taken a perverse pleasure in frightening me. Even now I shuddered, no matter that it was the end of December in another millennium, and I was older and wiser.

The memories lingered. Once there had been two doghouses outside the back porch. They were now gone. A short distance from the cabin Aunt Celia's neighbor, Fred, had built a tree house for visiting children. All that remained of it were some old boards clinging to the branches of an ancient maple.

A few tall evergreens grew among the oaks and birches. They weren't as plentiful and shapely as the ones beyond the barns, but being balsams they had that sweet distinctive scent that always defined Christmas for me.

I wasn't entirely over my fear of being ambushed by the archer killer. In spite of Mark's dire warning about turning myself into a target, I felt safer here with the cabin to shelter me.

I had taken the precautions of stationing Tasha at the side of the house for protection and leaving the shotgun outside the door where I could reach it at a moment's notice.

When I found the tree I wanted, I sawed it down and left it lying in the snow while I cut branches for swags. There. It was done without any fanfare or rude interruptions from would-be killers.

I was about to drag the tree and branches inside to the porch when I heard the hum of a car engine in the deep silence. It came closer and then died abruptly. A car door slammed.

Tasha tore around to the front of the cabin. I followed her, nearly tripping over the saw in my haste to grab the shotgun from the porch and follow her.

I heard Craig's voice shouting. "Whoa! Get away! Krista! Call off your wolf."

"Tasha! Come! Craig is a friend." I dropped the gun and grabbed her collar. She swung her head around as if to bite me. Quickly I released her and moved back a few feet to a safe distance.

That wasn't bright. I knew enough not to let a dog know I was afraid of her. Not that I thought Tasha would attack me. I was just startled. She was watching both Craig and me now with wary blue eyes that would strike terror into the heart of a man with evil intentions.

"That's a good dog now, Tasha," I said in a soft, soothing voice. "I don't know why but you bring out the worst in her, Craig. How did you know I was outside?"

"I didn't. When I saw that vicious dog running loose I hoped you weren't too far away. What's the gun for?" he asked.

"Marauding bears."

"No, seriously."

"For protection. You never know what's lurking in the woods."

"Probably only hungry deer. You're not really afraid, are you?"

"It never hurts to be prepared," I said. "Come in. Let's go around the back. I've been cutting down my Christmas tree."

Craig walked over to the fallen fir. "This is a beauty but it's almost twice your size."

"I'll saw a few more inches off the trunk."

He said, "Let me do it. Then I'll help you put it in the stand."

"No, I can…"

"It's easier when there are two pairs of hands. You can hold the trunk straight, and I'll tighten the screws."

What he said made sense and he only meant to be helpful. It would be rude to refuse.

"I'll make some hot cocoa, then," I said. "Putting up the Christmas tree and drinking cocoa was a tradition in our family, until my parents—until I lost them."

I didn't want to talk about my mother and father now and Craig seemed to understand.

He said quickly, "It's a good one. With us, it was popcorn. I came over for your RSVP," he said.

"My what?" Clearly I was missing something. I had no idea what it was.

"To have a Christmas drink at my house tomorrow," he said. "I thought I'd spare you having to drive over in the snow."

"I'm afraid I don't know what you're talking about, Craig." At that minute though, I remembered the cards Estella had given me. I'd slipped them into my shoulder bag and promptly forgotten about them.

"I didn't open my cards yet. Is the one in the green envelope from you?"

"If it doesn't have an address on it, yes. I enjoyed our last evening so much I want to do it again. I'm roasting a goose on Christmas and since we're both alone, I thought you might like to join me. Unless you've made other plans."

"I haven't. But you've already cooked me dinner once. I can't go on accepting your hospitality. You said something about a drink…"

"That's a separate invitation," he said. "You'll be doing me a favor, Krista. I like eating at the American Legion but not on a holiday."

There was no way I could refuse graciously. And why should I? I had planned to go to midnight mass on Christmas Eve and spend the day alone reminiscing about the past and dreaming of the future.

Alone in the cabin with somebody else's dog for company? That's as pathetic as it gets.

"I'd like to come, Craig," I said. "You'll have to let me bring something—dessert, maybe."

"If you will, it would help. I'm not much of a baker. Now, let me help you put that tree up."

AFTER CRAIG SET the tree securely in its stand and went home, I worked until mid-afternoon making swags and tying them together with red velvet ribbon. I filled vases with balsam branches and cut remnants from the steamer trunk into shapes vaguely resembling bells, stars, and candy canes. Although I didn't have any lights, the final effect was colorful and nostalgic, and the cabin was fragrant with balsam.

When I was finished, I spread a snow-white sheet around the trunk but left the silver sleigh on the sideboard with the candles and the radio. It looked as if it belonged there now.

Everything was ready for a real country Christmas. I hadn't felt more at home in a place in years. I vowed to find a way to keep the cabin, even if I had to amend my college plans.

Since there was a lull in the snowfall, I decided to treat myself to a trip to town. Craig had happily accepted my offer to bring dessert to his Christmas dinner, which left me two choices: create something sweet and festive in the small kitchen or head to the Station Bakery. That decision I made quickly.

I left Tasha lying between the stove and the tree (no doubt eyeing my homemade ornaments as potential tug-of-war toys), cleared the snow off the car, and drove to town on roads that were only a little slick in spite of the last snowfall.

Main Street was crowded with pedestrians and the stores were outdoing themselves to draw in the holiday shoppers. The window of Blooms from the Past was filled with antique toys and miniature potted firs decorated and strung with tiny lights. Even Nichols' Drug Store was doing a brisk business.

Since Estella had closed for the holiday, the bakery was making an attempt to fill the void with ice cream tables and chairs set out near a coffeepot. Inside a small group of people sat talking and eating doughnuts, pastries, and a holiday confection the bakery sold by the slice. They were probably café regulars but the only familiar face I saw was Cindy's.

She was one of the two clerks behind the counter, busily filling orders.

Three people waited in line ahead of me, which gave me an opportunity to view the array of baked goods. Gingerbread cottages decorated with candy, elegant cakes, and trays of delicate bow ties dripping powdered sugar onto lacy paper doilies—my choices were endless. Mixed together, vanilla, ginger, sugar, and chocolate could easily rival balsam as the quintessential scent of Christmas. Someone should bottle it.

While I waited for my turn I wondered why Craig had issued individual invitations for separate days. I would have thought the Christmas drink would be part of the dinner. It couldn't be that he simply wanted to see me twice in one week. I hoped that wasn't the case because I didn't want him to think that I was interested in forming a relationship with him. Maybe I should have tried harder to find a gracious way to decline his dinner invitation. It was too late now.

I still hadn't found any evidence to support Mark's claim that Craig was strange other than his quirky aversion to women in pants and his fascination with murder, which, for a writer, wasn't really unusual. When I saw him tomorrow I would make it a point to quiz him discreetly about his background and interests. Perhaps I could find out why he disliked Mark. Then, although my suspicions of him seemed faint and faraway, I might learn something that would finally put them to rest.

Cindy wore jeans today as did every other woman in the bakery, including me. Embroidered on the front of her sweater was a charming woodland scene of three wolf cubs playing at the edge of a frozen stream.

She looked older and sleeker than she did in her orange café uniform.

"What can I get for you, Miss Marlow?" she asked.

"I'd like a fancy dessert," I said. "Something nice enough to take to a Christmas dinner."

"We have pineapple cheesecake with holly berries on it, strawberry torte, all these cakes…"

Each one of the seven cakes was frosted and decorated a little differently like the deer in my silver sleigh. With their bright Christmas colors all were festive. Tiny cards placed in front of them described the batter and gave the price.

"Is it too early to buy one today for Christmas?" I asked.

"It should be fine. These came out at three and the frosting seals in the freshness. You should buy one today. They'll be gone by tomorrow and it's too late now to take orders."

"I'll have the chocolate cake on the end, then, with the poinsettias and green snowflakes," I said, "and a dozen gingerbread men." I couldn't possibly stop there. "A dozen of the bow ties, too."

"The *chrusciki?* You'd better take two dozen. They're as light as air and just sweet enough."

As she lined up three boxes I said, "That's a pretty sweater you're wearing. It's really unusual."

"I bought it at Brecht's. They're having a 'Going out of Business' sale. I heard that the store is bankrupt. After Mr. Brecht lost his partner we were expecting it."

I remembered Mark telling me that Randall Scott and Hal Brecht had been partners. "It's too bad Mr. Brecht couldn't go on alone."

"I guess he wants to concentrate on his other affairs," she said. "Would you like anything else?"

"Maybe. Let me look over here."

At the refrigerated counter I saw three days' worth of meals set out with the holiday breads and coffeecakes and chose a spinach tart, a broccoli quiche, and a vegetarian pizza. That should take care of dinners for the rest of the week.

I wanted to wrap up my bakery business quickly and think about this interesting bit of information Cindy had given me. According to Mark, Hal Brecht was a born gambler who was often broke and he still had political ambitions. Most importantly he had a connection to Randall Scott.

These might be isolated facts but they could also be relevant. And the bankruptcy news had come my way when I hadn't even been thinking about the mystery. Also, thanks to Craig's dinner invitation and my love of baked goods, I wouldn't have to cook for a while. I had a feeling that with the approaching blizzard, the coming days were going to be too busy to waste time cooking. As with the shotgun, it was always best to be prepared.

TWENTY-THREE

ON THE WAY OUT OF TOWN I took a detour and drove by the Sheriff's Department. Mark's second story office was brightly lit and several cars were still in the lot. Wishing that I had some reason to visit Mark, I slowed down. If only I had a clue or piece of evidence that had to be delivered in person.

Cindy's revelation of Brecht's financial loss wouldn't be news to Mark. He must have investigated the people close to Randall Scott and I was sure he knew about the store's bankruptcy. If Hal Brecht was still free to roam the county's gambling halls Mark had no reason to suspect him.

Still, the possibility that Brecht might be involved in the murder tugged at me. It would be better to work it out on my own, though. And why give Mark a reason to think that I regretted turning down his offer of a night of lovemaking?

That's a novel way to look at it, I told myself. *Now drive on.*

Snowflakes dissolved on the windshield of the Taurus and the air in front of me grew thicker. I turned on my lights and slowed down even more. For some reason I was reluctant to go home just yet. I passed Brecht's but they were already closed for the day. Then, while waiting to turn right, I saw Saint Sebastian's Church ahead, a ghostly gray building that appeared to be floating through the folds of snow fog.

I'd always meant to view the nativity scene by night when the lights were on but had never been in Huron Station after dark. Now I brought the Taurus to a stop in front of the church. Albert had done a fine job of illuminating the display. But from the street overgrown evergreens obscured my view of the manger. I hesitated, wondering whether to go closer and perhaps even inside the church or to hurry home before nightfall.

Soft Christmas music streaming out through the open doors helped me to decide. I parked in the small lot and followed the path that angled through the yard to the entrance, pausing to admire the manger on the way.

Snow fell on its slanting roof and covered the life-sized figures outside with a new mantel of white. Blue floodlights shone on Joseph, Mary, and the Baby safe inside. Some distance from the adoring angels and shepherds, the Wise Men paused near a stand of silver poplars as they neared the end of their long journey. This was historically correct since they had been miles from Bethlehem on the night of the Christ's birth.

I wasn't the only one here today. It appeared that a pageant rehearsal was about to begin. Children in long robes and veils hurried past me like diminutive guests on their way to a costume ball while a young black-clad priest stood at the door waiting to greet them.

Unnoticed, I slipped into the church and knelt at the altar of Saint Sebastian. The statue was exactly as I remembered it— a smooth white body pierced through with arrows and bathed in the light of the vigil candles. It felt right for me to be here.

Then I saw something I hadn't noticed on my previous visit. On either side of the statue were three wall murals, each one depicting an event in the life of the saint. From his days as a noble Roman soldier through his suffering and martyrdom to his triumphant entrance into heaven, St. Sebastian's story was laid out in bold bright colors.

The artist had a gift for capturing the true nature of his subjects in paint. Sebastian was as noble and pure as the angels who hovered over the gates of heaven and the ruthless Roman Emperor and his soldiers were evil incarnate. Even those unfamiliar with the saint's story couldn't possibly confuse the good characters with the bad.

I wished that I could read people as clearly as the artist did.

I had met and talked to several of Randall Scott's associates but all I'd seen were the faces they presented to the world. If one of them had committed the crime, he'd kept his secret well. And if he was the same person who had tried to kill me, so far I had thwarted him.

Whether it was through saintly intervention or luck, I didn't know. But I needed all the help I could get. Saint Sebastian would make a good ally. I said a silent prayer to him for protection from arrows and all other evils and felt that I was no longer alone.

I remembered a passage from Shakespeare's *Hamlet* about the absence of evil during Christmastime: "No spirit can walk abroad; The nights are wholesome; then no planets strike, No fairy takes, nor witch hath power to charm, So hallowed and so gracious is the time."

Bad things happened throughout the year, but the concept of a moratorium was comforting. And wasn't this the season of comfort and joy?

On the way back to the parking lot, I passed the manger again. For a fragment of a moment, I thought I saw a man standing beside Joseph. He was dressed in white and arrows pierced his chest. Then I realized that the figure was a figment of my imagination caused by the whirling snow.

The time had come for me to go home.

A SUBTLE SCENT of balsam drifted out into the cold air as I opened the front door of the cabin. Tasha emerged from the still shadows beyond the dining room. She walked slowly toward me skirting the long table, and stood staring at me with those eerie blue eyes. At this moment she looked more like a husky or wolf than her collie ancestors.

I patted her on the head, glad for her company.

Whenever I came home after dark the first few minutes were always a little strange, almost spooky, until I turned on more lights and started a fire in the wood stove. Then with the dog by my side and the teapot whistling on the stove, familiarity returned. It was comforting to know that I could walk through the rooms without expecting a hand to come smashing out of the wall and grab me.

Good God, I never used to have such appalling ideas. But then I hadn't contemplated Christian martyrs and torture in years either. And I'd never been attacked by an unknown assailant. I was mixing recent events with factual historical accounts and Gothic elements, laying a firm foundation for a night of frightening dreams.

Tasha stayed close behind me as I put away the boxes of baked goods except for the small one that held the quiche. That was tonight's dinner. I turned the oven on and filled the teakettle with water. I was making a tray of aluminum foil when I heard a soft rapping at the front door. I knew at once that it wasn't Mark. He would never announce his presence so quietly.

Tasha started to growl. I attached her leash to her choke chain and led her into the living room. Through the window I saw a car parked behind the Taurus, but I couldn't determine the color or make through the snow. Deciding that a dog was as formidable a weapon as a shotgun, I opened the door.

Estella stood on the porch shivering and holding a red and white striped package. Snow dusted her long black coat and made the silver streaks in her hair appear wider.

"Merry Christmas, Krista," she said.

"I didn't expect...same to you, Estella. Won't you come in?"

She stepped across the threshold taking care to leave a good distance between herself and Tasha who was still growling.

"Isn't that Mark's dog?" she asked.

"Yes, her name is Tasha. She won't bite. She just wants you to think she will."

I didn't know that for certain. But if Estella recognized Tasha she must be aware of her temperament.

Ordering Tasha to stop growling, I dropped the loop of her leash over the back of a chair.

"Why do you have her?" Estella asked.

I took her coat and hung it on the rack. "Mark lent Tasha to me. She's good protection and he thought I needed it. Come in and sit by the fire."

"I can only stay a minute. I just wanted to drop off your Christmas present."

She followed me into the living room, her full black skirt swishing as she walked. "Celia always had dogs and she let them come inside the cabin." She fell silent as she stared at my tree with its homespun decorations. "I can't believe it, Krista. This is exactly how the room looked when your aunt was alive. That's where she always put her Christmas tree…right in front of the window. Couldn't you find her ornaments and lights?"

"I didn't look for them," I said. "I put this tree together in a hurry."

"I see you found the sleigh, though. Celia always set it under the tree next to the manger. And there's that wonderful old radio. If it still works, you can hear Christmas music on 7.189 all day long."

"I had it repaired," I said. "Didn't you say you were going to Detroit for the holidays?"

"I'm leaving in the morning, bright and early, a day ahead of the big blizzard, I hope. If I can't get back by New Year's I'll just take a longer vacation." She paused and gave me a sly smile. "You must be doing something right with Mark if he lent you his dog."

"Mark is only being a good neighbor. He lives nearby. But you must know that."

"Oh, I do, Krista. I definitely know where Mark lives."

Estella's soft laugh annoyed me as did her blatant attempt to let me know that she was on intimate terms with Mark. As well she might be. That wasn't my concern. I reminded myself that this was the Christmas season and Estella had brought me a present. I was being uncharitable.

"It's nice of you to stop by, Estella," I said.

"I have to go home and finish packing. But I wanted you to have this fruitcake for Christmas." She handed me the package.

"I used Celia's recipe. Her mother wrote it down from a radio program. If you like, I'll make a copy for you."

I took the fruitcake from her. The candy cane paper was cold and a little wet, and the cake weighed more than I thought. But I was almost reluctant to put it down. It seemed as if I were accepting a present from Aunt Celia.

"Fruitcakes have fallen out of favor lately, but I thought you'd enjoy it," Estella said.

"I'm sure I will. I don't bake much, but I'd like to have the recipe. Thank you."

My words sounded stilted to me, my sentences clipped and unfriendly. But Estella didn't appear to notice. Her gaze was riveted on my tree with its homemade decorations.

"It's amazing. Even without Celia's ornaments this is just like stepping back in time. Did I ever mention that I used to visit Celia often? We were good friends."

"You did, once or twice."

"She loved to cook and bake. I half expect to see her coming out of her kitchen any minute with a tray of coffee and a cake."

I looked toward the dining room, seeing in my imagination the exact image Estella evoked. "If only she could."

"I'm sorry if I upset you, Krista. I was just reminiscing. Everyone gets sentimental at this time of the year. I'll be on my way now."

Thank heavens, I thought. But remembering my duties as hostess, I asked, "Can I get you something to drink or eat? I made a stop at the bakery today."

"No thank you. I really have to go," she said. "I'll copy the recipe for you when I come back."

She walked to the door, taking care to stay out of Tasha's reach. I helped her on with her coat, not too quickly, I hoped.

"Drive safely," I said. "It's a long way to Detroit. Maybe you'll be lucky and miss the blizzard."

"That's what I'm hoping for. They say the snow will stay north of Saginaw. Have a good Christmas, Krista. I'll see you soon."

The relief I felt when I locked the door and freed Tasha from the chair was overwhelming. I didn't know what was happening to me. I used to enjoy having company. But this particular visitor had made me feel uncomfortable. Maybe it was because of her hint that she and Mark were much closer than I'd thought.

Once again I told myself that it wasn't my concern, that Estella might be baiting me for her own reasons. That was what I wanted to believe.

I'd believe it then as long as I could.

THAT NIGHT I HAD A DREAM that frightened me, even though it wasn't about Roman torture or assailants emerging from the snow.

I dreamed I was a child again, up north for the Christmas holiday with my family, stealing out of bed to help myself to a few more of the chocolate mints that Aunt Celia kept in her glass hen on the sideboard.

No one noticed me. They were all in the living room, sitting around the fireplace—my mother and father, aunts, uncles and cousins, all alive again in my dream and gathered in Aunt Celia's cabin for a family reunion.

The room had more furniture now, enough seating to accommodate a dozen people. And the arrangement was different. On a narrow bookcase in the corner the radio played familiar Christmas songs.

In spite of the moderate illumination in the room, the scene was dim and surreal. Candlelight, the crackling fire, and the multi-colored lights sparkling among the branches of the Christmas tree bolstered the low-voltage bulbs in the lamps.

The shadows had followed me out from the bedroom and were dancing madly around me. I tried not to look at them. At night the cabin changed, becoming a dark and scary place. For comfort I looked to the people in the room.

Dad sat on the sofa beside Uncle Chester who was loading his camera, and my nemesis, that diabolical Douglas, who should have been sent to bed with the rest of the children, was reading a comic book. My other uncles and Douglas' older brother were playing cards on the coffee table. In the corner near the radio, mother and Aunt Celia were engrossed in a private conversation.

I tried to hear what they were saying because I sensed that it was important, but I couldn't. Voices came from a distance. I seemed to be viewing an old home movie without sound, because all of a sudden I was older. Instead of flannel pajamas, I was wearing the long cotton nightgown I'd bought last winter and my hair felt lighter and fluffier on my shoulders.

The shadows were all around me now. Desperately I tried to ignore them and concentrate on the light from the candles. From where I stood I could see a miniature silver sleigh shining under the white lights on the lower branches, above a jumble of presents.

In my dream, I thought, *It was always under the tree. Why didn't I remember that?*

Then, as if on cue, somewhere outside the cabin I heard the clear melodious ringing of sleigh bells in the quiet night.

A dog came up behind me and gently nudged my hand, the one that held the mints. It was Ranger. I stroked his silky head and the dream ended abruptly.

I woke up. The cabin was dark and quiet, without even an echo of the bells, but my hand still felt warm from its brief contact with Ranger's fur. I lay still trying to remember, wishing I could go back into the dream because there was something undone about it.

I turned and raised myself on my elbow to check the time and the view from the window. Six o'clock and the usual morning snow was falling. I supposed this wasn't the real blizzard yet but another prelude.

Closing my eyes, I tried to recall the dream. Familiar faces, menacing shadows, people talking without sound, fire, radio music, and bells. What was wrong?

The sleigh bells confused me. Were they part of the dream or had I really heard them? They had seemed so real, but how could they be? I'd been in Huron Station for a month and had yet to see a sleigh. I could have sworn that I'd never set eyes on the silver decoration until I unpacked it last month.

You're missing the point. The dream is wrong.

I had never visited the cabin during the winter when I was a child. All of our vacations took place in the summer. Except one? I wondered.

A dream can't be wrong, I told myself. *It's only a dream.*

And yet there were other things I didn't understand. How could I hear that crackling fire, radio music and bells, but not what the people were saying? And what exactly frightened the child Krista/me? Was it the shadows or not being able to hear what mother and Aunt Celia were talking about?

I knew that often dream images have their beginnings in the events or thoughts of the previous hours. Last night, Estella had mentioned my aunt's Christmas decorations. Several hours later as I lay sleeping, my subconscious mind created a Christmas room and filled it with members of my family and images from the past.

Nothing could be simpler. Still, something continued to trouble me. All of my memories were of the summer. While I was almost positive that I'd never been up north at Christmas when I was a child, there was one way to find out for certain. The answer lay in Aunt Celia's old photograph albums. Fortunately, I had all of them.

TWENTY-FOUR

THE NEXT DAY Mark arrested Roy Yarrow again. I closed the album and turned up the volume on the radio, hoping to hear more details. Roy had confessed to the murder of Randall Scott but refused to reveal his motive. The next news flash concerned the blizzard that was still making its way toward Huron Station. It seemed to be taking an unusually long time to arrive.

Although I was relieved that the killer was behind bars, these meager facts didn't satisfy me. As I gathered the loose black photo corners into a neat pile, I tried to figure out how I could learn more. Specifically, I wanted to know if Roy was the man who had tried to kill me.

By now the afternoon edition of the *Station Press* would be on the stands with extensive coverage on the arrest. I would have to drive into town to buy a paper. I'd been looking for an excuse to set aside my search for a while anyway.

So far I had found dozens of snapshots taken during the summer at the farm and the beach. Those lakeside photographs were disturbing. I had no memories of swimming or playing in the sand on Lake Huron, but I didn't doubt that I was the little girl in the bathing suit. How much more of my childhood had I forgotten?

Instead of sitting in the midst of old pictures trying to disprove a dream, I should be taking action. I moved the unexamined albums to the sideboard and looked for my shoulder bag and car keys.

While I was in town I planned to stop at Mark's office. I had been looking for an excuse to do that, too, and now I had a legitimate reason to visit him. He might have more information about the case than the media did. Since ours was a sheriff-witness relationship in this matter, he would have to fill me in. Maybe. He could also invoke that confidentiality business. There was only one way to find out.

I was especially curious about Roy's alibi. Mark had never believed that Lily and Roy had been together at the time of the murder, and certainly Estella didn't. Probably Lily had retracted her statement before leaving town.

I wondered if Estella knew about Roy's second arrest. She appeared to care about him, but wouldn't her feelings for him change now that he was a confessed murderer? That was something I wouldn't know until she returned to Huron Station.

Tasha was outside running and barking in the snow. I called her name and started to pull on my boots. Enlightenment was half an hour away. It was a sure thing or rather, a reasonably sure thing. I still didn't know about Mark.

IT SEEMED STRANGE to drive down Main Street and not make a stop at Estella's Café. Although the café wasn't the only gathering place in Huron Station, it drew the largest crowd. When Estella was there, it was the best information and gossip source available for miles around. In her absence I would have to rely on the *Station Press*.

I stopped at Nichols' Drug Store to buy a paper. The headline 'Archer Killer Confesses' stretched across the top of the front page in blaring black letters. A picture of Roy taken at the Deer Kill protest occupied more space than the story.

He had the look of a man dedicated to his causes, but not that of a cold-blooded killer. Something about the whole affair felt wrong to me. Still, Roy had confessed. How could I argue with that?

I really needed to talk to Mark. The brief sense of relief I'd felt on hearing about the arrest was already dissipating. I didn't know why that should be, assuming that Mark had arrested the right man.

Before I left Nichols, I bought a bottle of chocolate flavored liqueur for Craig as a present to go along with the cake. This was the first time I had ever looked for a present in a drug store. But with only two more shopping days until Christmas the selection of cards and inexpensive gifts was dwindling. I considered myself lucky to have found something suitable to give him.

Shivering in the abrupt change from drug store heat to bitter cold air, I walked across the street to my car. The clouds were an ominous shade of gray and the air had a sharp, biting taste of snow. Everyone in sight appeared to move with a shared sense of urgency, of errands needing to be done. Christmas was coming and so was the blizzard. Both would arrive in a matter of hours now.

I set Craig's liqueur on the floor of the car where it would be safe and drove the short distance to the Sheriff's Department. The parking lot was emptier than it had been yesterday at the end of the workday. As I had done before, I entered the building unnoticed and took the elevator to the second floor without seeing anyone. The heavy silence made me feel like an intruder.

I thought the place would be crowded with reporters and lawyers, but the only person I saw was a man moving a mop down the hall in slow motion. Perhaps the media and legal team had been here earlier in the day. More likely, everyone was congregating in the courthouse or jail, in which case Mark might not be in.

Hoping that I was wrong, I opened the door to his outer office. Except for Mark's dispatcher, this room was empty, too. She was talking on the telephone in what appeared to be a personal call. Her red fingernail polish sparkled against the dull black surface of the receiver. She glanced up and said, "I'll be right with you."

I stepped back to admire the tiny plants in the brandy glass terrarium on her desk while she wound up her conversation. When she hung up the phone, her smile was as bright as her nail polish.

"You're Miss Marlow, aren't you?" she asked. "How can I help you?"

"I'd like to see Sheriff Dalby."

"Oh, I'm sorry. He's in a meeting. He specifically asked not to be disturbed."

I glanced at the wooden bench on which someone had left the morning edition of the *Station Press*. "Is it all right if I wait for him?"

"I have no idea how long they'll be. And then he has another appointment. Why don't you leave a message with me, and he'll get back to you when he's free?"

Trying not to sound as disappointed as I felt I said, "I guess I'll do that. Tell him it's nothing urgent. I'll see him later."

"I will. Have a nice Christmas, Miss Marlow."

"You do the same," I said.

Just then I happened to look up. Mark's visitor crossed the room to the wall where his certificates and awards hung. Through the glass portion of the partition I had a clear view of a blonde woman in a pink turtleneck sweater. Mark's meeting was with Renie Scott.

All the way to the parking lot I tried to convince myself that my trip to town hadn't been a failure. I had the newspaper and Craig's present. Why did I need a conference with Mark, too? I couldn't think of a single reason.

It made perfect sense that Renie would come back to Huron Station at this time. In any event, she had planned a return visit after her father's burial. I understood why she was here but I didn't like it. I felt frustrated and a little angry.

Renie Scott has more right to be in the sheriff's office than you do.

I was tired of listening to that aggravating voice of reason. As if it were an annoying television commercial, I turned it off.

Craig expected me at his house in a few hours for a drink. If I couldn't talk to Mark about the Randall Scott case, Craig would do. He was interested in crime and killing and had his own ideas about the identity of the archer killer. We could rehash the news story and exchanges theories.

That might not be appropriate conversation for a holiday

get-together but I didn't think Craig would mind. With the coming blizzard and Roy's confession and arrest this was going to be a very unusual Christmas.

CRAIG'S IDEA OF outside decorating involved stringing popcorn for the birds in the tall spruce trees that grew in front of his house and hanging three wreaths on the gray siding under the living room windows. This simple but festive display was exactly the kind I would expect from him.

I rang the bell and the chimes sent their music pouring out into the silence. Craig opened the door before the echoes of the ringing had died away. He reached for the cake box and the bottle of liqueur with its red velvet bow. "Come in out of the cold, Krista. Here, I'll take those for you."

"One is our Christmas dessert and the liqueur is a small gift for you. I hope you like it. I guess I should have checked with you first."

He held the bottle up to the firelight and smiled as he read the label. "This is an excellent choice. Perfect for a holiday or any day."

He closed the door behind us and set the cake on the dining room table and the liqueur under his tree. It was a large balsam fir decorated with strings of clear lights and garlands of popcorn.

"I like chocolate in any form, but I mixed a special Yuletide drink for us tonight," he said.

"Oh? What's in it?"

"That's my secret, Miss Marlow. Call it Craig's Christmas Surprise. Sit by the fire and get warm first. You look so pretty tonight. Blue and green are my favorite colors, especially when they're mixed together. How did you know that?"

"I didn't. And thank you."

Instead of my reliable black sheath, I was wearing my aqua turtleneck and matching skirt. My turquoise earrings gave the outfit a dressy touch. I wished that I had packed a sweater in a brighter color but winter pastel would have to do. And by happy chance my appearance pleased my host.

I leaned back against the soft leather of his sofa, enjoying the warmth and glow of the fire and the lights. "I like your tree, Craig. It has just enough ornamentation."

"It's a study in simplicity," he said. "I don't need anything else to celebrate the season except good company. 'Pastime with Good Company' is what it's all about."

Hearing Craig allude to the title of the old English carol made me realize anew how much we had in common. "Fancy trimmings are nice, too," I said. "I like old-fashioned glass ornaments from Germany."

My dream had forced its way into my consciousness. Somewhere, pasted to a page in an old album, I might still find a picture of me and my parents sitting under Aunt Celia's tree. That would prove that my memory was faulty, that I had indeed spent one Christmas at the cabin.

And the significance of that would be—what? In the process of searching, I'd almost lost track of my reason for doing it.

"Have you decided what you're going to do about your property?" he asked.

"Not yet. I'm still weighing pros and cons."

"Maybe you can find a niche for yourself up north the way I did."

"In writing, you mean?"

"Yes, or putting your own talents to work for you. There must be some way you could keep the cabin, if it means so much to you."

"It does, and I'm ready to try something new, but I can only live on my savings for so long. I'm going to decide right after Christmas."

"The real estate market is slow around the holidays anyway," he said.

I stared into the fire, wondering why I always found myself confiding in this man. "I thought I wanted to teach in college," I said. "Maybe it's more that I don't ever want to go back to a high school classroom."

"You didn't enjoy working with teenagers?" he asked.

"Not at all. When I was in high school I loved English. And in college I just drifted into education. When I started teaching I discovered that most kids were reluctant to learn and difficult to control. I felt like a babysitter or a referee sometimes.

"I wanted to be like my mother. She taught Elizabethan drama in college and she could make the oddest characters and stories seem real and interesting. I don't think I was very effective."

"Then you shouldn't do it," he said. "You have to want to be a teacher to be good at it. You'll figure out what's right for you. By the way, I have a present for you, too."

He took a package from under the tree and set it in my lap. It was simply but neatly wrapped in red and green plaid paper.

"May I open it now?" I asked.

"Please do. That's the reason I wanted us to get together before Christmas."

What I thought was Christmas wrapping was actually a box covered with plaid paper. I lifted the top and found a slender book, a reprint of *Christmas in Huron Station, 1890,* by the Michigan poet, Serena Holland.

"Oh, this is wonderful, Craig," I said, as I read the simple inscription written on the flyleaf. The date, my name, his name. "A book is the best present anyone can give."

"I think so, too. There's a selection in the beginning that reminds me of you, living in your log cabin with only that savage beast for company."

I had to smile, thinking of Craig's description for Tasha. "Yes, Serena Holland was a single woman who lived with her dog. She preferred it that way."

The flames in Craig's fireplace leaped higher, the fire crackled, and the room grew warmer by the minute. Everything fulfilled its purpose. After her husband was declared missing in action, Aunt Celia had lived alone. Sometimes I thought that I would do the same. However it wasn't a source of concern for me at present.

The timing was always wrong. I was still young. The man had never been right. Take this pleasant evening with Craig, for example. His qualities were as sterling as his gray hair and we were compatible. Although I was having a good time with him tonight, I wouldn't want to relive it a thousand or a million times more.

No, Craig wasn't the man for me. I thought I'd already settled that.

As he passed me a bowl of his special trail mix that resembled Tasha's kibble, I pushed the material of the sweater away from my neck.

"Do you miss Christmastime in the city?" he asked.

"Not really. I'm enjoying the north woods, even with all the turmoil."

"What turmoil is that?"

I had to keep reminding myself that Craig was unaware of my involvement in the Scott Randall case. He knew practically everything else about me.

"I was referring to the murder," I said. "Did you hear the news about Roy Yarrow?"

"Yes, this morning on the radio. I wouldn't have believed it if Yarrow hadn't confessed. I could have sworn that Renie Scott was the killer."

"I still think that idea is outrageous. Did you know that her father's store is bankrupt? I should say the one he owned with Hal Brecht."

Craig said, "No, I didn't, but it doesn't surprise me. Scott was the one with the money. If you don't like the trail mix, Krista, I have potato chips, walnuts, and peanuts."

"No, no, this is fine." I took a bite of the concoction in front of me. I suspected that all three of the above had found their way into the blend, but it was mildly tasty. I'd eat just enough to be polite and try not to look at it.

"I've been working around the clock on an article this past week," Craig said. "I'm not surprised about the store, though. That partnership was a bad joke."

I leaned forward, eager to hear more. If Craig didn't go on, I was prepared to launch a volley of questions at him. But apparently he had found a subject that intrigued him and an interested listener, that irresistible combination.

"You're aware of Hal Brecht's reputation," he said. "I don't know how he manages to stay afloat. Not through legitimate ways, I'm sure. Somebody must be protecting him."

"Somebody like Sheriff Dalby?" I asked.

"Maybe. They're friends. As for Randall Scott, all I can say is that tangling with him could be lethal. I don't know what he got out of working with a man like Brecht."

Craig had never offered his opinion of the murdered man. Hoping to learn some relevant information, I asked, "Did you ever have dealings with Randall Scott yourself?"

"I came close," he said. "When I first moved to Huron Station, we had a gentleman's agreement. Scott was going to provide the financing for a boat rental business I wanted to start, but he reneged on the deal and left town the day we were to sign the papers. He never gave me a reason and I didn't ask for one. In the end I managed fine without him."

"I thought he came to Michigan only recently," I said.

"He was here before, about seven years ago."

"Did you see him when he came back?"

"Did I ambush him in the woods with a well-aimed arrow? No, Krista, that's not my way."

"I never thought…"

He laughed. I was glad to know that I hadn't offended him.

"Of course you did. Maybe your true avocation is sleuthing. Now, if you were to go snooping in my study and came across my twenty-pound Randall Scott file, you'd be convinced that I was the archer killer. Especially when you found my bow and arrow collection."

Now he was teasing me, or so I hoped. "I don't snoop, Craig. I would never go into your study unless you asked me to get you something you left there, or…"

"Relax, Krista, I'm just teasing you. The file exists, though, and for a while I might have entertained the idea of revenge—through writing, not murder. As it turned out I dealt with the man by ignoring him."

"The news stories imply that Randall Scott was the best thing that ever happened to Huron Station," I said.

"In a way, that's true. He was rich and eager to invest his money in northern Michigan. People wanted to read about him. But I knew him well, and I wasn't fooled by the facade."

No matter what Craig said about his feelings toward Randall Scott, I sensed that he was concealing a deep-rooted anger toward him. It was in the sharp tone of his voice and the iron hard set of his mouth. I recalled his fascination with murder and my suspicions of him that I'd set aside.

He'd just admitted that he had a file on the murdered man, although I doubted that it weighed twenty pounds. What if he hadn't planned to skewer Scott in writing but with an arrow? His grievance was an old one, giving him time to plan his revenge carefully and then wait for an opportunity.

He was checking the fire now, wondering aloud if he should replenish it. Was there any way I could slip into his study and search for the file while he was outside getting another log?

At the moment I didn't see how, but the evening was young. Meanwhile, it was best not to let Craig know what I was thinking, which meant I would have to be on my guard against that odd sixth sense he seemed to have.

"I wonder if Roy Yarrow really murdered Randall Scott to protest the deer kill," I said.

"There's bound to be more to the story. But we'll have to wait until he's ready to talk. I think I'll get us something to drink now, Krista. While I'm gone see if you can figure out where I hung the mistletoe."

TWENTY-FIVE

CRAIG'S CHRISTMAS DRINK was clear red in color and icy with a gingery taste of fruit and rum and a warming power to rival the flames in the fireplace. He served it in wine goblets. Although Craig was usually agreeable he refused to reveal the ingredients, claiming that it was an old family recipe he'd promised to safeguard.

I drained the glass slowly, sip by sip, but declined a refill. For a moment, I felt as if I were standing outside my body watching myself drink. "This is good but it's very potent. I have to drive home."

"I'll be happy to take you," he said.

"I have my car and the cabin is just across the road."

"I can bring it over in the morning."

"Then you'll have to walk back. I'm fine to drive, but one drink of anything is my limit. I'm going to have to leave now. It's been a long day." To emphasize my intent I set the empty goblet on the cocktail table and stood up.

"So soon? It's not even seven."

"I left a major project half undone at home," I said. "I'd like to finish it before Christmas."

My mind had already leaped ahead to our Christmas dinner. While Craig was busy in the kitchen, I would offer to set the table or pour the liqueur, anything that would give me an opportunity to slip away and look for the file.

Tonight, after deciding that the fire didn't need reinforcement, Craig had stayed in the living room, close beside me. I hadn't stirred from the couch except to go to the bathroom, and I didn't see any room that looked like a study on the way. A casual question about the floor plan shouldn't arouse his suspicions, but I'd wait until Christmas to ask it.

Still, I couldn't help thinking that I'd wandered off in the wrong direction. Craig was so civilized and gentle that it was hard to picture him taking a life, but apparently he had done so during his years in Vietnam. In passing he had mentioned how his own experiences with death had helped him shape his violent protagonist.

I suspected that his young soldier was an extension of the man he had been. Was it so unlikely that forty years later he would kill the one who had betrayed him? I didn't know Craig very well. Quite possibly I didn't know him at all.

He held my coat for me. "I'm sorry you have to leave, Krista. There's so much more we could say about the motives for murder."

In order to end the evening on a light note I said, "It'll keep for another two days. I don't see mistletoe in any of the obvious places."

"You'll find it on Christmas," he promised.

A FEW SNOWFLAKES began to drift down as I walked to the Taurus. Their light sting felt cool and soothing against my face. After the heat of Craig's fire the sensation was welcome but it did nothing to clear my mind. I was as confused as ever.

While it was barely possible to see Craig Stennet as a vengeful murderer, I couldn't imagine him trying to kill me to conceal his deed. If he intended to do so he didn't have to lurk around in the underbrush with arrows. From our first meeting, he had established himself as my helpful, caring neighbor. I had no real reason to distrust him.

The day after tomorrow I was going to walk into his house, again of my own free will. He could easily dispatch me there. Although he might have trouble proving that the killing was accidental. Mark considered him strange and Estella had described him as a recluse. Maybe they knew something about him they weren't revealing. Maybe I should rethink that dinner invitation.

More snowflakes fell. They were larger now. If this was the beginning of the blizzard at last, we might be snowbound for Christmas. When two feet of snow trapped me inside my cabin, I would be safe.

Except that Craig had a tractor. He could plow his way to my front door.

I could tell him that I was sick. Now that I thought about it, I might be coming down with something. In retrospect, Craig's fire had been too hot. Although I'd been outside for only a few minutes, I was already freezing and my throat felt scratchy, as if I'd swallowed a cupful of thorns. Or was that just the lingering effect of the Christmas drink?

Oh, for heaven's sake.

I started the car, turned on the lights and windshield wipers and drove out to the road, planning to speed across to the other side before I could create another fantastic scenario.

From the east, bright headlights moved out of the darkness, traveling in the same direction as the slanting snow. The rapidly approaching car was so near now that if I had pulled out into the road without first looking, I would have collided with it.

As it came closer, I saw that it was a police cruiser. It slowed down at the path to the cabin and turned ahead of me. In the double glare of the two sets of headlights, I recognized Mark.

When I reached the cabin, he was waiting for me in front of the porch, a solitary but commanding figure in a sheriff's uniform. I turned off my lights, plunging us into a thick darkness broken only by the faint gleam of the lamp in the window.

As I walked toward him, he said, "Evening, Krista. Weren't you speeding down your drive just now?"

"I guess I was, but there's nothing to run over here. Tasha's inside," I said quickly. "I wouldn't have driven so fast if she was out."

He stood aside while I opened the porch door and then followed me into the frigid enclosure. My memory filled with bittersweet images of our last time in this place, the words we'd said, and the way the scene had ended too soon, like a movie cut off by a power failure at the most important part.

Tucking Craig's present under my arm, I fumbled with the door key. For the first time since I'd been living in the cabin, I couldn't turn it in the lock easily. Something was making me a little shaky tonight, either Craig's drink or the man standing so close to me.

"Here, give it to me," Mark said.

In the next instant he had the door open. Tasha jumped on him in an excessive display of canine emotion. I felt suddenly nervous. I couldn't be apprehensive at the prospect of being alone with Mark when only a few hours earlier I'd made a trip to town to see him. Or could I?

That was planned, and this visit was unexpected. Why that should make a difference, I had no idea. Trying to appear casual I asked, "Is this a social call? A holiday visit?"

We were inside now. Mark closed the door and ordered Tasha to sit and stay, which she did with reluctance. I turned on the light and looked for that teasing gleam in his blue eyes that would tell me everything was all right between us. I didn't see it. When he spoke his tone was brisk and business like.

"You stopped to see me at the office this afternoon."

"Yes, you were in a meeting."

I took his jacket and gloves, concentrating on how cold they were, how unlike the man who wore them. Although he was concealing that aspect of his personality well tonight.

"You didn't have to drive all the way out here in the snow," I said.

"I was already home. It's not that far."

"I only want to ask you about Roy. That was a surprise."

"I arrested him," Mark said. "He confessed, but he didn't say why he killed Randall Scott."

"Mmm, that's what the paper said."

"And that's all I know. Yarrow is waiting for some high profile lawyer from Detroit. With the holiday and the blizzard he may be delayed, so we're at a standstill. I stopped by an hour ago but I saw your car at Stennet's. I didn't know you two were friends."

"We're just neighbors. Craig invited me over for a Christmas drink."

"He did, did he? I wouldn't mind having one myself. Make it coffee, hot and black."

"Okay," I said. "I'll go get it started."

A familiar request, instant compliance, and the ice began to break—figuratively, that is. The temperature inside the cabin must be below fifty degrees.

"Your fire is dead," he said. "While you're in the kitchen I'll get us a little more heat."

"Thank you, Mark, and I'll light the candles. I use them more than the lamps."

Mark glanced toward the Christmas tree with its homemade decorations. "It sure smells good in here. You've made everything look cheerful, just like Christmas should be. I see you got your tree after all."

"I had better luck on my second attempt. No one tried to kill me."

I saw him look down at the albums lying in a jumble on the table and those neatly stacked on the sideboard.

"Are you going through old family pictures?" he asked.

"They belonged to my aunt. I may frame a few of the best ones."

"That's a good idea," he said. "Let me get that fire going."

"And I'll start the coffee and then light the candles."

Good Lord. Hadn't we just said that? Maybe the ice wasn't breaking after all and we were trapped in a time warp exchanging meaningless pleasantries. Next, we'd be talking about how much snow we were going to get. For a while I had better stick to the safer subject of murder.

In the kitchen, I filled the coffeemaker and stacked a plate high with bow ties, smiling to myself as I imagined powdered sugar showering down the front of Mark's crisp uniform. Maybe he knew how to eat the delicate confections neatly. I'd never learned the secret.

I stopped at the sideboard to light the candles and brought

one of them into the living room where Mark was kneeling on the floor alongside the wood stove, crumpling papers.

"When you're through have some *chrusciki,* homemade by the Station Bakery," I said.

"Thanks. I think I will."

I sat down on the sofa, and Tasha padded over to join me.

"So you're not going to give me any secret details about Roy Yarrow's arrest," I said.

"You know almost as much as I do, Krista."

"Did Lily's alibi for Yarrow go up in smoke?"

"That's something I can tell you. She finally admitted that she lied. When I reminded her of the penalty for giving a false statement she told a different story. She's crazy about Yarrow, but not enough to go to prison for him. It helps that they had a falling out. A quarrel about money."

"I'll bet it had something to do with Scott's stolen wallet," I said.

"I can't comment on that."

"I know it did."

When Mark had the fire well underway, he sat down on the sofa. Not exactly beside me, but not at the opposite end either. Tasha turned around so that she could lean her head on his boot.

"That's better now, isn't it?" he asked, as he stroked Tasha's head.

"Definitely. Firelight and candlelight are all we need."

I passed him the plate of bow ties. He took one and not a single grain of sugar fell off as he ate it.

"I guess I can relax now and not worry about getting shot by an arrow," I said.

Mark paused to swallow. Then he said, "Yarrow didn't admit to trying to kill you."

He broke another bow tie in two. This time a few grains of the powdered sugar topping drifted down onto his shirt. It was easier to think about falling sugar than the danger that had just made a return appearance.

"When I read about the arrest, I thought I could stop worrying," I said. "I've started to let my guard down a little…"

"Don't ever do that, Krista. Let's wait till Yarrow's lawyer gets here. Maybe we'll know more then."

"Did you ask Roy if he ever smokes a pipe with cherry-flavored tobacco?" I asked.

"He only said that he killed Randall Scott, and that he wasn't going to tell me why."

I wrapped my hands around the hot mug, wondering how I could grow as cold as the snow between one breath and the next. If Roy Yarrow had confessed to homicide, why wouldn't he admit that he had also made attempts on my life?

Roy was lying again. That there was someone else who meant to harm me was an alternative I didn't want to accept.

At the crime scene, after I'd found Randall Scott's body, Mark had touched my shoulder. We had come a long way since then, but not far enough. I wished he'd touch my shoulder again and not stop there. I didn't want him to leave at all.

I said, "I suppose Renie Scott is happy that you've caught her father's killer."

"You could say that."

"Will she go back to Detroit now, do you think?"

"She didn't share her plans with me." He stared into the fire and shoved his hand in his pocket. "Look, Krista, how about if we start all over again?"

So our fragile connection wasn't broken after all. I tried to keep the excitement out of my voice as I said, "I'd like that."

"My brother, Mac, is coming up for Christmas. We always have holiday dinners with my aunt. Would you like to join us?"

I'd like nothing better. I couldn't say that because of my promise to Craig. "I'm sorry, but since we last talked I've accepted another invitation."

"From Stennet?"

"Yes. He's roasting a goose."

"Well…and he gave you a present, too. We'll do it after

Christmas, then. Have another date. We can go some place fancy for dinner or anywhere else you'd like."

We sounded like high school kids making a movie date. If we continued like this we'd never get out of that time warp and I'd go on forever living with regret for things left unsaid and chances thrown away.

I took a deep breath and said, "The other night you were right, Mark. I do want you. But when the time is right."

He smiled at me. The warmth in his eyes and the heat from the stove banished a sizeable portion of the ice that had formed around me.

"I know," he said.

I NEVER CEASE TO MARVEL AT what a fool I can be. I had revealed my innermost desire to this man and he countered with a knowing smile and two words. All I could do was return to casual mode and say something to fill the awkward silence, even if it was a mundane remark about the weather.

"I'm leaving Tasha with you a little longer," Mark said.

Now there was no need. He had done it for me. "Do you think I'm still in danger?"

"I don't know. It's best to be on the safe side."

He walked over to the window and lifted the edge of the beige curtain. I followed him and stood, silently looking out into the night. It was still snowing and there was nothing to see except darkness and our reflections. I moved back into the shadows cast by the light of lamp and fire.

"It's really coming down out there," he said. "The big storm won't start until late in the day tomorrow, though."

"Just in time for Christmas Eve."

"It's going to make for a difficult holiday unless people stay off the roads."

"They never do where I come from. Do you know if anybody around here has a sleigh?" I asked.

"Not off hand. Unless you're talking about the kind that resorts have for rides."

"I was thinking about the ones farmers used for transportation in the old days."

"Why?"

"I was just wondering. I thought I heard sleigh bells the other night."

The teasing blue sparkle was back in his eyes. That was a good sign.

"Maybe you were dreaming about Santa Claus," he said. "Seriously, Krista, somebody must have an old sleigh parked in a barn, but I don't think he's been riding around in it."

Then, without giving the slightest indication of what he was going to do, he leaned over and put his arms around me, pulling me close to his chest. His kiss was so deep and thorough that I suspected my visions of love were closer than I'd thought.

"Try to stay out of trouble until after Christmas," he said. "We'll get together then."

It took me only a second to find my answer. "I think I can do that."

TWENTY-SIX

AFTER MARK LEFT Tasha walked over to the door. She stood there whining softly, with her nose pressed to the wood and her tail still. What she wanted was perfectly clear.

"I know you miss Mark, but you can't go home yet," I told her. "He said you have to stay with me for a while longer."

She turned to glance at me and then lay down in the doorway with her head resting on her front paws. If I let her out now, she would probably try to follow Mark home. I decided not to take the risk of having her wander away. After dinner I would go outside and play with her in the snow.

The best way to distract a dog is by feeding her. I went into the kitchen and fixed her dinner, making no attempt to work quietly. The clinking sound of the kibble as it hit the ceramic dish brought her instantly to my side. As she licked her chops her blue eyes grew bright with anticipation. So much for missing her master.

"I knew we were still friends, Tasha," I said.

For myself, I warmed the spinach tart in the oven and made a pot of tea. Humans, too, often find food a pleasant distraction. But without a salad or vegetable to accompany it my entrée from the bakery looked bland and unappetizing.

My thoughts kept returning to Mark. In spite of his arrogant reaction to my admission, I had been right to tell him how I felt. The only problem was that now he was sure of me. That wasn't good. Maybe I should take a few steps backward.

No, never. In a relationship, four steps forward is always better. I wanted us to move ahead.

While Tasha noisily devoured her dinner in the kitchen, I

took mine to the dining room table and resumed my picture search. I had twenty more albums to go through. If I didn't waste time in idle reminiscing, I could finish my project tonight.

I reached for the large blue volume closest to me. At one time it had been new and handsome. Now its cover was smudged and the black pages inside were coarse, almost gritty. Over the years the glue on the photo corners had broken down, leaving several pictures attached to the sheet by only one side.

Some day when I needed a mindless diversion, I would re-inforce them with Scotch tape and identify the people I recognized. Now I slowly turned the pages, skimming the images the way I would words in a book that I wanted to read in a hurry, looking for a family picture that might have been taken in the winter.

I found several color snapshots of Aunt Celia working in her garden or holding up a prized fruit or vegetable. There was Ranger sunning himself in front of his doghouse. I saw young calves outside the barn, the horse, Dasher, grazing in the meadow and assorted vacationing relatives in formal poses in front of the cabin. They were all ghosts from the past.

I paused over a picture of Douglas in the woods. Our families had never been close and as a child I had disliked him. But when he grew older he was only mildly obnoxious.

I was genuinely sorry when he and his brother had drowned two years ago during a late winter fishing trip. Although they had practically invited death by ignoring the Coast Guard's warnings of thin ice, their passing was still a loss.

But it was my gain. Had they lived, Douglas and his brother would have inherited the cabin, as they were Aunt Celia's nephews. I was the daughter of her niece, the next generation. Impatiently I pushed away the stab of guilt I felt that I had outlived those two vibrant young men. Well, I wouldn't be sorry that I was alive.

Between bites of spinach tart and sips of tea, I made my way through the albums and the years, turning pages, scooping up loose corners and revisiting remembered scenes. By nine o'clock I realized that I wouldn't finish my search tonight. What should have been a pleasant pastime had turned into an arduous chore, perhaps because I was so tired.

At ten-thirty I turned on the radio and found the Christmas music station that Estella had mentioned. To the strains of "Do You Hear What I Hear?" I replenished the fire, checked the candles, and walked briskly around the living room a few times in an attempt to stay alert.

In the next album I found the pictures I was looking for. There were two of them, taken from different angles. All the people from my dream were gathered around the dining room table except for Uncle Chester, the family photographer.

I was sitting between Aunt Celia and my mother, who looked only a little older than I was now. My father was there lifting a drumstick to his mouth, as were the ill-fated brothers, all dressed up in shirts and ties, for once behaving themselves under the watchful eyes of their mother. I was gazing into the camera and for a moment it seemed to me that I was looking back at my grown up self. In the background I could see the top half of the Christmas tree. I might have been looking at a picture of my dream, except that the people were in a different room.

Carefully I eased the photographs out of their corners and closed the album. I could no longer deny that long ago Christmas in the cabin since I now held the proof of it in my hands. It was only one of thousands of events from my past that I had lost. That was the infuriating way of memory. Bits and pieces of dialogue, emotions, people, and places stayed as clear and whole as if they were a part of yesterday, while large chunks of time vanished into oblivion.

Now what? And why had I been so determined to find the pictures?

It wasn't only to satisfy my curiosity. There was an underlying reason of which I hadn't been fully aware until now. Somehow, it was connected to the dream. All I knew was that

I had forgotten something very important. It was essential that I remember it soon.

"Now what?" This time I said it aloud. Tasha came up to me and nudged my hand with her nose, no doubt thinking I was talking to her again.

"Let's go outside before bed, girl," I said. "We both need some fresh air."

THE NEXT STEP WAS to retrieve the lost memory. I didn't know if that was possible, but I was going to try.

I set the stage by taking a hot bath and drinking a cup of tea. Then I set the pictures on the cedar chest beside the bed. Before turning out the light I studied them carefully, making a note of the seating arrangements and dress styles, saying the names of the people at the table, and even trying to identify the contents of each serving bowl.

Like a camera, my mind captured the images it could find. I lay still, hoping that I would remember the missing pieces or, when I fell asleep, call back the dream.

Christmas, the cabin, turkey, Dad, Ranger, Lincoln Logs, a stuffed toy, fruitcake, the Monopoly game—one by one I dropped the words into my mind, waiting for sleep, willing the dreams to come…

Strong hands pulled me toward the middle of the bed and pushed down the sleeves of my nightgown. For a brief moment I felt a cold rush of air on my arms and chest and then a warm enveloping sensation.

"I came back to make love to you," Mark said. Suddenly the wood stove was in the bedroom with us, sending out its heat to wrap around us as we twisted and turned on the flannel sheets…

The dream changed.

Like a multi-colored ball in motion, the years turned in dizzying revolutions. I followed them back into the past to a night in late December and another decade.

I was miserable. I had pulled the comforter up to my chin

and tried to fall asleep but I was still too cold to relax. I didn't think I would ever be warm again. Instead of lying alone in this chilly bedroom, I wanted to get up and sit on the sofa in front of the wood stove where the tree lights twinkled in the dark.

I didn't know where my father was, but the radio was playing in the living room, with the volume turned up high. The news was on, so he was probably there, listening to it. Mother and Aunt Celia were in the kitchen talking while they washed our dinner dishes. Over the splashing of the water in the sink I could hear their voices clearly.

My mother was saying, "This is my last trip up north in the winter. I thought we were going to freeze to death in that snow bank."

Aunt Celia responded, "Nonsense, Kristina. That would never have happened. When you didn't show up I called Fred to go out and look for you."

In spite of her no-nonsense words, I could tell that Aunt Celia had been worried, too.

"I was never so happy to see anybody," Mother said. "It was fun riding up to the cabin in a sleigh, almost like being in a Christmas parade."

"A horse-drawn sleigh is more reliable than a car. I wish I had one. It's a good thing the others won't be here until tomorrow. Maybe the snow will stop by then. How is Krista?"

"I think she'll be all right now that I've gotten her to bed. I hope she doesn't catch another cold. She's just getting over one."

My aunt laughed softly and said, "It wouldn't be a holiday if one of the kids didn't get sick."

"As soon as we're through here let's go in and check on her."

I heard the concern in my mother's voice, but I knew it was going to be all right now. In just a moment my mother and aunt would be in to check on me…

I woke with a start, half expecting to see the spirits of my mother and aunt hovering over my bed. I was back in my own time, in the cabin, without my family. They had all gone away.

My memories of that night were so clear now that I wondered how they could ever have slipped out of my mind. It had started snowing in Standish. Three or four miles outside Huron Station, the car had spun off the road. We were stuck in a snow bank. Mother and I huddled together in the back seat under the emergency blankets, while Dad tried to shovel snow away from the tires, but it was a losing battle. That was what he had said later.

Finally Aunt Celia's neighbor, Fred, had come to our rescue with his ancient sleigh and his horse. I recalled my father lifting me out of the car and onto the sleigh. The rest of the night was a muddle of ringing bells, lights in the window of the cabin, hot chicken noodle soup, cold flannel pajamas, and being put to bed in the cabin's spooky bedroom.

I had dreamed about the conversation in the kitchen. But on that long ago winter night, I'd also heard it. I was certain of that.

I leaned over and turned on the lamp. The sixty-watt bulb coaxed the shadows out of hiding. Tasha lay asleep in the doorway, my sixty pounds of protection never stirring at the sudden appearance of light.

Remember, I commanded myself. *There must be more.*

My mother had always been close to Aunt Celia, who was her father's only sister. He had died when my mother was four. That was part of the reason for the special bond between them. They were also very much alike, both of them warm and loving women who made the world beautiful and secure for those around them.

When they had a chance to visit each other they were inseparable, exchanging gifts of canned goods or foodstuffs, working together in the kitchen and filling each other in on the news of their lives. They lived hundreds of miles apart. Sometimes I liked to sit near them with a book or a toy and listen to what they said.

Try to remember. It's so important.

I didn't know why exactly, but recalling the forgotten images was essential. My life might depend on it.

I remembered Aunt Celia and my mother having a conversation about seeds, but I didn't think it took place that night.

"Sweet peas, mixed colors?" Aunt Celia said. "A dozen packages? What a lovely gift, Kristina."

"Plant them in the spring." That was my mother's voice. She loved flowers but had little time for gardening. "They'll come back every year. You have to give them something to climb on, though."

I could almost hear Aunt Celia's soft laugh. "I know, dear. I was growing flowers before you were born."

While that was a pleasant memory, it couldn't be the important one.

If I turned out the lamp and went back to sleep, I might have another dream, but my waking thoughts were more reliable. The excitement of remembering had energized me, and I suspected that this was only the beginning.

I put on my robe, stepped over Tasha, and made my way into the living room, turning on lamps as I passed. Firelight and candlelight were the magic essentials for a perfect winter evening in the cabin and summoning lost memories.

I made a new fire in the wood stove using an elm log but decided not to light the candles in case I accidentally fell asleep. I wished now that I had searched for Aunt Celia's ornaments and lights, but I'd make the best of what I had.

She used to say something about that, too. "It was the best way to be happy," she claimed.

I had done everything I could think of to encourage the memories to reveal themselves. When I held the last vital piece of information in my hand I would be able to go back to bed and sleep. Maybe, if my luck held, I would return to my first dream and finish the night in Mark's arms.

Until then I was going to stay awake and think.

I SAT ON THE SOFA, sipping my tea and staring at the stove as if by doing so I could find answers in the flames. In the end, I could only recall one other conversation. This one was difficult to reconstruct because I hadn't heard much of it to begin with. I suspected that this was because my mother and aunt were talking about something scandalous or tragic, perhaps both, and they knew I might be listening.

At the time I had been lying alongside Ranger in front of the Christmas tree playing with the tiny nativity figures. I only managed to hear a sentence or two, pieces of a narrative that didn't fit together into a sensible whole.

Aunt Celia was saying that she—I didn't know who—must have inherited it from her mother, and it was a shame because she was such a beautiful girl and so young with her whole life ahead of her. I couldn't hear my mother's answer but I recalled Aunt Celia's next words vividly.

"It's in the cards, Kristina. There's no getting away from it, but I'll say this. I'm glad I moved away from Pinegrove. I'll swear there's a curse on that block."

There the memory shut down, leaving me with only a few tantalizing fragments.

I finished drinking my tea and isolated the pieces. I could examine them one by one and use them as building blocks. Perhaps I'd be able to add more at a later time.

They were talking about a girl who might have inherited something unfortunate from her mother, most likely a disease. She was young and beautiful but doomed to some dire fate because…she was the daughter of an afflicted woman and lived on an unlucky street?

It sounded like the plot for an old Gothic novel. What was significant was the name of the street that had appeared on envelopes addressed to both Estella and my aunt. Estella had admitted that Pinegrove was the street where her cousin owned an old Victorian house. She might have heard or read something about a tragedy that had befallen someone who lived on Pinegrove, even if it had happened some years in the past.

I couldn't ask her about it until she returned. But I could read Aunt Celia's letter. I had taken it to the trunk of the Taurus along with the box of cards. I wondered if I should go out to the car and get it now or wait until it was light out.

I would go now. As I started to reach for my coat, I heard a plaintive howling from outside. Tasha howled in response from the bedroom. Mark's dogs certainly knew how to create an illusion of impending doom. As the sounds died away I decided that the envelope would keep until morning.

Since I didn't want to add a haunting to the eerie night sounds, I left the radio on and went back to bed. It was midnight, the witching hour, but the next day was Christmas Eve, the beginning of that hallowed and gracious time when good cancels out evil.

The station was playing classical music now. It was a selection by Schubert, Parvarotti singing, "Mille cherubini in coro." Tomorrow I would go to midnight mass at Saint Sebastian's church, have a traditional holiday dinner with Craig, and sometime after that get together with Mark.

These were all delightful prospects. But instead of looking forward, my thoughts kept returning to the past. Just as I was on the verge of falling asleep another memory surfaced.

On a warm day in the summer following our Christmas visit, my mother and aunt were sitting on the back porch shelling peas. They worked quickly, splitting open the pods, spilling the small green vegetables into a single large enamel kettle.

Watching this monotonous activity soon bored me. I had gone outside to play with Ranger who was always willing to keep me company. As soon as I'd left them alone, Aunt Celia lowered her voice and said, "I had a letter from Madeline yesterday. They don't expect her sister to live much longer."

I moved closer to the cabin, studying the blue wildflowers that grew near the foundation and listening.

"Probably it's for the best, Celia," Mother said. "She could never live in the real world again after being locked up for all those years. She's lost most of her life."

"Madeline said the same thing. It's too bad no one knows where her daughter is. Did you hear anything new about it?"

"Not a thing, but after what happened, I can't say that I blame her for going away."

Aunt Celia said, "Neither can I."

There was a brief pause during which I could hear the thud of each pea as it fell into the kettle. I thought they were finished until Aunt Celia added, "But still, Margaret is her mother. She ought to come home now."

That was all. I didn't have total recall, but that was the gist of the conversation, and I was reasonably certain it was accurate. Also, I strongly suspected that it had something to do with the secret information I had to remember.

In the morning, as soon as it was light, I would bring the boxes inside and start another search. Perhaps the letters sent to Aunt Celia from Pinegrove would reveal more of the story.

TWENTY-SEVEN

"THIS IS THE LAST of the warnings. It's up to you now, Krista."

The voice was in the bedroom with me, a startling sound in an all-encompassing silence. It seemed to come from under the bed and inside the closet and in through the frost-encrusted window all at the same time.

I opened my eyes and looked around the room. No one was there. I must have been dreaming.

The voice was unfamiliar. Or perhaps it only seemed so because of the odd distortion in the tone. It reminded me of the radio's broadcast, transmitted over the years, losing a portion of its clarity as the sounds traveled through time.

I lay still, reluctant to get up and face the chill of this unusual Christmas Eve morning. It was so quiet in the cabin that I could hear my breathing and Tasha stirring in the kitchen.

The radio! I had left it on last night. Someone had turned it off. Someone like—whom? I was back to square one again, asking the same questions.

Before concluding that the radio had reverted to its haunting ways only in reverse, this time turning itself off, I considered all the rational explanations I could think of. The most logical one was a power failure. But I could hear the droning hum of the refrigerator in the kitchen and the bedside lamp came on when I pressed the switch. That wasn't it then.

I could also rule out the loose wire theory because Albert Drayton had pronounced the radio in perfect working order. Perhaps the station had ended its broadcast and I was listening to dead air. That was a distinct possibility that I could easily verify. Maybe the plug had slipped out of the outlet when Tasha tugged at it. Or a mouse had run over it, pulling it loose.

Those last two explanations were the weakest. Tasha was too big to squeeze behind the sideboard where the outlet was located, and no sane mouse would show its face with a predatory dog in the house. I was trying too hard to find an explanation for the inexplicable. It was better just to accept the fact that the radio's strange workings had their origin in another realm and move on from there.

Still, I got out of bed and made my way through the early morning shadows to the sideboard. Gingerly I touched the radio's surface. It was cold and silent with its knob in the 'off' position, as if moved there by an invisible hand.

Whether I had heard the voice in my dream or out of it, the message was clear. The warnings were over. From now on, I had to proceed on my own. In a way I was relieved. It would be easier to fight a flesh and blood antagonist than one from another world. I only hoped the coming confrontation wouldn't prove me wrong.

I was ready to get up and start the day now for I knew exactly what I had to do. As I walked back through the kitchen to the bathroom, Tasha danced around in front of me. I stopped to let her out through the porch door and watched her dart crazily among the trees, scooping up the snow with her snout and tossing it into the air.

I'd always thought that dogs have a special connection with the other world, a canine sixth sense, but Tasha hadn't barked to alert me when an unfamiliar voice began talking to me in the cabin. Nor had she noticed when the radio suddenly died, without a human hand to turn it off. She was one hundred percent earthbound and playful, a real dog in a haunted cabin.

While the water boiled for tea, I made a fire in the wood stove. Then I turned on the radio, wondering if I would tune in the past. The dial was set at the station I'd been playing last night. The song, "Have Yourself a Merry Little Christmas" anchored me firmly to my own time.

With the cabin back to normal, I set two doughnuts on a paper napkin and poured my tea. I could hear Tasha barking, telling me to hurry and join her outside. That was a good idea and exactly what I wanted to do.

You have to hurry, I told myself. *Time may be running out.*

I LIFTED THE LAST BOX of letters out of the car trunk and slammed it shut.

As I turned around I almost stepped on Tasha's paw. She had come up behind me so quietly that I hadn't heard a sound. That wasn't good. Even on this hallowed day and with my borrowed protector dog at my heels, I couldn't afford to be unaware of my surroundings.

She threw herself at me playfully and nipped my coat sleeve, collie fashion, in a blatant attempt to lure me into a play session. I held on to the box and did my best to evade her.

"After lunch, girl," I said. "I have a busy morning ahead of me." I held the porch door open for her. "In, Tasha. We'll play later."

Not getting the response that she wanted, Tasha began to bark. I hoped that Mark wouldn't accuse me of spoiling his dog since obviously she'd been that way when he gave her to me.

The sky was dull and overcast, and a promise of snow was blowing in with the west wind. Possibly the long awaited Christmas blizzard was already nearing the border, in which case it was hours ahead of the latest schedule.

I might as well leave Tasha outside for a while longer since that was where she wanted to be and I didn't feel like chasing her. Once it started snowing heavily, she would be happy to come inside the cabin and lie by the wood stove.

I couldn't wait to start going through the letters. Ever since I had remembered the summer conversation over shelled peas, I'd been wondering if the missing daughter had returned in time to be reunited with her mother. It promised to be a sad story. This was certainly a strange way to spend Christmas Eve. But since I couldn't go to church in a blizzard, I might as well make good use of the time.

I moved the rest of the albums to the sideboard where they would be out of the way and spilled the letters out on the dining room table. I found six envelopes, all from Madeline Varner, 253 Pinegrove, Detroit, Michigan, and arranged the letters in chronological order. The earliest was dated April 30, 1965. Skipping over the salutation and a boring description of spring flowers, I began to read:

> *Since you moved up north, Sundays aren't the same without the two of us getting together for coffee at your house after church. I miss our conversations so much. I don't have anybody to confide in and I feel completely alone. The girls are usually busy playing or reading, but people have been cool to me since Margaret's trouble.*
>
> *Having another child in the house at my age keeps me busy. Estella is easy to take care of. She's almost too quiet, not like my Cathy. Sometimes I wonder if she knows where her mother is. But there's no way she could have found out. I'm going to tell her some day, but not yet. She's still too young to understand.*
>
> *The new people have moved into your old house. They're an elderly couple and not very friendly. The neighborhood is changing. This street has been unlucky for our family. I wish I could go somewhere else, but I need to live close to Margaret so I can visit her.*

ESTELLA. NOW THAT I knew the name of Margaret's daughter, an inevitable connection tugged at me, refusing to go away until I had examined it. The name was pretty but old-fashioned and not often heard today. Until I had walked into the café, the only previous time I had come across it was in the Dickens' novel *Great Expectations*.

Would it be too much of a leap to assume that the young girl described in the letter was the Estella I knew as the owner of a café? I tried to remember what Estella had told me about herself. Her last name was Marten. She had come to Huron

Station seventeen years ago for the winter sports and liked the area so well that she decided to stay. The time fit with the date of the letter.

Estella received mail from a Pinegrove address and had gone to Detroit for the holidays. She claimed that she had met Aunt Celia when she first came to Huron Station. But if Madeline and my aunt were once neighbors on Pinegrove, could Estella and Aunt Celia have known each other before then? I was unsure of the time line, but this was definitely a possibility. If only I could ask my aunt.

I couldn't see anything tragic about Estella, but I didn't know her very well. She presided over the café where she provided Roy Yarrow with free meals and gave the lawmen extra eggs and pancakes with their breakfast. Practically from the start Estella had been interested in my life, so much so that she'd caused me to back away. But she never talked about herself unless she couldn't avoid it.

If by chance Estella were Madeline's niece, I might find evidence of it in the letters. Then I could go on from that point. I found a red pen in my shoulder bag and unfolded another letter. From now on I would underline every mention of Estella and anything else that appeared to be relevant. When I was finished reading the letters I would know more about Estella's past life than she would ever tell me herself.

That was assuming Estella Marten was Madeline's niece, I reminded myself.

The next letter was dated four years later. I wondered why Madeline had waited so long to write to her friend. Had Celia received other letters from Madeline, or did Madeline only write to her when she had a problem? That was the subject of the next letter.

How I wish you were here to advise me! You always know exactly what's best to do. Estella has been asking questions about her mother. At thirteen, I think she's still too young to know the truth, and I can't bring myself to tell her that her father left the state for good. He gave me five hundred dollars, told me to buy Estella whatever she needed, and said goodbye. We both knew he wouldn't be back. He doesn't want to deal with Margaret's illness. I don't even know where he is.

Estella is growing up too fast. She's going to be a beauty just like Margaret. Sometimes she's willful, the way her mother was. She's always in trouble with the nuns at school. I allow her to wear makeup but she overdoes it. Unlike the other girls, she likes to wear dark red lipstick. Sister Mary Perpetua always tells her to wash it off. Estella says that she hates school, but she's getting interested in boys. There are a lot of them at Saint Agnes.

She's nothing at all like Cathy who loves school and gets all A's. But the girls get along well. They're more like sisters than cousins.

I went to see Margaret today. I brought her a purple crocus plant and a box of chocolate covered cherries, her favorite. That's all I can do. She didn't know me. I'm afraid that her memories are completely gone, but I hope that wherever she is, the sun is shining. She used to hate rainy days.

The third letter, written in the following year, began with a two-page description of an ice storm and the discomfort of living without power for five days. I skipped over most of that, along with Madeline's apology for not being a more faithful correspondent, to the heart of the letter. Again, Madeline was having a problem.

I took Estella to see her mother today. As I feared, Margaret didn't recognize her. Estella was only two when Margaret had her breakdown. I'll never forget that day. Sometimes I have nightmares about it. There wasn't a single warning, or maybe I should say none that we recognized.

I came over to bring Estella a little dress I'd made, and there she was crammed into the toy basket with her own dolls. She was crying while Margaret calmly arranged daffodils in a vase. She thought the baby was just another one of the dolls.

She didn't remember that she had a child. She didn't know who I was. Everything had slipped out of her mind, and to this day, it has never come back.

I was worried about them meeting today, but Estella spoke to her mother kindly and said all the right things. Later, when we were home, she asked me the question I'd been dreading for years. "Do you think I'm going to go crazy like my mother some day?"

I'd had a long time to prepare my answer. I said, "No, I don't. You have your father's blood in you, too, and he's as normal as they get."

"How do you know?" she asked. "He's been gone since I was a little girl."

Estella was right. I don't know. But how could that response reassure her? What can I say if she asks again? In my place, what would you say, Celia?

There was another long gap. The fourth letter was short and happy in tone.

These past years have been quiet and happy although I haven't been feeling well. It's nothing serious, only arthritis, they say. We're not getting any younger. Cathy is taking a business course, and Estella is working full time in a dime store now, spending most of her money on clothes and makeup. She saves very little and doesn't know what she wants to do with her life.

Last month she met a nice young man named Ted at a dance and she's happier than I've ever seen her. I think our family is going to have some good luck at last.

Attached to the last letter was an uncashed check for fifty dollars, made out to Estella. The explanation was heartbreaking.

> *I have to return your generous gift, Celia. The wedding didn't take place. Ted decided that he was too young to settle down, but he waited until the last minute to tell Estella. She doesn't believe him, and I'm inclined to agree with her. She's convinced that he found out about her mother, and it scared him off. I wanted her to tell him about Margaret before they got engaged, but she was determined to keep it a secret. I respected her wishes. What else could I do? It was a mistake. I know that now.*
>
> *She hasn't said much, but she spends a lot of time in her bedroom. She tells me she's reading. Also, she quit her job at the dime store to look for something better. I think it would be a good idea if she'd take a short vacation and then enroll in school in the fall.*
>
> *I'll admit I don't like the signs. I'm so afraid for her.*

I set the letter down with a sigh. Although I couldn't know for certain, the jilted girl who had taken refuge in her bedroom after a devastating experience was unlike the Estella I knew. The woman who presided over her own café had beauty, confidence, success, and apparently plenty of male attention. But if Estella was the girl in the letter, one thing stayed the same. She still overdid her makeup.

The last letter was a sequel to the story of the wedding that never took place. Madeline had written it a month after she'd returned the check.

> *There was a tragedy on our street last week. Ted was killed in a hit and run accident. When I showed Estella the story in the paper, she didn't seem surprised. Without a trace of regret, she said, "I know. I heard about it."*
>
> *"Maybe it turned out for the best, Estella," I said. "You might have been a widow now."*

'That wouldn't have happened, Aunt Madeline," she replied. "If Ted had married me, he would still be alive."

"You can't know that."

"I do," she said, "because I would have taken care of him."

Something about this incident has been troubling me. At first I was afraid that Estella was denying her true feelings. But then something happened to drive that thought clear out of my mind.

The police questioned her yesterday. Somebody reported seeing her car near the scene of the accident. She denied that she had anything to do with it and claims that her car was stolen.

"Now they'll all be talking about me again," she said. "It isn't fair. I wish I could go away somewhere."

The police may be suspicious but have no reason to hold her, especially since the car is missing. They consider the case unsolved vehicular manslaughter. But I can't rid myself of a terrible suspicion. Maybe she did it. But is it possible that someone did steal Estella's car? What do you think?

I separated the remaining letters from their envelopes, hoping to find one with a later date, but, if it had ever existed, it wasn't here. I wished again that I could have read Celia's reply instead of being left with two tantalizing questions. Was Estella Marten Madeline's niece? And did she run Ted down deliberately because he had jilted her?

It might have happened that way, or it might have been a co-incidence that brought Estella to the street where Ted was to die. After all these years, how could anyone know? I thought that if the police had the evidence to charge Estella, they would have done so. About the allegedly stolen car I had no idea. Working with what I knew and the remembered conversations, I created my own afterward.

Estella left town either to avoid the police and the pos-

sibility of new evidence turning up or to get away from the
people who knew she had been jilted. Some time later, she'd
come to Huron Station and opened the café. Presumably in the
interval her mother had died and possibly also Madeline. With
the names and the Pinegrove address, I could find out.

By then Estella might not have recognized Aunt Celia who
had been gone from Pinegrove for several years, but she would
have remembered her name. Most likely she'd forged a new relationship with my aunt based on old neighborhood ties.

It could have happened that way.

I wondered why Aunt Celia had chosen to keep these few
letters, while others were missing. It was a reasonable assumption that Madeline had written more frequently to her friend over
the years. But unless Aunt Celia had stored boxes of correspondence in the barn with the cast off furniture, these were all I had.

Suppose Aunt Celia had kept only the letters that traced the
highlights and lowlights of Estella's unhappy story. Perhaps my
aunt, too, had suspected Estella of murder. But what purpose
had Aunt Celia intended the letters to serve? She couldn't know
that some day I would read them and try to piece together the
puzzle of Estella's life.

I decided to proceed on the assumption that Estella and the
girl in the letters were the same person. The real mystery
revolved around the woman as she was today. I knew more
about Estella's past now, and I sympathized with her. But I
didn't like her any better, especially now that I knew she might
be a murderess. Somehow, I had to find out the truth.

TWENTY-EIGHT

AT NOON I warmed the vegetarian pizza, made a pot of hot tea, and mulled over an alarming new thought. Assuming that Estella had deliberately run Ted down, what if some years later she had killed again?

I was thinking about Randall Scott. The name of the new woman in Scott's life had never been revealed. But from the first, I had sensed that Estella cared for him. Maybe she was the mysterious bride to be. What if Estella had murdered Randall Scott? Maybe like Ted, he had betrayed her. Estella had once referred to betrayal as an unforgivable sin.

Unfortunately I couldn't take this theory very far until I knew more about Estella. It made sense, though. I wished that Madeline had written more about the broken wedding plans. Did "at the last minute" mean at the altar, or the days or night before the ceremony? Also, did the guests know that canceling the wedding was Ted's idea? Whatever the circumstances, Estella would have been humiliated. She must have felt unloved and abandoned once again.

I tried to put myself in her place. If I had been jilted, I'd deal with my feelings and then move on. I knew that I wouldn't murder the man who rejected me. But then I couldn't kill anything, not even a deer.

Continuing this speculation was pointless. Estella and I were different people. And although it might be far out in left field again, I couldn't let the idea go. I remembered that I hadn't seen Estella on my first visit to the café, just before I'd found the body. Had she been back in the kitchen at the time of the murder or out in the woods shooting an arrow into Randall Scott? Hadn't Albert said that Estella had been among his archery students?

As I ate my lunch I continued to think about the other suspects. From the beginning, I had assumed that the killer was a man, probably because the people I suspected were male. First was Roy Yarrow who wanted to protect the deer from men like Scott. Then Hal Brecht with his debts and his dependency on Scott's generosity, and finally Craig who had counted on Scott for financial backing and been let down. From their various points of view, all of them had good reasons to want Randall Scott dead.

Of all the motives I was tossing about in mid-air, I considered Hal Brecht's the strongest. If Scott's loans to him were personal, no one else would know how much he owed. With one well-aimed arrow, the debts would disappear, leaving him free to pursue his dual interests of gambling and women and run for public office again. Yes, Hal was definitely the frontrunner.

But I always returned to a possible Estella-Scott connection. How ironic it would be if the killer turned out to be a woman scorned with a history of insanity in her family. Before I could pursue this angle, I had to know the exact nature of Estella's relationship with Randall Scott.

The teapot was empty. I didn't want any more pizza or even the rest of my tea. I wondered what Mark was doing today. He should have this new information. I had better go into Huron Station at once before the storm grew worse.

SOMEWHERE BEYOND the barns I heard Tasha barking. I stood on the top step and called to her, keeping one hand on the porch door to prevent it from slamming shut in the force of the wind. Icy needles of snow hit my face, momentarily obscuring my vision. As I turned to get a better grip on the handle, I almost slipped on the slick wood beneath the snow.

All I heard was the howling of the wind and I saw nothing except blowing snow and the slender young trees closest to me bending toward the earth. The storm was in its beginning stage and I could still see the dark shapes of the barns.

I raised my voice, making no attempt to hide my impatience. "Tasha, you devil! Where are you? Come! Now!"

This was a husky's favorite kind of weather, but Tasha couldn't stay outside indefinitely. I'd promised Mark that I wouldn't coddle his dog. It hadn't occurred to either one of us that I could lose her. There was only one thing to do, and I wasn't looking forward to it.

Inside the cabin, I pulled my boots on and grabbed my jacket from the coat rack. I made a stop in the kitchen to tear the rest of the pizza into bite-size pieces and wrap them in a napkin. Then I put on two pairs of gloves, stuffed Tasha's leash into my pocket, and pulled my hood snugly over my head. If Tasha wouldn't come to me, I'd have to bring her back, storm or no storm.

IN THE BRIEF TIME it had taken me to get dressed and prepare my bait, the snow had thickened and the winds increased. I could hardly see the barns now. In my haste I walked into a low hanging tree branch. The sudden jolt knocked my hood back. Crying out more in surprise than in pain, I felt my forehead. There was no blood. The rough bark had only scraped the skin. Snow blinded me and instantly soaked my hair, but the cold lessened the discomfort of the impact. If I didn't manage to stay out of the path of a tree, I'd never make it to the barns and back in one piece.

Once again, I called, "Tasha, come!"

I couldn't stay out in this swirling white hell while that spoiled creature played in the snow. Changing my approach, I made an attempt to sound excited.

"Do you want a piece of pizza, Tasha? Pizza!"

She might be back at the cabin. Sometimes when her fun-loving collie side took over, she would play a game with me, pretending to be lost. When I went looking for her, she'd slip back to the starting point and wait for me at the door.

I suspected that I was the only one she played with in this way. I couldn't imagine Mark putting up with such nonsense.

I didn't want to think about Mark now. This was his dog I had lost track of. But more importantly I'd grown attached to her. I cared that she was out running around in this wild storm and I wouldn't be able to rest until she was safe inside, lying by the fire.

I left the pizza pieces in the snow beside a stump, hoping that the smell would lure her out into the open. In the meantime, I'd go back to the cabin and find a scarf to cover every part of my face except for my eyes.

If I had to stay outside until Tasha decided to come within catching range, I would. But once I had my hands on that wretched canine, I'd take her back to the cabin. The next time she went outside she would be on a leash.

I STOPPED IN MY TRACKS at the sight of the arrow. It lay in the snow, a long, sinister object bearing an unmistakable message. In a few more steps, I would have stumbled over it because I was looking straight ahead, trying not to run into a branch again.

Since it had only a light dusting of snow, the archer must have shot it recently, which meant that he was still in the area— which meant...

Oh, my God. Tasha! I hadn't heard her barking since I'd first stood on the porch calling to her.

As my heartbeat vaulted into a mad, irregular motion, I attempted to block out of my mind the picture of Mark's dog lying dead in the snow with an arrow through her body. Under all the protective layers I wore, I felt a new kind of cold. The very wind seemed to be screaming 'Danger!' Still, I couldn't move.

"Never let your guard down," Mark had said, but that was what I had done.

So much time had passed since the attack in the balsam grove that I'd been lulled into a false sense of security. Neither a blizzard nor this hallowed and gracious time could keep a determined killer from striking.

Nausea gripped me and I regretted the slice of vegetarian pizza I'd eaten for lunch. I tried to swallow the hard lump in my throat but couldn't get past it.

That won't help you now—or Tasha. Stay optimistic. Focus.

I felt as if I'd been standing in the wind and the snow for a long time, paralyzed by the sight of the arrow as if it were a snake come up out of the frozen ground to inject me with poison. It couldn't have been more than a few minutes, though. Time enough for the archer to shoot another arrow at me if that was his intent.

He might have another plan. Maybe he had left the arrow for me to find as yet another warning and taken off. But what would be the point of that? How would he know that I would notice it before it vanished under the drifting snow?

He couldn't, unless he'd been watching the cabin, knowing that sooner or later I would come outside to find Tasha, the same way he'd watched before launching his attack in the balsam grove. Tasha was the lure, and I had fallen right into his hands.

Since I couldn't see anyone moving around the barns, I assumed that I was safe for the moment, but I couldn't stay outside making myself a target again. Safety lay at the end of the long walk back to the cabin where the rifle was.

Still hoping to find Tasha waiting for me in front of the porch, I started walking, fighting my way back through the wind-whipped snow, trying to step in the deep footprints I'd made earlier. With nothing to hold on to, occasionally I veered off balance. But I didn't fall, and nothing interfered with my slow progress.

Then the cabin was in front of me, solid and safe, only a heartbeat away. Tasha wasn't there. As I neared the stairs, I realized that I hadn't locked the door, thereby allowing the archer instant access. But I decided to go on in anyway and hope for the best. The alternative was freezing to death.

In my absence, the snow had drifted over the stairs. I cleared the way with my boot and pulled open the door to the porch.

The wood floor was slick at the entrance, but the wind couldn't find me here; and I had only four more steps to safety—I hoped.

The cabin was exactly as I had left it, with the wood stove filling the room with blessed heat and my empty plate and teacup in the midst of Aunt Celia's letters. I leaned against the door, letting my breathing and heartbeat slow to normal. No place had ever looked so good to me. I vowed that I would never sell the cabin, no matter what sacrifices I had to make.

What about the back entrance?

The question sliced across this sentimental resolve. The intruder could have come in through the sleeping porch.

Impossible. The door was locked. A sense of security slowly drifted back, but I walked quietly through the kitchen out to the porch anyway and made sure that it was. Then I checked the windows. Everything appeared to be secure.

The shotgun was in its accustomed place above the fireplace. I took it down and ran my hand over the cool barrel. In all the days that had passed since I'd brought it back from the hardware store, I hadn't once taken it outside to test it, but it would work. It had to. I trusted Albert Drayton's expertise. Perhaps I should fire a few shots now to announce to the archer that I could protect myself. First, though, I'd call Mark, and then Craig…

No, not Craig. What if he were the archer? I couldn't take a chance.

I'd just call Mark then.

No sooner did the thought form than I realized that I had left my cell phone in the car. That was why I'd bought it in the first place—not for idle conversation but for emergencies such as a breakdown on the freeway or the discovery of a body hanging in a tree. But I should have brought it inside.

All I had was the gun.

My mouth was so dry that I couldn't swallow. There was still a little tea left in the cup. I took off my extra pair of gloves and forced the cool flat liquid down over the painful lump in my throat that had appeared with the first image of Tasha lying dead in the snow.

That was all the fortification I would allow myself, but it helped me to focus. I had a weapon, but I needed the cell phone, too. Fortunately, I had left my jacket and boots on. Without giving myself time to think, I found my car keys in my shoulder bag.

Why couldn't I just drive away from here, call Mark from the car and take refuge in Huron Station? The roads would be treacherous but probably not yet impassable. It might work, but what if the archer had a car nearby and tried to run me off the road? Barricading myself inside the cabin with the doors and windows locked seemed safer.

It was only one o'clock, but it seemed as if I had lived through a week of tortuous trekking through snow and trying to elude a killer. I was nowhere near safe yet.

WHEN I GOT OUTSIDE, I realized that the archer had been there before me.

I stared at the flat tires that were rapidly sinking into the snow, taking the body of the Taurus down with them. All four were pierced through with arrows. One alone would have disabled the car. This was more than a warning.

My enemy was very close now and had been for some time. He must have shot the arrows into my tires before the blizzard started or he wouldn't have been able to see to hit his targets. By the time I had passed by on my way to the barns, I'd been so intent on finding Tasha that I hadn't even glanced at the car.

Brushing the snow away from the lock, I inserted the key.

Don't let it be frozen shut, I prayed.

The key turned and I pulled the door open and leaned across the seat, expecting any minute to feel the pain of an arrow driving into my back. It didn't happen. I closed my hand over the cell phone and backed up.

I was still alive. In a minute I would call Mark. If I had a minute left.

I was closer to the cabin now than I had been before, only about four or five yards. I closed the car door as quietly as I could and made my way back, heartened by the thought that if I couldn't see the archer through the snow, probably he couldn't see me either.

When I reached the porch, my breathing slowed down. I was going to be all right.

Up the stairs, in through the porch, inside again.

For now I was safe. As I had done before, I leaned against the door for a moment, letting the heat and the solitude of the cabin return me to a state where I could function rationally.

I dialed Mark's number.

TWENTY-NINE

MARK'S VOICE over the phone was brusque. "Stay inside and lock the doors. Do you still have that old shotgun?"

I glanced at the table, just to make sure it was still there. "It's right beside me."

"Okay. Use it if you have to. I'm on my way, and Krista…"

For a second I thought I heard Tasha wailing outside the back door, but it was only the wind, combined with my imagination.

"Krista!"

"I'm here," I said.

"This is almost over."

His voice sounded reassuring. I needed to believe him.

The line went dead. I set the cell phone down on the sideboard next to the radio. I wanted to keep busy until Mark arrived, but my only immediate task was to wash the lunch dishes. A tiny sliver of pizza remained on my plate. It was cold and soggy, but if Tasha were here, she'd be underfoot begging for it.

I could almost hear her stirring in the living room, padding over to her favorite spot beside the stove. Soon I would be telling myself that she was waiting for me in the shadows, a spirit dog come back from the world beyond to protect me.

That couldn't be. Tasha had to be alive. She was a mix of two hardy, self-reliant breeds. She might have eluded the arrow and taken shelter from the blizzard in some abandoned outbuilding or a den formed by fallen logs.

I needed to hold on to these thoughts. If she were dead, the responsibility was mine because I had let her run free. But these last hours were already the past, and I couldn't change what had happened. Mark was on his way to the cabin. I had the shotgun. I couldn't afford the luxury of even a moment's inattention.

Trying not to dwell on Tasha, I made a fresh pot of tea and gathered all the candles together on the sideboard where they would be handy if the power failed.

I was lighting one of the pillars when I heard a soft clicking sound in the lock. With the match still in my hand, I whirled around. Estella came through the door, shedding enormous amounts of snow in all directions. For a moment, I was too startled to say anything.

She wore tan wool pants and a man's brown corduroy jacket. Her hair was hidden under a fur hat, with only a few silver streaks escaping. Even though the snow had washed some of the rosy color from her lips and cheeks, she looked as vibrant as ever.

But her eyes frightened me. They were cold and unnaturally bright, almost feverish. Even more ominous was the strong odor of cherry tobacco that clung to the jacket. It drifted across the table and mixed with the fumes from the burning match.

"Merry Christmas again, Krista," she said. "I'm so glad to see that you're not hurt."

I decided to let her think that I was fooled. She had her right hand in her pocket. That must be where she had the gun. I wondered where she'd left the bow and arrows.

I would have to tread carefully. My best defense would be to pretend to go along with whatever she said. The shotgun was at the opposite end of the table. It might as well be a mile away from me. I still held the match.

A flame licked hungrily at my fingers. Quickly I turned the match sideways. Its deadly power could destroy a forest, but I couldn't use it to defend myself without taking the risk of burning down the cabin. I had to get my hands on the gun.

"Blow out that match before you burn your hand," Estella said. "It's wicked outside but you have it nice and warm in here. There's simply nothing like a wood burning stove to heat these old cabins."

Tread carefully now.

"What brings you out in this storm, Estella?" I asked. "And I didn't know you had a key."

"I'm sorry I startled you, but I just heard that the archer killer struck again. I was worried about you because you can identify him."

There was only one way Estella could know that, and she didn't seem to mind that she was giving herself away. That couldn't be a good sign.

A memory rose to the surface of my mind. *Hair swept up under a cap, streaks of silver showing. A white cap?* Was I looking at the driver of the Crown Victoria at last? A woman, not a man? It was possible, even probable. But once again, I couldn't remember the face.

I blew out the match and walked toward Estella, trying to reposition myself nearer to the gun, making a concerted effort to speak in a casual tone. "That doesn't explain how you have a key to my cabin."

"Oh, that. Celia gave it to me years ago. I used to bring meals to her. I think I mentioned that once. Toward the end she was too weak to get out of bed, so I would just let myself in."

"I was surprised that you didn't knock," I said.

"I apologize. I should have. Here, I won't be needing it any more."

As she placed the key on the table, she stared at the letters.

Damn. I should have put them back in the box as soon as I'd finished reading them. But how could I have foreseen this development?

Trying to appear as if I hadn't noticed Estella's interest, I walked slowly past her to the window. The air had turned to pure snow. If her car was there, I couldn't see it.

"Surely you didn't drive all the way out here in the storm just to check on me," I said.

"I told you, Krista, I was worried about you. The roads are just starting to get bad. I'm in no hurry go back out there, though."

In good weather, the drive from Huron Station to the cabin would take thirty minutes. Unless the sheriff's cruiser had special powers, the trip in blizzard conditions would be twice as long. The storm was growing worse. The wind howled like some frightful monster running amok.

I didn't know how long I could keep Estella talking, or why she was stalling. It was obvious that she planned to kill me. Let her take her time. As long as she didn't realize that I knew her true intent, I had a slight advantage.

"I thought you went to Detroit for the holidays," I said.

"I drove back this morning, just in time to miss the snow."

"You must be tired, then. Won't you sit down? Would you like something to drink? Maybe a cup of tea?"

"Not right now." She moved her hand slowly toward the table.

"What are these, Krista?"

"Some old letters I found. Nothing you'd be interested in."

"Such pretty stationery. I love pastels. Did you read them?" She reached for the letter closest to her, the last one I had read that ended with Madeline's suspicions of her niece.

"Not yet. Estella, please put that down. It's personal."

As Estella unfolded the letter, I seized my opportunity, grasping the rifle as if it were a lifeline. I could aim it at Estella now or wait to hear what she had to say. I decided to wait. "Here, let me get this old relic out of your way. It doesn't belong on a dining room table."

Estella was so absorbed in the letter that she made no move to stop me. Nor did she look up when I laid the gun carefully on a chair, with the trigger positioned close to my hand. She was reading rapidly, and when she was finished, she threw the letter down on the table with such violence that one of the pages fell to the floor.

"This is about me, but they're all vicious lies. Everything that woman wrote is a lie. You have read these, haven't you, Krista?"

"Yes."

"Then you know what they say. Aunt Madeline never liked

me. After my parents died, she raised me, but she treated me more like a maid than a niece. She was unstable. You know—delusional. It ran in her family. I've spent years trying to forget her."

"Mental illness is nothing to be ashamed of," I said.

"No, I suppose it isn't. But nobody can know what she wrote about me. I thought I had them all."

"Are you talking about my aunt's letters?" I asked. "How could you have them?"

She didn't answer, but the explanation was simple. If she had a key, she could have searched the cabin at any time during the past two decades, except when the doctor and his hunter friends were in residence. I wondered what else she had helped herself to.

"I'm glad you understand," she said. "You don't mind if I take these, do you? I don't have anything to remember Aunt Madeline by."

Without waiting for permission she stuffed all six letters into her left pocket.

She wanted to keep a remembrance of a relative who had never liked her, a woman she'd spent years trying to forget? Didn't she realize that didn't make sense? Or had she passed the point of caring?

"Take them then, Estella," I said. "I don't mean to be rude, but I can't have company today. Sheriff Dalby is going to be here in a few minutes."

She moved closer to me, bringing the vile cherry odor with her. I stepped back and swallowed, desperately trying not to be sick.

In a deceptively soft voice she said, "I doubt that, Krista. He'll be busy with other matters." Her eyes were colder and brighter, if that were possible. I watched her hand as it moved slowly toward her right pocket. "I knew I could trust Celia, but you're different."

"You don't have to worry," I said quickly. "I would never gossip about your personal affairs."

"You might. I could never make up my mind about you. You pretend to be friendly, but you're secretive and devious."

"So that's what you think of me? I'd say that was a fair description of you. I won't say a word. You have the letters now. Do whatever you like with them. As far as I'm concerned, I never saw them."

"That isn't good enough." She drew a small handgun out of the pocket and aimed it at my head. "This is the only way I can make sure that my past stays buried."

I stared at her, looking for some sign of the vivacious, talkative woman I thought I knew, the woman who had pretended to be my friend. She had disappeared.

"What do you think you're doing?" I demanded.

"That should be obvious. I'm going to kill you."

I glanced at the rifle on the chair. As I'd planned, it was within my reach, but I hesitated. What if I couldn't move fast enough? Estella already had a gun in her hand. Perhaps I could think of some way to defuse the deadly situation.

"You can't be serious," I said. "You're going to shoot me over some old letters that nobody but you and I know about?"

"No, I have to get rid of you because of what's in them. I've made up my mind. I don't trust you. You've had a whole month to snoop around in the cabin. There's no telling what else Celia left lying around."

"I don't care about your delusional aunt," I said. "That's your business. I have people and events in my life that I wouldn't want anybody to know about either. Everyone does."

"It isn't that easy. There's too much at stake here."

I took a deep breath and listened to the wind. It was screaming now.

"It's you or me," Estella said. "I'm going to save myself. We're going to go outside now. I'll be right behind you with the gun. You won't need a coat. I promise it'll be over soon."

"I'm not going anywhere with you, Estella. You'll have to shoot me here."

She didn't speak. Nor did she move. I sensed that her resolve was weakening slightly, but I couldn't be sure.

About now I could have used a little help from the supernatural. If only the radio would turn itself on or the bells on the silver sleigh would start to ring Estella would be startled and I'd have a chance to disarm her. But I could only rely on myself.

My survival had come down to time and distance. Approximately fifteen minutes had passed since I'd talked to Mark. I tried to visualize his patrol car skimming over the slippery roads, plowing through drifted-over lanes. Allowing for a three-minute run from his office to the parking lot, he should be pulling up in front of the cabin in ten minutes. In my present desperate situation, that was an eternity.

In the meantime the rifle rested on the seat of the chair, out of sight under the table. I hoped that Estella had forgotten about it. When she had advanced on me, I'd moved backward toward the kitchen. Only four steps forward would bring me close enough to the handle that I could reach it.

I would have to be quicker than Estella who already had her finger on the trigger. I didn't know if I could do it. In despair I threw out a distraction. "You're the one who's delusional, Estella."

I was gratified to see the flash of anger in her eyes. I had hit a nerve. Now, to build on what I'd said. "You've been trespassing on my property, spying on me, arranging accidents, and leaving a trail of arrows that was supposed to do what? Intimidate me? Send me back home?"

"I don't know what you're talking about," she said.

"No? What did you do to Tasha then?"

"Mark's dog? I just neutralized her. I wouldn't hurt an animal. You're the one who's the threat."

One more step forward, another second, and I'd be close enough to pick the rifle up and fire.

Quickly, or she'll shoot first.

"Mark knows I'm here," I said. "That's the truth. I expect him any minute. And I'm having Christmas Eve dinner with

Craig Stennet tonight. What do you think they'll do when I turn up missing?"

Her smug smile infuriated me. "Are you sure about those social engagements, Krista? That's a lot of comings and goings in the storm of the century."

"You can always wait and see."

"I'd better hurry then. They won't find your body until spring. When they do, they'll see the arrow through your heart and think it was the work of the archer killer. As for myself, I'll be long gone by then. I've been waiting for a nice little blizzard to deal with you. Snow conceals a multitude of sins, don't you think?"

She had said something similar before. I still didn't understand what she meant, but it didn't matter because I saw a way to use it. I only hoped it wouldn't backfire.

"By that I suppose you mean crimes? The two murders you committed?"

She hadn't expected that. I added, "This isn't about letters and a family secret at all. You killed Randall Scott, didn't you? And years ago you killed Ted."

I saw that I had surprised her and, even better, wounded her. She still had a fragment of composure left, but I could tell by the way her hand shook that it was about to crumble. Then she rallied.

"Ted never existed. My nutty aunt made up that whole incident. And I don't know where you got the idea that I killed Randall. Roy confessed."

"But you're the one who did it. By the way, that arrow through the heart was an inspired bit of symbolism. Did Randall Scott abandon you too?"

I knew I had discovered the truth by the fleeting look of pain in her eyes. She managed to keep her voice steady.

"I don't know what you mean. It was all Roy's idea. All his doing."

I aimed my final blow. "You can kill all the men you like, Estella, but that won't make any of them love you. Look at your track record. Two men murdered, and you're still alone."

"It was Roy's fault, I tell you. He was supposed to hide the body, not leave it hanging in a tree for everybody to see." Instantly, she realized her mistake and her hand tightened around the gun.

And now while I had her...

I said, "They're going to catch you, Estella, and when they do, you'll be locked away for life, just like your mother."

Quickly—now!

She fired just as I ducked down under the table, inadvertently knocking the rifle to the floor and out of my reach. I grabbed the chair and flung it at her while dodging another bullet. With an enraged scream, she fell backward, into the coat rack. Her gun slid across the dining room floor, following the direction taken by the bullets.

Before she could scramble to her feet, I grabbed the rifle and aimed it. Even as she lunged toward me, my finger froze on the trigger. I couldn't shoot Estella.

Yes, you can. Do it!

As her hands reached out to close around my throat, I stumbled out of the way, turned the shotgun around and jabbed the handle into her chest with as much force as I could muster. The cherry odor washed over me like an obscene shower, but I fixed all my concentration on the woman in front of me and pushed her again, farther toward the door.

She cried out and ran her hand across her rib cage.

Slowly and deliberately, I returned the gun to its proper position and moved my finger a fraction of an inch toward the trigger. "Get out of my cabin now, Estella, or I'll fire."

For the first time since I had known her she seemed unsure of herself.

"I can't go out in that blizzard," she said. "Krista, please. I don't have a car."

"Then you couldn't know how bad the roads are. I don't care. Go back the same way you got here."

Estella didn't move. She kept her hand to her ribs, and her pain-filled eyes narrowed. "You can't mean to send me out of

Celia's house in the middle of this storm. I wouldn't last an hour in those wind chills. You'd be committing murder—and you don't like to kill anything."

The way she emphasized those last words led me to suspect that she had sensed my reluctance or even guessed my secret. I had to change her mind quickly.

"That goes for helpless animals, not my would-be killer. Get out now."

"No."

Her tone was defiant. She wasn't going to budge, just as I had refused to leave the cabin with her earlier when she'd ordered me outside at gunpoint. Confidence had replaced the pain and pleading in her eyes. She was daring me to shoot her. I had to convince her that I could indeed pull the trigger. And convince myself.

I raised the rifle slightly, forcing my hand to hold it in a steady grip. I tried to match her defiance and ignore the quiet voice inside me that said *She's right. You'll never be able to shoot her.*

I couldn't let her realize that. I pulled the trigger.

The bullet sailed past Estella and disappeared in the shadows beyond the table.

Estella took a resolute step toward me. Behind her the front door opened. Mark and Gil stood on the threshold, their bodies covered in snow, their guns drawn. I hadn't heard a single telltale sound, not even a creaking of the old wood as it rubbed against the frame.

Estella whirled around, saw them, and instantly switched to her alternate role. She was the congenial café owner again, baffled by a strange turn of events and grateful that the lawmen had arrived to take charge of a situation that had spiraled out of control.

"Mark, I'm so glad to see you!" she said. "Something must be wrong with Krista. I'd swear she was going to shoot me! It must be all the isolation and the snow getting to her. She actually thought I was an intruder."

"Why you lying witch…"

"Save it, Estella," Mark said. "Roy Yarrow has been talking. He tells a very interesting story."

"You never believed him before. Roy is just angry with me, but I can't tell you why. It's personal."

Mark's face was grim. "I'll find out who's telling the truth, Estella," he said. "For now you're under arrest for home invasion and attempted murder."

As Mark read Estella her rights and secured her wrists with handcuffs, I set the shotgun down on the sideboard. I felt as if a tremendous burden had been taken from me. As soon as I could, I was going to return the gun to the wall above the mantel. I hoped I'd never have to aim it at anyone again.

Estella changed her approach. "If I misunderstood, I apologize, Krista. I hope we can get past this little unpleasantness— for Celia's sake."

"Unpleasantness? You were going to kill me." Suddenly I remembered. "Mark, she did something to Tasha. You have to find her. It may already be too late."

Mark's eyes were as hard and cold as ice. "Where is she, Estella?" he demanded.

She shrugged. "Your dog is perfectly all right. You'll find her asleep in the barn."

"Gil, escort Miss Marten out to the cruiser and watch her. Krista, you stay here and wait for me," Mark said.

He went back out into the cold and Gil followed with a subdued Estella. Her hair had fallen loose from the man's cap she wore and the silver strands at the sides of her face shone in the light. In spite of the mannish clothing and the scent of tobacco that still clung to her, she had regained a measure of her former poise and confidence.

I had no doubt that she would give Mark yet another version of the day's events and that she would probably believe her own story.

THIRTY

THE BLIZZARD CONTINUED. I waited for Mark inside, watching through the window while the wind whipped the snow into high drifts around the cabin's foundation. Although the power was still on, I had lit all of the candles and added a log to the wood stove. As the friendly shadows danced around me, I breathed in the fragrance of apple wood and hung the rifle back up in its accustomed place.

The middle of the afternoon felt like night. Mark, Gil, and Estella had only been gone from the cabin for ten minutes but it seemed like an hour. The radio played softly in the kitchen. It was on with the volume turned down low. After a brief update on the blizzard, the program of Christmas music resumed with "In the Bleak Midwinter." I had a feeling that from now on the radio would wait for a human hand to turn it on and the broadcasts would be firmly rooted in the present.

The weather forecast was for six more inches before the snow tapered off and the wind died down sometime during the night. We were going to have a white Christmas with a vengeance. I hoped that someone would plow the way to town so that I could go to church in the morning and visit the altar of Saint Sebastian again.

It was a true Christmas miracle that I had escaped the fate Estella had planned for me. I was glad I finally understood the reason for the haunting of the cabin.

In some way Aunt Celia had come back to warn me of the imminent danger by forcing me to remember that long ago Christmas at the cabin. I had arrived with my family in a horse-drawn sleigh, listened to the radio, and overheard snatches of adult conversation that eventually led me to Estella.

The final clue was in the letters. As I sipped a cup of fresh hot tea another memory came to me. I *had* seen the silver sleigh before unpacking it a few weeks ago. That same year of the visit my mother had given it to Aunt Celia as a Christmas gift. They had laughed about having two sleighs, one a decoration and the other real.

I found only one problem with this theory. In the beginning, when the radio had traveled back in time, it had aired protests songs and news about the war in Vietnam. I couldn't possibly have heard such broadcasts that December, as they were already several years in the past.

My only explanation for this was neither scientific nor particularly satisfactory. From my mother's stories, I knew that in the early years Aunt Celia had talked constantly about her husband. She had played war protest music on her phonograph and never doubted that he would come home. That hadn't happened, and in later years she rarely mentioned him.

But perhaps these feelings were still with her when I was a child and somehow they came through to me, along with the other memories. I wished that I could discuss my experience with someone, but I didn't think that would ever happen. Not many people would be ready to believe in a radio that turned itself on and off or a transfer of memories over time and space.

Curious and restless with the sudden inactivity, I bundled myself into my coat and boots and went out to the porch to wait for Mark. I was tempted to ignore his order to stay in the cabin, but decided against it.

I stood in the doorway, feeling the sear of the wind on my face and letting the blowing snow batter my body. The lights of the cruiser formed an island of brightness in the swirling snow. Although I couldn't see her, I knew that Estella was inside the car, waiting also, restrained by handcuffs and guarded by Gil.

Literally, it wasn't a fit night out for man or beast. But I had been ready to force Estella out into the storm. And I'd said some terrible things to her. No matter that I'd been fighting for my life, I wished I hadn't called her delusional or mentioned her mother. Now that I knew the story of her background, Estella's reaction to the remark made by the rowdy hunter in the café made sense.

"Krista, get back inside, now!"

Mark's voice carried over the wind. I saw him coming through the thick wall of snow. As he crossed in front of the cruiser, I saw that he was carrying Tasha. She looked as limp as a large stuffed toy that had been long abandoned to the elements.

I held the door open for him as he brought her inside and laid her down on the floor beside the wood stove. "She isn't dead, is she?" I asked, almost afraid to hear his answer.

"No, but she's been drugged. I found a half-eaten piece of meat by her side. Estella must have lured her into the barn and left her there. I think she'll be all right, but she's very sleepy and cold."

"Are you sure she'll be okay?"

"Pretty sure."

I knelt down beside the unconscious dog and touched her head. When she didn't stir, I took the plaid throw from the sofa and covered her with it, tucking its edges around her shoulders.

"Are you all right, Krista?" Mark asked.

"I am now."

His face was burned from the wind and his jacket appeared to be made out of snow, but he looked fine and handsome to me. I watched him take his leather gloves off and trail his hand slowly over Tasha's head and ruff.

"I should deputize you, Krista," Mark said. "The police are looking for Estella all over Detroit, but you led us right to her. She was camping out in your barn, using that old furniture that's stored there. She even had a battery-powered space heater and some food. We found her car about a mile down the road." He paused and laid his hand on my shoulder. "I found a bow and a stack of arrows, too. Estella is out of commission now. She'll be spending Christmas in jail with her partner in crime, Yarrow."

"I thought they were good friends. How did you convince Roy to implicate her?"

"I can be very persuasive, but Yarrow was ready to talk. He thinks Estella left him to take the murder rap alone."

"Are you going to drive back to Huron Station now?"

"Sure, I've got a prisoner to lock up. Estella says you attacked her with a shotgun. Is that true?"

His voice was stern but I knew the sparkle was in his eyes, even though he was looking down at Tasha, still stroking her.

"You could say that. Did she tell you that she came here to kill me?"

"She didn't have to."

"I'm glad you showed up when you did," I said. "When it mattered, I couldn't bring myself to shoot her, even to save my life. She knew that. I'd be hopeless as your deputy—if you were serious, that is."

"I wasn't. Krista, are you sure you have to have Christmas dinner with Stennet?" he asked.

"Well, yes, I promised. He's cooking a goose."

"But it's dinner he invited you for, right? How about afterwards—later? Are you free for the night?"

"I can be."

"Good. You'll be here in the morning, won't you?"

"I guess so, until somebody plows me out. I'd like to go to church."

"I'll bet your friend, Stennet, will do that. The snow is so high that we barely made it through on the way here. I'd better hit the road again while we still can. I'll know more tomorrow. We can compare notes. Make sure you have the coffee ready, plenty of it, okay?"

"I will," I said, marveling that Mark never changed. Not even capturing a murderer and battling a killer storm could faze him.

ON CHRISTMAS DAY Mark and I sat at the little table in the kitchen while Tasha, who had awakened briefly, napped in the doorway. It was almost noon. The blizzard had dwindled down to a few flurries flying through the air, and the blue sparkle in Mark's eyes was a satisfactory substitute for the sun that had yet to make an appearance.

"I thought Estella was giving away all those free cups of coffee and pancakes out of the kindness of her heart. But maybe she was staying on the good side of the law as a kind of insurance policy," I said.

"She worked hard to build a new life for herself in Huron Station. When you showed up, you were a double threat to her. You saw her fleeing the crime scene, and when she learned you were Celia's niece, she was afraid you might find evidence of her past in the cabin. She was willing to kill to keep her mother's insanity a secret."

"Also, she was afraid that she'd go mad some day herself," I said. "I learned that in an old letter. You certainly can persuade people to talk, Mark. I'm impressed."

"That's true, I can. But Estella was willing to talk. She thinks I can make all this go away for her. That's why she's been so cooperative."

I poured Mark's coffee and wished I had something good to give him—pancakes, maybe, or bacon and eggs. From now on we would all be eating at home until some enterprising soul opened another café.

I said, "A while back, Estella mentioned a mirror Aunt Celia kept in her bedroom. I couldn't find it. Do you think she took it?"

"We'll find out. I'll bet she wanted you to think that thieves had made off with it, just in case you noticed something missing. After your aunt died, Estella admitted that she'd made several trips to the cabin to take back what she called her personal property. Mostly old pictures and letters, she claimed."

"I hope she really was a friend to Aunt Celia," I said.

"I think she was. Estella had nothing to fear from her."

"My mother always said that Aunt Celia could keep a confidence. Can you tell me what part Roy played in the murder?" I asked.

"He helped Estella every step of the way as long as he could. The way he tells it, she met Randall Scott in the summer. Roy knew she had fallen for him, but nobody else did. They were very discreet. Then, Scott met a woman he liked better and Roy found out about it."

"That was the woman Renie thought her father was going to marry. Did you find who she is?"

"She's a lawyer practicing in Lansing who wants to be kept out of this mess if possible. When Scott dumped her for this other woman, Estella decided to kill him."

"That's as good a way as any to deal with a man's betrayal," I said. "Don't frown, Mark. I'm only joking."

"There's nothing funny about murder, Krista. Scott wanted to build a new house near Huron Station. Roy's job was to lure him to a prime site in the woods and see to it that he looked toward the east. Estella was waiting across the road with a bow and arrow. She was a real sportswoman in her younger days and apparently she didn't forget anything. Afterwards, Roy sent her on her way, promising that he would get rid of the body."

"That was when our cars passed on the road."

As Mark spoke, I reconstructed the scene. In her haste, Estella hadn't taken the time to brush the snow off the windows or push the silver strands of her hair up under the cap. All she wanted was to get away. She didn't care how fast she drove or how recklessly. How likely was it that she would meet another car on this deserted roadway?

But I was there and she saw me. It was only natural for her to think that I had seen her, too.

Mark said, "It was Roy's idea to hang Scott's body in the tree to make it look like the work of the anti-hunting activists."

"Didn't he realize he'd be attracting attention to himself?" I asked.

"He thought he could count on Lily to give him an alibi."

"Until she discovered that he'd kept the money in Scott's wallet and was spending it. She knew he would be caught and she'd be implicated for giving him a false alibi."

Mark sat forward in his chair. He was frowning again. "I didn't tell you that, Krista, did I?"

"No, but it makes sense. That must have been Roy's corduroy jacket that Estella was wearing tonight. So he was the one who locked me in the barn."

"Or it was Estella, wearing the jacket again. We're not sure who did what yet. Roy and Estella are telling different stories."

"But why would Roy confess to a crime Estella committed?" I asked.

"Apparently Estella promised to find him a good lawyer who would get him off with a light sentence."

"Probably Roy was at the Hollow Oak Casino the night we were there," I said. "I wonder who shot an arrow at me in the balsam grove."

"It could have been either one of them. My guess is Estella. But as of today, the only sure thing is that Roy likes cherry tobacco and Estella shot the arrow that killed Randall Scott," Mark said.

"Don't forget. Years ago, she might have run down Ted."

"She wouldn't admit to that. But the case will be reopened."

"It's ironic," I said. "Estella killed Randall Scott because he betrayed her, and all the time she had Roy. He must have cared for her very much to help her commit murder and terrorize me."

"There's no love lost between the two of them now," Mark said.

I refilled our cups and made another search for something to serve him. There was Estella's fruitcake, but I didn't want to eat anything she had baked or serve it either. That left two nutty dunkers nestled among crumbs and sprinkles in the bakery box. They seemed to signify an end, but that was wrong. This was a joyous day and a time for a new beginning.

Quietly I set them on a plate and placed them in front of Mark. "I came to this cabin to think about what I want to do with my life, but I've been so busy dodging arrows and bullets that I haven't had much time for solitude."

"You'll have it now. With Estella locked up things will go back to normal."

"And what's normal for Huron Station?"

"Four more months of snow and cold weather, skiing, quiet nights by the fireside, maybe the Station Roadhouse or the Hollow Oak…"

"You left out the toasted marshmallows," I said. 'And I have a wood stove."

"There's an open fireplace in my house. That's better. Then the next thing you know, it'll be spring. It's different up here in the north woods, slower and greener. You have to experience it first hand. Then, in the summer, there's Lake Huron and fishing…"

He was serious now, but I couldn't help but laugh. "I'll soon be pining for a faster pace. Don't forget that I'm a city girl at heart, Mark."

"And I'm a country sheriff…"

"Who always gets his man," I said. "I remember. You told me."

"I always get my woman, too." That devilish sparkle was back in his eyes.

I hoped I hadn't misunderstood. To be certain I said, "That's right. The archer killer turned out to be a woman. And yes, you did get her, with a little help from me, as you just said."

The sparkle in his eyes intensified, or maybe it was the light of the sun that had finally appeared from behind the last of the storm clouds.

"I wasn't talking about Estella," he said. "I can make you another promise, honey. No matter what's going on in Huron Station, you'll never be bored with me."

He reached for my hand across the table and squeezed it.

I decided to let the honey pass this one time. "I'll hold you to that."

"You do that." He got up and stooped to pet the still sleeping Tasha. "I'm going to let you keep Tasha for a little longer. You two look good together. Now I'd better get over to my aunt's for Christmas dinner. She likes to eat at two. Mac didn't think his little brother could solve the case so soon. I want to make sure he has all the details."

"Craig wants me there at four. I'll see you later then?"

"You sure will. Let's say around eight. I'll show you how we celebrate Christmas night in Huron Station. Hell, I think I'll show you now."

As he pulled me up into his arms, at last I knew exactly what to say. "I think I'll let you. Merry Christmas, Mark."